G.I. JOE: TALES FROM THE COBRA WARS

IDW Publishing presents an action-packed collection of all new, high-velocity prose from today's top crime and thriller writers. This is adventure fiction designed for Joe fans of all ages.

Flint, Scarlett, Duke, Snake Eyes, Hawk, Destro, and the Baroness. All your favorite Joe characters are here, as well as a host of new heroes and villains.

The global covert conflict between G.I. JOE and COBRA is explored from every angle and viewpoint, and ties directly into IDW's exciting comic book reboot of G.I. Joe continuity.

This exclusive collection features two short stories and five novella-length tales, from writers Jonathan Maberry, Jon McGoran, Duane Swierczynski, Matt Forbeck, and John Skipp & Cody Goodfellow. Chuck Dixon, IDW's main G.I. JOE comics scribe, makes his prose debut with a new Snake Eyes adventure.

COBRA WARS is edited by best-selling author Max Brooks (*World War Z*), who also supplies an introduction and a new story.

Illustrated by new IDW discovery, Michael Montenat.

A G.I. JOE ANTHOLOGY
TALES FROM THE
COBRA WARS

EDITED BY
Max Brooks

ILLUSTRATED BY
Michael Montenat

COVER PAINTING BY
Gabriele Dell'Otto

SAN DIEGO, CA
2013

FOR JOE FANS EVERYWHERE

—————— TALES FROM THE COBRA WARS ——————

Executive Editor: Jeff Conner • Associate Editor: Andy Schmidt

Consultant: Shane Davis • Book Production: Robbie Robbins

Special thanks to Hasbro's Aaron Archer, Michael Kelly, Amie Lozanski, Ed Lane, Joe Furfaro, Jos Huxley, Samantha Lomow, and Michael Verrecchia for their invaluable assistance.

ISBN: 978-1-61377-664-3

16 15 14 13   1 2 3 4

www.IDWPUBLISHING.com

Licensed By:

Ted Adams, CEO & Publisher
Greg Goldstein, Chief Operating Officer
Robbie Robbins, EVP/Sr. Graphic Artist
Chris Ryall, Chief Creative Officer
Matthew Ruzicka, CPA, Chief Financial Officer
Alan Payne, VP of Sales

DUTY ROSTER

Introduction

MAX BROOKS

TALES FROM THE COBRA WARS is an all-original story collection that expands and deepens the G.I. Joe experience as only quality fiction can. The seven main tales featured here recount various skirmishes and battles in the ongoing Joe-Cobra conflict. It's a covert global war that has the very soul of freedom and democracy hanging in the balance.

For nearly half a century, G.I. Joe has proven itself to be one of the most enduring, multi-generational, cultural phenomena in American history. For the last 29 years, that phenomena has focused on the epic struggle between G.I. Joe and, in the words of the early 80s TV show: "A ruthless terrorist organization determined to rule the world." That organization is COBRA. Their battle with the Joes has played out in comics, cartoons, a live action movie, and now this collection of stories.

A band of writers, all with diverse and award-winning backgrounds, contributed their talents to the creation of these stories. And while their Joe world conforms to the re-imagined comic book series from Hasbro and IDW Publishing, fans should not worry about having to read those series first. Likewise, readers shouldn't worry about any retreads or "novelizations" contained in these pages. These stories are as original as they are thrilling.

The first tale comes to us from none other than Joe comic alpha scribe Chuck Dixon. His debut on the prose stage follows

Snake Eyes in his desperate attempt from stopping the Baroness from using a kidnapped economic genius to engineer a global financial meltdown.

Next in line is *New York Times* best-seller Jonathan Maberry who contributes a novella-length adventure pitting man against machine as the US Army's most brilliant inventor, and his masterpiece combat exo-suit, turn on the Joes on orders from Cobra Commander.

Duane Swiercynski's "Speed Trap" races across the American Southwest with G.I. Joe's top driver, Skidmark. Caught between emergency orders from Hawk, and the hyper-armed SUV driving assassin Interceptor Three, the lone Joe must foil a nationwide threat from behind the wheel of…a Prius.

Matt Forbeck's "Just a Game" comes next. As a novelist and video game writer, Forbeck combines his prodigious talents into a tale of online gaming infiltration in a fashion that is frighteningly plausible.

The action shifts to south-central Asia with "Unfriendly Fire" from crime novelist Jon McGoran. In a novella hauntingly reminiscent of true events, the Joes learn quickly that there's no such thing as a purely humanitarian mission.

Closing out the selection is "Message in a Bottle" from the writing team of John Skipp & Cody Goodfellow, who have three novels out and are known for their dark, often transgressive yet visionary work. Their novella views the Joe/Cobra conflict from an entirely different perspective, namely that of a Cobra code monkey whose dirty digital deeds have begun haunt him.

The collection is illustrated by Michael Montenat, a young artist whose amazing talent is sure to make a lot of future jealous enemies.

COBRA WARS is more than a simple collection of stories; it is a rallying cry for seasoned writers to capture the innocent luster of their youth. As America matures, so must its heroes and the authors of COBRA WARS have attempted to portray just that. The goal was to evolve beyond the archetypes of a simpler, more comfortable time and forge a deeper, more nuanced, less cartoonish Joe World for the real world we now find ourselves living in. Hopefully, you the reader, will decide if that mission was successful.

YO JOE!

MAX BROOKS
LOS ANGELES,
JANUARY 2011

Snake Eyes

CHUCK DIXON

Dr. Averill Hanover never considered himself to be a ladies man. Mathematicians don't get the chicks. Especially frumpy, fiftyish, balding academicians. But the woman in the third row at his presentation was showing him a flattering degree of attention.

The conference in Geneva was attended only by those deeply devoted to numbers and how they related to life, existence, and everything else. Most of the chairs in the hall were empty. Those attending were either bored, dismissive, or simply holding their seat for the appearance of the next speaker: a best-selling author who made a name for himself on chat shows by providing dumbed-down, simplistic explanations of difficult mathematic principles as applied to socks missing in the laundry and finding lost pets. A phony with an expensive haircut and even more expensive smile.

But the woman in the third row watched with true interest as Dr. Hanover presented his theorem in a PowerPoint show crowded with charts and number sets. She seemed to be absorbing the complex algorithms and rows and rows of symbols with understanding and appreciation. She was a very attractive woman with long dark hair worn loose to her shoulders and designer eyeglasses that took nothing away from her shocking beauty. Rather, they accented it. She wore a black business suit that even someone as fashion-unconscious as Hanover recognized as haute couture.

Hanover did everything he could not to openly stare at her and several times lost his place in his presentation. In the end, he could only concentrate by looking everywhere but where she was seated. When his lecture ended to polite applause he was disappointed to see that her chair was empty and she was nowhere in sight.

He packed up his laptop and made his way from the hall through the crush queued up to see the charlatan who would follow him. He wondered why he even attended these events. He needed attention for his published formulas. The university insisted on it. He had no interest in attending the talks, luncheons, or panels. Each time he went to one of these gatherings, he spent half the time dreading his time on stage and the other half hiding, bitter and deflated, in his room.

That same woman from his presentation was alone on the elevator as Hanover stepped on board. She smiled at him in a friendly way. He turned to tap the number for his floor and stood pretending great interest in the floor display over the door.

"You're quite brilliant, Dr. Hanover," the woman said behind him. A lovely contralto voice.

"Um...I haven't had the pleasure," Hanover said and half turned to her.

She held out a hand for him to grasp.

"Anastasia deCobray," she said. She wore soft leather gloves. Perhaps that was the style now? He took her hand and searched for something to say. She saved him from the awkward pause by continuing.

"Your equation for creating predictable growth in the economy of a developing nation is fascinating," she said. "It seemed counter-intuitive at first but all makes perfect sense when viewed in hindsight."

"Well, as long as there are no radical changes in a nation's political ideology," he said. "My algorithms, if followed, would provide a steady, reliable growth and a leveling of debt loads and trade deficits."

"But if you could create a formulation that creates a positive economic model, could you not also devise an equation that would destroy a stable economy?"

"I suppose I could," he began.

"Because we would be interested in such a theorem," she said.

We?

His last memory was the touch of her suede gloved fingers to his neck.

Then nothing.

FRIDAY 22:30 HOURS

MOSCOW

YURI KOLIABSKAIA was past the age for leaping about on rooftops. Or crawling about one, as was the current case. The snow-slick surface far above the traffic noise and lights was unforgiving. His smooth-soled dress shoes weren't up to the job. The crocodile-skin loafers, custom fitted in Rome from a mold of his feet at a cost of two thousand Euros, slipped on the slush-coated tiles. He would have traded them in a heartbeat for the pair of combat boots he wore in Kabul all those years ago. Those would be more suited for crossing the roof of the Moscow Grand Hotel in a mid-winter snowfall.

An inch of snow underfoot and twelve stories above the street. He sweated under his suit despite the cold. Too many years of the soft life since the end of the Soviet Era.

Twelve men were paid to protect Koliabskaia from his past. Twelve hard men handpicked by himself and paid well by him. Ex-Spetsnaz. Former mafia. Each one a man more dangerous than anyone Yuri's enemies might send against him.

They were all dead now. He was certain of it. There was no longer the sound of gunfire from the floors below.

Moments before, Yuri was shoved roughly into an elevator

when a man dressed entirely in black materialized among his entourage in the lobby. The two women he'd picked up at the club ran screaming. His guards were too late defending themselves and Yuri saw at least three of them go down in the roar of point-blank fire from what appeared to be an Uzi. Mossad?

Four of his men bundled into the elevator car with him and readied their weapons as the ripping, pounding sounds of automatic fire followed them up the shaft. The thunder from below stopped long before they emerged onto the penthouse level. Two of his men rushed Yuri to a secure room in his suite and told him to stay put while the others tore heavier weapons from a concealed cabinet. Alone in the master bathroom, Yuri stood at the door and listened. Magazines snapping home. Bolts clacking. Muttered curses and whispered grunts of confidence. Men psyching themselves for action. Girding for what was to come next.

He leapt back as his ears rang with the deep thump of an explosion from the next room. Someone blew through a wall or doorway to gain entrance. Then gunfire. The boom of shotguns and freight train sound of an automatic weapon magnified to a deafening degree in the enclosed space. Then the thuds of furniture and the shush of breaking glass.

And silence.

Yuri used a brass towel rack to break out the bathroom windows and made his way out onto the roof.

The roof was a trap. There was nowhere to hide. Only the big steel boxes of air units. Satellite dishes. He moved breathless around the roof looking for another exit. A ladder. A skylight. It was bitterly cold outside but he didn't feel it. He clambered over sloped surfaces and gullies, fell and cracked a hip on the decorative shingles.

Was it really only one man who pursued him? There had to be more. Who would send anything less than a team to bring down the best bodyguards his wealth could buy?

Yuri reviewed the list of those he'd crossed in the past as he moved as swiftly as caution allowed over the slick roof. There were so many in a lifetime of betrayals and lies. He was old enough to have been an officer in NKVD but they were never his true employers. He received payments into a Swiss account to act as a servant of the KGB, paid by one master to spy on the other. The civilian intelligence service wanting to know what their cousins in the army were up to at all times. Spies spying on one another within the same house. Nothing changed in Russia. Always a people who could not trust themselves. Too preoccupied with looking behind themselves to ever make progress. The list of his NKVD comrades who were sent to Lubyanka or worse (based on his detailed reports) was a long one. He betrayed still more of his comrades when the old regime fell and he used his amassed fortune and the dirty secrets he knew to secure himself a place among those protected by the ruling elite.

And that was to be the end of it. He was out of the game and free to retire to a dacha on the Black Sea with the funds earned through deceit and compounded through theft and extortion. That was when he learned that he was never in the pay of the KGB all those years. The money placed in his accounts was put there by a shadow organization, a dark cabal who shunned the light and moved people about as though they were pieces on a chessboard the rest of the world was unaware of.

Cobra.

Yuri was never told the name of his true masters. He had to learn it by a process of elimination, by sifting through whispers and rumors across the global intelligence network. There was a void there. Wherever that void appeared, Cobra benefited. There were inexplicable occurrences and irrational alliances. Cobra provided the missing piece of the narrative that brought all into focus.

A force was always there pushing events for ends that were

invisible even to someone looking for them. Like an object only seen in peripheral vision. Turn your eyes to it and it was gone.

They kept him in the game he thought he'd left behind. He was expected to maintain his contacts and create new ones. In recent years they had him facilitating contacts between terrorist and crime organizations to some unknown purpose. He was expected to use his knowledge and influence to maintain and control his own network of cells, most of which had no idea they were part of a larger scheme and would kill him if they knew how they'd been used. And all the while he knew that his web of contacts were only a single skein in the immense tapestry weaved by Cobra for an agenda known only to themselves.

Was it Cobra who had sent this man in black? Was Yuri's usefulness to them at an end? Is this how they rewarded loyalty?

Yuri realized as he skidded and crept along a ledge that he was not only reviewing a list of his enemies. He was looking back on a lifetime, a lifetime of treason against his fellows, his oath, and his country. This was what a man does when he knows his life is to end.

A shadow fell across him. He turned to see the man in black standing above him. Was that a sword in the man's hand? A sword?

Yuri's movement caused him to lose his tenuous balance and his foot gave under him. He slid toward the edge of the dark roof and toward the bright lights beyond the edge. His heel caught on the strip of party-colored neon that described the rooftop. He could feel it bending, cracking, under his weight. He pounded his hands flat on the icy metal slope for purchase to take the weight from his feet but only slid farther.

His wrist was pinched in an iron grip and he craned his neck to see the man in black crouched firm on the forty-five-degree angle above him. The man had his sword driven into the metal roof as an anchor, his fist wrapped firmly around the long shark-skinned handle of a samurai katana. The man's face was hidden by a mask that covered his head. His eyes were concealed behind a grill of steel. What looked to be a form-fitting Kevlar suit covered his lean form. Blood glistened cold and black on the fabric and Yuri knew that none of it was from his pursuer. The grip on Yuri's wrist was strong, strong enough to easily pull him from the ledge and to safety. But the stranger did not do so.

The man was not here to kill him. The man was here for something Yuri could tell him.

The man was not from Cobra. Yuri allowed himself the luxury of hope even as the neon strand beneath his foot snapped with a brittle sound. The man's grip remained firm. He would not let him fall yet.

Yuri Koliabskaia searched his mind for something, anything, he might say to this man to spare his own life. It had to be a current operation.

"Is this about Dushanbe?" Yuri said.

The man was silent. The only evidence that he was not a statue was the thin wisp of vapor that drifted from his mask.

"Or perhaps Hanover—the mathematician?"

The grip grew firmer.

"I only know a part of it," Yuri said and felt the grip press tighter on his wrist. Painful but encouraging.

"I only suggested his name. Had some people verify his calculations. He was easy to find. His travels were a matter of public record. They made contact in Geneva."

The grip tightened. Painful. The sweet pain of security. Keep talking and the stranger will not let me fall.

"My contact was the woman. The one in glasses. I do not know her name."

The grip shifted slightly. Blood flowed unrestricted to his hand. Displeasure.

"No! Let me think! There may be something useful to you!"

The vise-like pressure was restored.

"I...I..." Yuri searched his mind for anything, true or untrue, that would buy him a few moments more.

The fingers relaxed. The slightest change in pressure.

"There's an operation in Nepal. I've heard rumors. If you let me go I can learn more for you!"

The grip relaxed further.

"I've told you all I know! All they would let me know!"

His fingers tingled as blood rushed back into his hand.

Yuri screamed now, high and shrill. He was past disgrace now. An animal in a trap shrieking for its life.

"I can find out more! I can work for you! I can spy on the spies! It's what I do!"

The grip released and, as he slid the final few feet to the edge, and the roar and hum of traffic grew in his ears, Yuri looked up to see the man was gone.

And then Yuri was gone.

SATURDAY 04:00 HOURS
NEVADA
UNITED STATES NAVY GEOLOGICAL STATION N-99
A DUSTY SERVICE ROAD stretched across a hundred miles of empty desert to end at a sad collection of Quonset huts. The steel buildings were beginning to bake in the early morning light. Sagging cyclone fence and razor wire enclosed them. Heat haze rose from the rocks and sand that were soaking up the first light of the rising sun. A solitary Marine stood at a corrugated steel shack. Unmoving. Not a bead of sweat on his immaculate BDUs. He cast no shadow. Occasionally he fluttered. His holographic image flickered.

Like everything else about this lonely base, the jarhead was not real.

A thousand feet below USNGS N-99 was the Pit. Blasted from solid rock, it housed vehicles, ordnance, and self-sustaining living quarters for five hundred. It was built to not only withstand a nuclear strike but to keep its occupants fed, armed, and safe for the day they would take the fight to whoever dared to nuke their beloved country. This was the super-secret subterranean base of G.I. Joe. The American secret weapon made up of men and women who were dead to the world but lived a second life as the vanguard of a force that defended their country from the dangers of a world of harm.

That's what the recruitment brochure would say. If there was a brochure.

Florescent lights flickered and hummed and bathed the room along Barracks Block A. She sat up in her bunk. Squinted eyes found Shareware standing timid in the doorway. He didn't want to approach and startle her. Last guy who did that spent two months in rehab with a broken collar bone.

"Sorry, Scarlett. You said to come get you anytime."

"Snake Eyes?"

"Yeah. Mainframe has a text."

"Give me thirty seconds."

Mainframe was already seated at the main console in the intel center when Scarlett entered. High-res monitors surrounded a massive table top touchscreen—all of the high-frontier weapons of cyber war. The current field operations were being directed by General Hawk's staff in CommCon (Command and Control) on another level. Intel's background work was done for those ops, and only one intel specialist was required to hold the fort.

"Been up all night, Mains?" Scarlett said as she filled a coffee mug behind him.

"Night. Day. My circadian rhythms march to a different drummer, Red," he said without turning from the triple array of monitors. "I know we're supposed to stick to military time. But I never go topside so it's all good, you know?"

"You have Snake Eyes' contact?" she said and took a seat and keyboard by him.

"Read for yourself," he said and tapped a key. On the monitor appeared:

h/-\n0\/3R /-\8d|_|CtI0N G3N3v@ iNtel?

"It's Leet Speak," Scarlett said.

"Abbreviated multi-byte Leet Speak," Mainframe agreed. "And then encrypted. Our silent buddy is quite the one for hacker cool."

"He's in Moscow and wants an update on a math egghead who disappeared in Geneva?"

"What's his interest in a guy like that?"

"Snake Eyes concentrates on the micro," Scarlett said and tapped in her access code to open her JOEweb account.

Scarlett keyed and scrolled through intel reports from Swiss FCP and INTERPOL. Averill Hanover was a UK native attending a Global Mathematic Solutions Initiative conference and was not seen after delivering an address over a week ago. Swiss cops had it down as a missing persons. No sign of foul play. No evidence of a crime. Hanover was reportedly depressed. He was either on a drunk or was a suicide. Neither of which was illegal in the land of chocolate and coo-coo clocks unless you did your business in public.

Snake Eyes thought otherwise.

Dark hints that this incident was a cover for something more sinister. But that was the world of intel. The glass was always half full. Of cyanide.

"If Snake's into it then it means something," she said.

"Ping him then?" Mainframe said. Fingers poised.

"I'll do it. Translate it to Leet for me and send." She began tapping.

Reliable intel on Hanover?

No active police investigation

What are your needs?

How do we help you proceed?

Mainframe keyed the conversion program and they waited. Fifteen minutes passed with neither of them speaking. A text message opened on monitor:

r3lI@8L3 iN73l. |-|@n0₩/3r ab|)|_|C73d.

₩/al|_|/-₩8le a$s37?

PRi0Rity?

"Snake has reliable intel that it's an abduction," Mainframe said. "There's a Cobra connection."

"What's he want from us, Mains?" Scarlett said.

"An evaluation of the situation," Mainframe said.

"Sounds like Snake wants to go hunting and needs to know the game and the stakes," Scarlett said.

"What do we text back?" Mainframe asked.

Scarlett tapped.

> Hold for ten.
> Will have analysis.
> Your twenty?

Seconds later:

> 3N Rou73 G3n3v@

"On his way to Geneva," Mainframe said.

"As always," Scarlett said as her fingers flew over the keys and the powerful Snakehunter program booted up. "Into the fire."

She settled in for a long day and night.

Saturday 10:24 hours

Dr. Hanover awakened on a bed in a room straight out of a fairy tale. The bed was a four poster of hand-carved wood in an ornate theme of vines and grapes. The other furnishings were old and heavy and dear as well. The room's ceiling was vaulted with exposed oaken beams carved to match the bedposts. One wall of tall windows of leaded glass allowed sunlight in. On another wall was a stout wooden door banded in iron. So he was a prisoner. He was wearing crisp new pajamas, which troubled him more than anything else. His bare feet touched the broad-beamed wooden floor and it was cold. He found woolen slippers that were just his size, again disconcerting, and padded to the windows.

The view through the thick blown glass was a vista of snow-covered mountains. He was in the Alps. No other mountains look quite like them. And he was at an elevation. Standing on his toes with forehead pressed to the glass, he could see the room he occupied was on the upper floor of a medieval building set atop a peak with a sheer edifice dropping hundreds of meters to a rocky defile dotted with evergreens.

On his tip-toes and peeping out the window in his PJs like a child watching anxiously for Father Christmas was how the Baroness found him.

"You'll find your clothes in the wardrobe, Doctor," she said. She was dressed differently than when they last met. Some kind of outfit that looked of a military nature. Dark blue with red piping but without insignia. A stylish outfit that complemented and hugged her slender form. She also wore a pistol belt and boots. Her demeanor was more martial as well. The charm offensive was over.

"Get dressed and I will take you to your workroom. You will have breakfast as you work. We will make productive use of your time, I assure you."

The door closed and Dr. Hanover opened the massive mirrored wardrobe to find his own clothing, cleaned and pressed, hanging in a row.

Troubling.

Saturday 23:30 hours
Snake Eyes maintained a speed just above the limit for the ride south to Torino. The Volvo he was driving was a car he took from the long-term parking lot at the airport in Geneva four hours ago. He watched from the concealing darkness as a fat couple emptied the rear compartment of a half dozen pieces of luggage. A long trip. The car would not be reported missing for a week or more.

He took the Route de Marlagnou south and pulled into a rest stop north of the Italian border crossing. He left the Volvo parked at the rear of the lot where trucks were parked with engines running to keep their cabs warm in the frigid night.

He watched a driver get into a car-carrier truck with Italian plates. He climbed on the back of the trailer as the truck started forward with a jerk and exited the lot. As the truck re-entered the highway and motored south toward the border, Snake Eyes picked the lock of one of the new Audis on the top level of the carrier and ducked inside.

The truck was waved through the Swiss and Italian customs stations and arrived in Milano with no further stops. It was not until the following morning that one of the new Audis was discovered missing.

SUNDAY 05:00 HOURS

THE SHADOWS between the mountains were receding as the sun rose in the sky over the peaks. Snake Eyes guided the Audi along a sidewinder mountain road that hugged a cliff on one side and a two-thousand-foot drop on the other for most of its length. He pushed the car to the limit of its speed and maneuverability as the slick road climbed and climbed in a winding path toward a dead end high above. This section of road was privately owned and would not be monitored by law enforcement. Speeding was not an issue here. As he drove, he maintained contact with the Pit.

"We've reviewed surveillance video from the conference center around the time of Hanover's disappearance," Scarlett's voice came through the receiver built into his helmet. "We see him get on the elevator but we never see him get off. There was some kind of interference with the video signal. That would be Cobra covering their tracks."

Without removing his eyes from the switchback road swerving before him, Snake Eyes tapped keys on a sending set strapped to his wrist. He texted:

EYWITNSSES

"There were a few. A half dozen of them remarked on a woman who attended Hanover's address. Tall. Black hair and eye-glasses. And not the kind of babe who hangs out with math geeks."

BRONESS   CNFRMS MY DESTNTN

"Mainframe worked his magic. If Hanover was taken to the nearest location related to Cobra it would be Monte Verdi. A former Franciscan monastery scammed off of Pope Innocent XIII back in the eighteenth century by the deCobray clan. One of the holdings the Baroness married into."

CERTNTY?

"Mains gives it seventy percent. They could have yanked him to one of their secret sections. If they did, we lost him. We only know the location of a few of them, and most of those were closed once they were compromised. This is the best bet within driving distance. It might be why they grabbed him

DTA ON HNOVER

"Except for why Cobra snatched him, the guy is an open book. He works in theoretical economics. Making projections and predicting trends. His latest work is in fiscal dynamics. Macro economics stuff. Nothing dangerous there. No weaponry or anything that goes boom. Cobra's interest in him doesn't exactly jump out at us."

LVERGE

"Hanover is a widower. He's estranged from his grown daughter. She's the wandering type. The perpetual student type. We're narrowing down her current location."

ETA MNTE VRDI WITHN THE HR

SNKE OUT

"If you hold position and re-con we can send—"

He tapped the temple of his mask and the transmission went dead. He pressed the pedal, shifted down, and drifted around a hairpin turn. This turn fed into a run of straight road that climbed upwards at steep angle. The sun glinted for just a second to his left as he flashed past a dark car parked on a runaway lane.

A check of the rearview showed the dark car was in motion and pulling onto the two-lane road in a shower of dust and gravel. Snake Eyes pushed the Audi harder and tore around a curve to put him out of sight of his pursuer.

SUNDAY 05:16 HOURS

THE ROOM had probably been a grand dining hall at one time. But in place of serving tables and sideboards there was an impressive computer station. A young man in a T-shirt sat absorbed by the images and words on the three big monitors before him. Several tablet computers were on the table before him. Against a wall painted with a mural of Saint Francis and his trial by fire were eight-foot whiteboards on rolling stands. Boxes of markers were open and ready. Seated at a table near the door were the two men in dark clothing who had brought Hanover to this room. They sat sipping espresso with the bored expression of sated lions.

The Baroness stood before the mural.

"Saint Francis was freed by the Sultan after he stepped through the fire unharmed," the Baroness said.

"Is that a promise?" Hanover said.

"Merely a story." The Baroness turned to the young man

"You two will work together," said the Baroness. The young man reluctantly turned his attention from his monitors. He wore a black T-shirt with ERROR 404 on the front in block letters. His hair was studiously unkempt and he wore a permanent sneer of derision. A pair of rimless glasses were perched low on his nose. This tyro was a type Hanover had become familiar with in his years as a teacher.

"Whatever you need to crunch the numbers, Doc," the young man said and shrugged elaborately.

"The white boards will be enough," Hanover said.

"Too slow. Too slooooooooow," the young man said. "You do the big thinking and let me handle the interstitials, know what I mean?"

"I worked ten years on my equation with only chalk and a blackboard. It is not a simple matter of reversing the formula."

"We don't have time for that old-school approach, Doc. Life is short. We need results yesterday."

The Baroness interceded.

"We are on a timetable, Doctor," she said. "We don't have the luxury that a university tenure affords you. Your equation presents a convincing model for how to build a stable economy from a faltering one. It should be the work of no more than a few days to deconstruct that equation to provide guidelines for collapsing an existing stable economy. Particularly with the aid of our computers."

"Theoretically, yes," Hanover said. "But how are you to determine that the results I give you are effective? How are you to know that I am not just stalling, only to give you a useless formulation in the end?"

"That would not be in your interest," the Baroness said. She gestured to the young man who turned to the computer station and touched a screen.

The largest monitor filled with a high-definition image of a modest living room. Messy bookshelves lined one wall. A sofa and an armchair. An Indian weave throw was over the back of the sofa. The setting was familiar to Hanover. A cat, bushy-tailed Persian with dappled white and black fur, strolled into the image area and climbed up on the sofa.

His daughter's cat.

It was a live shot of his daughter's apartment in Paris.

"You see that you have a reason to share our urgency," Baroness said.

SUNDAY 05:29 HOURS

THE BLACK MERCEDES SL 600 rounded a turn on the Via Monte Verdi to find the Audi pulled onto the gravel of a scenic lot overlooking an Alpine valley. The Audi was running and sat alone in the pullover area.

The Mercedes pulled up and stopped thirty meters behind the Audi. The driver and passenger emerged with automatic weapons in their fists and fired controlled volleys at the Audi. The car bucked and twitched like a live thing under the impacts, the windows exploding out in all directions. The interior was filled with a haze of pulped upholstery fill and dusted glass as three- and five-round bursts of nine millimeters tore through the car in an expert crossfire pattern.

The men inserted fresh magazines and approached the Audi from either of its blind sides. With one standing cover, the other stepped to the driver's side and, leading with the barrel of his MP5, craned for a look inside the Audi. It was empty.

As both men turned to scan the park around them, a dark figure rolled from beneath the Audi.

Neither of the men had a chance to turn to see what had disturbed the gravel behind them.

SUNDAY 08:01 HOURS

"LET ME see her," Hanover said. He tried to keep a note of pleading from the request.

"Since you're playing nice," the smirking young man said.

The young man touched the screen and the view of Caroline's apartment appeared again, the cat still dozing in the late morning light.

Hanover turned from the second white board he'd filled with the figures of his formula. He was transfixed by the monitor.

"We have full audio," the young man said. He touched the screen and a volume control appeared. He dialed it louder.

The faint sound of Paris traffic came from the speakers on the wall. The ambient noise of an unoccupied apartment. Then a clinking sound. The snicking of locks. The creak of a door opening off screen. A voice called an indistinct word. Repeated it. The cat mewed in answer and leapt from the sofa to trot off screen. A shadow fell across the room as a figure moved in front of the windows.

"That's enough for now," the young man said. The screen

returned to windows displaying progress bars for the many tasks Hanover had set it to.

Hanover turned to his figures and wiped the last row away with the sleeve of his sweater. He heard her. She was alive. They were only letting him know that they were watching her. That they could reach out whenever they wished. Now or in the weeks to follow, should his equation prove unworkable.

"Any more numbers for me, Doc?" the young man said.

"In a few moments."

SUNDAY 08:18 HOURS

IT WAS SNOWING now as the Mercedes came to a level patch of road just short of Monte Verdi's peak.

The car came to the end of the road and turned onto a broad circular drive before a stone building at the foot of the mountain. There was no one in sight but two black SUVs were parked near the entrance. From the rear of the building a set of rails ran up the slope to the monastery above. It was a mile-long track at a steep thirty-degree angle that clung to the incline and bridged a fissure before it entered a tunnel carved from the rocky wall of the mountain. At the other end of the tunnel, the tracks crossed an open area and then vanished into a broad opening in the cliff's face that would access the cellars of the medieval abbey. A single cable car was drawn by a cable up the tracks with the pulling motors at the top of the run.

Snake Eyes punched the gas and aimed the Mercedes at the decorative double doors of the stone building. The car jumped the steps with a shower of sparks and slammed the doors from their hinges. Snake Eyes leapt from the car as is it continued across the lobby to slam into a stone pillar with a force that shook the entire building.

He was on his feet and moving through the building toward the open cable car platform at its rear. With his Uzi in one fist and a long-slide custom 1911 automatic in the other, he trotted toward the open platform where the six-seat car waited.

Six men, professionals all, leapt from their positions with automatic rifles and shotguns drawn up toward him.

Seconds later he stepped over their bodies and boarded the cable car.

SUNDAY 08:31 HOURS

"MADAME, I may interrupt?" The man stood in the doorway of the monastery's library, where the Baroness was indulging in a cup of hot tea.

"What is it, Emil?" She stirred fresh cream into the china cup.

"Bruni and Paltz radioed. An unauthorized car coming this way on the access road. They found it pulled over on one of the scenic cut-offs."

"And then?" She was growing impatient.

"Then nothing. The men at the base cable station have called to say that Bruni and Paltz's car has arrived but they are not responding to either radio or cell calls."

The Baroness was up and brushed past Emil.

"Follow me!" she called as she stormed down a corridor toward a broad flight of steps.

In the great room she pulled open a cabinet concealed in the paneling to reveal an impressive armory of automatic weapons, ammunition, and explosives. She drew two Panzerfaust 3 rocket-launchers from their place. German designed, one-use projectile weapons. She handed one to Emil and, carrying the other, trotted through French doors and out onto a broad battlement that overlooked the cable car tracks.

She braced herself between two stone crenellations and aimed through the scope at the cable car slowly trundling up the tracks from below.

"It could be our own men," Emil said.

"It is not," she said and squeezed the trigger.

The 60mm anti-tank round took the cable car head-on and burst inside blowing windows and doors out in a fiery blast.

The cable continued drawing the flaming and smoking mess up the side of the mountain.

"Another!" she said and held her hand out for the next launcher.

The second round impacted the tracks below the car and tore away the supports of an old wooden bridge that carried the rails over a rocky depression. The bridge collapsed and the car tumbled to the rocks, where a secondary explosion ripped it in half. All that remained was a greasy fire that sent thick smoke drifting up the mountain side.

Baroness tossed the smoking rocket tube aside and addressed Emil in a flurry of orders. She gave these as she walked back into the monastery and he trotted behind her like a faithful dog.

SNAKE EYES crouched on a ledge and watched the remains of the cable car burn below him. The smoke offered further cover for his ascent, as did the increasing snowfall. He climbed to within a hundred meters of the monastery's cellar entrance after setting the car's departure for a thirty-minute delay. With the most obvious path to Monte Verdi closed off, the Cobra agents in the abbey would believe they were safe for a time.

The way was steep but there were plenty of reliable hand and foot purchases. His chosen path would bring him to some ancient iron steps leading directly up to the broad cable car entrance carved in the mountain's face.

"WE'RE GOING!" the young man announced. He stood before the white boards and used a small camera to take HD images of the equations Hanover had already written there. The pair of armed watchdogs had already left the room in response to commands over their radios.

"But the work—" Hanover said.

"We have to leave, Doc. Now," the young man said and

turned to his keyboard to open a program that would transfer the data they'd created to the COBRAnet. The hard drives here would then fry, leaving no way for others to retrieve their work.

Baroness had given the orders. This place was compromised. Whoever was on that cable car was just a scout. Whatever agency he represented (anyone from Delta Force to the Italian Carabinieri or even Mossad) there would be more on the way. And they'd come in hard and not spare the ammo.

Cobra existed this long by never leaving themselves open to a direct fight with law authorities, especially in a European Union member nation.

Hanover stood transfixed by the image on the large monitor. It was afternoon in Paris and the shadows in the apartment were lengthening. He watched as a slender young woman entered the frame. Unruly blonde hair and dressed in the loose-fitting silk robe top that he'd sent his daughter from a conference he'd attended in Cairo. She shooed the cat from its resting place on the chair. The cat leapt down.

His heart skipped a beat when he heard the voice through the speakers as though she were here in the room with him.

"Get down, Napoleon. You've slept enough."

"Come on, Doc!" The young man was jamming equipment into padded cases. "We're out of here!"

"My daughter…"

"We'll maintain the link. She'll be fine. But we gotta move, okay?" The young man stood holding the door and looking warily down the hallway outside.

Hanover lifted a heavy external hard drive from a table. It was warm in his hands. He brought it down on the back of the young man's head with all the force he could manage.

SNAKE EYES reached the opening in the cliff face and hugged an interior wall as he crept along the shadows under a steel-ribbed loading platform. His hands felt along the granite surface. This was the winch room for the cable car. The cable looped through a massive wheel powered by twin gasoline engines. There was a reservoir tank for gasoline mounted on the floor beneath.

Voices and the clang of footfalls above. Ten men. Maybe more. In a mix of three languages they discussed their status. The Baroness had ordered an immediate evacuation. A small force would be left as a rearguard to ensure her escape along with the hostage. Their job was to prevent any follow-up force from gaining access through the tunnels beneath the monastery while the evac was in progress.

Snake Eyes crouched in the dark and moved across the grease-slick floor toward the winch. He placed a full block of Semtex on the outside of the gasoline reservoir. Two hundred liters at least if it were filled to capacity. He stabbed a stick timer into the block and set the countdown.

He drew throwing blades from a scabbard on his thigh and slipped toward a ladder that led to the walk above.

The first two died quietly with throwing blades deep in the place where the cervical spine joins the base of the skull. The third turned in time to see a dark figure leap over the corpses of his comrades. The only sound he made was a truncated hiss as the long blade of a katana cut short his life.

The rest, eight in all, realized too late that they were under attack. By then Snake Eyes had positioned himself between them and the only exit from the winch room. A spray of fire from his Uzi dropped two of them and sent the rest to cover. He leapt through the doorway and kicked it shut as answering fire swept the spot he'd occupied a half second before. He secured the heavy wooden door and dropped an iron-studded bar across it. He could feel the impact of hundreds of rounds being pumped into the door from the other side, to no effect.

They wouldn't get through the door to trouble him further. Especially not in the fifteen seconds they had left.

*   *   *

A BIG HELICOPTER sat idling in the courtyard of the monastery. A fat EH-101 with no markings. The four rotors created mini cyclones of dust and snow powder as the Baroness ran low toward it with a trio of armed men.

"Error! Respond!" She shouted into a handheld radio. "Where is that geek?"

As if in answer, the young man stumbled out into the courtyard holding a hand to his bleeding scalp. He fell to his knees as the Baroness reached him.

"The old guy clocked me and ran off," the young man said with a wince.

"The formula?" she said.

"Uploaded to the COBRAnet," he said. His eyes swam as he fought to remain conscious.

"Can we finish his work?" The Baroness was shouting now and shaking the young man by the shoulders.

His head lolled back and his mouth went slack.

"Get him on board," Baroness said. Two of the men lifted the young man under the arms and dragged him to the bay doors of the waiting chopper.

"What are our orders?" said the armed man who remained by her.

The flagstones of the courtyard shook. From beneath their feet came a growing rumble. The winch room. It had to be. They were here.

"We leave," Baroness said.

"What about the old man?" the armed man said.

"He didn't hold up his end of the bargain, did he?" she said with a bitter smile. "Make contact with our Paris operatives and give them the green light."

SMOKE WAS FILLING the monastery from the fuel fire raging in the cellar. It provided cover for Snake Eyes, who moved through the haze-choked corridors with the help of optical equipment. It cut through the cover of smoke to give him a clear digital image of the armed men rushing in confusion about the interior of the abbey. Most of these fell silently to his blades as he slipped up close to them in their blindness.

A rack of an action being drawn back. Twenty feet away. Maybe less.

Snake Eyes dived behind a heavy wooden balustrade just as a belt-fed weapon opened up on him. Bullets sent splinters flying over him and racked the plaster walls all around. The gunman was firing blind, sensing the presence of the intruder rather than seeing him. This killer had a hunter's instinct, a predator's wariness.

Five- and six-round bursts followed one after another and expertly swept past Snake Eyes' position. He moved as the rounds reached the farthest point of their arc from him. Low and soundless. The opticals revealed a big man blocking the entrance to a courtyard and firing an FN Minimi hung from a combat sling. The man was bringing the big gun around for another sweep, but Snake Eyes was already in motion and dove into the hallway to plant three rounds from his .45 in a close pattern on the man's chest.

Snake Eyes snatched up the Minimi and followed the stream of the oily smoke that poured up from the floor vents in every room. It was being drawn toward open air. He could hear the thrum of a helicopter's rotors powering up ahead of him. The smoke haze was being blown clear by a big chopper lifting off from the courtyard in the flat light of a snowy afternoon.

Dropping to one knee, Snake Eyes trained the Minimi on the ascending bird and let fly with a long burst that struck sparks from the chopper's undercarriage until the massive vehicle disappeared over the monastery wall trailing smoke. Its barrel burnt out, Snake Eyes tossed the weapon aside. He saw the chopper regain altitude and move, nose down, toward the mountains in the distance. It made a grinding racket but was still air-worthy, and getting farther from his reach with every second.

He whirled, .45 gripped in both hands, and laid the front sights on a figure stumbling from the dense fog of smoke roiling from the abbey. It was a disheveled man in his fifties in a suit that had seen better days. The man bent over and leaned on his knees to retch. Snake Eyes holstered his handgun and approached him.

"May I assume," the man said between coughs, "that since you are at odds with my captors that I may count on your friendship?"

In response, Snake Eyes snapped open a flip phone and held it out to Dr. Hanover. The face of an attractive red-headed woman of serious demeanor appeared on the tiny screen.

"Dr. Averill Hanover?" she said.

"Yes?" he said.

"You're safe with our operative, sir," she said. "Italian authorities will be there within thirty minutes."

"My daughter…" he started.

"She's in no danger, sir. We dispatched a unit to watch over her as soon as we'd determined your situation. There's no reason to worry."

"I suspected so," Dr. Hanover said with a weary smile. "After all, her cat's name is Mimieux."

SUNDAY 22:21 HOURS
PARIS, 14TH ARRONDISSEMENT
THEY WERE relieved to get the call. Eight hours of cramped quarters in the rear of the van with only one another for company were quite enough. The two men stepped from the rear doors and crossed the street to the apartment block in which their target waited unawares. They were dressed in workman's coveralls stenciled with GDF SUEZ, the logo for Gaz de France Suez, the country's primary natural gas utility.

As they climbed the stairs to the fourth floor, they each drew handguns and held them close to their sides. The 9mms were equipped with silencers and special rounds with reduced

powder loads. Execution rounds. For when your target was close and helpless and time was not an issue. They counted off the numbers in the dim hallway until they reached the fourteenth doorway.

They stood before the door and one of them banged on it.

"Mademoiselle Caroline Hanover?" the man called out. "Gaz de France!"

He leaned an ear to the door and could hear movement within. Then:

"*Oui?*"

"There is a reported gas leak. We must speak to you, Mademoiselle. It is urgent."

"Just a moment."

The men took a step back and raised their weapons to train them on the doorway. They had decided that one would take the center shot and the other would deliver the coup de grace. They each took in a breath and slowly released it as they heard footsteps approach the door from the other side. Pulses steady. Eyes trained.

The hallway filled with a cloud of splinters as a dozen heavy slugs exploded through the door from inside the apartment. The door crashed open even as both men were flung across the hallway. A woman with a mop of unruly blonde hair and dressed in a silk robe worn over a Kevlar jumpsuit stepped into the hallway with a matched pair of automatic pistols in her fists. She pumped a three-round burst into each of the fallen gas men.

"Caroline's not home," she said to no one who could hear her. "But you can call me Agent Helix."

Flint and Steel

JONATHAN MABERRY

ONE

The Island – High Security R&D Facility
Near Area 51, Nevada

IT WAS ALL coming apart. Gunfire tore holes in the night. There were screams and the constant rattle of automatic gunfire. Fires burst through the roofs of a dozen buildings, sending showers of sparks into the sky so that it looked like the stars themselves were dying and falling.

Flint ran fast and low, using hard cover instead of shadows, moving from tree to rock to wall, his pattern random and unsymmetrical. He was hurt, he knew that much. The warmth running down the inside of his clothes wasn't all sweat. He could smell the sharp copper tang of his own blood.

His blood and the blood of others.

Doc. Law. Scarlett, too. God knew how many others. In his mind all he could see was blood.

Blood... and those *things.*

He ran and ran, his breath burning in his lungs.

He stumbled and went down, hitting chest-first and sliding, tasting sand in his mouth. He came to rest in the middle of the east parade ground. Exposed, vulnerable.

The screams began to die away. They did not fade like volume turned down on an iPod. They were cut off. Sharply, abruptly, in time with new bursts of gunfire.

Flint felt his consciousness begin to fade as fatigue or damage took hold of him.

"No," he mumbled, spitting sand out of his mouth. "No!"

If he passed out now, he knew that he would never wake up. Not in this world. *They* would find him. Find him and tear him apart.

He tried to get to his hands and knees, but weakness and nausea swept through him.

"No!" he growled, louder this time, and the harshness in his own voice put steel into his muscles. He rose, inch by agonizing inch until he was upright on his knees.

In the distance he could hear one of *them* coming.

A metallic clang, the squeak of treads.

How far? A hundred yards? Less?

Flint set his teeth and tried to get to his feet. No way he was going to die like this. If this was his last firefight, then by God he was not going out on his knees.

Pain flared in his side. He couldn't remember what had hit him. Bullets? Shrapnel?

It didn't matter; he forced one leg up, thumped his right foot on the ground, jammed the stock of his M5 on the ground, and pushed.

It was like jacking up a tank.

He rose slowly, slowly.

The squeak of the treads was closer. All of the screams had stopped.

Even the gunfire seemed to have died away.

"No!" he snarled and heaved.

He got to his feet and the whole world spun around him. He almost fell. It nearly ended right there, but Flint took an awkward sideways step and caught his balance.

The world steadied.

The squeak of treads was close. So close. Too close.

Flint turned.

It was there. Massive, indomitable against the firelit columns of smoke. It rolled to a stop ten feet away, and with a hiss of hydraulics the black mouths of twin 7.62 caliber miniguns swung toward him. He raised his own gun.

The miniguns could fire more than four thousand rounds per minute, per gun.

He wasn't sure he could even pull the trigger.

Flint bared his bloody teeth in a grin that defied the machine, defied logic, and defied the certainty of death that towered over him.

"Yo Joe!" he yelled.

And fired.

TWO

The Island – Conference Room #3
Three Hours Ago

"I'M NOT comfortable with this."

Dr. Allyn Prospero tossed the sheet of paper onto the table with a dismissive flick of his hand. The others at the table watched as the paper spun on a vagary of air and then slid halfway across the polished hardwood surface, coming to a stop almost perfectly equidistant between Prospero and the soldier. Then everyone looked from the paper to Chief Warrant Officer Dashiell Faireborn like spectators at a chess match.

Faireborn—known as Flint among his fellow Joes—had a face like a stone. His jaw was square and set, his nose straight, his eyes as uncompromising as those of a hunting hawk. Flint did not look at the paper, but he tapped the table in front of it.

"That's an Executive Order," he said quietly. " 'Comfort' isn't part of the standard phrasing."

"This is my project."

"That's not what it says on the pink slip. The U.S. government pays for two-thirds of this, and the rest of the light bill is funded by NATO. You're an employee," said Flint, "not a stockholder."

Prospero was as resolute as Flint. "This project would not even exist without me. I *am* the project."

Flint almost smiled. Almost. "Well, that means you must have the same tattoo on your ass that I have on mine."

Prospero frowned.

" 'Property of Uncle Sam,' " explained Doc Greer, who sat to Flint's right. He grimaced. "A little military humor."

"I'm not a soldier. I don't work for the Army, I don't work for G.I. Joe, and I certainly don't work for General Hawk." He loaded that last name with enough acid to melt tank armor.

"That's true," admitted Flint slowly. General Hawk had warned him that he and Prospero were old political sparring partners with a relationship closely resembling a mongoose and a cobra. "However," he said, "you work for the DOD."

"I'm a private contractor," replied Prospero sharply. "I am *not* a rah-rah supporter of the military machine. My work is designed to save American lives, not find new wars in which to discard them."

"You're building war machines—" began Greer, but Prospero wheeled on him.

"What I'm building will ultimately take humans *out* of the combat equation. Does *anyone* in Washington actually read my reports?" When no one spoke, Prospero turned back to Flint. "Perhaps the real issue here is resistance in some quarters to projects that would deny certain persons the opportunity to pull triggers."

Flint said nothing for a moment. The small muscles at the corners of his jaw bunched and flexed. Before he could speak, Doc spoke. His voice was gentle, conciliatory.

"This kind of debate isn't productive, gentlemen," he said. "Politics, ethics, and philosophy aside, the real truth is that we all answer to the man in the Oval Office. With the military budget coming under fire in the press and in Congress, the President needs to be able to justify the kinds of expenditures that have been allotted for Project Caliban."

"My reports are—"

"Yes," cut in Flint, "your reports are fine. Detailed, exhaustive, and to most of Congress, incomprehensible. There are no scientists in either the House or Senate, and what they don't understand they won't support. Sure, back in the Reagan years they'd line up to throw money at a project with a cool nickname, but nowadays everyone's pinching pennies, and Department of Defense research projects are the first on the chopping block."

He bent forward and placed his forearms on the table.

"Dr. Prospero, you're not facing enemies here. I'm an advocate of your program. Hell, I'm an advocate of *any* program that will reduce the risk to men in the field. Cutting-edge drone programs like yours will save lives. American and allied lives. Civilian lives, too. We all know that. But we need to have a clear evaluation statement that will convince Congress of that, or this program is going into mothballs. This isn't a debate. The decision has been made by the President. NATO follows America's lead when it comes to funding."

Prospero said nothing, but he pursed his lips, clearly thinking it through.

"And more to the point, Doctor," said Flint, "there is a long list of other projects begging for the kind of dollars you've been given. If there is any hint of resistance or obstruction on your part, the money train is going to get switched to a different track and within six months the only thing that will be in development out here will be tumbleweeds and cacti."

Flint knew that this had hit home with Prospero. This facility, codenamed the Island, was really a bunch of buildings built into the unforgiving Nevada desert. Twenty years ago there were more than fifty active projects in development out here. Now there were Prospero's team and a few ancillary projects. It was an enormously expensive facility to maintain and only results could keep the lab open.

The doctor looked at the others seated around the table.

There were three members of the Joe team present—Flint, team medical officer Dr. Carl "Doc" Greer, and flame-haired Shana O'Hara, whose call sign "Scarlett" was hardly a "covert" choice. None of them had shared their real names with the team here at the Island. Even though this was not a combat mission, General Hawk had ordered that only rank and call-signs be used. Part of Hawk's policy of professional detachment.

The others at the table were members of Prospero's staff here at the Island. To his immediate left was Professor Elsbeth Miranda, once his most promising grad student during his days at MIT, then his protégé, and now the most valuable senior researcher on staff. Her knowledge of unmanned combat systems was only slightly less profound than his own. She was tall, slim, and had that blend of pale skin and foamy dark hair that usually made Flint's heart flutter like a jazz drum solo. She wore a lipstick that was a shade too bold a red for this kind of meeting, and her blouse was unbuttoned one button too low to have been anything but a deliberate move to attract attention. At first Flint thought that she was a hot-blooded woman who was taking a rare chance to attract something other than lab-coated geeks, but as the meeting progressed he changed his view. Her attention was clearly—and entirely— focused on Prospero, and it was at once possessive and protective.

Office romance, he wondered. *A May-December thing…or a female predator laying claim to the alpha in her environment. Had to be something like that.*

And yet he knew that the lipstick and the abundant cleavage she had on display was for his benefit—his and the other Joes.

A distraction? Sure. But to distract them from what?

He quietly studied the other scientists. Like Miranda they were lions in their fields—microsystems, software integration, computer engineering, nanotechnology, artificial intelligence, and tactical weapons sciences. None of them, however, were on Prospero's level, and probably not on Miranda's either.

They were strong members of a pack. And, like Miranda and Prospero, they resented outside intrusion of any kind, and evaluations in particular.

However, no one spoke. Everyone was aware of who the true alpha—at least in terms of scientific genius—was. Allyn Prospero had graduated from high school at age fourteen, college at sixteen, and had earned his first PhD at nineteen. Since then he had lost track of the many degrees, awards, and accolades he had collected in fifty years as the leading light in cybernetic combat. He had pioneered more new fields of study than anyone alive, and was named on over six hundred patents. He had four times been senior researcher on teams that won the Nobel Prize.

Flint knew all of this. He had Prospero's resume memorized. It was in the scary realm somewhere between "impressive" and "freaky," though Flint tended toward the latter category.

Prospero sighed.

"Very well," he said heavily. "When do you want to begin?"

Flint kept a smile off of his face. "Now would be good. Our weapons and equipment have all been off-loaded and should be set up out on the sand."

"What kind of equipment?"

Flint spread his hands. "It would make a more effective and convincing test if you didn't know ahead of time. And, let's face it, the best way to guarantee the biggest slice of the pie from the budget committee would be for me to be able to tell them that I saw the system in full operation."

Professor Miranda shot Prospero a sharp look. "We're weeks away from a practical test—"

The scientist narrowed his eyes. There was some murmuring among his staff. None of them spoke directly to Prospero, though one or two bent close to whisper to Professor Miranda. After a moment's consideration she and Prospero leaned their heads together and hid their mouths behind their hands to exchange a few covert words.

Flint, Scarlett, and Doc exchanged quick looks, but did not comment.

Prospero held up a placating hand. "If that's what will get this over with and allow us to get back to work, Chief, then I think we can provide a demonstration that will satisfy *any* Doubting Thomases."

Miranda furrowed her brow at him. "You mean...*Caliban*?"

Prospero smiled. "Yes," he drawled. "I think Caliban would provide a very adequate demonstration of our potential."

Miranda studied him for a moment, and then she, too, smiled.

THREE

"WHAT WAS all *that* about?" asked Scarlett once the team of scientists had filed out of the conference room.

Flint leaned back in his chair and blew out his cheeks.

"Hell if I know. Spooky bunch, every last one of them."

Doc said, "Prospero's oddly aggressive for someone who's ultimately goal is the end of war."

Scarlett closed the door and parked a shapely haunch on the corner of the table. "Prospero would make a wonderful mad scientist. Give him a white cat and a hollowed-out volcano and he's all set."

Flint grunted. "When you're that far out on the cutting edge, a little eccentricity is expected."

"Scary smart," agreed Scarlett.

"Speaking of scary," said Doc. "Did you catch the mood dynamics of that team? There's a weird pecking order there. Prospero almost never looks at them. He looks at Professor Miranda, and she relays Prospero's moods through her own expressions and body language to the rest of the team. They in turn make quiet comments to her, and she conveys *some* of the comments to Prospero. Like a filtering process."

"He doesn't deign to speak to the little people?" suggested Scarlett.

"So it seems."

Flint shrugged. "Runaway ego is also pretty common with guys in his class. I'm not really worried about whether he rules his staff with an iron fist. It's an extension of the university model, so he probably picked that up at MIT. He was top dog there, too." He glanced at the closed door. "No, what concerns me is how possessive he is about this."

"Surely that's pretty common too among top researchers," said Doc. "Especially guys pioneering their own fields."

"Maybe," Flint said dubiously, "but it comes off more as arrogant and secretive. I could accept that a bit easier with an egghead running a software lab—you know, fear that someone else will copy the idea and rush another version to market. Happens all the time in the gaming industry. Can't say I'm fond of seeing it in a weapons designer working for us."

Scarlett stood up. "I know what you're saying, Flint. Prospero's attitude has been *noticed*. Duke said as much during our briefing. It's not just the viability of the program that's under the microscope."

"No joke," nodded Doc. "Last thing we need is an *actual* mad scientist going off the rails with forty billion dollars worth of automated killing machines that only he knows how to control."

It wasn't meant as a joke, and no one laughed.

Flint got to his feet. "Okay... we asked for a demonstration. Let's go see what he has."

FOUR

The Island – Dead Lake Testing Area

Dr. Prospero stood in the middle of the empty desert, surrounded by red flares that burst above him like fireworks and drifted down to encircle him like one of the rings of hell. As each new flare burst, the scientist could see the clouds of white phosphorous smoke hanging in the sky, and then as the flares drifted down on their tiny chutes the sky above him faded again to utter blackness.

The desert at night was usually so quiet. He loved coming out here to think, to work things through. To consider the past and plan for the future. The emptiness and vastness of the Nevada desert was his sanctum, his cloister for years.

Now it burned with red fire and the silence was torn by the hollow, steady crack of automatic gunfire and the occasional deep-throated boom of missiles. Hellfire missiles, which Prospero thought was a fine irony.

He waited. Dragonflies flitted around him. They always made him smile. They swirled around him, buzzing on green wings that gave off a faint electric hum. Anyone unfamiliar with the tiny biomimetric machines would think they were really insects. Prospero extended a hand and one of them landed on it, antennae twitching, miniature legs bending and walking in an almost perfect imitation of life.

"Go play," he said and shook it off. The words sounded playful, but they keyed the search and observe protocols in their microchips. The dragonflies turned and flew into the darkness, hunting the monsters that hunted him, their beating wings recharging their batteries as they flew. Not quite a perpetual motion machine, but as close as he had been able to manage so far.

Prospero had also launched a half dozen of the larger but still man-portable SkyLite observation drones. The lithium-polymer batteries on the stealth drones only held a four-hour charge, but it took only a few minutes for them to reach thirty-six thousand feet. The Joes had satellites that could be targeted and destroyed by any number of air-to-space or space-to-space weapons, but Prospero had swarms of tiny machines that were harder to see, harder to catch, disposable and replaceable.

"Fly, fly, fly," he said in an almost dreamy voice.

There were gunships in the blackness above him, running silent and dark; and even though he could not see the wicked mouths of the miniguns pointing at him, he could *feel* them. At least a dozen of them, each capable of firing six thousand rounds per minute through their rotating six-inch barrels. Enough firepower to wipe out a company.

Because there was no possibility of escape, Prospero did not care about them.

There were other monsters in the dark, and he turned his head slowly from side to side, trying to decide the approach vector for the drones. He knew that at least two of the unarmed combat air vehicles would be zeroing in on him. There was a Phantom Ray II up there, the newest of Boeing's Phantom Works craft. Armed with the Hellfires and other goodies, some as experimental as the drone that carried them.

And if that psychopath Hawk had anything to do with planning this attack, then there would be a General Atomics Avenger up there, too, laboring under the weight of Paveway bombs, Hawk's personal favorite.

Prospero could try to run, but where could he go? They were drawing a circle around him, closing it tight like the neck of a drawstring bag. With him inside.

He smiled.

On his way out here he had carried two large metal cases that looked like dog carriers. Each case had a spring flap keyed to a pedometer built into his exosuit. Every fifty yards the flaps opened and dropped half a dozen Sprawlers. These small hexapedal devices dropped like spiders onto the sand, immediately activated ground sensors, and scuttled off into the dark. They were unarmed, but they were fast, and long before the Joes found *him* he would know where *they* were.

Professor Miranda's soft voice whispered in his ear.

"They're coming."

"And about time, too," he replied.

"Are you ready?"

He hit a keypad and a hologram of a topographical map appeared in his visor. The map sparkled with blue dots that identified his Sprawlers and Dragonflies and SkyLites, and glowed with larger yellow dots that showed what his mechanical friends had found. "Completely."

"Be careful," she cautioned. "I don't trust them. I think they're determined to take you down."

Prospero laughed. "They're welcome to try."

"Then watch your back, because they're going to try right *now*!"

The world of darkness turned to blinding noonday brightness as missiles punched into the desert floor and burst. Twin fireballs curled upward and the concussive crossways blast of the shockwave hit the man with bone-crushing force, lifting him, throwing him like a doll into a sandstone wall sixty yards behind him. The force of the impact was enough to splinter bone and rupture muscle tissue, bend steels and shatter hardened polymers.

Except that none of this happened to the scientist.

He slammed into the wall and slid down, but only into a crouch. Fire and hot dust swirled around him, but he was safe and whole. And smiling.

He pushed off the wall and stood, turning left and right to watch for the next attack.

"Gunships!" cautioned Miranda's voice, but Prospero did not need the warning as fifty-caliber rounds pounded into his chest, driving him backward against the wall. Hundreds of hits. Thousands.

Then another salvo of rockets turned the sandstone wall into a rain of jagged debris, knocking him over, burying him to the waist. In the nearly constant muzzle-flash he saw the Blackhawks hovering ten feet above the desert floor, side doors open, miniguns swung out on electric turrets and opened up, their roar louder than thunder.

The guns hammered him until they fired themselves dry, then they rose slowly, moving upward and sideways, turning to bring their rocket pods to bear.

Prospero fought his way out of the waist-deep rubble. He grabbed a rock the size of a mailbox, lifted it with a grunt, and threw it to one side. Then he straightened, rising to his full height of nine feet.

"Night vision," he said, and instantly the world transformed from black and red to green and black and white.

"SkyLites," he said, "talk to me."

One side of his vision was suddenly filled with images taken from the drones that circled like buzzards over the desert.

"Thermal overlay." Dots appeared on the image. He counted four Blackhawks and three fixed-wing drones. Hawk had sent *two* Avengers to back up the Phantom Ray. All of the military drones were circling back toward him, their systems apparently ignoring the smaller UACs that Prospero had launched. Other signatures showed a phalanx of fast-moving desert patrol vehicles converging.

It was anyone's definition of a worst-case scenario. A pair of Abrams tanks couldn't fight their way out of this. Which is why he'd sold his General Dynamics stock last month. The Caliban exosuit he wore was about to put the tank manufacturer into the antiques business.

"Are you all right?" asked Professor Miranda, her voice twitchy with stress.

"I'm perfect," he said and then laughed. "They've shown us what they can do. Now let's show them what *we* can do."

"Prospero… Allyn… please," she said urgently, "don't take any unnecessary risks. You—"

"Hush, darling. Hush. This is what we wanted. This is what we *needed*. We've been wracking our brains trying to figure a way to give a practical demonstration to our overseas friends. This was *handed* to us on a silver platter. A full system demonstration, and the government is not only paying for it, but mandating it. What could be more perfect?"

"I know, but these people, these Joes… just because they're military don't fool yourself into thinking their collar size is bigger than their IQ."

He laughed again, and there was a wild quality to it. He even heard it, and didn't care. It was a time to be wild, to be fully alive!

"They're dinosaurs, my dear; they just don't yet know that they're extinct. Besides, the Joes will see only what we want them to see."

"Don't underestimate them—"

"Miranda, hush. Just make sure everything is fed to the secure uplink. I want our *friends* to see the Joes throw everything they have against us."

"Be careful, my love. The Joes are coming in for another run."

"Let them come," said Prospero. Then he switched from external to internal voice mode. "Caliban combat systems to voice control."

"System on." Caliban's computer voice was the only part of this he didn't like. It was an older computer voice system that manufactured words instead of compiling them from a programmed library. The new voice software package had not been installed yet. He was sorry about that. The voice choices included Morgan Freeman, Mark Hamill, or Joseph Gordon Levitt. Hamill would have been fun. Luke Skywalker guiding him through this would be fitting. It all seemed like science fiction anyway. Even to him.

"Laser targeting."

"Online."

"Uplink to enemy tactical satellite."

"Uplink established."

He stepped forward. The servos attached to his boot straps lifted the forty-pound foot as easily as if he wore a pair of flip-flops.

"Skyjack online," he said.

"Booting," said the computer voice. *"Skyjack system online."*

The whine of the chopper rotors increased as the Blackhawks tilted for a strafing run. They'd hammer him again, allowing the laser-sighting system of the drones to acquire him for another rocket attack.

"Initiate Skyjack protocol Prospero One Nineteen."

"Initiating."

The satellite display board flashed and cleared, removing all of the identified combat craft. Then one by one they popped back on, but this time each dot was surrounded by a white circle. Before they had all reappeared, the circles were overlaid by white crosses.

Caliban's dispassionate computer voice began counting it off.

"Blackhawk one acquired."

"Blackhawk two acquired."

"Blackhawk three acquired."

"Blackhawk four acquired."

"General Atomics Avenger one acquired."

And on and on until all of the vehicles and aircraft surrounding him were logged.

Prospero smiled. "Prepare to accept command code."

"Ready."

" 'Tempest,' " he said. Instantly the computer voice rattled off a stream of command codes.

"Destroy all enemy warcraft," said Prospero. He did not need to give that command, and in truth it did nothing to increase the lethality of the Skyjack program. The virus software would now be rerouting the systems of every automated vehicle, on land or in the air. In seconds the machines sent to *test* him would obliterate each other. All of that was written into the code…but it felt good to speak the order; when the destruction began it would be at his command.

Pleased, the old scientist sat down on the rock he had thrown and waited.

There were three seconds of silent darkness.

All around him the skies blossomed with white light. Gunfire roared. Rockets fired one after the other. Bombs fell.

The whole desert seemed to explode.

None of the bullets struck him. None of the missiles flew in his direction.

He smiled.

"Destroy them all," he murmured. "Burn them out of my sky."

On his helmet's monitor the blips indicating the Blackhawks and the drones and the fast attack vehicles flickered and vanished until only one craft was left. Then, it too burst into flame and fell like a meteor through the night. It struck the sandstone eighty feet from where he sat. Prospero didn't even bother to raise an arm to protect himself from the flaming debris.

FIVE

The Ice House
Kaffeklubben Island, 440 miles from the North Pole

THE MAN sat alone, draped in soft shadows, his shoulder and face etched by yellow firelight. Pine logs hissed and popped in the stone hearth. The air around him was troubled by the almost maniacal complexity of Rachmaninoff's *Piano Concerto No. 3 in D minor, Op. 30*, and yet the man in the chair found the music deeply soothing. It was like sailing through the eye of a hurricane—chaos all around and yet deep insider there was perfect stillness. And with stillness came clarity.

A glass of wine sat forgotten on the table beside his chair.

The man reclined in the chair, fingers steepled, eyes narrowed, lips pursed as he studied the images that played out on the flatscreen monitor that filled most of one wall. He watched with professional interest as a Phantom Ray veered off course and slammed its eighteen-and-a-half tons into a General Atomics Avenger. Both drones exploded in a massive fireball and fell onto the desert floor far below. Unmanned tanks swung their turrets and laid down continuous fire at fast attack vehicles. Machine guns in remote-controlled Blackhawks turned their guns on other helos flying in attack formation. All of it within seconds, all of it in a beautifully coordinated ballet of self-immolation and mutual destruction.

When the last of the guns fell silent, the man in the chair

took a deep breath and let it out through his nostrils, puffing like a contented dragon. In the upper left corner of the screen a smaller pop-up screen showed the face of a beautiful woman with long brunette hair and glasses that hung around her neck on a silver chain.

"This completes our demonstration, sir," she said. Her voice trembled and she was clearly nervous. No, almost certainly afraid. Although she did not know the name, or even the codename, of the man to whom she spoke, she knew enough about who he was and what he represented to be properly terrified. That pleased the man; it was as it should be.

The woman stared at him—or at the screen saver of a coiled snake, which was all that she would ever see of him—with expectation in her eyes. Was she waiting for praise?

Probably. He smiled. The next ice age would come and go before he would spoon out praise to a *vendor*. And a potential vendor at that.

"What is your asking price?" he said. There was at least a fragment of tacit approval in that question. Let that be enough for her. Let her suck what juice there was out of that.

But she was undeterred. She leaned toward the camera, double vertical lines forming between her brows. "Price is secondary," she said. "Your assurance is paramount."

"Of course," he replied with only the barest hesitation, "and you have it. I respect and endorse your ideals. Ending global conflict is our shared goal. How did Prospero himself phrase it? 'When no human hand touches a weapon of war, then war will not touch human hearts.' Elegantly phrased. Much better than my own clumsy 'Wage a war to end all wars.' So... rest assured that I will always bear in mind that this is the cornerstone of any arrangement between us."

The woman hesitated for a moment, then nodded.

"Now," the man said, "I believe we were discussing price—?"

The woman had enough grace and good taste not to speak the number. Instead she looked down and tapped some keys.

A price appeared in a discreet corner of the screen. There were a lot of zeroes. Some might say an absurd amount.

The man in the chair considered the price.

"I'll let you know," he said, and before she could say anything he disconnected the call.

He sat in silence for a thoughtful few moments and then turned his head ever so slightly to the other small pop-up screen.

"You may comment," he said.

"That bonnie lass and her auld—and, I might add, quite daft—Frankenstein boyfriend are trying to rob ye blind, and ye damn well know it," snapped a slender man wearing an ermine-trimmed robe. His eyes were alive, but in a face that gleamed like old silver.

"Is that your professional assessment of the demonstration?"

"Oh, aye, I like it well enough. Lots of lovely pyrotechnics. Hooray for the Red, White, and Blue... but ah dinnieken why ye want another vendor. Which of my bloody systems have underperformed for ye?"

"What's the matter, Lord Destro? Don't you *believe* in capitalism?"

"I believe in loyalty. From vendor to customer as well as from customer to vendor."

"Mmm, that's one view, but it's self-corrupting. Competition, on the other hand, encourages innovation, shortens time to market, and allows for more rational discussions of price."

"Don't be daft. I'm fair scunnered with these games. There's a trust issue here as well."

"Trust is earned."

"And haven't I earned your trust?"

"Allow me to modify that statement. Trust needs to be continually earned."

The man with the silver face said nothing.

"Dr. Prospero is offering some exciting new technologies. His hybrid Skyjack/ Tempest intrusion software is probably worth the price he's asking for the whole package. I don't really need the exosuit, though admittedly there are some members of the Crimson Guard who would enjoy field testing it." He paused. "Really, Destro, if you had a mobile tactical command unit like Caliban we might not be having this conversation."

"I can make one, as ye damn well know."

" 'Can make one' is far less appealing to me than 'have one now.' The schematics for Dr. Prospero's technology will be uploaded to my servers within minutes after a wire transfer to the Caymans. Can you do that for me?"

Lord Destro's face was inert steel, and yet it seemed to convey both anger and menace.

The man in the comfortable chair chuckled. "I thought not."

"You know you can't trust him," said Destro. "Unless you're so soft that you *believe* that he's doing this all for morality and greater good."

"Mmm, and all this time I thought *you* were an idealist, and yet you are always willing to take my money. What are you saying? That idealism is merely a candy coating over a poisoned apple?"

"Don't compare me to that maniac," demanded Destro.

"If you're uncomfortable with the question, then forget I said anything. Contact me when you have something for me to consider."

"'Consider'? In the name of the wee man! What about our agreements?"

"Free market," said the man with an airy wave of the hand. "Sadly, it's become a free market."

He disconnected the call and reached for his wine, sipped it. And smiled.

SIX
Destro Castle
Scotland

LORD DESTRO reached out and tapped a key to disconnect his end of the call. The white static vanished on the screen.

He slowly stood and walked slowly across the room, his steps measured and his posture thoughtful. His two dogs—great brutes of black hounds named Cu Sith and Boky—lifted their heads and watched him. They knew their master and his moods, and they were not at all fooled by the calm façade, just as they were not surprised when their master suddenly snatched up a silver and crystal goblet and threw it the length of the room.

Boky *whuffed* softly.

Cu Sith bared a fang and growled low in his throat.

Destro sighed and bowed his head.

Honor was a ten-ton weight at times. He'd known about Prospero for years and had worked with him off and on. A gentleman's agreement was supposed to be in place. Prospero would bring his drones and software systems to him and Destro would in turn broker them to Cobra. Now it was clear to a blind man that Prospero had no intention of including Destro in any part of this exchange. Not even so much as a finder's fee for having introduced the old tosspot to the Commander. And Destro had lent Prospero some of his own systems and even one of his top men, Han Kong, to speed the development along. Kong, of course, had finessed a few things according to Destro's requirements, none of which were shared with Prospero. That wasn't dishonorable, that was common sense self-defense.

This presentation... now that was so sharp a slap in the face that Destro swore he could actually feel it on his skin.

"Damn ye for a Sassenach!" he said in a fierce whisper, conjuring images in his mind of that old bastard being torn to red rags by the dogs.

He felt insulted, betrayed. Hurt.

He had even tried to give Prospero a chance to make it right. He'd gone through that witch Miranda to suggest very quietly and discreetly that the old man stop hunting on another man's preserve. When that hadn't worked he'd appealed directly to the egotistical old swine. Nothing. Not even a returned phone call.

Instead, the Commander calls him and offers him the opportunity to covertly observe Prospero's impromptu test.

There were times he wished he was a mackerel fisherman. This life could be so bloody frustrating.

"Honor among thieves," he said aloud. "Aye, and pigs may fly."

The dogs got up and came over to him, leaning their huge shoulders against him, whimpering softly. Destro bent and stroked their flanks, doing it slowly, letting the action soothe him. Dogs were always the best of companions, and no joke. Loyal by nature's design and incapable of guile.

"Ye shaggy monsters," he said with rough affection. They licked his hands and chuffed.

Destro took a long breath and let it out. Then he cocked his head to one side as if listening to an inner voice.

"Ah... you are a glaikit moron," he told himself. Beneath his mask, he smiled. Then he turned back toward the computer and looked at the screen as if he could still see Prospero in his metal suit. And still hear the Commander's velvet mockery of a voice.

"Free market be damned."

He stalked back to his computer terminal and began hammering keys. He used a signal re-router to spin-worm his way into the Department of Defense database, blank-trailing his entry by a code-rewriter that wiped out all traces of the intrusion. Then he accessed the inactive employee data files and brought up the login for Dr. Han Kong.

Still smiling, he tapped in the password.

"*Welcome, Dr. Kong,*" said a soft computer voice.

Destro laughed softly to himself. "Free market is it, ya bas? I've got your number and no mistake. Let's all make free, and devil take the hindmost."

* * *

SEVEN
The Island
Tactical Observation Room #1

FLINT STARED through the reinforced glass at the flaming wreckage and gave a low whistle. "That's... beautiful."

"I don't think that would be the adjective I'd choose," muttered Doc Greer.

Flint grunted. "The pacifist doesn't like things blowing up. Enormous surprise, Doc."

"It's not just that. One man did all that. Granted the attack vehicles were all automated, but from what I can see it wouldn't have played out any differently had there been real men and women on the field. One man."

Scarlett added, "One man in a half-billion-dollar combat suit cross-linked to targeting satellites and using counter-encryption intrusion software."

"My point exactly," agreed Doc.

Flint turned away from the fires still burning out in the desert. "What adjective would you prefer?"

"Offhand?" said Doc. "Terrifying."

"Then you're going to live in fear, Doc, because this is the new face of warfare. Congress and NATO are going to line up to shovel money into this project."

Something caught their eyes and they both turned toward the window as the man in the combat rig walked by. Light from the observation deck spilled out through the window and traced the outline of the stalking figure. Prospero was totally encased in armor painted with the alternating pixilated slate gray, desert sand, and foliage green of the universal camouflage pattern used by the U.S. Military. The exoskeleton was neither sleek nor handsome. Instead it looked like an ugly and improbable collection of pipes and plates fuse-welded in a way to be deliberately unpleasant to the eye. However, its massive height gave it grandeur and its performance in the field inspired a sense of dread.

It stopped and turned toward them. From outside, this viewport blended into the landscape, invisible even to infrared and NVG, but the blank steel face of the titan swiveled around so that it was facing the Joes inside.

"God almighty," breathed Doc.

Then the massive metal arm came up into a formal salute, snapping it off with a touch of swagger instead of the crisp military precision that would have been more in keeping with the thing's robotic appearance. But the Joes knew full well that this was no robot, nor was it a drone. A man hung suspended within the metal body, his slightest move instantly activating a reciprocal move by the exoskeleton.

And though they could not see the face of Dr. Allyn Prospero, they knew that the old scientist was smiling.

"Okay," said Scarlett as the thing turned and stalked away. "I'll go with 'terrifying,' too."

"I might have understated it," murmured Doc.

The hatch door behind them hissed open and they turned to see Prospero in the exoskeleton. Desert winds whipped tendrils of residual smoke around him and he looked like a statue of one of the Greek titans standing there. Immense, impossibly powerful.

With a hiss of hydraulics, the iron giant stalked into the room and stopped a dozen feet away. A robotic voice spoke from external speakers.

"Powering down. Caliban combat systems off-line."

A golf cart came whirring out of a side corridor and as it rolled to a stop the -tech crew jumped out, each of them holding tools. Professor Miranda was with them, her expression neutral. Two men with impact wrenches went to work on the chest plate. Another unlimbered a heavy cable and plugged it into a socket on the back of the suit. Professor Miranda unfolded a short metal step ladder and mounted it to reach the face plate. The team worked with practiced efficiency as Flint and Doc watched, and with the speed of a race team pit crew, they had the major components removed and set aside to reveal Dr. Prospero suspended in the sling harness.

"How did Caliban perform?" Miranda asked.

The old man was bathed in sweat but grinning like a happy child.

"He was magnificent!" said Prospero. "Absolutely magnificent."

Professor Miranda smiled with obvious relief and pleasure.

Scarlet nudged Flint with an elbow and mouthed the word *he*. Flint had caught it. *He,* not *it.* He turned to Doc, but Doc was already up to speed on that. He had his lips pursed in thought. Flint knew that they weren't happy thoughts.

Miranda disconnected the last of the straps and then descended the ladder to allow Prospero to disengage the harness straps and step down. She offered her hand to steady him, and when he was off the ladder she fetched a cane from the golf cart and handed it to him.

Prospero leaned on the cane. "Thank you, my dear."

"And how do *you* feel?"

It took a moment for Prospero to answer that. He turned and stared at the dissembled mechanical monster. While it was clear that he was physically exhausted, his face came alight with a complex series of emotions. He cut a quick look at the Joes standing nearby and then touched the woman's cheek.

"I feel *wonderful!*" he said. "Young and alive."

Doc cleared his throat and entered the little bubble of their private conversation. "I'd like to give you a brief post-action exam, Doctor."

Prospero stiffened. "Nonsense. I'm perfectly fine as you can see."

"You're flushed and perspiring heavily and—"

"The suit was hot and I just ran four miles," interrupted Prospero.

"—and you're seventy-four years old."

Prospero laughed aloud and nodded toward the machinery. "Not when I'm in there! It's very much like sky-diving, or driving a Formula One. After a while you can't tell where you end and the machine begins. It's so exhilarating. I was a *god* out there!"

Doc nodded. "Sure, but you're not in there all the time. And right now it looks like your blood pressure could pop rivets out of plate steel."

"I'm fine."

"I'll be the judge of that."

Prospero met Doc's eyes and the moment stretched around them. Professor Miranda shifted to stand next to the old man, using body language rather than words to show her support.

Flint watched all of this and very nearly stepped over to stand beside Doc, but that would turn the moment into bad drama. Instead he said, "The test was pretty amazing, Dr. Prospero, and you have a right to be proud of the Caliban exosuit. Consider me a fan. However, our friends in Congress aren't paying us just to watch. Our team is here to evaluate everything, and that does mean *everything*. If Doc Greer wants to examine you, then let's all put it down to dotting the I's and crossing the T's."

Prospero opened his mouth to say something, and from the taut pull of his lips it was likely to be something biting. They had been warned that the old scientist was a cantankerous SOB, but Flint wasn't interested in enabling cranky behavior.

It was Professor Miranda who broke the tension of the moment.

"We understand completely, Chief," she said with a smile, touching Prospero on the arm and then turning the full wattage of her smile on Flint. She stepped closer to him, pitching her voice as if they shared a private conversation. "Chief Warrant Officer Faireborn, as a soldier with significant field experience you must be familiar with the exuberance that comes with combat exertion."

"Somewhat," Flint said neutrally.

Professor Miranda stepped a bit closer, looking up into

Flint's eyes, and Flint was suddenly very aware of how truly beautiful the professor was. He made his face turn to stone.

"All those juices flowing," Miranda continued, "the awareness of your own power. The understanding of your potential for great things."

Flint cut a look at Doc, who was trying so hard to hide a smile that the effort looked painful.

"Um, yes, ma'am," mumbled Flint. "I suppose I do."

"Call me Elsbeth, Chief *Flint*." She loaded his name with enough hidden meanings to sink a battleship.

A few feet away Scarlett softly cleared her throat. She had been watching with amusement and professional interest as Miranda attempted to dazzle Flint. She shifted her posture as a way of breaking the trance through distraction, and in a very businesslike tone said, "If everything plays out the way it looks like it will, once we crunch the numbers...I think we can safely say that you just changed the face of warfare for the next generation."

Professor Miranda began to say something else, but Flint stepped sideways—out of the potent energy of her personal space—and angled himself to address both her and Prospero.

"When Doc is done with his exam I would love to sit down over coffee and hear everything about what went on out there." He looked at Prospero. "I've never seen *anything* like that."

Prospero studied him for a few moments, clearly trying to determine whether he was being "handled" or if the praise was genuine. Then a smile seeped slowly onto Prospero's mouth as he considered those words. He took a deep breath and let it out slowly, deflating the ball of tension he'd been holding in his chest.

"It's encouraging to know that you are a person of vision," he said.

"Are you kidding?" said Flint. "We're all certified soldier geeks. We love gadgets."

"You have no idea how much," Scarlett said under her breath.

"So," Flint concluded, "this stuff is straight from heaven."

Prospero's smile became genuine. He nodded and offered his hand to Doc.

"Forgive my terseness."

Doc's hand was only a microsecond slow in responding, but they exchanged a firm grip.

"Perfectly understandable. Just watching you had my own blood pressure nearly off the scale." He gestured toward the side corridor. "Shall we?"

Doc and Prospero walked away together. Professor Miranda lingered for a moment, giving Flint an enigmatic look and a very appealing pink-lipped smile. Then she turned and followed. The tech crew finished their work and piled back into the golf cart and vanished, leaving Flint and Scarlett alone in the observation chamber. Silence filled the room, and they turned and walked slowly over to the window. The fires had burned down to embers out there on the sand.

"How's *your* blood pressure, cowboy?" asked Scarlett.

He laughed. "Don't start."

"Me? *I* wasn't starting anything, but you looked like you were ready to drop down on one knee and propose."

Flint snorted. "She's cute, but her only interest in me is in how much she can run interference for Prospero."

"So, you're not smitten by the geeky brunette with glasses?"

"I think we all know what a slippery slope *that* is."

Scarlett gave him a knowing wink and sat down on the edge of a desk. "I think Miranda is every bit as formidable as her boss."

"Agreed. Which means everybody needs to keep their eyes open at all times." Flint tapped the topmost button on his uniform shirt. "You get all that, guys?"

"Every word," said a man's voice.

The receiver bug looked like a freckle on the inside of Flint's left ear. Scarlett had an identical one on her right ear. The voice belonged to Christopher M. Lavigne. "Law" to the rest of the

Joes. In the background his dog, Order, gave a single sharp bark as if he, too, was acknowledging.

"I heard it, too," said a second voice. Laser Rifleman Anthony "Flash" Gambello.

General Hawk had sent a full team. Law and his canine partner were reviewing the facility security systems, with two computer experts—a Brooklyn tech-geek called Jukebox and a Japanese woman codenamed Schoolgirl—as backup. Flash had been running the drone systems from a truck parked way out in the desert, and his team included the beefy and always-grinning Australian Bruiser and Shock Jock, a sniper from San Antonio. The last two Joes here at the Nevada base were a diminutive man who was, despite the unfortunate call sign of Teacher's Pet, a first class shooter; and Monster, a hulk of a kid straight out of Force Recon and three tours in the Middle East. They were all listening in on the call, though only team leaders chimed in on the conversation.

"Opinion?" Flint asked.

Flash said, "I think you and Professor Miranda will have lovely children."

"Secure that crap, soldier," barked Flint, though he was smiling. "Give me your *professional* opinion."

"Of what?" asked Flash. "The Caliban unit? Totally kicked my ass, and that's somewhere between very cool and very, very scary."

"Agreed," said Law. "I was watching the whole thing from the security office. I had the action on fifteen screens and it was scary as hell on every screen."

Scarlett said, "On the other hand, considering that this is a military system, 'scary' is what we want."

No one responded to that for a moment, then Law said, "Y'know guys, this is a pretty strange back road for anyone who's ever been a pair of boots on the ground. On one hand we all dig the idea of replacing vulnerable flesh-and-blood soldiers with metal and motherboard drones. On the other hand...have these guys even *watched* science fiction? Automated systems? Artificial intelligence combat machines? That never ends well."

"It's not AI," corrected Scarlett. "They're drones. Remote operated and—"

"Yeah, yeah, I know. Short step from remote to automated, though. I mean...it's the next natural step in development. Congress ups the budget for Prospero and next thing you know it's '*Ahll be bahhk...*'"

"Geek-centric paranoia noted, Law," said Flint. "That'll look good in the report."

"So," said Flash, "what's *your* take on the good Dr. Prospero, boss?"

"On or off the record?" asked Flint.

"Off."

"He's halfway to being nuts."

"Only halfway?" asked Flash.

Flint chuckled. "Hey, I just met the man a few hours ago, guys. Jury's still deliberating."

"Well, from where I'm sitting," said Flash, "which is out here trying to figure out how one old dude in a friggin' tin suit handed me my ass...I'm going to put my vote in right now. Guy's scary *and* nuts. And I'll bet a shiny nickel that he was grooving on it, too. Sitting there in the middle of all those fireworks like he was conducting the *1812 Overture*."

Scarlett raised an eyebrow to Flint. "He's got a point. Prospero took a bizarre risk just now. He could have used a less valuable subordinate for that test. Instead he put his own life on the line to prove how effective his system is."

"Personal pride?" suggested Law. "The Caliban unit is a major career high."

"Maybe. We'll go into that later."

"Couple other things to go over later, too," said Law. "The security systems are a little weird."

"Weird as in vulnerable?

"Weird as in totally *in*vulnerable. I've never seen any system with this many safeguards and redundancies."

"Better safe than sorry," quipped Flash.

"I suppose," Law said, but he sounded uncertain.

"Okay... team meeting in thirty minutes. My quarters."

"We all going to compare our homework?"

"Yeah, and then we'll braid each other's hair and have a pillow fight."

They were all laughing as the call was disconnected.

Outside, the last of the fires was out now and the desert was in total darkness.

Scarlett turned to Flint. "At the risk of sounding like a cliché," she began, "something about this place gives me the creeps."

"Yeah," said Flint, "I know what you—"

Anything else he was going to say was suddenly cut short as screams tore through the night. They whirled toward the access corridor.

"What the hell—?"

Those words were likewise drowned out. This time by the harsh rattle of automatic gunfire.

And then all of the lights went out.

EIGHT

THE ROOM seemed to explode around them.

"Down!" Flint and Scarlett yelled it at the same moment, and then they were diving for cover as someone with an automatic weapon opened up from the side corridor. Bullets chopped into the desks and chairs, tore jagged chunks from the poured linoleum floor, hammered into a Coke machine and blew sparks out of it, and burned through the air above their heads like a swarm of angry bees.

Flint hit the floor in a chest-first dive that sent him sliding toward the wall with the Coke machine. Soda hissed and sprayed from a dozen holes in the casing, but Flint couldn't see it. Except for the nearly continuous muzzle flashes at the far end of the room, there was no light.

"Who the hell's firing?" yelled Scarlett as she rolled behind a heavy desk. She had her pistol out but the barrage of rounds was too heavy to risk leaning out to return fire.

"What's happening?" everyone on the com-link was yelling at once.

"We're taking fire," barked Flint. "We need back-up!"

"Yo Joe!" bellowed several Joes at once.

Backup was on its way, but Flint didn't feel comforted. The automatic gunfire was continuous. He kept waiting for the pause as the shooter or shooters swapped magazines, but there was no break at all. He pressed his head to the floor and risked a quick look. Almost instantly the gun barrel fanned around to chop the exact spot. He jerked his head back amid a swarm of splinters and ricocheting lead.

"That's belt-fed," he shouted, and Scarlett nodded. "Minigun on a cart, I think. I can see some of it in the flashes."

"Cover me!" she snapped, and without waiting for his nod, Scarlett got into a crouch, racked the slide on her weapon, and threw herself sideways toward another desk eight feet away. It was a powerful dive but not a pretty one, lacking her usual athletic grace. She twisted in midair as she jumped, firing toward the minigun, each recoil warping her flight path. In the darkness and thunder it was impossible to tell if she hit any of the hostiles.

The gun instantly pivoted to track her, but as it did Flint rose up fast and opened up on it, aiming for the shadows just above the muzzle, knowing it was where the gunner had to be. Every shot hit home, every shot was true and straight.

The minigun kept firing.

"The hell…?"

Scarlet landed hard and slewed around while continuing to fire. When the slide locked back, she rolled behind the desk and fished out another mag.

There was no break at all in the gunfire.

The desks behind which they were hiding were disintegrating and pretty soon it would be like trying to hide behind Swiss cheese.

Flint would have given his left hand for a couple of fragmentation grenades.

And, as if wishing could make it so, there was a tremendous explosion that rocked the entire room and a red fireball that punched into the ceiling and then flattened out. The sprinklers and the security lights both came on at the same time and it looked like red tears falling from a black sky.

The minigun was finally silent.

"Clear!" bellowed a deep bass voice. Monster.

Flint and Scarlett rose up together from their hiding places and their laser swept over the hulking form of Monster—who held a combat shotgun with over and under grenade launchers. Water from the sprinklers danced along the gnarled lumps of his massive arms and shoulders. He was not a handsome man, but at that moment both Scarlett and Flint could have kissed him.

"Clear!" called another voice as Teacher's Pet skidded into the room from the far side. He had his M5 in his hands and whipped it back and forth as he checked the corners and behind obstacles. "Clear!" he yelled again.

Suddenly then the lights came on, flooding the room.

The sprinklers shut off with a hiss.

The red emergency lights dimmed.

Silence settled around them.

As if everything was normal.

NINE

TEACHER'S PET lowered his shotgun. "Flint, Scarlett ... what the bloody hell happened here?"

Flint got carefully to his feet and scanned the room. His ears still rang with the thunder of gunfire. Amid the phantom echoes he heard Law and Flash yelled at him.

"Dial it down," he growled. "No casualties here. Anyone else taking fire."

"No, but it sounded like you were in a war zone," said Law. "What the hell—"

"Unknown," cut in Flint. "We have zero intel and that's got to change. I want everyone to hold tight until I give the word. Stay online."

"Look," said Scarlett as she carefully crossed the room. Flint joined her, and Pet gave a long whistle.

The minigun was a tangled mess of twisted metal that sagged from its pedestal. The vehicle on which it had been mounted looked like a golf cart except that there was no seat for a driver.

Monster hurried over to it, his shotgun ready to finish what his grenades had started... but there was no need.

There were also no bodies.

He looked up in puzzlement.

"Zero hostiles," grunted Monster. He was six-feet-ten and built like a tank. His bulk filled the corridor and he looked around irritably, as if annoyed there was no one with a pulse he could shoot. "Where the hell'd they go?"

"I don't think they went anywhere," Scarlett said as she poked at the rubble with the toe of her boot. The floor was carpeted with spent shell casings. Thousands of them. Huge drum magazines anchored each side of the cart.

"Huh?"

She didn't answer right away. "Never saw a minigun like this. Dual belts leading to a central firing chamber that feeds into the same set of rotating barrels.

"Worse than that," said Flint. He tapped a scorched metal box that hung from the pedestal on a tangle of wires. "Look at this."

Teacher's Pet bent forward and peered at it. "Is that a CPU?"

"Ah," Scarlett said as if she was expecting that.

Pet looked at the others, his eyes filling with anger as he

realized what it all meant. "Ah… c'mon, man, you frigging kidding me here?"

Scarlett studied the wiring. "There's an antenna array, too." She straightened. "This is—"

"What in God's name is happening here?" interrupted a fierce voice and they turned to see Dr. Prospero come sweeping into the room. He wore trousers and an undershirt. Doc was right on his heels and it was clear they had just run there from the medical suite. Professor Miranda was a half step behind them. She had a small .25 automatic in her hands, but she held it with professional competence. As soon as they saw the ruined desks and the mangled remains of the minigun they stopped in their tracks.

Prospero's face went purple with rage and he wheeled on Flint. "You maniac! You destroyed a four-hundred-thousand dollar prototype and—"

"Hold it right there, Doctor," interrupted Flint with steel in his voice. Prospero paused. Flint kicked at the shell casings and sent a score of them skittering toward the scientist. "In case you've suddenly gone blind, that prototype of yours just tried to kill us."

"Nonsense. The Kobold 118 is incapable of—"

"Scarlett and I would be dog food if Monster hadn't taken it out."

"Impossible."

Flint felt his control slipping. "I'm sorry… did you say 'impossible'?"

Prospero was not one for backing down. He stepped close so that he and Flint were almost nose to nose. "Yes, *Chief*," he said in a way that suggested that Flint's rank was of less consequence than a used Kleenex. "Kobold is a drone system. It can't 'try' to do anything. *Trying* is an act of deliberate will."

"No kidding," said Flint icily. "So what does *that* tell us about what just happened?"

Prospero's eyes cut back and forth between Flint and the drone. Doubt clouded his features. "I…" he began, but did not finish the sentence.

"Let me check the system," said Professor Miranda quietly. She stepped forward at an angle that forced Flint and Prospero to shift away from each other. It was a deliberate move calculated to dial down the tension, and everyone allowed it. A shouting match was not going to increase operational efficiency. She unclipped a small toolkit from her belt and selected a screwdriver, then quickly undid the four tiny screws that fastened the faceplate to the CPU casing. There was a small *pop* as she pulled it off.

"The security seals were intact," she announced. "I had to break them to take the faceplate off." She showed the cover to the Joes. The security tags were slowly turning color from beige to red. "Breaking them releases chemicals that change the tags' color. They were normal when I opened it."

"Always the same color?" asked Scarlett.

Miranda shook her head. "No. Beige was Monday's color, which is when I last worked on this unit. I select a new color for every day."

"How many people have authority to install the security tape?" asked Teacher's Pet.

"Only Dr. Prospero and myself," she answered. "And we're under constant video surveillance when either of us does that. The digital files are stored in the security office."

Flint tapped his ear mike. "Law, you get that?"

"Copy that. On it."

Prospero scowled as he realized that others beside the Joes in the room were party to their conversation. He said nothing, his expression conveying his displeasure eloquently enough.

Flint managed not to fall down and die.

He tapped his earbud again. "Yo, Joe! Headcount and location. Did anyone take any fire?"

Immediately the other Joes scattered in and around the Island sounded off.

"Bruiser on deck—I'm outside with Flash. We're checking the perimeter. Zero hostile contact."

"Shock Jock here, Chief. Quiet as church out here. I'm running scans on the drones Dr. Prospero tore up. No one around but us Joes."

"Schoolgirl in the house. I'm down in Operations," Schoolgirl replied. "No one home, everything shut down and locked."

"Good," said Flint. "Jukebox...where are you?"

"I'm in the generator shed, Flint," Jukebox said. "Got a lot of boards fried down here. Halo never kicked in, so I've been putting out fires."

"Deliberate?"

"Could be...but it's hard to say. Looks like a mother of a power surge."

"Okay, everyone stay on station and stay on the line." He gave them a brief rundown of what happened. A lot of theories got thrown around but nobody came up with a reason to think that they were experiencing an actual attack.

"Hope the Doc's toys are still under warranty," quipped Flash.

Flint grunted and turned to Prospero. "I want a complete rundown of every single malfunction you've had that resulted in a weapons discharge."

But the scientist was already shaking his head. "Malfunctions? No, no, no...there haven't been any."

"Not one?"

"No," insisted Prospero, "and there *can't* be because as I said, this system is a drone, it has not autonomous capabilities."

"I know." Flint smiled thinly at Prospero. "As you've heard, my team is on the line with us right now and a full-scale search is underway."

"Affirmative," said Flash in his ear.

"This is sabotage, Chief," said Prospero. "Odd that it only happened after your team arrived."

Flint took a challenging step forward. "You want to explain that comment—?"

"Wait…" said Professor Miranda in such an urgent tone that everyone turned toward her. She held a penlight and was using it to examine the inside of the CPU. "Oh my God! Doctor… look at this."

Prospero and Flint gave each other two seconds of the Alpha Dog glare and then they turned to see what the professor had found.

"What is it?" demanded Prospero.

Miranda handed the unit to the senior scientist, who immediately frowned as he laid eyes on the inner workings. "This isn't right," he said softly.

"What isn't?" asked Flint.

Prospero ignored him and instead directed his comments to Professor Miranda. "This is one of Kong's devices. The AI256?"

"I think it's the 257," said Miranda. "Look, it has a smaller microprocessor unit and—"

"Whoa—stop right there," ordered Flint. "What is an AI256, and why do you two look like you just swallowed scorpions?"

Prospero plucked a plastic-coated unt the size of a button from the CPU and held it up between his thumb and forefinger. He waved it in Flint's face. "This is your villain, Chief."

"What is it?"

"It's an artificial intelligence module designed for the next generation of unmanned tactical combat vehicles."

"Artificial intelligence?" Flint's heart sank. In his earjack he heard Flash curse.

"Yes, Chief," said Prospero.

"One of your toys?"

"I don't *do* AI," he said as if that field of science was akin to selling crack in middle school playgrounds.

"Who does? AI was on last year's budget report. You signed off on it."

"Dr. Kong's team did all of... that." Prospero still looked like he was sucking a lemon. "Kong was working on full automation systems. It was a small department and I had no plans to include it in this year's budget request."

"And yet it just *happens* to be in the CPU of one of *your* combat drones?" asked Scarlett, one eyebrow arched.

"I obviously had nothing to do with that," said the scientist, dismissing even the possibility of such a thing. "I said Dr. Kong's team *was* working on this. Kong had a stroke five months ago. He's in a coma in Las Vegas and is not expected to recover. I believe that is in the same report from last year."

In Flint's ear, Law said, "Yep, it's there. Blink and you miss it, though."

Flint said, "Who's continuing Kong's project?"

"There were only three people on his team," explained Prospero. "None of them is advanced enough to lead the project. They're all a half step up from lab monkeys. Kong never used top people. He didn't like to share the byline on any potential patent, so most of his team are graduate assistants with low-level clearance. They only worked on peripheral aspects of the hardware. None of them wrote code for the operational systems. Besides... I shut the whole project down until a suitable replacement could be found."

"And—?"

"I haven't spent a lot of time looking. As I said, AI is not the primary goal of this project. The Island is a drone shop."

Flint digested this. "Who has access to their research and materials?"

"I do."

Flint gave Miranda a hard look. "Who else?"

She shook her head. "Only Dr. Prospero. We certainly didn't plant the AI unit."

That served up a moment of silence as the Joes and the scientists processed the implications.

"Swell," said Doc with a sigh.

Flint touched his earbud. "Law, it's confirmed that we have a breach. Lock this place down. Bruiser, you stay outside with Flash. Seal the perimeter. Nothing gets in or out. Shock Jock, I want you inside with Schoolgirl. I want all staff locked into their rooms. Personally check all doors. Law—initiate J-94 security redirects. Blank all keycards and replace them with our team code."

"You can't do that—" began Miranda, furious.

"Shut up," barked Flint. "Jukebox…lock yourself into the power shed. I don't want another lights out."

"On it."

Immediately, red lights mounted high on the walls flashed with crimson urgency. A recorded female voice spoke from speakers mounted below the lights:

"THE ISLAND IS GOING INTO LOCKDOWN. ALL STAFF WILL OBSERVE SECURITY PROTOCOL ALPHA ONE. REPEAT…"

To Monster and Teacher's Pet, Flint said, "Coordinate with Law. Everyone is on two-man patrol. You find anyone— *anyone*—from senior staff to pot-washer third class that's not locked in their assigned quarters and obeying all of the Alpha Security protocols, you bag 'em and drag 'em. I will want to have a talk with them."

They saluted and headed out.

"You copy all that, Law?"

"On it. I'm downloading the fingerprint and retina scans of the whole staff to team PDAs. Everyone should verify the identities of every single staff member. Anyone can wear a nametag."

"Good call."

Flint eyed Prospero and Miranda. He debated locking them in their rooms, too, until his team had a chance to sweep the entire facility. The Island was a big place. He also wanted to get out of there and think it through alone. He was still jumpy from all the adrenaline that had been dumped into his bloodstream during the brief but harrowing firefight. It made it hard to maintain the air of detachment that he preferred to show, especially in front of a touchy high-maintenance jackass like Prospero.

He took the device and held it up.

"So what does it mean, doctor? If this thing had an AI predecessor then there isn't a need for an operator, correct?"

"Correct," said Prospero. "Under normal circumstances the drone would have an operator uplinked to a satellite or a plane, or perhaps a ground spotter. As the operator received intel he would direct the flight-plan or drive-plan of the drone. Our latest generation has better optical systems, including the Ariel series of airborne cameras. They're too agile to be hit by most conventional weaponry and too small to appear on radar." He paused. "I released twenty of them when I went out into the desert for our test."

Flash, who was still an invisible audience to all this, murmured, "News to me, boss. I never spotted them."

Flint did not acknowledge the voice in his ear, but he knew that the rest of the Joes heard it. None of them would like the idea of tiny spycams flitting around.

"There was nothing in your quarterly reports about these Ariel units, Dr. Prospero."

Prospero shrugged. "The Ariels are biomimetric units— small drones designed to look and behave like insects, birds, or animals. In the case of the Ariels, they look like fireflies. They're new."

"So new that you have working prototypes in the field since your last report, which was—what?—six weeks ago?"

Prospero dismissed it with a wave of his hand. "I'm sure they are in the report, Chief. They'll have had a number-letter code. The nickname 'Ariel' was picked recently."

Although that was probably a legitimate answer, Flint was not leaping to accept it. His skepticism must have shown on his face, because Prospero bristled. "You don't believe me?"

Flint looked at him, then down at the still-smoking machine and the carpet of spent shells. Then his cold eyes refocused on Prospero.

"Right now, Doctor…I don't trust anyone who didn't come on the chopper with me. That means if you're not a Joe, you're a suspect." Prospero turned livid and opened his mouth, but Flint beat him to it. "If you don't like it, Dr. Prospero, then that's just too damn bad. Before you explode all over me, take a second to remember whose name is going to be on the report that goes to NATO and the President. If you want me to sign off on a positive report, then dial down the pompous attitude and try working with us. That means full disclosure. No more of this 'oh, I forgot to mention it' crap. You'll tell me everything and you'll goddamn tell me up front and when I ask for it. Is that understood?"

"That's outrageous. This is blackmail, it's—"

"The word you're fishing for is 'extortion.' "

Silence crashed around them and Scarlett thought she could feel the temperature of the room drop about forty degrees.

"Very well," Prospero said eventually, but it looked like speaking those two words was more painful that having teeth pulled without Novocain.

Flint studied him, and then gave a curt nod.

"Then tell me about this thing." He held up the AI processor. "Does this require any real-time human assistance?"

"No. That replaces the need for spotters of any kind. Kong's field within artificial intelligence was learning computers and their tactical uses."

"How advanced is this thing?"

"It has generational memory and has an extrapolative assessment hunter-killer subroutine based on established predator-prey behavior models."

"Oh boy," murmured Doc. "I'm not a computer expert, but even I can tell how bad that could be."

Prospero sniffed. "Well, it *is* designed to replace individual soldiers in the field. The whole purpose of such weaponry is to reduce human assets and—"

"We know," said Flint. "So are drones. But what you're describing here is an autonomous killing machine."

"*Ahll be bahhk,*" Law repeated in his ear.

Flint winced.

"Don't be naïve," said Prospero. "Computers and robots are only as autonomous as we allow them to be. Humans program them, and every AI system that exists or ever will exist will have override commands and failsafe systems."

"You're sure about that? Are there limits to the autonomy in self-learning systems?"

"No. Autonomy is a word we deliberately misuse. The autonomy goes only as far as the parameters written into the operational software."

"They can't evolve beyond that?"

"Absolutely not."

Flint looked at Scarlett. She gave the tiniest shake of her head. She wasn't buying Prospero's rant either.

"Then that leaves us with only one option," Flint said. "And I think you already know what that is."

"Impossible," Miranda said under her breath.

"A saboteur within the Island," Prospero said flatly.

"Yep. Either an infiltrator, in which case your security isn't as good as it should be—"

"Impossible," snapped Prospero.

"—or one of your people is working for the bad guys," concluded Flint.

Prospero was already shaking his head. "No, no, no, no…"

"Got to agree with him, Flint," said Law in Flint's ear. "Like I said, there are safeguards on the safeguards with this stuff."

"No." Prospero said it a final time and without the possibility of contradiction. He folded his arms and stared at Flint, defying him to argue.

"We need to keep an open mind," began Scarlett, "because any—"

That was as far as she got.

Something small flitted past her face—a tiny fluttering thing that glimmered like polished steel. She waved at it in annoyance. There was almost no sound. Just a tiny *pop!*, like a bubble bursting—and then Scarlett uttered a soft cry and fell forward. Tiny bits of metal debris fell like glittering dust.

Flint reflexively stepped forward and caught her.

"Hey, what's—?"

Scarlett's eyes were wide as saucers and filled with terror and pain. She opened her mouth to say something but instead coughed bright red blood onto Flint's shirtfront.

"I…"

Her eyes lost focused and she went totally limp in his arms.

Then the lights went out again.

And the gunfire started once more.

TEN

The Ice House

THE COMMANDER poured himself another glass of wine. The big central screen displayed a shaky green-and-black image from a hovering night vision camera. He watched Scarlett fall, saw her blood seed the air like drops of black oil.

Other monitors showed different views of the Island compound. Inside and out.

Small devices flew or rolled or scuttled through the darkness toward the Joes.

It did not matter to him if the Joes lived or died. There were some tactical advantages either way.

It did not matter to him if Prospero or Destro won this round, because there was no way for a completely clean win. However it played out, it would shave millions off of the asking price of anything they brought to him.

He smiled.

This was real entertainment. This was an entirely new spin on the concept of a "price war," and he was delighted.

* * *

ELEVEN

Observation Room

ONCE MORE the darkness was absolute except for flashes from gunfire.

Except this time the flashes were not the rapid-fire growl of a minigun firing from a fixed position. Instead they were smaller, almost delicate *pops* that seemed to appear randomly from different parts of the room.

"What the hell is this?" bellowed Doc as he fumbled to find Flint and Scarlett in the dark.

"Sprites," yelled Professor Miranda. "Oh my God...someone launched Sprites at us. Get down... get down!"

At the same time Prospero hissed: "Don't move...freeze! They're motion trackers."

But something did move in the dark.

"Flint...I saw Scarlett, is she—?"

There was another *pop!*

"Ah...*God!*" and in the tiny muzzle flash Flint saw Doc stagger as something hit him between the shoulders. He collapsed against Flint and drove him and Scarlett to the ground in a tangle of too many arms and legs.

Pop! Pop!

Doc's body trembled as he was hit twice more, and then he lay totally still.

Flint was buried under Doc's solid weight and the muscular heft of the unconscious Scarlett. He was also afraid to move.

He was wearing BDU's but he wasn't in battle dress. No Kevlar, no spider-silk weave in any of his clothes. He had a sidearm, but from what he had seen in the flash the machines were tiny, about the size of a chicken's egg.

"Keep perfectly still," said Prospero slowly in the uninflected way a person does when he speaks without moving his lips. "They can only track movement."

"Heat...infrared...?" demanded Flint.

"No. They're prototypes."

"Drones?"

"Drop and Pops," whispered Miranda.

Flint's heart sank. Drop and Pops were a covert anti-personnel device that had been in development for years. Small, self-contained units with tiny filament wings, a motor, and a barrel loaded with a single shot. The bullets were low-caliber hollow-points. Deadly if they hit the head or chest cavity, potentially crippling everywhere else. They were intended to be dropped by a fixed-wing drone over a mass of troops. Each device—*Sprites*, as they were called—would seek out the first moving target, close to within a meter, and discharge its round. As it fired it would use gunpowder boosted by a single discharge of all the juice left in its battery. They were single-use and disposable, and were supposed to be at least eighteen months away from practical field testing.

He listened to the darkness and heard a swarm of them overhead.

Dammit.

Warmth was spreading over his throat and chest, and with horror he realized that Doc and Scarlett were both bleeding, their blood seeping into his clothes. Just the thought of it burned him like acid.

Lying there, immobile and helpless was maddening, but he knew that even with the lights on the tiny hunter-killers were too small to bring down with small arms fire.

"What's the battery life on these things?" he whispered, keeping his own lips from moving. He didn't know if the Sprites were really sensitive enough to pick up on the movement of lips, but if Prospero was being careful then so damn well was he.

"Less than five minutes," answered Prospero.

Five minutes could be four minutes too long if the Sprites had clipped an artery in Scarlett or Doc. Worse if one of them had a head wound.

At the same time the thought of lying still for five minutes felt like a life sentence.

How long had it been already?

Twenty seconds?

Thirty?

Certainly not much more than that.

"Law—?" he whispered.

The voice was right there. "What the hell's going on, Flint?"

Speaking very slowly and softly, Flint told him.

"God! Monster and Pet are inbound to your twenty. One minute."

Flint almost yelled for him to stop them. Then he had an idea.

"Frag the doorway."

A pause, then Law said, "Copy that."

Time dragged and Flint's nostrils were filled with the sharp coppery smell of fresh blood.

Come on, come on, he said to himself, willing the two Joes to get here, and willing Doc and Scarlett to hold on. *No Joe dies on my watch, damn it.*

A booming bass voice yelled from across the room: "Frag out!"

And a second later the double doors leading to the main corridor blew inward as a fireball shattered wood and twisted metal and threw pieces fifty feet into the room.

A split second later the air was filled with dozens of *Pop-Pop-Pops!* The Sprites blasted the flying debris, each round creating more flying debris.

Pop-Pop-Pop!

There was a second big explosion as another fragmentation grenade struck the wall by the Coke machine. The soda dispenser seemed to leap into the air and pirouette, and before it landed there were more small shots.

Pop-Pop-Pop!

Then silence.

*   *   *

TWELVE

The Island – Security Office

CHRISTOPHER M. LAVIGNE—"Law" to the Joes—was trapped in a black box.

When the main lights all through the Island went out, so did every electrical system in the security room. Order, a muscular shepherd, stood somewhere in the inky nothingness to his left and barked steadily. Deep-chested warning barks.

Law fumbled at the gadgets on his vest until he found his flashlight and he turned it on, dialing the lens from beam to full blaze so that the security room was suddenly filled with pale blue-white light.

"Hush," he snapped to the dog and Order instantly obeyed. The shepherd's eyes were as black as a desert demon's in the gloom, their pupils reflecting pinpoints of light.

Law tapped his earbud.

"Law to Flint, over?"

There was a burst of static, then a sound like a fragment of an explosion and part of a yell, then more static. He dialed through a dozen command and team channels and got nothing but white noise.

"Screw this," he said and grabbed for the door handle.

It turned an inch and stopped.

Locked.

He knew from his analysis that the security ops room was essentially a modular vault built into one corner of the Island facility. It had a GSA Class 5 vault door capable of withstanding up to sixty minutes of penetration delay against battering attacks, and intense and concentrated hand tool attacks, and both 7.62mm and 5.56mm multiple-shot ballistic attack without penetration. In short, Law wasn't going to force it open or shoot off the lock. There was supposed to be a failsafe system for emergencies of this kind, allowing trapped security officers to open the door using a special day code.

Law had the day code, but the touchpad on the inside of the

door was dark. Even with the backup generators out, that shouldn't be possible. The touchpad was operated by batteries.

"Uh oh," he said. "We are in deep doo-doo."

Order barked again. The sound was loud and the echoes banged around inside the vault with nowhere to go and no way to escape.

THIRTEEN

Observation Room

FLINT TURNED at the sound of running feet and the jiggling beams from two gun-mounted flashlights. Hands reached out of the dark and suddenly the oppressive weight on Flint's chest eased as Monster pulled Doc off of him and then Scarlett. Teacher's Pet kept watch, moving his weapon in perfect time with the alert back and forth turn of his head.

"I think we're clear," he said under his breath. "Gimme some good news, Monster."

"Oh… man. Doc's bad. Count two… no three wounds. Two are through-and-throughs, upper back and love handle. Those aren't the problem. He's got a third hole off center of his spine, right between the shoulder blades and no exit wound. Let me work."

He had his first aid kit open and his big hands were busy. All of the Joes were qualified as medics. In their line of work it was crucial.

Flint crawled over to Scarlett. Pet kept looking over his shoulder at her, his expression a mixture of anger and alarm.

"Boss?" called Pet. "How's—"

"I'll live," growled a female voice.

"Scarlett?" Flint grinned as he put the light on her face.

She was awake and her eyes, though glazed with pain, were clear.

"Where are you hit?"

She grunted and then hissed. "Left thigh."

"You went out…"

"Something hit the back of my head. Crap...I think I bit my tongue."

Flint examined her scalp. There was a bloody groove across the middle of the occipital bone. "Good thing you are the stubbornest woman I ever met."

"What?"

"Hard head. Bullet creased your skull. You were out for almost five minutes."

Five long damn minutes, he thought.

Scarlett cursed, then a wave of nausea hit her like a punch and she turned aside and threw up.

"That's attractive," Flint said, and Scarlett replied with a particularly obscene gesture.

Monster was still busy with Doc Greer, so while Scarlett was still wiping her mouth, Flint flicked out his lock-knife and slit her pants leg, cutting it from boot to upper thigh and tearing the flaps back.

"Don't fall in love down there," Scarlett said, giving him an evil glare.

"I'll restrain myself." He set down his knife and tentatively probed the wound. "Missed the artery."

"Halle-freaking-lujah," she said, then snarled and bared her teeth. "Damn, Flint, why not just hit it with a goddamn hammer?"

"Stop being such a girl."

Scarlett picked up his knife and tapped him on the upper thigh with the tip of the blade. "You're one flick of the wrist away from being a girl yourself, mister."

"Noted."

"Chief," said Teacher's Pet in an urgent whisper.

"Busy."

"Chief...you better look."

Flint turned and shone his light. Professor Miranda was sprawled in a heap a dozen feet away. She seemed to float in a lake of blood. Nearby Prospero was staring at her, his eyes wide, mouth hanging open in an almost comical expression of complete shock. Then he turned to Flint and there was such a deep sense of helplessness and need in his eyes that it struck Flint to the heart.

"Please…" Prospero whispered. "I don't…I…I don't…"

"Go!" said Scarlett, pushing his shoulder.

Flint scrambled over to her, knee-walking through the blood. Miranda's brunette hair lay spread around her, her glasses on the floor by her cheek. Flint pressed his fingers into her throat, found a pulse, but it was weak and thready.

"She's alive…"

"Thank God," gasped Prospero.

Flint bent close to see if he could hear her respiration. Then he heard it. A wet hissing sound, very faint. He tore open her jacket and listened. It was there, louder. Wetter.

"Crap, I've got a sucking chest wound here." He tore open the woman's shirt and there was the wound. The bullet had gone in low on her torso, right at the bottom of the lung.

"Monster… is Doc stable?"

"Yeah, but—"

"Then leave him. I need hands over here. Right now."

But Monster was already there, opening a field trauma kit. They moved fast.

"Can you help her?" begged Prospero, his voice trembling at the edge of breaking.

"Shut up and let us work."

The bullet had punched a hole in Miranda's chest cavity, effectively unsealing the normally airtight lung sac. With every breath, Miranda's lung took in blood and collapsed a bit more. Flint wasted no time cleaning the wound. That was far less important and could be done later. If there was a later.

"Patch," Flint said, and instantly Monster tore the cover off of a prepackaged chest seal. Flint took it and pressed it gently into place, making sure the seal was tight. The seal had a one-way flutter valve so that with each exhale, air in her chest would be pushed out from underneath the patch, while each inhalation would pull the patch firmly against the wound to seal it and keep air from coming in through the bullet hole. Once it was in place Flint could hear Miranda's breathing begin to settle in a relatively normal rhythm. As normal as it could be until a real medic was found.

"I think she's stabilized," Monster said.

Flint tapped his earbud. "Law…we need a medic down here."

The only reply was silence.

"Law!"

Nothing.

"Jukebox…Schoolgirl. Report, damn it."

Nothing but static.

"I got nothing either," said Pet. "White noise."

Flint rolled Miranda onto her wounded side so that gravity would help keep the seal in place. He checked her airway and leaned back.

"Damn," Monster whispered. "What the hell are we into here?"

Flint got to his feet and walked over to Prospero. "She's lost a lot of blood and we need to get her to medical."

The old man shook his head slowly, his voice a faint mumble. "This wasn't supposed to happen. No more blood… no more death…damn it…this wasn't supposed to…"

Without knowing that he was going to do it, Flint grabbed a handful of Prospero's undershirt and held him there. "Listen to me…I don't know what the hell is going on here, but whatever it is it's happening with your toys."

"This wasn't supposed to happen…"

Flint drew his pistol and shoved the barrel hard up under Prospero's chin. "What wasn't supposed to happen? Start talking and I swear to God, if you lie to me I will kill you. Look into my eyes. Tell me if you believe me."

"Y-yes."

"Then you tell me what the hell is going on."

Prospero licked his lips. Flint pushed the barrel harder.

"Tick tock."

Prospero spoke a single word. It answered everything and at the same time asked a thousand more questions.

He said, "Cobra."

FOURTEEN
Dead Lake

THE MACHINE rolled through the night in near silence. The low-pressure tires barely chuffed the sand and the battery-driven motor was in a sound muffler. Bruiser never heard it coming.

His first warning was when the drone rolled past a perimeter sensor and a small red dot flashed to life on the computer screen on Bruiser's forearm.

He whirled, bringing his M5 up, calling it in.

But there was only static on the team channel.

Through the green clarity of his night vision, Bruiser saw the machine. Recognized it for what it was.

He opened fire immediately.

But he was a tenth of a second too late.

The silence and darkness were torn apart by the continuous roar of the minigun.

Bruiser—or the thing that had been Bruiser—was flung against the corner of the wall, and the barrage of bullets was so intense and heavy that his body stood erect and at attention as thousands of rounds tore him to rags.

FIFTEEN
Observation Room

FLINT BENT close and snarled.

"Talk fast."

"I needed the money and—"

"Really? You want to play that card with me. Do I look like a sympathetic man?"

Something changed in Prospero's eyes. They lost some of their fear and it was replaced by a jaded coldness. "Very well. It doesn't matter why I did it. I did it."

"Did what?"

Prospero told him. He had been approached by a man he originally thought worked for the security division of the Department of Defense. That was both true and a lie—the man did work for the DOD, but he also worked for a black market weapons broker who had been hired to reach out to Prospero. Him, and men like him. At first Prospero turned it down. He turned it down a dozen times over a two-year period, not so much out of patriotism but out of fear that it was a government sting of some kind.

Then he started believing in the man. Money was involved in that process. Money was always involved. But over time Prospero felt his heart change. The money became less important than the nature of the work, and its potential. His drones could effectively remove man from the combat field. No lives would ever have to be lost. Wars would become a contest of technology, and ultimately mankind might step away from the need for war.

The other man seemed to share this impassioned view, this Big Picture perspective that justified any covert or clandestine steps taken to achieve such a noble end.

Once they had struck a bargain, the man said that his boss wanted to acquire the Caliban combat system. Not the hardware. Just copies of all schematics and the complete Skyjack/Tempest software system. They haggled over the price for another seven months. During that time the broker himself emerged and introduced himself. He was a foreign national who had himself sold weapons systems and other technologies to the same client.

"Who was he?"

"I never knew his name," said Prospero. "I never met him. He was a voice on the phone."

"What *do* you know about him?"

Prospero hesitated. "He's a Scotsman."

Flint cursed.

"You know him?" asked Prospero, surprised.

"Unfortunately, and I plan to hang his head on my wall. Unless you want your head to be hung next to it, keep talking. If you're working *for* this client, for Cobra…why are your systems going off the rails."

"I don't *know!* It has to be sabotage."

Flint studied him, looking for the lie, but seeing only outrage and fury.

Prospero *didn't* know.

"Tell me something I can use, damn it."

"First…you have to understand two things."

"I'm listening."

"You saved Miranda's life. You may think I'm a cold-hearted bastard, but I…I love her. *We* are in love. I know the age difference is—"

"Save it for Dr. Phil."

"My point, Chief Flint, is that you *had* to save her, which means *they* betrayed me. Betrayed us. They tried to kill the woman I love."

"You looking for revenge?"

"Of course," Prospero said coldly. "I'm a man, just like you."

Flint almost slapped him with a sarcastic comeback, but he held his tongue.

Prospero nodded. "The other thing I need you to understand is that…while I admit that at first this was about the money, it became about the work. About the goals. The Caliban unit, the other technologies…they really will save lives. American lives at first, and then as combat becomes mechanized to the point that these systems cancel each other out it will save lives on all sides."

"Bull. If the machines stop working, then people will go back in the field."

"No…the machines would deadlock each other, but they

would make the actual field of combat too dangerous for men. It would end the game in a stalemate."

"That's it? Your newfound higher motives are about creating a new Cold War?"

"A Cold War is better than endless slaughter." Prospero's eyes glittered. "We are a warlike and savage race, and you know that every bit as well as I do. Just because out intellect has evolved to the point where we can appreciate and even defend ideals, it doesn't change the aggression built into our DNA. We're a predator species. We *take* what we want. Look at America's history. Eminent domain? That is a polite label for centuries of landgrabs, slaughter, and genocide."

Flint said nothing.

"Once I realized that the Caliban systems could bring us to a bloodless stand-off, I saw that, however dubious my initial motivations may have been, I had *found* my purpose."

"Tell it to Congress and the U.S. Attorney, Doctor. I'm not your lawyer, your confessor, or your friend. I'm going to ask you one more time and then I'm going to show you just how savage a human being can be." He bent close. "How can I stop these things?"

The old man stared at him for two long seconds, then he licked his lips. "Nothing I did could possibly be responsible for this. It has to be the AI chips. Kong only made a few of the chips. They were very difficult to make, and they're too big to fit into the Sprites. Those are still drones and someone had to have launched them. There has to be somebody *here*, there has to be a handler."

"On site? What's the operational range?"

"A few miles, but the fences have jammers. Otherwise the prototypes might pick up all kinds of confusing signals. Nothing from outside the fence can get inside. And there's one more thing, Chief."

"What?"

"None of the drones have the articulation needed to enter the generator shack and blow out the fuses. And it can't have been an EMP or the drones themselves would—"

"Yeah, I got it." He stepped back and eyed Prospero in the dim glow of the flashlight's beam. "I'm going to bury you for this," he said.

The old scientist said nothing.

Suddenly gunfire erupted from the doorway.

Flint spun in time to see Teacher's Pet go flying backward as another of the minigun Kobolds rolled into the room.

There was movement to Flint's right and he cut a quick look just as Prospero vanished into the darkness.

Doc was helpless on the floor.

Scarlett pulled her sidearm and returned fire. Monster knelt in front of her and was firing his big shotgun. He was screaming Pet's name like a war cry.

"Monster!" Flint bellowed over the din. "Frag it!"

Monster yanked a fragmentation grenade and rose up to throw it. He was strong and he had a good pitching arm. The grenade flew into the flash-lit shadows. But Monster never lived to see it hit the target. Bullets tore into the big man's chest and he fell backward, landing at the same moment the minigun drone blew up.

Flint ran to where Monster had fallen, but the Joe was past all help.

Grief and rage were like a furnace in Flint's chest. Even so, he couldn't pause to mourn his friend's death. Instead he took the remaining grenades—frags and flashbangs—and all remaining ammunition.

He turned to Scarlett and gave her half of the grenades.

"Look," he began, but she gave a fierce shake of her head.

"Go!" she snarled. "Find them... *stop* this thing."

* * *

SIXTEEN
Inside the Island

FLINT RAN through the darkness. He had looted Teacher's Pet as well and wore the dead Joe's helmet, and his pockets were heavy with grenades and magazines. The NVD allowed him to move fast.

Once he was out of the observation wing, he had to cut down a long access tunnel to get to the security vault. The comlink was still dead, but between bursts of gunfire he could hear voices. Screams.

It had to be the staff.

"Yo, Joe!"

The cry came from his left and Flint skidded to a stop and wheeled around. Two figures emerged from behind a stack of crates. Law and Order.

The security tech was covered with blood and his left arm hung limp at his side. Order limped beside him and the dog's eyes were wild with a predatory gleam that looked more like a wolf than a German shepherd.

"How bad are you hurt?"

"Shrapnel in the shoulder," Law answered. "What the hell is happening?"

In a few terse sentences Flint gave him the basics.

"That doesn't make sense. It was Doctor Prospero who just got me out of the vault. Him and that weird iron suit of his."

"*What?*"

"Yeah, just now. He ripped the door right off the hinges. Wouldn't have thought it was possible. He told me to get to the observation deck and help Professor Miranda. Said she was hurt…"

There was another burst of gunfire, down the corridor and around the bend.

Law nodded. "Prospero went that way. One of those minigun drones attacked us. Prospero charged after it and tore it apart. Literally. By hand. It exploded, which is how I got nailed. He left me here and said he was going to Ops."

"Okay. Get to the observation deck. Doc's out, Miranda's down, and Scarlett took one in the leg. Keep 'em safe."

"Count on it. But... where are you going?"

"That way," Flint said and ran off in the same direction Prospero had taken.

Order's fierce barks seemed to chase him through the darkness.

An explosion shook the whole place and the shock wave nearly knocked Flint off his feet. When he rounded the corner he saw four more of the minigun drones. Two were smoking, their parts twisted from the blast. The others looked like they had been torn apart by an angry giant.

Along one wall was a row of doors and Flint realized that he was in the first chamber of the staff wing. Most of the doors were still locked shut, but a few had been torn open and there were bodies slumped inside and out. Two or three white-coated figures staggered dazedly through the smoke, their faces smudged with dirt, their clothes singed and streaked with blood.

Flint ran.

He was following a trail of destruction. Prospero had somehow managed to get into his Caliban exosuit and was hunting the drones in his own facility. The power of the Caliban unit was incredible. Steel doors had been ripped from their hinges, doorways smashed to allow the monstrosity to pass through. And everywhere there were dead bodies and drones.

With a sinking heart Flint realized that his team had not been able to get everyone into their chambers before the drones attacked. Men and women lay sprawled like broken dolls.

And in the mess hall, Flint saw a heartbreaking sight. Jukebox and Schoolgirl, two of the newest members of his team, had apparently tried to mount a defense in order to protect a dozen staff members. They had tossed heavy tables onto their sides and set up a firing position. The floor was littered with countless spent shell casings. Jukebox's M4 and Schoolgirl's M5 were still in their hands, the barrels still smoking. But both of the Joes were down. They had taken round after round and gone down fighting.

Behind them, nine of the staff still huddled—weeping and trembling—in a corner between the kitchen entrance and the juice bar. Flint read the scene as he rushed through it. His Joes had destroyed five of the miniguns. Five.

But there had been six.

The last one was smashed flat as if a gigantic fist had pounded it into debris.

Prospero.

Had he gotten here too late? Had he tried to save the Joes as well as the staff? It looked that way, but it didn't make sense to Flint. Prospero had to know that if the drones were stopped then he was going to jail for the rest of his life.

Yet he was trying to save people.

Why?

Flint ran on. Eating his grief, clamping down on his pain.

Something hit him hard in the side and Flint felt himself tumbling, spinning. He struck the wall and slid to the floor, his whole left side ablaze.

I've been shot, he realized.

Darkness and nausea washed over him, but he fought it down, shoved it back.

The shock of the impact erased the immediate awareness of the shot. He had no idea where it had come from.

Then there was a second shot. It pinged off the wall near his head, missing him by inches.

Flint could use his right arm well enough and he sent six shots downrange with his Sig Sauer. There was a scream and then the sound of running. His NVG were askew and by the time he straightened them all he saw was a flash of white.

Not a soldier. Had to be one of the staff. The traitor.

He was sure of it.

The only one? Or part of a sleeper team?

He was inclined to think that there were more. Too much was happening too fast.

He got to his feet and probed his side. The bullet hadn't penetrated, but had instead hit at an angle on his ribcage and slashed him as surely as if he'd been hacked with a sword. When he took a breath he almost screamed. At least two ribs were broken. He could feel the jagged end of one of them tenting the skin. He took a deep breath and pushed it back into place.

He did scream then.

The world danced a sickening jig around him, but he ground his teeth. If he fell, he knew he'd never get up.

He began limping forward, forcing his mind to think through the problem. That was how to defeat the pain. That was how he'd survive.

"Kong's team," he said between gritted teeth.

What about them?

Kong had built the AI chip. Was Prospero correct when he said that Kong's team was all third rate? Or was arrogance clouding the man's judgment. At that moment Flint would have bet a month's pay that it was one of Kong's team who had installed that chip. And that some or all of that team were finessing this situation.

Why?

He staggered on, following a trail of bloody footprints. He'd scored a hit. Nice. As he ran, Flint thought about Prospero's mention of a Scotsman.

Destro. Had to be.

Destro *was* known for AI systems, as well as other weapons that smudged the boundaries between "in development" and "science fiction."

That fast Flint understood it. The competing weapons designers. The "client." Backstabbing and sabotage were not exactly unknown to that crew of maniacs.

If Destro was afraid that another top-of-the-line weapons manufacturer would come and crowd him out of the market, what better way to handle it? Let the man finish his masterpiece—the Caliban exosuit and the Skyjack intrusion software—then discredit him during an inspection and take the system for himself. He could then sell it to Cobra without losing the broker's fee, and Destro was genius enough to retro-engineer it.

It made sense, though Flint wondered at how twisted *he* was becoming if this made sense to him.

He rounded a bend and saw the open sky and the vast, black desert.

He saw Flash running at him, the smoking ruin of a laser rifle in his hands, his face flash-burned and bloody. There was an explosion and Flash was flung twenty feet through the air. Flint tried to dodge, but Flash was a screaming missile that struck him full in the chest.

SEVENTEEN
Outside the Island

FLINT COULD barely breathe.

He crawled out from under Flash's body, reached down to touch his friend's throat, felt the pulse. Weak, but still there.

Pain was everywhere. Flash's damaged laser rifle had struck Flint in the face, and blood dripped from a deep gash on his cheek. One eye was puffed shut and the whole world had a distant, tinny sound.

And the pain.

It was hard to find somewhere to put his thoughts that was not already flooded with agony.

It was all coming apart. Gunfire rattled on and on. There were screams from inside the complex and then a huge series of explosions.

Flint was down on his knees, bent over, trying to breathe. Trying to stay alive. Blood dripped from his face onto the ground. He fought the darkness that wanted to pull him down.

They were coming but he was damned if he was going to take it on his knees.

"No!" he snarled and heaved.

He got shakily to his feet and the whole world took a sickening sideways spin. Flint took a hard step forward and caught his balance.

The squeak of treads was closer.

Flint turned, and there it was. Massive, indomitable against the hellish glow from the burning building. As it rolled forward two miniguns swiveled toward him, their black mouths promising awful things. Each gun could spit out more than four thousand rounds per minute.

Flint raised his gun. It felt like a ten ton weight and he didn't know if he even had the strength to pull the trigger.

The killing machine moved forward, offering death, promising nothing. Not mercy, not compassion for the lives lost. Not regret for the slaughter.

Somehow the emotionlessness of it infuriated Flint. Somehow that seemed to dishonor the fallen by refusing to offer even token acknowledgement.

Flint bared his bloody teeth as the metal monster towered over him.

"Yo Joe!" he yelled.

And fired.

Then something came out of the darkness to his left and slammed into the drone with the sound of a train wreck. There was a scream of twisted steel and one of the guns fired, but the rounds chopped a line through the sand a yard to Flint's right.

From the tangle of wreckage a monster rose, gleaming and ugly and huge. It punched down at the drone, shattering the gearbox; it grabbed the active gun and tore it from the pedestal and flung the smoking weapon a hundred yards into the dark.

Then silence collapsed around Flint, and he sprawled onto the sand, his gun falling from his nerveless fingers.

The giant moved toward him, clanking with each step, its metal skin smoking. There was a hydraulic hiss and the faceplate rose to reveal the madman inside the monster.

"It's over," he said. "I set an EMP bomb. It will detonate in two minutes. The drones are done. Everything is done."

Flint tried to speak, tried to form a word.

"W—why?"

Prospero smiled. A strange, enigmatic smile.

"You didn't believe me when I told you earlier, Chief," he said, "but I really have come to believe in the work. There will be blood—there *has* been blood, and I regret that more than I can express... but eventually this technology will make open warfare impossible. My drones were meant to fight other drones. That's the point. Let the machines battle over politics and oil and religion. Let men be safe." He shook his head. "There will be a new Cold War. It's inevitable. Cold as steel, Chief. The drones and iron giants will become walls between men, and ultimately men will have to stop killing each other."

"Sounds nice," gritted Flint, "but I have dead friends here who wouldn't think much of that plan."

Prospero waved his gigantic arm. "None of this was supposed to happen. This was sabotage. This is a perversion of everything I stand for."

"You got into bed with Cobra," Flint said with a cold sneer. "What did you *expect* would happen?"

Prospero's eyes shifted away. "I had his word. The Commander. He gave his word that my systems would never be used against human assets. Only against other machines of war."

Flint turned his mouth and spat blood onto the sand. "You're a goddamn liar," he said. "Or you are the greatest fool who ever walked the earth."

Prospero shook his head again. "You love war, Chief. You're incapable of understanding the higher purpose in all of this."

"Maybe. I know people, though, and you can tell yourself whatever fiction will get you through the night, but anyone who does this does it for one purpose only. Money."

Prospero's eyes were unreadable in the glow from the burning buildings.

"Believe what you will," he said. "But then why did I save you?"

Before Flint could answer, the faceplate slid back into place and the Caliban unit stalked off. Flint could hear its clanging footsteps as it headed away—not into the desert, but back into the burning building.

Then the darkness and shock and blood loss reached for Flint and took him down into the world of shadows.

EIGHTEEN
The Island

A JOE RESCUE team landed thirty-one minutes later.

By then the EMP had done its work and all of the drones lay still and silent. Merely machines now.

Medical teams were flown in from Area 51. Doc Greer was in the worst shape and he was airlifted to a Las Vegas hospital for emergency surgery. Scarlett, Law, Flash, and Flint were all battered, but none of them were in any immediate danger. Order would need a vet's attention.

The only member of the team unaccounted for was Shock Jock. His body was never found and the search was ongoing. Had he been with Kong's team? A mole inside the Joes? It was a horrible thought.

Or would his body be found buried under the tons of rubble of what was once the Island?

Flint thought about that as the chopper lifted him and the other survivors into the air.

Monster, Schoolgirl, Teacher's Pet, and Jukebox were still down there. Bodies in black rubber bags. Heroes whose real names would never appear in any headline. Heroes who had died fighting a battle the public would never know about. What had happened at the Island was classified. The death toll would be attributed to an industrial generator explosion. There would be no medals awarded.

There would be four more photos on the wall of the Pit. And the world would move on.

Flint sipped water to wash the taste of blood from his mouth.

Prospero had gotten away. He had gone into the burning building and taken Professor Miranda in his steel arms and then…vanished. Walked out through the smoke, leaving a hole big enough for Law and Scarlett to pull Doc Greer's body out to safety as the building collapsed in flames around them.

From the air, Flint watched the last of the buildings go crashing down. There wasn't enough water in the desert to fight that kind of conflagration. It would all be ash and charred metal.

It was a defeat. The Joes had lost before, but this felt somehow worse. Dirtier.

Prospero was out there. The Caliban unit was out there. So was Skyjack.

Destro, too.

And Cobra.

Flint stared down at the destruction and ate his pain and endured.

This was a defeat, but the war would go on.

NINETEEN
The Ice House

THE COMMANDER sat in his chair and sipped a lovely red wine. The *Goldberg Variations* played softly, filling the room with beauty. On the screens in front of him Destro and Prospero were screaming at each other from two separate secure locations. Each of them had called him within twenty-four hours after the Island incident, each of them boiling with righteous rage. They screamed about betrayal, about the sabotage of efforts. They each vowed revenge and retribution. And seeded through their diatribes, each threw covert pitches at the Commander about how their particular technologies were the only sane course worth pursuing, and they fired off coded e-mails with revised prices. Over and over again, even as the war of screams and threats raged.

The Commander conferenced their calls together and sat back to watch the fireworks.

"Ah," he said to himself, "I do love the free market."

Speed Trap

Duane Swierczynski

PART ONE: CHALLENGER

1.

GROUNDED.

There was nothing worse than being grounded.

Skidmark had always hated it as a kid—hated it more now.

As he wiped away some of the condensation from the bar top, Skid listened to the endless drone of the talking heads on the flat screen mounted high up in the corner. All flights in and out of Texas and the Southwest U.S., grounded until further notice. Skid tapped his fingers nervously as he half-watched images of confused and angry commuters, but Skid didn't need the TV to show him that. He was seeing it live, at Amarillo International in Texas.

He had the urge to walk outside, rent another car, and just peel away into Texas, all the way out to the middle of the Nevada desert where he could resume his usual life.

However, until Skid got the clearance, he had to stay right here—this faux-Mexican-themed bar catering to commuters who wanted to get plastered on neon margaritas before they stepped onto their short flights to major hubs.

But nobody was going anywhere now.

Including Skid.

They were all grounded.

* * *

2.

A SOFT VOICE, to his right, snapped him out of his reverie.

"Can I borrow your phone for a minute? Mine's dead."

Skid looked at the woman seated one bar stool away. Lustrous red hair, pulled back to show her bright green eyes and flawless skin. There was a bottle of Shiner Bock—*Made in Texas, for Texans*—in front of her.

"I promise," she said, "it'll just be a quick text to my supervisor."

Skid looked down at the phone in his hands.

"Uh…"

Well, this was going to be interesting.

How do you explain that your phone is biometrically programmed to work only at your specific touch and the sound of your voice? That the phone, in the hands of anyone else, was nothing more than an inert chunk of plastic and metal?

This was an amazing security feature that came in handy if you happened to lose it. But he couldn't tell this pretty girl any of this.

So instead Skid said:

"Mine's out, too. Too much texting the last few days, I guess."

She smiled. He was off the hook.

"I hear you," she said. "I take it you're stuck here, too?"

Skid supposed he was. Which was a strange feeling. He wasn't usually stuck anywhere. Not with the incredible capabilities of the G.I. Joe force behind him. As one of their top drivers, he was always on the move. Always transporting people or weapons or bombs or tech gear or live animals—yeah, that had happened more than a few times—or whatever else Joe needed moved from one place to another as fast as humanly possible.

But for the last three days Skid had been on an extremely rare leave of absence. For the first time in a long time, he found himself a civilian again. The only physical link between himself and G.I. Joe was the phone in his hand.

Fortunately he wasn't like most other members of Joe—thought to be dead, reborn into new identities. Skid still had a life out there. As far as his family—and the world—was concerned, Cyril Colombani was a career solider, always on assignment, always moving. Anyone who knew Cyril—before he took on the code name "Skidmark"—wouldn't be surprised by this. He was not the kind of man who liked to sit still. For anything.

Ever.

Now the redhead was watching cable news, shaking her head. "You hear anything about when the situation might clear up?"

A good question.

"I was wondering the same thing," Skid said.

3.

THE FIRST announcement came within seconds of Skid's arrival at Amarillo International. He was headed back to base—the Pit, they called it—and he'd arrived early, as usual. He couldn't stand being late for anything—a movie, a flight, dinner, anything. He'd rather wait in silence than risk being even a moment late.

But then Skid watched the electronic display notices—

> DELAYED
> DELAYED
> DELAYED
> DELAYED
> DELAYED

—begin to stack up, one at a time, until they included Skid's own commercial flight to McCarran in Las Vegas. Right away Skid checked with Dial Tone in the Pit, and she told him to stay at the airport until further notice.

"You might be needed in the field," she said.

In Amarillo? he thought to himself. *Away from my usual pool of vehicles?*

This was a surprise. Skid was looking forward to being back at the base as soon as possible. Three days away had felt like an eternity to him. He didn't have much experience being off duty. In fact, he had to work hard to appear like just another soldier on leave, happy to be around his family again. Not that he wasn't truly happy to see everyone. He just wasn't entirely at ease around them. Like he'd wandered into a play during the third act, and he'd completely forgotten his lines.

Small talk about work? Forget it.

If he told his family even the smallest bit of what he did on a daily basis, their minds would melt.

Now Dial Tone was telling him there was a situation evolving; operations were still figuring things out.

"What's going on?" Skid asked.

"All I can tell you is," she said, "the situation is evolving."

Skid hated that euphemism. *Evolving.*

Evolution took centuries.

Eons.

Forever.

And in the meantime, Skid was grounded, watching the cable news just like everyone else.

The official word from the TSA was that it was a freak weather pattern over much of the Southwest. But the talking heads on cable were going on about terrorist plots, and a series of "experts" were trotted out to talk about the weakness of airline security. Some even wondered if it was another Eyjafjallajokull—even though there was zero trace of any volcanic activity anywhere in North America. Conspiracy theorists claimed something awful had already happened, but the U.S. government didn't want anyone to know about it yet.

Skid knew it was none of the above.

Commercial planes were one thing. If G.I. Joe couldn't put a plane in the air, that was something altogether different.

Something, frankly, kind of scary.

*   *   *

4.

"So what's in Amarillo?"

The redhead was leaning over, looking at Skid, hint of a smile on her face. "I mean, you don't end up here accidentally."

Skid shook his head. "No, that's true. I was here for a funeral."

The smile disappeared instantly. "Oh, I'm so sorry to hear that."

"It's okay. It was my great uncle. He retired here—he was sick of Los Angeles. He loved the panhandle, loved the old Route 66. He'd driven it back and forth between Chicago and L.A. back in the 1950s. For some reason, this area caught his fancy. So he moved here. Met a girl. Fell in love. Had a family."

Skid was surprised to hear himself gush. So much of his life was kept under lock and key, it felt good to talk about stuff that was on the public record. He did have an uncle—Uncle John. Anybody could look that up. Even the obituary that appeared in the *Globe-News* a few days ago.

John Michael Colombani, 1926–2011.

And his Uncle did indeed love Highway 66. Skid could remember being a kid and looking at the walls in Uncle John's den with the kind of reverence you usually save for churches. Old highway signage, advertisements, model cars, mugs, shot glasses, patches…anything at all to do with Highway 66. "The Mother Road," Uncle John had called it. Skid had no idea what he meant by that until he was old enough to drive it himself —only by then, the Mother Road was broken up, bypassed and fallen to ruin. Skid had driven as much of it as was possible, and saw what had appealed to his uncle. The lure of the open highway, and the real America waiting for you at every stop. There was nothing better.

Even the names were poetic:

Rolla

Tulsa

Shamrock

Amarillo

The redhead smiled again. "I've never heard anyone talk about Amarillo that way."

"What brings you here?"

"Audits. I'm an accountant, so I'm always traveling around to the satellite offices. Though guess that's not going to happen today."

"No, not for a while at least."

They sat and sipped their drinks. His, a Coke. Though he very much would like to be able to join this pretty girl in drinking a Shiner. He'd had one with his cousins after the funeral—the first beer Skid had consumed in years, probably. It was cold and dark and slightly bitter and good.

But Skid never drank when there was even a remote possibility that he'd be driving. And Skid *always* needed to be ready to drive.

As soon as he had the thought, his phone rang.

See?

5.

SKID EXCUSED himself, tilted his body away, hit the screen—which triggered a secret partial fingerprint scan and security check in microseconds—then held the phone to his ear, painfully aware of the lie he'd told the redhead.

Mine's out, too. Too much texting.

But it wasn't as if Skid could just ignore the call, either. Not with it coming from the Pit. It was Dial Tone again.

"Okay, got your assignment," she said.

"Shoot."

"Head towards the Pit immediately."

The Pit was in the middle of Nevada—exact location classified. Your average citizen didn't realize how many blank spots were on the map of the United States. Usually in the most inhospitable, miserable corners of the country. Places like these, Skid called home.

"C'mon, boss," Skid half-whined. "You know all flights are grounded."

"Boss?" Dial Tone asked. "Oh, I get it. You're in public. Anyway, I'm not talking about flying, Skidmark. I'm talking about doing what you do best."

Dial Tone meant *driving.*

Skidmark was—if he allowed himself this much—the best driver G.I. Joe had. It was all he thought about, all he focused on, all he wanted to do. He'd taken after his Great Uncle John that way.

Except that for Skid, the open road wasn't Highway 66. It was the secret highway between nations around the globe. Places most people wouldn't even think of driving—and even if they did, couldn't without risking death.

"You're on," said Skid.

Ordinarily, Skid would answer with a curt, professional "affirmative"—but not in mixed company.

"I'll call with more details on the way, but we need you on the road, heading west, ready to answer the phone. You're going to be picking someone up and transporting them safely back to base. But time is critical, and the logistics are tricky. You need to go now."

"Already gone," Skid said.

"We need you here by sundown."

It was noon.

"No problem," Skid said.

6.

SKID DID SOME ultra-quick calculations:

Amarillo, Texas, to the secret Pit location in Nevada was about 950 miles, give or take.

Pushing the speed limit, and skipping bathroom breaks, you could make it in about fourteen hours.

He had roughly eight.

With one pickup along the way.

The very thought would panic most ordinary people. Not Skid. This mission already had his heart racing and blood pumping. His fingers were already twitching with anticipation.

All at once... *he wasn't grounded anymore.*

And man, there was no better feeling.

Skid stood up, sped through his options. He'd just turned in his rental car—and boy, did driving that thing hurt the past few days. Skid was used to being behind the best vehicles in the world, maintained by the best mechanics, and tuned to his body perfectly. Not some prefab tin can that passed itself off as an automobile.

But at this point, he'd be lucky to have even that. Trying to book another rental—especially with every flight delayed— would be insane. People were already in lines twenty deep to try to book the last few cars available.

No. He needed something else.

What Skid needed was a cab back to his Great Aunt's house.

He'd have to explain the situation quickly, without revealing any specific details. And he'd have to beg her for her trust and understanding. This was the worst day to do something like this, Skid thought. Just yesterday, Great Aunt Maria watched her husband of fifty-five years be lowered into a hole in the ground. He hated the idea that she would think he was circling around his great uncle's possessions like a vulture.

But really, it was the only sane option.

Especially if he was going to make it to Nevada by sundown.

7.

"Guess your phone had a charge after all," the redhead said.

"I'm sorry," Skid said. "Waiting for a call from work, and I knew I only had just enough juice to..."

"Hey, I'm teasing," she said. "Honestly. I wouldn't lend my phone to a stranger, either. What if I suddenly decided to text Dubai, or something?"

There was a moment where her eyes brightened, her playful

smile widened, as if sheer charm would force him to relent and let her use his cell phone.

Because, after all, they weren't strangers anymore, were they? How could they be, when death and family were discussed?

Skid knew his mother, if she were alive, would urge him to slow down a minute and talk to this pretty girl. His mother used to always beg him to *slow down already*, maybe give her a grandchild.

But no.

Not this time.

Not any time, really.

Because there was no time—not with what he did for a living.

Skid slid the phone into his pocket, picked up his go bag. "Great talking with you, miss."

Her eyes tried to hide the hurt. "Guess you found a way out of Amarillo?"

"Yeah," Skid said. "The hard way."

8.

IF ONLY THE Target had let her use his phone, this would all be so much easier.

Then the Watcher could have entered a quick sequence that would have instantly enslaved his device to hers.

Instead, she had to file what she had, and her superiors would have to make other arrangements.

File quickly, that is.

The Watcher figured she had about ten, fifteen seconds before the bartender finished mixing up a frozen margarita.

She took the clear plastic-like sheet from her clutch as she slid two seats down the bar to where her Target had been sitting. She peeled off the backing, pressed the sheet to the pint glass containing his half-finished Coke, waited one second, then peeled it off. She carefully placed the sheet inside an analyzer that could easily be mistaken for a compact makeup kit. While the analyzer did its thing, she pressed the side of her silver watch and uploaded the voice sample.

Fingerprints.

Voice sample.

And now, from the top of his straw, a DNA sample.

The Watcher already managed to snap many photographs of the Target with her cell phone—which, of course, was not out of power.

She also had managed to capture eye shape, color, facial structure, even the shape of his ears—which was just as good as fingerprints when it came to telling people apart.

Everything that made a person unique. Collected and uploaded after a thirty-second encounter in an airport bar.

By the red haired Watcher, who was really a blonde.

She would have liked to have had more than a few minutes with her Target, another context entirely. For a moment there —as loathe as she was to admit this—she forgot herself, listening to him talk about his dead uncle. For a moment she thought she was just a girl in just another airport bar, talking to another guy, and the possibilities were endless.

That, of course, wasn't the case.

9.

SKID FELT LIKE a jerk even as his aunt handed him the keys without a word, eyes glistening a little.

"Your uncle always told me he was saving his car for a reason," she said.

Skid started to protest. "I wish I could explain, Aunt Maria, but I really—"

Aunt Maria cut him off. "You don't understand, Cyril. I know *you* were that reason. You were the only person who loved that car more than your Uncle John."

"I promise—there won't be a scratch on it."

She smiled and squeezed his hand—the warm metal keys inside his own hand. It was a blessing, as if it had come from his Uncle John himself.

Which made no rational sense.

There's no way his Uncle John could have known what he did for a living—or would do for a living—when he bought that car.

Still…

Life was full of weird signs sometimes.

When he slid the key into the padlock and opened the door to the stand- alone garage, Skid felt even more like a jerk. His Uncle John had spent so many years inside this room, toiling on this car…

The clock was ticking. He could feel like a jerk on the road. The thing he had to do now was get behind the wheel and go, go, go, go, go…

The wheel of his Uncle John's beloved '70 Dodge Challenger.

10.

BLACK, OF COURSE—paint code T-X9.

Two-door hardtop.

Vinyl bucket seats.

Split "sad mouth" grille.

Big block 383-cubic-inch V8 engine with a 4-barrel carburetor—his uncle had modified it to match the specs of the Dodge Challenger used as the pace car of the 1971 Indy 500. Able to nail 99 mph in a quarter mile.

The 1970 Challenger.

Great year.

The first year.

It didn't get any better.

Don't misunderstand; 1971 was good.

But from 1972 on…*meh*.

To put it diplomatically.

But 1970, man. That was the Challenger's *year*. It was the car Skid drove when he dreamed.

* * *

11.

IT WAS ALWAYS a special, rare thing when his Uncle John would take him to the garage to look at the Challenger. Skid's family travelled to Amarillo so infrequently, it felt like entire stages of Skid's life would pass by between visits—grade schooler, awkward pre-teen, straight-A high schooler, then finally... unrepentant speed demon.

The last one had been a surprise to his entire family.

Skid—whose birth name really was Cyril Colombani—had been a good kid most of his life. Excellent grades. Polite. He brushed his teeth, combed his hair, said his prayers at night...until he held his first driver's license.

And all at the once, the mischief most kids bleed out of their system in small doses came gushing out of him like a tidal wave. He'd racked up more speeding violations than most adults would accumulate in a lifetime.

Uncle John somehow had understood.

And he never treated him differently, even after his great nephew's many scrapes with the LAPD and CHiP on the highways and byways of Southern California. Racking up enough tickets to pay for two years of a junior college somewhere.

Uncle John was trusting; he even left Skid alone in the garage with the '70 Challenger—his most prized possession— even though he knew his great nephew might not be able to resist the temptation.

But Uncle John would know instantly if anyone ever took the Challenger out of his garage for a little joyriding. That's because there were only forty-four miles on the odometer.

Four of those miles are what it took him to drive it home from the dealership back in 1970.

The other forty: short test runs over the years, just to make sure everything was in perfect order.

No road trips.

No races.

No rallies.

No nothing.

That was the big family mystery—why he'd never driven the Challenger. Like, for real. Uncle John never said. Even at the funeral, all of the grandchildren buzzed about what would become of the car.

The car that nobody ever drove.

Aunt Maria didn't say a word about it, other than:

"Uncle John told me what to do."

12.

SEVENTEEN MILES northwest of Amarillo, someone else opened another garage door.

This one had more than a padlock. This one had biometric security systems, DNA checks, a half-dozen armed guards.

That's probably because it contained something a little more valuable than a '70 Dodge Challenger.

This was an experimental armor-plated vehicle, designed with urban riots in mind. Able to move at speeds that could make your gums bleed. Equipped with enough firepower to raze an entire city block without stopping to reload. Utterly impenetrable.

And on the outside, it just looked like another obnoxious gasoline-wasting SUV.

A man who had been given the designation "Interceptor Three" sat behind the wheel, his throat still hurting. Just thirty minutes ago he'd received the call, and within five minutes he was in surgery. Nothing major—just an implant on his voice box, and laser modifications to his fingers. Instant coagulants, synthetic skin, no trace of the surgery left behind.

The surgery that turned part of him into a guy named Cyril Colombani.

Unfortunately, the surgery came with no anesthetic. How could he be expected to drive on it? That would dull his reflexes, fog his mind.

So Interceptor Three's throat hurt like he'd been gargling with broken glass.

Then again, this was why Cobra paid him an exorbitant retainer—to be ready and available for anything. To do what was asked flawlessly and without question.

Three was mentally prepared to drive a suitcase nuke into the middle of the city. Just so long as he was far enough away from the blast.

You couldn't collect a retainer if you were blown to atoms.

13.

So SURREAL, this feeling:

Driving his Great Uncle John's Challenger, at long last—brand-new wheels whining on asphalt.

It didn't seem like reality. It all still felt like a dream.

That didn't mean Skid didn't immediately start to punch it.

The engine purred to life. Skid didn't anthropomorphize his cars. But if this one could talk, it would probably express gratitude. Finally. Being used according to its purpose and design.

To go really, really, really freakin' fast.

Within minutes Skid was merging onto I-40. The speed limit: 70.

The Challenger going: 90.

Not all that fast, but he had to be conservative while still near Amarillo. Once Skid was out past city limits, he could really open her up.

He loved the feel of the engine in front, the metal cocoon of the car all around him. Shame his Uncle John'd never had the pleasure.

Except for those first four miles.

As Skid rocketed down I-40, the strange art exhibit known as the Cadillac Ranch whizzed by in his peripheral vision, to the left. Skid had visited there once with his parents. His father thought he'd dig it. But young Skid was totally turned off by it.

Ten formerly beautiful Caddies, buried headfirst in the middle of a pasture, defaced by a jackass with a spray paint can who happened to wander by? No thank you.

Skid was no Neanderthal. He realized the whole thing was supposed to be artsy or something. But he took it as an insult —like smashing a Stradivarius, surrounding it with velvet ropes, and asking people to *appreciate the beauty.*

Cars weren't meant to be buried in the earth.

Cars were meant to be *on the road.*

Headlights blazing the way forward. Tail lights warning all comers from behind. Engine humming at peak performance. Accelerator mashed to the floorboard. The brakes, used sparingly.

Driving the Challenger was the first real joy he'd known since before receiving the news about his great uncle.

Hammering the accelerator, his heart straining to go faster, faster, faster. Driving to the point where his body and his vehicle merged into one physical form, screaming down the asphalt.

On the road, all was good.

On the road, he was in his element.

On the road, he was unstoppable.

Why would he want to do anything else?

14.

INTERCEPTOR THREE located Colombani's Challenger just after the New Mexico state line.

Three's SUV was packed with enough ordnance to turn both the car and its driver into little more than a steaming grease spot on the asphalt. Armor-piercing rounds, grenade launchers…all at the touch of a finger.

Sadly, it wouldn't be that easy.

Because Three's handler had made it clear—they needed the cell phone in working condition. Colombani didn't matter.

But the phone was *everything.*

15.

SKID'S EYES flicked to his rearview. A black SUV, tinted windows, was rocketing up his backside. Skid refused to move to the right lane to let him pass. He hadn't let anyone pass since Amarillo, wasn't going to start now. Skid nudged the accelerator, gave the Challenger a little more.

The speed limit on I-40 in New Mexico was 75.

He was going above 100 now.

Not only did the SUV keep up with him, it zoomed closer. Must be going 105.

All right, tough guy. You want a shot at the title?

Speeding on an interstate was a high-intensity dance. Fortunately, Skid knew all of the steps. As G.I. Joe's top driver, he made a point to study and know all of the speed traps and state trooper patterns. He memorized them like some guys memorized sports statistics. All of the free space in his brain was committed to road conditions and downhill grades and construction zones and traffic trouble spots and, yes, speed traps everywhere.

There were obstacles, yes.

But so much of the roads was open.

Nobody realized that.

Skid thought of them as *freedom zones*. In freedom zones, you could go as fast as you wanted.

They were in a freedom zone now.

You could go 105

110

120

…sometimes more.

But this particular freedom zone, a few dozen miles past the state line, was coming to an end.

Two miles up ahead, just outside Tucumcari, was a speed trap.

That was fine, and all part of the cross-country speeding dance. It was like a breath between exercises.

The guy in the SUV behind him clearly didn't know the dance.

Skid couldn't risk getting pulled over—not in a civilian vehicle like a 1970 Challenger. He had no special G.I. Joe card he could pull, and having the trooper call his commander could put this mission—still undefined—in jeopardy. His agency counted on his ability to be loose in the wind, ready for action whenever needed.

Being pulled over, or possibly arrested, counted as failure.

So he had no choice.

Skid signaled, decelerated, moved over into the right lane. Let this idiot pass. Let *him* get nailed.

16.

THE SUV followed closely.

Sped up.

Mere yards away.

Bumper close to bumper.

Even closer now…

What the hell? Skid thought.

17.

INTERCEPTOR THREE prepared his front-mounted guns. When he hit the pre-engage button, panels in the grill retracted, and four steel barrels emerged a few inches.

The guns were meant to blow out enemy tires. You could manually adjust it for the type of vehicle you were pursuing. Although Three had once used it to slice through the shins of a dozen armed Mexican cartel thugs. That had been a sweet moment: the popping, the screams, the splattered blood…then, goodbye.

No need for such firepower now.

Just a few rounds, into this guy's back tires. Let him fight for control for a while, then give him a kiss, sending him right off the Interstate.

18.

RIGHT ABOUT the moment Skid realized something was hinky about the SUV, the sounds of automatic gunfire ripped through the air.

There were twin pops.

The shattering of tail lights.

Rims on the asphalt.

Skid, losing control of his Uncle John's '70 Dodge Challenger.

WHAT THE HELL?

His first thought, swear to God, was not about his mission or Joe or God or country.

It was of his Uncle John, looking down from Heaven, shaking his head disapprovingly.

19.

ONE OF UNCLE JOHN'S favorite Americana stories was about Casey Jones, the train engineer who sacrificed his own life to save every single one of his passengers.

John Luther "Casey" Jones was a railroad engineer totally dedicated to the Illinois Central. Just four months into the new century—April 30, 1900—fate put him on a collision course. Near Vaughan, Mississippi, double-header freight train No. 83 and long freight train No. 72 had more cars than a passing track could hold, and Jones's 382 was speeding around a curve at 75 miles per hour, totally oblivious to the danger ahead. When Jones finally could see what lay ahead, he encouraged his fireman to jump to safety…but he himself stayed on board to slow that train down.

Jones reversed the throttle.

He slammed the airbrakes.

"Ole 382" collided at exactly 3:52 a.m.

Casey Jones was killed instantly.

Legend has it, his dead hands were still clutching the whistle cord and the brake handle when they were pulled from the wreckage.

But that's not the remarkable thing.

The remarkable thing is that every single one of his passengers *lived.*

Even the fireman who'd leaped from the train.

20.

SO AS THE CHALLENGER seemed to break up around him, Skid couldn't help but think of Casey Jones, doing everything he could to slow down that train before impact. Same deal here. Skid wasn't so much concerned for his own body as he was the phone call he was supposed to receive.

He needed to be alive to receive it.

He needed to be able to carry out his orders.

Skid had no idea what the orders might be, or what he might be asked to do. That didn't matter.

So he fought the wheel, trying to convince the Challenger to bend to his will, just for a little while. Do not flip. Do not break apart.

Do not explode...

21.

INTERCEPTOR THREE smirked.

Colombani was an amazing driver—he had to give him that. With both back tires blown out, off the road and into the scrub, he was still managing to keep the vehicle in control.

Hats off to you, buddy, Three thought.

But I've got a job to do.

So time for another kiss.

Three found the button on the control panel, mouthed a silent *Sorry, buddy*, then pushed it.

22.

FOR A MOMENT, Skid thought he was going to be all right, that he would be able to bring the vehicle to a halt, then deal with his attacker. He had no gun, but Skid was sure he could improvise with something in the trunk or his go bag.

And that's the moment something exploded and the car flipped over

and over

and over

and over

and over…

23.

WHEN HE CAME to his senses, Skid crawled out of the shattered window, felt the dirt and dried grass under his hands as he pulled himself forward. His life's credo echoing in his skull…

Keep…

Moving…

And he had to reach the Pit. Call this in immediately.

Skid blinked blood out of his eyes, felt around for his phone —which had flown out of his pocket, apparently.

Whoever had just shot at him and blown him up was clearly aware of the mission. This wouldn't be the first time there would be a security leak in the Pit. Seems that Cobra's reach extended nearly everywhere.

Once he finally found the phone in the space between the dash and windshield, Skid crawled a dozen feet away from the wreckage, rested his back against a boulder. Cars almost never just exploded like they did in the movies…but there was still a chance.

Out on the highway, a dozen cars had pulled over to the side. He should yell at them to keep moving, to get the hell out of here. But the priority was contacting the Pit.

He was about to key in the emergency sequence when—

The whole world seemed to fall down on him.

*   *   *

24.

THREE TOOK no pleasure beating Colombani into unconsciousness. The man was clearly a good driver. Not as good as Three—he'd just proven that. But the poor guy deserved better than this savage thrashing.

Cobra would probably want Colombani dead. Off the road permanently.

But Three was a driver, not an assassin.

He'd been asked to incapacitate, not kill.

Besides, the shame of losing would probably nudge this "Joe" off the playing field for good. Let him limp home, lick his wounds for the rest of his life.

Which was the fate he deserved.

Three held the cell phone in his hands, pressed his thumb to the keypad.

The fingertip augmentation worked.

The phone lit up.

Three spoke into the phone: "Time and temperature please."

The call went through.

Clearly the voice box implant worked as well; the call was patched through. Three wasn't up on all of the particulars of the technology, but it was fairly amazing that a short sample of speech could be used to replicate someone's voice perfectly.

Now all he had to do was wait for the call, and the next part of his job.

PART TWO: CAPTIVES OF THE ROAD
25.

ONE SECOND Becky Campbell was headed to the Grand Canyon, the next a stranger was jumping into the seat behind her.

As the suspension rocked, Becky spun around, one hand still on the steering wheel.

"Hey…" she said.

Something pointed and sharp dug into Becky's side, directly

on the narrow band of skin between the upper edge of her jeans and where her shirt lifted a little.

"I hate to do this," the stranger said, "but I don't have a choice."

Becky's first thought:

Oh God he has a knife.

Becky sucked in warm air and squeezed the wheel. Her bare hand floated just above the gearshift, fingers trembling.

"I'm not going to hurt you. I just need you to drive down I-40 West right now, as fast as you can."

Becky said nothing. The car engine idled, the red needle of the tachometer floating just above zero.

"Do you understand me?" the stranger asked, his voice sounding pained.

The springs in the backseat groaned slightly. The man groaned slightly, then leaned in closer still. His mouth was inches away from Becky's right ear.

"Please tell me you understand what I'm saying."

"Yes."

"Good. If you stay calm, everything will be fine. Got it?"

"Yes. Got it."

The man—keeping his right hand near Becky's side—reached over with his left to grab the handle of the open door and quickly pulled it shut. The slamming sound made Becky jump.

She cursed herself for jumping.

"Just the door," the man said.

"I know."

"Put your foot on the brake and put the car in drive."

Becky lowered her bare hand to the gearshift. She hesitated. Oh God. What was going on? What had happened in the past sixty seconds? Even worse: what was going to happen in the next sixty, when she put the car in drive and started moving forward? Oh God.

"Now," he said, "please."

Becky touched the cold faux leather of the gear shift handle, which was still cold. Squeezed the left-hand button with her thumb, releasing the lock. Pulled the handle down to DRIVE.

"Look, I know you're afraid."

Becky exhaled quickly.

"Yes," she said. "I am.

Yes of course I'm afraid. What kind of question is that? That's the kind of question that makes someone more *afraid.*

"It's understandable," he said. "I'd be afraid, too, if I were in the driver's seat, and a stranger was sitting right behind me."

The man leaned closer.

"But here's the thing. Right now I very badly need you to *not* be afraid. Right now, I need you to drive out of this parking lot, and back onto the interstate."

"Okay."

"You know the way back to the interstate, right?"

"Yes," Becky said. "We were on it before we stopped here."

She wished she could stop sounding like an idiot.

Phillip's 66 was bustling at this early hour. The station already had the makings of a line behind each of its eight pumps. There were very few empty spots in the lot. The whole world seemed to be out in their cars this morning. Even here, high up in New Mexico's mountains.

"Okay."

Becky drove slowly across the lot, paused at the entrance, then turned right, following the signs back to I-40—the most direct route to Flagstaff, and then, beyond that, the Grand Canyon. She'd never seen it. She wondered if she ever would.

26.

IT WASN'T a knife, of course.

Skid had merely touched the edge of his military driver's license to her skin, letting her imagination do the rest.

He'd chosen this woman, and her 2010 Prius, because it was the best choice of the six vehicles at the service station.

For one, she had just finished filling her tank—unlike four of the other cars at the travel plaza. The only other car that had just finished up was a late-model Honda weighed down with two adults, two children, Pennsylvania plates and a ton of luggage—not exactly the vehicle you want to use during a hot pursuit.

Skid had pulled himself to his feet and—after getting over his utter astonishment that no major bones were broken—limped quickly across a scrubby field to a Phillips 66 service plaza. He'd climbed up the embankment, eased himself over a metal guard rail, and starting looking.

He scanned the cars and spotted the Prius—as well as the young woman easing herself behind the wheel.

There was only a second to decide.

As he made his way to her car, Skid could hear his Great Uncle John's voice in his head:

You really going to do this, Cyril? Abduct a poor young woman out here on I-40?

But I have to, Uncle John. No other choice. The guy who shot me up, ran me off the road—he knows about my mission. He took my phone. Chances are, he'll be able to intercept the call. He's Cobra, Uncle John.

Cobra, rattlesnake, whatever. I'm thinking of that poor woman in the car.

I'm not going to hurt her.

Geezus, Cyril—I know that. But she *don't know that.*

I know.

And for the record, you drove my baby what...an hour before you managed to get it all shot up and destroyed?

I know, Uncle John.

27.

AFTER AN 18-WHEELER passed, Becky drove the Prius down the hot, cracked asphalt of the ramp leading back down to the highway.

The man moved his hand away from Becky's side and settled back into the seat.

"Good."

Becky drove onto the Interstate proper, embarrassed to be so terrified. She should be going ballistic on this guy. She shouldn't have let this happen in the first place. She should have sat down, turned on the ignition, and auto-locked the doors. Three seconds would have changed everything.

But now there was a man with a knife.

In the seat behind Becky.

Right next to her son.

28.

SKID HAD NO idea there was a five-year-old boy in the backseat.

Swear to God, Uncle John.

His head was down, face buried in a large visual reference book—something about the solar system—when Skid jumped in behind the driver's seat, license in hand.

The whole time he pulled his escaped-lunatic-with-a-knife routine, the little boy said nothing. Regarded Skid with a mild curiosity.

Maybe that's because he could see there was only a tiny rectangle of plastic in his hand.

29.

BECKY TURNED and looked at Kyle, strapped in behind the passenger seat.

She'd put Kyle in without a car seat—there had been no time to buy one this morning.

This was not their car. At the time, Becky rationalized it. Kyle was a tall kid; it's not as if a booster seat did much to make him safer. And this morning, it was kind of an emergency situation.

A sudden decision not to take it anymore.

An impulse, after a cancelled flight. They couldn't fly away for a few days? Fine. They'd drive. Nobody could stop her from filling her tank with gasoline and pushing her foot on the accelerator and putting a serious number of miles between herself and her troubles.

A road trip.

Just what she'd needed.

Until a few seconds ago.

Kyle looked defenseless back there. And so, so small—despite being a tall kid.

"You okay, sweetie?" Becky asked.

"I'm okay, Mommy."

"Everything's going to be okay."

"I know, Mommy."

Becky wanted to turn her head just a little bit more, so she could see more of the stranger. But she didn't dare. It might piss him off.

"Mommy," Kyle whispered.

"What sweetie?"

"You should tell the man to put on his seat belt. That's a safety violation."

Becky heard the man in the backseat move.

"You're absolutely right," the stranger said.

"Of course I'm right," Kyle said, with a tone of voice that suggested *well, duh.*

Becky heard the stranger pull the fabric band across and snap the latch into the buckle. "Better now?"

"Better," Kyle said.

Becky cleared her throat. This stranger shouldn't be talking to Kyle. Becky had to keep him focused on her. She looked in the rear view.

"Where do you want to go?"

"Just drive," he says. "As fast as you can. Please."

. Becky turned to her right and looked at Kyle in the backseat.

"It's okay, sweetie. Everything's going to be okay."

Becky tried to focus on the road ahead—the hot shimmering asphalt that bore traces of the sudden rainstorm from an hour ago. The heat outside, though, was nothing compared to the black pit of cold forming in Becky's chest, spreading like cancer.

It was far too easy to imagine the man in the backseat roar with psychotic rage, then turn his knife to Kyle and start slashing away.

And there was nothing Becky could do about it, except hammer the brakes and bring the Prius to a skidding stop fast and turn around in her driver's seat and reach into the backseat with one goal: grab the dirtbag's arm and pull it back before it's too late…

No.

Stop it.

Becky looked at the stranger in the rearview. She could see most of his face, except for his mouth. He had brown eyes, framed by perfectly manicured eyebrows and a crew cut. A handsome guy. A nice young man.

But weren't they all.

All the nice young psychotics.

30.

"WHAT'S *YOUR* name?"

"Rebecca."

"Do you have a last name, Rebecca?"

"Campbell."

"Okay, Rebecca Campbell. I know you have a lot of questions. But I promise this will all be over soon. You and your son are not in danger. I need to borrow your cell phone, if you have one."

"I do. Right there."

Skid saw it in the center panel. He reached forward cautiously, realizing that she could snap an elbow into his face instantly, break his nose if her aim was lucky.

But he picked up the phone without incident, then settled back into the seat to call the Pit.

To see how bad he'd messed things up.

31.

"DIAL TONE," Skid said.

"Something wrong, Skid? Need clarification on something?"

"Yeah, I'd say so," he said, then quickly recapped what had happened in the past fifteen minutes—careful to keep the details not too grisly or scary for the benefit of the boy sitting next to him. Skid could remember being that young, growing up in L.A. He'd heard a lot of things he wished he hadn't.

"Wait," Dial Tone said, "you just talked to us a few minutes ago."

"No, I didn't."

"I mean you were terse, but I figured that's just because you were driving. We told you…"

"That wasn't *me*, Dial."

"Oh hell." Dial Tone cursed under her breath. "Then we have a problem."

32.

DIAL TONE told him that Skid's instructions—which had been intercepted by his attacker, apparently—were to proceed as fast as possible to Flagstaff, Arizona, and make contact with a source who needed transport back to the Pit immediately.

Before sundown.

This "source" would be on the campus of North Arizona University and would only agree to go with a driver who showed him a certain image on his cell phone.

The image was now on Skid's stolen cell phone, in the hands of an unknown enemy.

"Who's the source?" Skid asked.

"Negative," Dial Tone replied. "You're on an open cell."

"Damn it. Can you get anybody in the air right now to intercept that SUV?"

"No," Dial Tone said. "Nothing can fly out of the Southwest right now. Not even a Cessna. Nothing."

This made no sense. What kind of no-fly order was this? Even in the darkest hours of 9/11, military aircraft were allowed to fly and protect the country. What could keep the full airborne might of G.I. Joe out of the sky?

"What about ground forces?" Skid asked.

"They're deploying now. Getting your location from your cell now, and someone will scoop you up in a couple of…"

There was an incredulous pause before Dial Tone continued.

"Wait…are you moving!?" she asked.

"Yes. I'm in pursuit of the SUV now. Whatever you sent out isn't going to reach the Flagstaff in time. Not on roads, anyway. I'm the only one who can do it. Do not give up on me. I can do this."

"So your vehicle is still operational, despite the shots and the rocket?"

"No. It's totaled."

"I hear the hum of the road."

"Yes, you do."

Confused pause.

"So how are you driving?"

"Someone's giving me a ride."

"Someone? Someone *who*?"

"Don't ask questions you don't want answers to," Skid said.

Skid thought about how many miles down I-40 that black SUV must be by now. Speeding with glee, thinking nobody could catch him.

"We can't make contact with the source again," Dial Tone continued. "You're going to have to beat this unsub to the source."

"I'll do it," Skid said, though he wasn't sure. He was still dizzy and lightheaded from the crash and the attack—and in no condition to drive. Chances of a concussion were excellent. God forbid he pass out at the wheel while going 90 mph on I-40 West…

There was only one thing he could do.

33.

BECKY COULDN'T help but eavesdrop. When you're held captive by some nutcase with a knife who just hopped into your backseat at a Phillips 66 in New Mexico—a nutcase who oh-so-politely asked to borrow your cell phone—the rules about privacy kind of go out the window. What was she supposed to do? Hum a happily little road song in her head?

Of course she listened. To every single word.

And tried to figure out who this guy was, what he was doing.

Someone's giving me a ride. Like they were old friends, and she was just giving him a lift back to his place.

But other snatches of the conversation—

Intercept that SUV

Ground forces

Whatever you sent out isn't going to reach Flagstaff in time

Now that was flat-out strange. He sounded like police. Or military. Or something.

Yeah, a total nutcase who thinks he's a cop or a soldier.

Now that he hung up, he leaned forward again and told her:

"Rebecca, I'm going to ask you something more than a little crazy."

34.

FOR A WHILE there, Skid had been assigned to teach new recruits. *Extreme Driver's Ed.*, if you wanted to give it a name.

But Skid quickly realized that he wasn't exactly the best driving instructor in the world. That's because so much of what he did was hardwired in his system, and it was difficult to come up with a translation.

Intellect was a large part of it: you had to know roads, conditions, your vehicle. And you could teach that. The average Joe could absorb it.

But the rest—those tiny decisions you make every microsecond—the interplay of your hands on the wheel, your foot on the accelerator, your eyes on the mirrors—

It was almost impossible to teach it, without crawling into someone else's skin and *showing them*.

Now, Skid had no choice.

He was going to have to teach this poor woman how to drive like a total maniac.

35.

"I KNOW this is overwhelming, Rebecca, but it's very important that you stay focused on the road. I promise, I am *not* going to hurt you or your son. I just need you to keep driving."

"Okay."

"And I need you to follow my exact instructions."

"Okay."

"So when I say…"

There was a strange pause. After a while, Becky looked in the rearview.

The stranger was wincing, holding his hands to his head. She couldn't see his mouth, but the rest of his face was twisted up.

"If you're hurt," Becky said, "I can take you to a hospital."

The stranger's eyes flicked up. He looked like he was caught in the act. "No," he said, then blinked. "I'll be okay."

"Okay."

Becky wished she could stop saying *okay* like an idiot, let this guy know she had a brain in her head. Make him understand she wasn't this weak.

The stranger continued.

"I'm going to tell you when to hit the accelerator, and how far you can push it. I'm going to ask you to reach speeds that are going to sound crazy—but trust me, you'll be okay."

Becky heard a laugh escape from her lips.

Why did she laugh?

The situation wasn't even remotely funny.

The shock was finally starting to fade away. It had acted like a shrink-wrap around Becky's personality, choking it, depriving it of oxygen. Now it was slowly disintegrating, probably thanks to the laughter. As well as the passage of a few minutes. Shock, by definition, can only last a certain amount of time.

Becky was quickly moving from shocked to pissed.

"Who are you?"

"Nobody."

"No," Becky said. "You have a name. You have at least one friend in the world—you were just talking to her on my phone. I heard her; a little bit of her voice seeped through. But you're not a couple. She's your boss or something. Am I right?"

The stranger seemed to ignore her. He was looking out of his window at…something. But what?"

"Okay now—get it up to 100," he said.

"Did you even hear me?" Becky asked. "Are you crazy?"

"One hundred—please, now. You've got a late-model Prius. It can handle it."

"Who the hell are you?"

Now Kyle piped up from the backseat:

"Mommy—going 100 is definitely a safety violation."

The stranger turned to Kyle.

"You're right, little man. But this is a special circumstance… do you know what that means?"

Kyle nodded.

Of course he knew what it meant. Kyle knew definitions, details, names, places, dates…everything. He was a human Wikipedia page. She was in love with who Kyle was, what he knew, how he spoke. But not everyone agreed. Including her ex-husband.

Now she was alone in a car with a maniac. It was up to her to take care of Kyle. No one else.

And then it hit Becky.

Yeah.

You want 100 miles per hour, you headcase?

I'll give you 100 miles per hour.

36.

IN NEW MEXICO, the speed limit along much of I-40 is 75 miles per hour.

You could go 80, even 81 or 82 without too much trouble.

But 100?

One hundred miles per hour will get your ass pulled over, pronto.

And that's what Becky was counting on.

Let them get pulled over, and then watch as the New Mexico state police haul this guy out of the backseat. There might be a moment of drama, but the guy would have to know he had no way out—no choice but to surrender. He didn't seem violent, other than the whole knife-in-her-side thing.

And then maybe she could resume her miserable life, already in progress.

So yeah.

I'll give you 100...

37.

THE PRIUS reached 101 mph in less than six seconds.

Mile markers and signs and shrubs and other cars and the red and brown mountains seemed to whip by faster than her eye could comprehend them.

Becky Campbell had never been in a land-based vehicle that moved this fast before.

And if she weren't so scared and angry, she might even admit to being a little exhilarated by the experience.

38.

"MOMMY, this is definitely a safety violation."

Skid turned to the kid next to him. "You're absolutely right, Kyle. You should never go faster than the speed limit, and your mother knows that. But you know what? I know roads better than anybody. And sometimes, if you have a really good reason, you're allowed to go fast. Especially if it's to help people."

"Like the police?"

"Exactly like the police."

Rebecca, behind the wheel, said:

"So you're some kind of law enforcement?"

"No," Skid said. "Not exactly. Forget I said that."

"Well that's really hard to forget. And it would be kind of reassuring if you would explain it to me. Are you an undercover FBI agent?"

Skid looked at Rebecca for another second or two, then turned to stare out his window. What could he say? Under no circumstances could he discuss G.I. Joe, in any way. He could tell her that he was with the military—which was true—but that begged all kinds of questions, like why would a soldier be out here alone, on the road? Start lying, and you're on a slippery slope. The fewer details Skid shared now, the fewer that would have to be contained later.

"Something like that," he said.

"Uh-uh. Either it is that, or it isn't that."

"It's not that."

"But something like it," she mocked. "Look, I'm the one going a hundred freaking miles an hour with my son in the backseat and a total stranger who won't tell me a damned thing."

"It's for your protection," Skid said, even though he knew that was hollow comfort.

"Yeah," his captive driver said. "I feel really protected now."

The car hit a slight bump.

The pain almost brought tears to Skid's eyes.

Every tenth of a mile or so, the car would hit a newly-patched joint in the asphalt. Just a minor bump to most people.

To him, though, the bump sent a shock wave of pain up through the tires, the frame of the car, and right into his bones.

Skid swallowed hard, tried to ignore the pain...then noticed the mile marker slide by. Damn—he'd almost missed it.

"Okay, take it back down to eighty."

"Why?"

"There's a speed trap two miles ahead."

"How do you know this?"

"I just know."

39.

OKAY, so we'll slow down.

Sure thing.

Take it all the way down to the extremely slow and safe speed of 80 miles per hour. Heck, it'll feel like we're hardly moving.

But let's just count the mile markers, shall we?

If the nutcase in the backseat is telling the truth, and there is speed trap just up ahead, what...1.7 miles?

1.6 miles now?

Kyle would know the exact mileage. He was probably ticking it down in his head. But Becky didn't dare ask, and she'd looked at the odometer too late.

She wasn't as brilliant as her son. All she could was guesstimate.

40.

THE SOUND tipped Skid off. The sudden hum of the engine, the RPMs working faster. Goddamnit, he thought. She was accelerating. The needle was racing towards—

—*90*—

—because she knew there was a speed trap up ahead.

She was trying to get pulled over by the New Mexico state police.

Which was clever as hell—Skid had to give her that. Were he in her shoes, he'd probably try the same thing. But if they got pulled over, the mission was over, with zero chance to reach Flagstaff.

So he had no choice.

Even as he heard his Uncle John's voice in his head—

You're going to frighten that poor woman again?

—he touched the edge of his military license to the narrow band of skin on her side.

"Don't," he said.

"What?"

"Slow down to 80."

The needle still fluttered up around 85, 86...

"Please," Skid said.

After a few tense seconds, she gave in. Her speed dropped back below 80. Skid glanced to his left and saw two state police interceptors by the side of the road, partially hidden behind a rocky hill.

"Thank you," he said. Then after a few moments, added:

"Don't do that again."

41.

SKID TRIED to do some calculations in his head. According to his watch (now with a spiderweb-cracked face) he was unconscious for six, seven minutes. Took him another seven to make his way to the service plaza. Another minute or so to hijack Becky Campbell and her son, get her to the road, which meant:

Fifteen minutes, at 80 miles per hour—

About a 20 mile lead.

If his attacker kept going the limit. For all Skid knew, his attacker could know the roads and speed traps and conditions just as well. He could be flying ahead at 100 mph or more.

Skid needed an edge. Some way of slowing that SUV before he reached Flagstaff.

Then it occurred to him.

And it was all thanks to Becky Campbell.

"I'm going to make another call," Skid told her.

"Sure," she said. "You're the guy with the knife."

42.

INTERCEPTOR THREE was buzzing along I-40, trying to ignore the pain in his throat, just thinking about the 400 miles or so left until Flagstaff, when he saw the flashing cherries in his rearview.

Oh hell.

A speed trap?

No, he'd been going the limit. Just a touch above 75.

He was just past Santa Rosa—a small town a couple hours southeast of Santa Fe. And now he had a state police car behind him.

Three thought it over. It would be no problem to just keep speeding ahead, all the way to Flagstaff. This SUV could outpace pretty much anything on the highway if it came down to it. They could put up roadblocks, and he'd blow them apart. They could leave IEDs in the road, and he'd run 'em over on purpose. Whatever.

But a high-speed, high-profile chase would be a bad move.

His employer did not want attention.

And his Target would definitely be scared away like a spooked rabbit.

No, the only thing he could do would be to pull over.

Accept his ticket from whatever jerk hadn't reached his monthly quota yet.

Then keep moving.

43.

SKID PRAYED the phone call to the New Mexico state police had worked.

He walked the fine line between specific and vague—black SUV, Texas plates, going west on I-40.

But he hit all of the important red-flag words—

terrorist

bomb

"something about Muhammad"

—for the state police to track down that SUV and see what was what. Let that psycho behind the wheel try and explain why he has machine guns mounted in the front, and rocket-propelled grenades and god-knows-what-else.

Skid hoped the jerk in the SUV would play nice, and not try to kill a bunch of cops just to prevent blowing his cover. There were already enough innocent civilians caught up in this.

Skid caught Rebecca Campbell's eyes in the rearview and saw that she was completely. Freaking. Terrified.

"Were you serious about that?" she asked in a small, almost whisper-like voice.

"Serious about *what,* Mommy?" Kyle asked.

"No," Skid said. "There's no threat like that, I promise. But I need that guy off the road."

"Why?" Rebecca asked. "Who is he? Who are you, for that matter? How do I know you're the not the bad guy here?"

"I'm not."

"You're the one who jumped into the back of my car with a freakin' knife! That's not exactly good guy behavior, you know?"

Told ya, Uncle John said.

"I'm not the bad guy," Skid said.

Kyle said: "Mommy."

"What?"

"He doesn't have a knife. It's a little card!"

44.

INTERCEPTOR THREE rolled down the window. He knew the drill. Be docile, be apologetic, don't try to fight it. Take your ticket, move on.

"Sorry, officer—I must have been going a little faster than I thought."

The trooper's face remained like stone.

"Step out of your vehicle, please."

In Three's rearview, he could see another set of flashing cherries—no, two more sets, pulling up on the road behind them. It was turning into a regular road party.

Which meant this was about more than a speeding ticket.

Damnit.

"Please step out of your vehicle, sir."

It had to be the driver of the Challenger.

Must have regained consciousness, made it to a phone, called this in. God knows what he'd said to them, didn't matter now anyway. The police were here, and nothing was going to change that.

"Sure thing," Three said, then reached on his panel to engage a particular button.

One he'd never used before—one, in fact, that triggered a kind of prototype.

One he wasn't quite sure would work.

45.

THE JIG was up. Now the driver knew Skid had pulled off this ridiculous car-jacking with little more than a military driver's license.

The question now was: what would Rebecca Campbell do?

Skid started talking.

Fast.

"Listen to me," he said. "I'm not the bad guy here. I can't tell you what I do for a living, because I'd be breaking the law. But I can tell you about myself. That I still own. My name is Cyril Colombani. I grew up in L.A., joined the military young to escape some jail time."

"For what?" Rebecca asked.

"Speeding," Cyril answered, honestly.

Rebecca said nothing for a moment, then started to giggle. Skid suspected it was more out of some strange sensation of relief than actual humor. It was kind of funny, considering.

This was good. He needed her to feel relaxed.

"I noticed you have Texas plates," he said.

"Yeah. We're from Shamrock."

"My Uncle John used to always talk about Shamrock. Until he died, he lived in Amarillo, and loved riding Route 66. His favorite stretch of land was the Texas panhandle. I was here for personal reasons, but then it suddenly turned into a work assignment. Something bad happened to me along the way, that's why I'm banged up, and unless I make it up the road in a hurry, something even worse will happen. Does that make sense?"

Rebecca nodded, said:

"You mentioned Flagstaff."

"Yes."

"You have to go to Flagstaff."

"As fast as humanly possible. Before sundown. Or else…"

"Yeah, I get it," she said. "Funny thing is, we were headed there anyway. We wanted to see the Grand Canyon. Lived in Shamrock almost all of our lives, and never saw the Canyon. Kind of sad, isn't it?"

"Rebecca," Skid said, "I promise you, you are going to see the Grand Canyon. You and Kyle will be there to watch the sun set over it. I promise."

"You can tell me when to speed, and when not to speed?"

"I'll tell you all of my road secrets."

"Just one thing, Cyril."

"What's that?"

"Nobody calls me Rebecca. It's Becky."

"Thank you, Becky. Now take it up to 105, if you don't mind."

A beat later, Kyle reminded them that this was a serious safety violation.

46.

"PAIN RAYS" were still technically experimental. But this SUV had been equipped with the latest prototype.

They weren't pain rays exactly, but a hot-modded ADS:

Active Denial System.

As in:

Actively denying your ability to stand up straight without feeling an intense burning sensation all over your body.

Much like a microwave oven on steroids, an industrial-strength beam of electromagnetic radiation "cooks up" the top layer of its targets' skin. No burns, no blisters. Just pain. A serious amount of pain. Enough pain to make you drop to your knees and think about the last mean thing you said to your mother.

Range of the ADS in this vehicle: 100 yards.

All outside the vehicle, of course: the ADS protype had been mounted directly onto the SUV's grill, right in the middle, and resembled little more than a design feature. The driver inside was completely insulated from the effects of the rays.

Which was a very good thing.

You couldn't drive when waves from the ADS were smashing into your body.

Interceptor Three flipped the switch just as the officer outside his door drew his weapon and began to aim it through the open window, barking another order to—

Please exit your vehic

—and then he hit the switch.

47.

THE PROTOTYPE worked better than expected, Three had to admit.

All six cops who had gathered at the scene suddenly fell to their knees, then tried to crawl away. As if they could somehow move away from the source of such extreme heat. The burning pain was cranked up to *unreal*.

What made it worse was that the targets had no idea where this sudden, awful, crazy, nuclear-blast-effect-like sunburn from hell was coming from. There was no mushroom cloud in the sky, there was no explosion, there was just

hideous

inescapable

awful

crazy

god kill me now

BURNING

But the ADS waves didn't stop with just the cops. Unfortunately, they also spread to whatever vehicles were passing through I-40, scorching the skin of the drivers with an invisible heat blast, causing them to lose control of their vehicles at about the same time, and that meant...

A forty-car pileup on the highway.

No, forty-one.

Broken glass, crashing metal, squealing brakes, smoke, screaming, skidding...

Forty-two now.

Forty-three...

48.

"CYRIL," Becky said.

"What?"

"Something up ahead. Something big."

Skid held onto Becky's seat and looked out onto the highway. There was a huge multi-car pileup, bigger than he'd ever seen in his life. The SUV had to be in the middle of it. What had he done?

There was no time to analyze it now.

He could easily be out there, speeding towards Flagstaff, leaving all of this destruction behind.

"Drive onto the median."

"What?"

"The median strip. It's grass and dirt, not too many rocks. We'll be okay."

We have to be okay.

"Are you sure?"

"Slow down to 60 and take the median, quick!"

The Prius went over the rumble strip, and an awful buzz ran through the car, and Becky drove right into the freshly mowed strip of land between the two asphalt ribbons of the I-40.

Even Kyle was too stunned to mention the ramifications of this blatant safety violation.

49.

ADS OFF, Interceptor Three stepped out of his car.

My God, what had he done.

Wrecks everywhere. People writhing on the ground, some of them vomiting.

Well, whoever had invented this damned thing should be proud of himself. Works like a charm. If urban pacification is your game, then this should definitely be on your holiday shopping list.

The only problem was, stray car—an old, battered Toyota Corolla—had rammed itself up his backside. No real damage to the SUV, of course, but he had to figure some way of prying it loose before he hit the road again. And he would have to think of something quick. With the ADS off, the cops were coming to their senses again.

And they would be *pissed*.

As Three walked up to the Corolla, he saw something buzzing by on the opposite road.

It was a Prius, slowing down just a little.

A face appeared in the back passenger window. A face that was bloodied, and covered in bruises, but smiling.

Goddamnit—it was the driver from the Challenger!

And he was giving him a salute with

just
one
finger.

PART THREE: THE EMPTY SKY
50.

BECKY DROVE all of the way to Gallup, not far from the Arizona border, by which point Skid felt like it was safe for him to take over. He hadn't passed out once, or even felt dizzy, in a couple of hours. He was probably out of the danger zone. Becky, however, was fading. Her lower back hurt and her legs were cramping.

And poor Kyle needed a bathroom break.

He'd been a good soldier for the past 250 miles. But when a boy has to pee, a boy has to pee.

They pulled into the first place they saw off I-40—which turned out to be the El Rancho Hotel, a local landmark. Not just another kitschy roadside motel; this was a Hotel with a capital H. Rumor had it that the founder passed himself off as the brother of a movie mogul, which attracted stars like Reagan and Bogart and Cagney to this otherwise nothing town in the middle of the Southwest desert.

As Becky took Kyle inside, Skid could hear the strains of a player piano inside. It didn't feel right, stopping. But what was he going to do—ask the boy to go in his pants?

Skid called after Becky:

"I know you know this, but…"

"I know," Becky said. "We have to make this quick."

"Super-quick."

"Come on, sweetie."

Skid didn't dare go into the hotel—better to keep watch on the road.

The man in the black SUV would be racing like hell to finish *his* assignment.

51.

THE COROLLA had really been wedged under there. Rocking the SUV back and forth only seemed to make the problem worse. And the New Mexico state troopers were starting to pull themselves together, cursing and fumbling for their guns. Citizens would be reaching for their cell phones, to snap pics or record some video. Both no-nos.

So Interceptor Three really didn't have much of a choice.

He' gave everyone another five-second dose of the ADS.

Moans.

Screams.

Prayers.

(Sorry, my bad.)

Then he dragged the Corolla's driver out of the front seat and put his unconscious body behind another car.

Then he brought out the rocket launcher.

Because while the SUV was fully loaded for urban pacification, you never knew when you had to exit the vehicle and do a little *mobile* pacification.

swwwwwwwshhhhhhhhh

BOOM

The resultant blast didn't harm the SUV whatsoever; the armor was too thick.

Same couldn't be said for the Corolla, which was now in at least a hundred different pieces, many of them charred like a set of baby backs.

A final hit of the ADS later, Three was back on I-40 West, racing like mad.

Three was not a man of revenge—it was simply unprofessional. But when he caught up with the driver of the Challenger, he hoped there would be an opportunity to put him in a garage somewhere with the SUV and the ADS, set on high…

…for, like, an hour or so.

Cook that sucker like a campfire marshmallow.

52.

SKID DIDN'T know what was taking so long—maybe number one had turned to number two, or Becky had been kidding about trusting him and was calling the police right now…but he knew he couldn't wait any longer.

He quickly pulled a leather folder out of his go bag, scribbled quickly, then handed it to the guard at the front desk, asking him to give this to Becky Campbell.

G.I. Joe's didn't make too much—that's not why you signed up for the gig.

But Skid had pretty much saved everything over the years.

And his Uncle John had left him some money, too.

So it wasn't a problem to leave Becky a check—written from a dummy Joe account, set up for such emergencies—for $30,000 that would cover a new Prius, and maybe even their trip to the Grand Canyon. Joe would pay Becky. Skid would pay Joe the money from his Uncle.

Time was short, so Skid simply wrote:

B—

Thank you for the ride.

Tell Kyle to keep looking out for those safety violations.

—C

And hoped that she wouldn't think he was too much of a bad guy.

53.

INTERCEPTOR THREE decided *to hell with the speed limit*; he was already responsible for a traffic pile-up from hell, dozens of counts of assault and battery (if using an ADS was even covered in New Mexico's penal codes), assaulting state troopers, carrying unlicensed explosives…you name it.

So what was a speeding ticket, on top of all that?

Anybody came near him, he'd blow them off the road.

He had a job to finish.

54.

THERE WAS nothing like being behind the wheel again.

Even this Prius, which felt like a dime store kiddie ride—
the kind you pump a quarter into to rock you back and forth
for three minutes. Still, driving it was better than being in its
backseat. Skid couldn't remember the last time he was in the
passenger seat of a motor vehicle, let alone the backseat. He
always drove.

And while Becky had done an outstanding job on the road,
following his backseat directions like a pro—

Okay, take it down to 70

Punch it

Even more, you can do it

There was nothing like doing the road dance yourself,
taking it to the absolute limit before cycling back down…

And repeat.

Skid crossed into Arizona quickly, and after a brief show of
an outstanding mountain display, I-40 settled into an ugly,
deal-with-it landscape. The temperature shot up twenty degrees
in just as many minutes. Rest stops were fewer and farther
between. Everything felt tired, including Skid.

But it was only 170 miles to his target in Flagstaff.

Once the source was safe with him, he could race back to
the Pit.

Then, sweet, sweet sleep.

The only acceptable alternative to driving really, really fast.

55.

JUST OUTSIDE of Holbrook, Three saw a Prius. Same color—
gunmetal gray. Single guy behind the wheel.

Had to be him.

56.

SKID HAD Dial Tone on the phone, but she wasn't telling him
a thing.

"I can't," she said. "You *know* this. We already have compromises."

"I can't exactly stop and call you from a landline, Dial. Come on! I'm going to be in...*the location* within the hour."

"We also have a team headed towards you."

"Where are they?"

"Near...*the border.*"

"I'll make it to Flagstaff long before they will. Tell me again why Joe doesn't have planes in the air?"

Dial Tone made an exasperated sound, followed by a pounding that very well may have been her forehead on a flat surface, such as a desk.

"Okay, okay," Skid said. "I know you can't say anything. So give me an option here. I can still complete this mission!"

She paused, then told him: "We'll go old school with this. By the time you get to your...destination, I'll have instructions for you. Somehow."

"Good, because..."

And then, like a black nightmare in his rearview—

57.

INTERCEPTOR THREE opened fire. No short rounds, no little kisses anymore. Three was going for total destruction. He'd cover up what needed to be covered up later. Right now he wanted that little gray Prius perforated like a paper silhouette on a shooting range.

But the little bastard zoomed to the right, just in time. The rounds chopped up the asphalt in his wake.

Three adjusted, came up hard and heavy, and fired again...

POK

POK

POK

POK

POK

POK

Only now the Prius dropped back and to the side, expertly, cleanly, shooting around the SUV and coming within millimeters of a collision.

None of the bullets hit their intended target.

58.

THIS JERK wasn't going to get the drop on him twice.

Did he think this was the first time he'd been shot at on the road, going 100 miles per hour? Please. Skid specialized in being a moving target.

A target you couldn't hit.

His mistake earlier was that his mind had been in half-civilian mode, thinking that fast driving was enough to get the job done, that this wasn't a war zone, that all he had to do was dance with the accelerator and the brake all the way to Flagstaff. Skid hadn't thought anyone would be coming after him.

Now he knew different.

They were almost alone out here on the open road—which was fortunate, because bullets were spraying all the hell over the place. Skid thought he'd be breaking out the rocket launchers soon enough, too—that seemed to be his pattern. Shoot first, then escalate until the target was destroyed.

And then, like clockwork…

Out came twin rockets, straight from the back of the SUV.

PHSHEWWWWW

PHSHEWWWWW

Locked on the heat of the Prius's engine.

coming

right

FOR

HIM

59.

SKID STEERED hard to the left as he accelerated, then darted to the right. The trick was to give the heatseekers a nice fat burning target...

...then deny it.

As the Prius jolted to the right, Skid gritted his teeth and prayed—*Uncle John, if by any chance you're up in Heaven and have any influence over physics down here on Earth...*

One rocket slid to the left of the Prius.

The other, to the right.

Missing completely.

The rockets tried a last-second course correction, which only had the effect of slamming them into each other with a loud single

THWOOOOOM

behind him.

Skid's fingers twitched, searching for weapons that weren't there. He was in a gray Prius, not one of his Joe vehicles. He had no counter-offensive capabilities. All he could do was dodge...or try to zoom ahead.

So that was the only thing he could do. Pray he could outrun the behemoth SUV in his little darty Prius.

He pushed down on the accelerator, knowing that he couldn't stomp full-bore. This car needed to be coaxed into outlandish speeds. Somewhere in her engine was the capability, only the Prius didn't know it.

Skid did some crazy math in his head that went beyond numbers and into the realm of instinct—

—and shot past the SUV, bullets snicking and spacking along his wake.

60.

THREE WAS getting frustrated.

The Prius driver was like quicksilver—seemingly dancing around his bullets and rockets with ease.

Fine. Let's see him dance around an ADS blast.

Projection range: 100 yards.

Hard to drive when you feel like every cell in your body is ablaze.

61.

AT FIRST, Skid thought the Prius had somehow caught fire.

Maybe he'd pushed the engine too hard, and the whole thing was ready to go up. But no, the temperature gauge was within normal range—despite the blazing Arizona heat outside. What the hell was going on? Couldn't be an AC malfunction, because Skid had turned off the AC the moment he left Gallup—consumed too much gas.

So why did his skin feel like he'd just received an instant sunburn? A burn that worsened by the second? There wasn't even time to sweat, to react, to do anything…because the burn just got worse. Not only his exposed skin. Everywhere. His back. His legs. His chest. His scalp. His face. *Everywhere.*

After only a few seconds the pain was so intense Skid went into a kind of shock, which was his worst fear. You could not drive—you could not do the dance—when you were in a state of shock.

Keep it together.

Ignore the burning.

Keep driving.

Keep on the road…

62.

THREE HAD the Target deadbang.

The Prius slowed down a little, zig-zagged. The driver was feeling it. Let's see him evade my kisses now.

He primed the guns, swerved to a position behind the Prius…

63.

THE INTENSE PAIN made the wheel and the car and the road and everything blur away to the point of abstraction. Skid didn't know if he was still driving or already dead and his corpse was burning up in the middle of a flaming wreck.

Still, he forced himself to focus. If he was still driving, then there was still a brake pedal somewhere down there.

If he still had a foot, he could stomp on the pedal.

If he could stomp on the pedal, then maybe he could ram his Prius into his pursuer and take both of them out. Skid might not make it to Flagstaff, but neither would his opponent. Ignoring the nuclear-blast-searing of his entire body, Skid

HIT

the

brakes.

64.

THE TIRES of the Prius screamed on the asphalt. The SUV came rushing up behind. No time to shoot—no time to react, really, except Three's involuntary slamming of the brakes.

The two vehicles collided.

The black SUV was designed to withstand full-on blasts to its tires, body, and all windows, which were triple-thick composite polymer. What good was an urban pacification vehicle if you could take it out with anything from a shotgun blast to a shoulder-perched Stinger missile?

So when the back of the Prius smashed into the SUV's grill, Interceptor Three wasn't unduly worried.

But he forgot about the ADS prototype, mounted on the grill.

The Prius bumper pushed into the grill, right against the radiator…

…past the insulation.

The pain ray waves filled the inside of the vehicle at what approximated point-blank range.

Three SCREAMED

his body suddenly on fire.

His last conscious act was simultaneously switching off the ADS and swerving to the right…

65.

WHEN SKID woke up, he had the most curious sensation. It was like waking from a dream. One minute he was in the throes of a living hell, and the next his eyes were snapping open, body jolting involuntarily…

And he was still driving down I-40.

As if his subconscious mind had taken over. There was no other explanation. The SUV was no longer in his rear view. He was still in his lane. The Prius—though making a funny rattling sound in the back, no doubt due to a missing bumper—seemed to be operating okay.

Skid couldn't believe it. Driving was so hard-wired into his system that he'd often dream about driving, and often joked he could do it in his sleep.

Well, he just had.

And his pursuer was gone.

Skid checked the mile markers. Only fifty or so miles to Flagstaff now.

With a trembling hand, he picked up Becky's cell and called Dial Tone. He started to apologize for the interruption, but Dial cut him short.

"You have a gas card, right?"

"Yeah, but—"

"When you get to Flagstaff," Dial said, "stop for gas."

66.

WHEN SKID got to Flagstaff, he stopped for gas. First station off I-40—pumps across from a brown brick building that looked more like a boutique Italian restaurant than a mini-mart. Flagstaff, at 7,000 feet, was a mountain town. The air was cool, the trees lush and green. A strange little oasis in the middle of unforgiving Arizona. No wonder his would-be passenger had picked it. If you had to hide out in the middle of Arizona, you'd want to hide here.

Slid in his gas card. Waited to punch in his PIN number.

But instead there was a message on the digital readout:

GEORGE SYKES Y/N

Skid, momentarily confused, hit Y.

ROOM 109 AMERICAN HOTEL Y/N

Then it hit him.

It was Dial Tone.

She'd found a way to communicate his mission without compromising any intelligence to the enemy. She'd hacked into his gas card, and was signaled the moment he used it, giving her the ability to talk to him directly over the digital readout. Which no one else could see or read, unless you happened to have hacked into Cyril Colombani's gas card.

Even the enemy wasn't *that* obsessive.

Skid hit Y.

OLD SCHOOL? Y/N

Skid chuckled. Yeah, Dial Tone, this was definitely Old School.

He jabbed Y, then took off for the hotel.

67.

DR. GEORGE SYKES was near dead.

Not physically; he was just *that* old.

Nervous, too.

First Skid had to show him his military driver's license through the eyehole. Then he had to answer a few questions, through the hotel door. Dial Tone had apparently given him specifics to ask. More Old School stuff. And then finally, Skid had to speak up loudly and clearly—to make sure the voice matched what G.I. Joe had supplied Dr. Sykes.

Skid's voice—being his own—matched perfectly.

"Thank God," Dr. Sykes said. "I was beginning to think you wouldn't make it."

"Me, too," Skid said. "Come on."

"I feel like I can finally breathe."

"It's not over yet. Let's get you out of here."

Dr. Sykes moved like a man shuffling off to death row. Skid tried to gently encourage him along, but it wasn't like he could drag him through the hotel and out into the parking lot. When they finally reached the outside, the sun was beginning its downward slide. Dr. Sykes looked around, blinked.

"Where's your vehicle?"

"Give me a second."

The Prius was no good to him anymore—too recognizable, too much damage.

Skid already had kidnapping, forcible detention, terroristic threats, and God knows what else on his head.

So what was a count of Grand Theft Camaro?

68.

THEY PEELED out of Flagstaff in their newly stolen vehicle, shot past Williams, and into the lands where the forest gave way to the desert. Skid kept checking the rearview; no sign of the SUV From Hell. No sign of anybody taking a particular interest in them at all.

One hour left until sundown. Skid had no idea what happened at sundown—all he knew was that Dr. Sykes had to be in Boulder City by that time.

The sun continued its descent.

Skid blazed down I-40, doing his dance.

After a while, Skyes said:

"Look."

Skid glanced over at him. Said nothing. Turned his attention back to the road. Going 110, you really didn't want to turn your eyes away for too long.

"Did you ever see something so beautiful," the old man said.

Better to say nothing. His mission wasn't to talk. His mission was to get him to Boulder City by sundown.

Now the old man was looking out of the passenger window. At first Skid thought he was gawking at the landscape, which was harshly beautiful. But no. The old man was looking up at the sky—vast, blue, clear.

"Nothing up there at all. That hasn't been the case for what…a century, at least?"

Something clicked in Skid's mind.

Who this man was.

And why G.I. Joe couldn't have sent a plane for him.

69.

AS INTERCEPTOR THREE feared, there was no Doctor Sykes at the hotel. Colombani had already been and gone.

Outside, parked in a space behind the hotel, was the battered Prius. He'd changed cars, too.

Either he had an accomplice…no, that wasn't right. The ultra-paranoid Sykes would only deal with one person from G.I. Joe. That was the reason for the voice implants, the stolen phone, the whole ruse…

But Colombani couldn't just pull a new vehicle out of nowhere.

Three put it together, and ran back into the hotel.

70.

"TAKE 93," the old man told him.

"I know the way," Skid said.

U.S. 93 would lead them right to the Hoover Dam. Great for tourists; awful for drivers on a deadline. They were still finishing the Hoover Dam Bypass—a 1,060-feet concrete arch that linked Arizona and Nevada about 900 feet over the Colorado River. Construction slowed traffic down to a single lane in areas, especially close to the dam. Ordinarily you should be able to zip over the dam in a few minutes. Now, it could take close to an hour. Or more.

They didn't have an hour.

If Skid was going to break all kinds of laws, he was going to have to know what kind of challenges he faced on the other side.

"The machine you built is tapped into the power plant somewhere, isn't it?" Skid asked.

Dr. Sykes looked over at him, guilty look on his face.

"There was no other place without risking blowouts," he said softly. "And I needed the desert conditions for the…"

"You don't have to explain any of that to me," Skid said. "All I need to know is—how long will it take you to shut it off?"

"Once I'm close, about three seconds."

"What happens if you don't turn it off in time?"

"The skies will stay open…indefinitely."

"That's all I needed to hear."

Skid hammered the accelerator. Dr. Sykes was thrown back into his seat.

It wasn't just coincidence that all planes in the southwest U.S. were grounded. Dr. Sykes had *made them that way*. Over the years, the U.S. government had been approached by hundreds of crackpots claiming the ability to change weather patterns. Such a thing would be a boon to the military—imagine being able to bog the enemy down in mud or a hurricane. Of course, such a thing was considered impossible.

Dr. Sykes, however, had apparently come up with the next best thing.

A way to keep planes out of the sky over a specific area.

71.

A STOLEN CAMARO—red (figured). V8 engine, Arizona plates DKZ 1932. Belonging to a very PO'd university professor who was at the hotel "visiting a colleague" (right) who wanted the car recovered, but it had to be kept quiet. At least, that's what Three learned when he presented himself as an insurance agent and talked to the Flagstaff police.

Oh, he'd recover the car all right.

When Three called his superior, he learned that unless he took out Colombani and Dr. Sykes, his services would no longer be required.

In other words: his life would no longer be required.

So now Three climbed back into the SUV and hit it, going max speed up I–40.

No need to recover any crazy weather scientist.

No need to keep any kind of phone intact.

He could just blow them off the road.

72.

"I DIDN'T MEAN for it to be this way," Dr. Sykes said. "But nobody would listen. I tried all of the usual routes, made all of the overtures…but nothing. Nothing until I actually did it."

The usual overtures, Skid thought. Which was how Cobra found out about it. They knew what operatives G.I. Joe had in the area. And when the test turned out to be the real thing, they were ready to strike.

This whole day had been a set-up.

"How does it work?" Skid asked.

"The explanation would take hours."

"Give me the 101 version."

Dr. Sykes sighed. "You know the Icelandic volcano? How no planes could fly through its ash? That was because the ash clogged the cooling components with a sooty silicate material. Such a thing presents a risk of engine failure. Well, this system does the same thing—only with smart particles, dispersed into the air all over a certain geographic area."

"So *nothing* can fly?" Skid asked, incredulous.

"With these modified particles, the risk of engine failure is too great."

"Why the hell would you risk so many lives?"

"The test was safe! No one was hurt! And like I told you, nobody would listen. Your government doesn't listen to anything but—"

Skid turned his attention back to the road. A sea of red tail lights was in front of him. The first traffic slowdown. This wouldn't work.

The problem was:

No shoulder.

There was no shoulder at all.

Across a short gap, Skid could see the virgin asphalt road surface which would be the next westbound lanes of US 93—*when they were finished.*

Damn it—Skid didn't count on this. This lack of shoulder must have been a new development, otherwise he would have never taken this route.

And that's when the explosions behind them started.

Skid checked the rear view. The black SUV.

Of course it was back. Racing towards them. At speeds that seemed insane for a vehicle that size.

"What is that?" Dr. Sykes said, turning around in his seat, completely rattled.

"Your other ride."

73.

THERE WAS no choice.

The virgin road was about to be devirginized.

Skid hit reverse, then blasted out around the cars in front, using what little of the shoulder there was left…which was not much at all. The right of the car started to tilt down as the speedometer needle climbed higher and higher…

"You're insane!"

"That's what the police always told me," Skid said, just before shifting and slamming the accelerator one last time.

For a few seconds they were

airborne

—and slammed down onto the other side of the road.

Open, freshly paved road.

Clear all the way to the bridge bypass…

He hoped.

(C'mon, Uncle John. These are your roads. It would be really great if you'd cut me a break right about now…)

Of course by now the Feds were scrambling into their vehicles, pulling them onto the road, offering pursuit. That didn't matter now, because the SUV was stuck on the other side, and there was no way it could make that—

Skid watched in the rear view as the SUV sailed over the same gap. That huge rolling behemoth must have some kind of propulsion system. The physics didn't seem possible, but Skid would worry about the physics later. Because now the SUV was blowing past the Federal vehicles, smashing through them, sending them off the fresh asphalt, and now it was

opening fire

SPAK

SPAK

SPAK

SPAK

SPAK

SPAK

grinding up the new road into little black chunks that seemed to be its own weather pattern.

"Hang on," Skid said.

The Camaro zoomed away.

But the SUV was keeping pace.

Perfectly.

Then…gaining!

Please let the road be there all the way

Please let the road be there all the way

Please let the road be there all the way

Gunfire echoed from the canyon. Skid could practically feel the rounds as they blasted apart the back of the Camaro—the trunk, part of the roof. Skid swerved. Tapped the brakes. Darted to the right.

The SUV was still gaining.

Dead ahead: the twin arcs of the bypass bridge. God help them if there was a piece missing…

SPAK

SPAK

SPAK

SPAK

SPAK

SPAK

Glass shattered on the passenger side—in another instant, the side view mirror was gone.

Dr. Sykes was screaming. Skid had little sympathy—didn't he know that it was statistically safer to fly than drive?

After a few seconds the gunfire temporarily halted. Skid knew what was next. Those goddamned heatseekers.

This guy was nothing if not predictable.

And in this case, it could be used against him.

Just as Skid never anthropomorphized vehicles, he never talked to them, either. Didn't have cute nicknames for his vehicles, didn't consider them to be sentient beings. They were machines. Extensions of himself, just like a prosthetic limb.

But this time, he made an exception as he slowed the car down.

I'm going to ask you for a performance miracle, Camaro. When I hit your accelerator, I'm going to want you to lunge like you've never lunged before. When it's over you can take it easy. Coast. Cool for days. I'll spring for the garage. But I need you to punch it hard right about—

PHSHEWWWWW

PHSHEWWWWW

two missiles were loose

locked on

screaming towards him

NOW

Skid punched it.

The missiles dipped, locked in on a phantom heat signature that was there a fraction of a second ago.

They blew up a chunk of arch, starting a cascading effect that broke up the road behind Skid as he rocketed toward the Nevada side.

And breaking up the road in front of the SUV following them.

There would be no propulsion now.

No guns.
No missiles.
No pain rays.
No nothing.
Just an oversized, overweight vehicle making a
900
foot
plunge
down to the mighty Colorado.

74.

THE TV INTERVIEWER put on a face that some how blended sympathy and incredulity—one that said, *I can't believe what you've been through.*

Becky Campbell nodded and said, "Desperate people will do desperate things sometimes. I can understand that. The important thing is that my son and I were not hurt. Cars can be replaced."

The interviewer mimicked the nod, meant to draw out more from Becky, and avoid speaking over her. This was TV gold, as far as the interviewer was concerned.

"Sometimes you've got to look beyond yourself. Whatrever this guy thought he was doing, he must have thought it was important."

After a few seconds of silence, the interviewer ventured a question:

"So are you saying, Ms. Campbell, that you forgive your kidnapper?"

Becky had to bite her lip to keep from smiling. She thought about Cyril and wondered if he'd somehow be watching this. Wherever he lived when he wasn't attending funerals.

"I don't know about that," she finally said. "Let's just say... I'm on the road to forgiveness."

75.

THE JOE FORCE was waiting for them at the device in Boulder City. As Dr. Sykes was escorted by armed guard to his own experimental unit so that it could be shut down, Skid crawled out of the driver's seat. He stretched his back and tried to make a list of all of the violations (*safety violations*, as young Kyle would say) that he'd racked up in the past seven hours. Destroying the still-in-progress Hoover Dam Bypass? That was probably the worst of them.

Still, it was his Uncle John's Challenger that haunted him the most. He would have to make arrangements for its burned-out shell to be brought back to his garage in the Pit.

A promise was a promise.

He'd have to return it to his Aunt Maria—not a scratch on it.

Unfriendly Fire

JONATHAN McGORAN

THE DUST rose up in front of them, a sinewy column twisting languidly into the sky. Every now and then a light breeze pushed it out of the way, revealing the trucks they were following, just for a moment. Duke could feel the soft wind through the open window, just long enough to remind him how good a light breeze could feel. Then it was gone, and the trucks disappeared back behind the choking cloud their own wheels were kicking up.

Duke was driving an SRAT, or Specialized Reconnaissance Assault and Transport System, a monster that could drive up an eighty-percent incline and reach speeds up to one hundred miles per hour. It was a sweet ride, but the novelty had long since worn off.

For six hours they had been driving the relief convoy over some of the roughest terrain in the world, distributing food and water to the civilian women and children of Tarkestan. The international peacekeepers and aid agencies were on their way, but it would take days for them to get through. That's why they had called G.I. Joe.

WHEN THE CONVOY stopped at a small cluster of ramshackle huts at the foot of a small craggy mountain, the Joes got out of their vehicles, sullen and stiff.

"How are you guys holding up?" Duke asked, slapping shoulders and trying not to cough from the cloud of dust that came off them.

"Just swell, Duke," said Tripwire, doing a couple of quick squats next to the water tanker he was driving. "Like riding on air."

Scarlett smiled and shook her head as she got out of the food truck, her red hair contrasting with the drab landscape. She immediately started distributing rice and water. Tripwire helped her while Heavy Duty, Flint, Footloose, and Stalker fanned out, forming a perimeter around the crowd of women and children clustering quietly around the aid truck.

This was not the first refugee situation Duke had been through. Usually, the civilians were quiet with despair or clamoring loudly out of hunger and frustration. These people had the hollow eyes and blank expressions of shock. It had been less than four days since their lives had been ravaged by sudden war, and some of them had suffered unspeakable acts of cruelty. There had been reports already of Azaki atrocities.

None of the boys were older than eleven or twelve, and the handful that were close to that age eyed the Joes warily, fingering strips of leather and rope that Duke recognized as shepherds' slings. Hundreds or even thousands of years earlier, slings just like them had been the weapon of choice in that region, but now they were just toys for children. Smooth pebbles littered the ground, perfect ammunition for a sling, and Duke tensed for a moment, wondering if those toys had seen action against the Azakis. Probably not, he figured, otherwise the boys would likely have been shot. Besides, their eyes might have been hard and wary, but they had the same hollow look as the rest of the villagers. Whatever fight they might have had in them had been knocked out of them, at least for the moment.

It would be a while before the villagers could even begin to process what they had experienced in the previous few days.

For the moment, all of them were hungry and thirsty. The parts of their brains that could function on autopilot moved each of them toward the food and water.

The one exception was a striking young woman with sharp, dark eyes, who hung back while the others got their food. Her face was drawn and alert, warily scanning the horizon.

The Joes watched as well, their backs straight and their weapons at the ready as they surveyed the dry, rocky terrain.

This was the sixth stop of a day spent mostly driving across the desert and up and down the foothills of the small jagged mountains. The work was tedious and depressing. Duke worried that the men might become complacent, but at the first sound of distant engines, they stiffened and assumed defensive positions before he could even call it out.

Scarlett and Tripwire continued to distribute the food and water, but their eyes swept the terrain.

The woman with the sharp eyes was finally taking her turn at the water truck, but she looked up and checked their surroundings as well, her eyes stopping briefly when they met Duke's. He gave her a reassuring smile, but she didn't look reassured.

Within a few seconds, the rest of the huddled crowd had snapped out of their torpor and were searching the valley as well, looking for the source of the sound.

A caravan of military trucks bearing the crest of Azakistan emerged from a narrow pass two klicks to the west: three troop carriers and an APC with a mounted machine gun and a paint job speckled with bullet marks.

The townspeople disappeared, scattering silently. For a moment, the boys with the slings stayed behind, but with a stern look from the dark eyes of the woman at the water truck, they too disappeared. In an instant, the Joes were standing there alone, watching in a silence disturbed only by the distant sound of the engines.

The caravan moved from left to right, curving slightly

around to follow the contours of the mountain. The only sign that they had seen the Joes was a lone Azaki soldier riding on the back of the truck, staring at them, his assault rifle pointing at the ground.

Duke watched the convoy until it disappeared behind a rocky outcropping left over from some ancient landslide. The squad relaxed the tiniest bit; it was reassuring that the rest of the Joes were taking the job seriously.

G. I. Joe was there in a neutral capacity. They weren't supposed to take sides, but it was clear who the bad guys were.

Tarkestan and Azakistan shared a long border and an even longer history, sometimes as allies and sometimes as foes, more recently in uneasy coexistence. Tarkestan was a young democracy. Azakistan had suffered under a string of brutal dictatorships, some worse than others but all of them bad, leaving Azakistan thoroughly corrupt and devastatingly impoverished. The Azakis had attacked without provocation.

As the clatter of the Azaki convoy faded in the distance, the Joes maintained their vigilance, but long after the last echo of the convoy had drifted away, the locals stayed disappeared. Even the woman with the dark eyes.

SCARLETT CHECKED her watch and then looked up at the sky. It wasn't late, but it was getting there. "We done here?" she asked.

Duke nodded. "Yeah, I don't think anyone's coming back for seconds," he mumbled, then louder, "Let's move out, people. And look alive … we're headed the same way they were."

Duke started up the Rat, then held back, waiting for the others to file out in front of him.

The lead vehicle was a JLTV, or Joint Light Tactical Vehicle. They called it the Jolt, partially because it was fun to drive, partially because on terrain like this it could do some serious damage to your internal organs.

Still better than a Humvee.

Once the convoy was moving, Duke pulled out of line and

drove up on the left, like a dog herding sheep. With the clouds of dust obscuring his view, it was important to get out to the side and take a look at things. He wanted to check on the rest of the squad, but it felt good to be actually moving instead of creeping along like they had been for the past seven hours. Once he got out in front of the convoy, away from the plume of dust, he could see the faint fog of dust from the Azaki convoy.

Ripcord looked over at him. "Lot of dust in the air."

"Not from us, either. We got company, and they're close."

Duke pulled up next to the Jolt. Heavy Duty seemed to be enjoying himself at the wheel, but next to him, Flint didn't seem to be having quite as much fun. With Flint it could be hard to tell.

"X-Ray Five, this is X-Ray One. You lonely up here? Over."

The radio crackled for a moment, and they could see Heavy Duty tap the radio on his shoulder. "Negative X-Ray One. Alpha Zulu convoy, maybe five klicks ahead. Over."

"Roger that, X-Ray Five. X-Ray One will assume lead off. You are now batting clean-up. Over."

"Roger that, X-Ray One. Don't let the pitcher get ahead of you."

Heavy Duty gave him an okay and immediately peeled off, decelerating so the rest of the convoy could pass him and he could take up the rear.

With a slight twist of the steering wheel, Duke pulled into the front position of the column and tapped his headset. "X-Ray Team, this is X-Ray One. We have a convoy of Alpha Zulus approximately five klicks ahead. Look alive, ladies and gents, these are not friendlies, but remember our ROE. This is a strictly humanitarian mission, and we are not taking sides. Do not shoot unless you are shot at. Over and out."

Ripcord laughed. "You know, a little bit of action wouldn't necessarily be a bad thing after a day spent driving a lunch wagon."

Duke smiled. "I hear you, Rip, but you know our rules of engagement. Unless we're fired upon, we're just a food bank on wheels, plain and simple."

FIVE MINUTES LATER they crested a small hill and slowed to a stop. The Azaki convoy, engines idling, was stopped next to a small cluster of earthen huts at the foot of the mountain. The trucks partially blocked the view, but from up on the hill, they could see that a crowd of people had gathered in the center of the village.

"Plain and simple, huh?" Ripcord asked.

Duke ignored him. "X-Ray Team, this is X-Ray One. We will proceed with caution to our objective. Do not, repeat, do not engage."

With Duke and Ripcord in the lead, the Joe convoy rolled down the hill, slowly pulling past the lead Azaki vehicle before coming to a stop.

"No sudden moves," Duke said quietly as the Joes slowly got out of their vehicles.

About thirty Azaki soldiers formed a circle in the village center. Inside the circle were an equal number of women. Children watched through windows cut in the walls of the houses. Their eyes were wide with terror and confusion. But one of the older boys stepped towards the door, his eyes burning with hatred. He looked to be ten or eleven, a solid boy with a scar across his forehead and a shepherd's sling swinging from his clenched fist. He stood there for the briefest moment before an adult hand grabbed the back of his tunic and yanked him back into the shadows.

The women cowered in a tight knot except for two of them. A slender girl in her mid teens was being pulled by the wrist by one of the Azaki soldiers. He was wearing sergeant stripes and seemed to be in charge. He looked about nineteen.

The woman with the dark eyes from the previous village was out in front, her arms spread protectively. A thin trickle of blood marked her cheek.

Ripcord pointed at the woman with the dark eyes. "Isn't that woman from that last village?" he said quietly.

"Got here fast, didn't she?" Duke noted.

Ripcord nodded. "Roger that." They both glanced up at the craggy mountain they had just come around. It had seemed impenetrable, but somehow she had come through it, and made good time, too.

The Azaki soldiers all turned to watch as the Joes climbed out of their vehicles. The Azakis looked mean and hungry, more like street criminals than the type of army who could pull off a lightning invasion.

The Joes stared back at them, and for several long moments, they stayed like that, then the young girl resumed her struggles and the soldier holding her backhanded her hard across the face.

Duke could feel the Joes stiffening behind him. "Easy Joes," he said softly.

The sergeant who had hit the young girl looked fearful for an instant, afraid of what reaction he was about to incite. Duke was worried about that as well, but to his relief, no one made a move.

Duke wasn't the only one relieved, and the sergeant started to grin, then he started to laugh. He mumbled something in Azaki, then repeated it, louder, drawing halfhearted laughs from the other soldiers.

"He's saying we're a bunch of cowards," Heavy Duty said in the radio, translating for the Joes.

"That hurts," Duke replied sarcastically.

The sergeant looked back at them, then turned and slapped the girl again. Her lip split, splattering her dirty blouse with blood. "*Irina!*" she cried, looking to the dark-eyed woman for help.

Irina, the woman with the dark eyes, moved to protect the girl, and one of the other soldiers grabbed her by the hair and put a knife to her throat.

The Azakis seemed sloppy and poorly trained, but a knife was a knife, and that close, he wasn't likely to miss. They had to be careful.

The sergeant laughed again, pulling the young girl away from the others. She yelped in pain and fear.

The rest of the soldiers looked on with bored, hollow eyes. They seemed dazed and indifferent. It was an expression Duke had seen before, and it was not from shock or battle fatigue.

Ripcord stepped closer to him. "This ain't right, Duke. We got to do something. I don't care about the ROE."

Duke shot him a glare and Ripcord rolled his eyes. "You know what I mean."

As they watched, the sergeant started to drag the young girl toward one of the huts.

"We're here to do a job," Duke said. "Scarlett, start unloading the food."

She glared at him. "You're not serious."

"Just do it," he snapped.

Scarlett glared at him again, then she stomped to the back of the truck and pulled back the tarp, revealing the sacks of rice and potatoes. "They're terrified," she said. "They don't want food."

"It's not for them," he said quietly. "Get ready, Joes."

Scarlett was right; the women on the ground showed no interest in the food. The Azaki soldiers, on the other hand, were transfixed. They might have been hungry for other things as well, but Duke hoped that what they wanted most was food. Even the sergeant forgot what he was doing, and his captive managed to pull free and dash into one of the huts.

The cluster of women no longer seemed important to the Azaki soldiers; their focus now was the food Scarlett had revealed. Careful not to make any sudden moves, Duke moved over to the back of the truck and hefted a bag of rice. The bag had 100 KGS stenciled across it, and it felt like it too, but Duke was careful to betray no strain or effort as he shifted it up onto his shoulder. He met Scarlett's eyes before he turned back to face the Azaki soldiers. "Line up your shots in case things get hot," he whispered. "And put that punk with the knife at the top of the list."

Before he could turn back around, Scarlett had slipped her crossbow around on its strap, subtly making it more accessible. Duke had been doubtful of the crossbow once, but he'd seen what Scarlett could do with it. Now he was a believer.

The rest of the Joes picked up on Scarlett's movement, and Duke heard a faint rustling sound, like a gentle breeze—the sound of a hundred subtle adjustments as each member of his team shifted balance and posture from ready mode to battle-ready mode.

It took an effort not to smile.

As he approached the circle of soldiers, they made no movement to get out of his way, and it took even more effort not to smile.

The closer he got, the more confident he was that he was going to survive the maneuver, but best-case scenario, he was still going to catch a ton of bad juju when all was said and done.

Through the gaps between the Azaki soldiers, he could see the women looking up at him, confused. The woman with the dark eyes was out of his field of vision, but he could feel those eyes burning on him. The soldiers themselves watched with a strange mixture of amused condescension and deadly serious hunger.

There were eight Joes and roughly thirty Azakis, plus a few more still in the lead truck. When Duke stepped up to the two soldiers in the middle, he could smell the battle on them: sweat and diesel fuel, fear and violence. The one on his left was six-two, maybe one-ninety. He looked like he'd be at least two-ten with a good meal in him. The one on the right was shorter and older, meaner looking, with a mustache doing a bad job of hiding a scar on his upper lip. They both had the Azaki mix of Eurasian features, but the one with the mustache looked more European. Duke paused in front of them, just for a second, then started to push past between them.

They stepped together, closing ranks, and Duke kept pushing, wondering which one was going to lay a hand on him first. It was the mustache, putting up an arm to block his way.

The instant they made contact, Duke slid the sack of rice off his shoulder. The Azaki with the mustache caught it, staggering under the unexpected weight, and Duke stepped backward, whipping his head back and crushing the nose of the soldier behind him. Hot blood splashed the back of his neck and he used the mass of the soldier behind him to give added force to the fist he drove into the face of the soldier holding the rice. Bone gave way under the blow and the soldier staggered backward, his mustache drenched in blood.

The sack of rice finally hit the ground as mustache reached for his holster. Duke snuck a glance at the dark-eyed woman, at the knife still at her throat, but not pressing any harder. He looked back as the soldier with the bloody mustache brought up his sidearm, a Russian-made Yarygin. The dark metal gleamed like it had never been fired.

Duke counted the beats, and when the gun had risen to a firing position, he swept his arm up, knocking the gun skyward so that it discharged into the air.

That first pop of gunfire was still ringing in the air when it was repeated, and then answered, like those first few kernels of popcorn, soon followed by a cacophony of explosions. Duke brought the butt of his gun down on the Azaki soldier's head, then quickly went through his progressions, scanning for his next target.

His eyes darted to the soldier with the knife. In a fraction of an instant, he saw the woman with the dark eyes holding her captor's wrist as if she'd been tensed to flip him, but had stopped, taken aback by the crossbow bolt that had split his forehead.

Next he found the sergeant, drawing his sidearm. Duke counted "one" and when the gun was fully drawn, he squeezed his trigger twice. The sergeant staggered backwards, firing wildly into the air as a pair of red dots quickly grew on his chest. Duke was already moving on to his next target.

But there were none left.

It was over in a moment, but moments like those can drag on for a long time. The women on the ground clung to each other in shock, all but one of them. Irina with the dark eyes had already disappeared.

All the Azakis were either down or in retreat.

The lead vehicle had sped off at the first shot. It had skidded to a stop a hundred yards away, the dust cloud it had stirred up slowly catching up to it as it waited for the soldiers running after it. The two men Duke had initially engaged were running along with the others, trying to stanch the blood from their broken faces as they ran.

When they reached the truck, the one with the mustache turned and shouted for several seconds in Azaki.

"He says we'll be sorry," Heavy Duty translated.

Duke and Ripcord turned to look at him.

Heavy Duty shrugged. "And some other stuff."

The Joes remained at the ready until the Azakis were on the truck and it had sped off once again.

As it disappeared over a low hill, Ripcord turned to Duke. "Well, now," he said with a wry smile. "I guess *you're* going to be in a little bit of trouble."

"I WAS DELIVERING aid to the noncombatants when the Azakis interfered," Duke explained. He was standing in the middle of General Hawk's tent, the setting sun showing red through the dust-caked window panel. "All I did was allow them to confiscate the rice. I didn't want to let them have it, either, but I did."

General Hawk looked dubious. "Didn't want to let 'em have it, huh?"

"The rice, sir." He bit the inside of his cheek. "I didn't want to risk an altercation."

Hawk stared at him, not believing him, but not wanting to push it any furthere. "Duke, I know this is tricky and not what we're used to, but the Joes are in a delicate situation. Our rules of engagement are clear: we do not use force unless attacked."

"I understand completely, sir. But we were attacked."

"That's not what the Azakis are saying."

"Well, then they're lying, and that does not surprise me a bit."

Hawk sighed. "I realize this isn't easy, especially when the bad guys are right there. I know it. These folks are in league with terrorists who have attacked the U.S. And there is nothing I'd like more than to go a few rounds with them myself. But that is not why we are here." He rubbed his temple. "We have to be disciplined. It's going to be even harder for the younger guys. That's why I need you to set an example."

It wasn't a question, so Duke didn't answer, but the rebuke stung.

"All right," Hawk went on. "The peacekeepers and the international agencies will be here in two days to take over the aid distribution and start the negotiations. Then we can go back to doing what we do. In the meantime, we need to make sure we don't get attacked, so we don't have to engage, so I don't have to get any more phone calls from the State Department. Is that clear?"

"Yes, sir."

"Go on and get out of here."

Ripcord was waiting for him outside the tent. "So how did that go down?"

Duke waved him off, striding past him, but Ripcord fell in beside him.

Duke sighed, annoyed at the missed hints, but he answered

anyway. "He wasn't happy, but he doesn't like this stuff any more than we do. You know how he is."

"Right." Ripcord was having a hard time keeping up with him, especially not knowing where they were headed. "Game of chess? Maybe throw a ball?"

Duke didn't look at him. "Maybe later, all right buddy?"

"Yeah, sure," he replied, slowing down a step while Duke strode away.

THE ATV was parked between two of the tents. If anybody asked, he was doing a perimeter reconnoiter. The real objective was to blow out some cobwebs.

He took it fast, pulling a long arc across the dusty terrain at the foot of the craggy mountain, crunching over the rocks and drifting across the desert sand. The speed and the wind made him feel better almost immediately, and after looping back almost to where he started, he headed straight for the steep incline of the rocky foothills.

The vehicle had an uncanny ability to climb, and at times he was sure he was going to slide straight back down, but he rode up the steep slopes, then moved side to side up the wide dry gullies that crisscrossed the mountainside.

When Duke reached a small plateau, he stopped, looking out over the basin below him as a few dislodged pebbles tumbled down the slope he had just climbed. The tents where the rest of the Joes were camped were plainly visible. Duke was glad for them that he was not an unfriendly sniper; a bad guy could have had a field day from up there.

Darkness was falling quickly and the cool night air was flowing in, chilling his sweaty skin. His better sense told him he should head back down to the camp, but he still had some stress to relieve and he found another dry mountain stream and continued farther up the mountain. It consisted entirely of dust and rocks; if not for the smooth stones it would have been impossible to imagine water ever flowing down it. It was good riding, though, and it felt satisfying to have his insides jostled around as he lurched up the incline. He was starting to laugh when he reached the top, going airborne as he crested it.

The laugh died in his throat as he landed, kicking up a spray of pebbles and dirt as he skidded to a stop.

The streambed widened out to a small plateau. In the gathering gloom, he could see it was crowded with tents and military vehicles, even a few horses. Directly in front of him, twenty feet away, three riflemen in Tarkestani military uniforms stood shoulder to shoulder with their rifles pointing at him. The weapons were World War II-era bolt-action Mosin Nagants, Russian. The wood was worn, but the rifles looked oiled and well maintained.

The soldiers themselves were in worse shape. But while they were dirty and gaunt, their eyes were sharp and the guns didn't waver.

The one in the middle said something Duke couldn't understand, then he spoke again, this time in English. "The engine. Turn it off."

He was a young man, but his shoulder insignia said he was a major general and his bearing indicated that he had earned the rank.

"Not looking for trouble," Duke said as he killed the engine. "Just here to distribute food and water."

"Of course you are," the young general said, his thick accent doing nothing to disguise his sarcasm. "Move away from the vehicle and put your hands up."

Duke did as he asked, stepping away from the ATV.

"You are with the Azakis," the general said.

"No, I'm not," Duke replied. "I'm here on a humanitarian mission." As he said it, he heard a faint rustling sound and sensed a presence behind him. In a flash, he grabbed the hand that was attempting to disarm him and spun around, putting the Tarkestani soldier between him and the men in front of him, using him as a human shield. Before the others could adjust their aim, Duke had his sidearm pressed into his hostage's neck. As he had spun, however, he had done a quick head count of the Tarkestanis gathering around him, their guns trained on his back. Unlike the Azakis, these guys appeared to know what they were doing.

The leader of the riflemen smiled grimly. "You don't seem like a humanitarian somehow."

"I'm not looking for trouble," Duke said evenly. "So how about we just go our separate ways."

"Sorry. You know the location of our camp."

Duke laughed. "I'd never be able to find this place again, if that is what you're worried about." The truth was, he was a little concerned about finding his way back to the Joe camp, even with GPS.

The commander smiled condescendingly, as if that didn't warrant a response. "Please hand over your weapon."

Duke grinned, but he didn't feel it. "I'm afraid I can't do that."

"Then I'm afraid we will have to shoot you." He nodded to one of the soldiers behind Duke and a sound of crunching gravel was followed by the feeling of a gun pressing into the base of his skull. Duke thought that if the guy behind him pulled the trigger, the guy in front of him was going to have a very bad day, but still probably better than Duke's.

"I will count to three," said the Tarkestani. "One."

Duke didn't like the way his hostage stiffened, as if he was taking the situation very seriously. As if this young general was the type who always followed through with his threats.

"Two. Hand over the gun."

The hostage started trembling. Duke planned his next move, figuring it would likely be his last one. If he could manage to head-butt the guy behind him, he could drop to the ground under this his hostage and take out the three riflemen without too much trouble. He could probably even roll over in time to take out a few of the others behind him. He didn't want to think about what would happen after that.

The Tarkestani was pursing his lips to say "Three," and Duke was tensing for the head-butt when a strong, clear female voice shouted out, "Stop!!"

All the soldiers froze, except for Duke and the Tarkestani general. Duke turned to the source of the command and saw the dark-eyed woman, Irina. She approached the Tarkestani commander and they had a terse but quiet exchange. After going back and forth a few times, she pointed at Duke and spoke again, and the general looked over at him, his eyebrow raised appraisingly. He considered Duke for a moment, then shook his head and they had another terse exchange.

Duke could tell the general was becoming exasperated, but she seemed to be swaying him. For all he knew, she could have been arguing that shooting was too good for him and they should really just skin him alive, but he found himself pulling for her side of the argument.

The Tarkestani general glared at her, then turned once again to Duke.

"My associate tells me you have been delivering food and water to our people."

"That's what I've been trying to tell you."

"But you are not an aid worker."

"Normally, no, but while I'm here I am."

"She says you protected the women of the village. Isn't that outside of your rules of engagement?"

Duke smiled. "I was delivering aid when I was attacked."

The commander turned back to Irina and after a brief exchange, he smiled and muttered an order to the soldiers behind Duke. The pressure at the base of his skull disappeared and Duke could feel his own captive relax. The riflemen lowered their weapons.

"You can relax," the commander told him. "And you can keep your weapon. I am General Aramen Alexi. It seems that we are now friends." He smiled, but his eyes remained wary. "I must demand that you never return here. But for the moment, come," he said. "I would offer you food, but we have none. Please, slake your thirst with us."

It was a short distance to the encampment, and Duke, Aramen, and Irina walked abreast, like friends, but Duke was very much aware of the soldiers that surrounded them.

"You are not an aid worker, I can tell," Aramen said again as they walked.

"My current mission is to deliver aid," Duke explained, "but you're right. That's not what I usually do."

"You are a warrior. And from what Irina tells me, quite an impressive one. The villagers you saved, that was my father's village. Thank you."

Duke smiled. "I'm happy to help."

"I am grateful for your help as well," Irina said. Her English was almost free of accent. "The Azakis have done terrible things to our people. They have destroyed our infrastructure and left us with no money for food."

"In two days, your country will be blanketed with aid and swarming with peacekeepers," Duke told her. "Then the negotiations can begin."

Aramen spat in the dust, his face going dark. "Peacekeepers! They do not keep peace. They cast evil in stone."

Duke had no idea what he was talking about.

"When the international forces arrive and peace talks start, we will be forced to negotiate from our current position," Irina explained. "It is a position of weakness."

"We were victims of treachery," Aramen said grimly. "The Azakis struck at dawn, unprovoked. Missiles took out our parliament and our military headquarters before we could even take up arms. Even after heavy losses, we were stronger than the Azakis and could have easily repelled the attack. Our army assembled to defend the presidential palace, with President Alexi in command. My father."

He went quiet and Irina continued the story.

"The police and intelligence forces took up the rear," she explained. "Commanded by General Grigori."

"My father's half brother," Aramen added, his eyes smoldering. "A fat pig with a bald head and a ridiculous mustache. I once called him uncle."

Irina continued. "When the Azakis rolled into Kutsk, the capital, the police opened fire on our own soldiers. Their own countrymen." She went quiet, as well, and for a moment they both stared at the ground, both of them still trying to understand what had happened.

Aramen cleared his throat and looked straight at Duke. "When the invasion started, the president went to his intelligence chief, General Grigori, my uncle, and asked many questions. 'Why did we not know this was coming?' he asked him. 'Why would the Azakis attack us, when they know we have superior military strength, and the advantage of home?' But Grigori had no answers. When the police force opened fire, General Grigori walked up behind the president and slit his throat with a dagger..." Aramen whispered. "He murdered his own brother, my father, and he vowed to wipe the Earth clean of any trace of him."

THE NEXT DAY started out much like the previous one: monotonous drives over rough terrain, hollow-eyed villagers dully accepting the food and water. Duke and Ripcord were riding point again, with Scarlett and Tripwire in the food truck, Footloose and Stalker in the water tanker, and Heavy Duty and Flint bringing up the rear.

Just before noon, they arrived at a village that looked just like all the others. The villagers, however, seemed different. Their eyes were furtive but animated, and they watched the aid convoy with excitement but also nervousness.

Duke got on the radio. "X-Ray Team, this is X-Ray One. Eyes wide, people. Something's going on here."

When Scarlett pulled the tarp off the food supplies, the

villagers drew closer, they always did, but one broke away from the others and stepped right up. Irina.

"Hello, Mr. Duke," she said, with a shy smile that softened her eyes.

"Hello, Irina." The other Joes turned to look at him, but he did not explain. Leaning closer to her, he smiled. "Thanks for your help yesterday. You probably saved my life."

"Perhaps you saved my life, too," she said with a shrug, pulling back a fold of her tunic to reveal a long dagger. "But perhaps I would have been okay."

Duke believed her, but he didn't say anything.

"Your team will be leaving soon?"

Duke nodded. "As soon as the peacekeepers arrive. Will you be okay?"

"We will be fine," she said with a knowing smile. With a glance to each side, she leaned even closer and lowered her voice. "I tell you this in confidence, so your people do not get caught in the middle, by surprise. The counter offensive is coming."

"But you have no firepower."

"It has emptied our coffers, but we have fixed that problem."

Duke hoped she was right, but he had his doubts. "Well, good luck to your people."

She bowed her head. "And to yours." Then she stepped back and lost herself in the crowd of villagers collecting food.

Duke started to help with distributing the food and water, but he noticed a presence at his elbow. When he turned, he saw it was Scarlett, staring at him quizzically.

"What was all that about?" she asked.

"What?"

"With that woman. What was that about?" Scarlett's orders were the same as the rest of the Joes, but her background was in intelligence, and she could tell when something was up.

He pulled her aside and told her about his experience the night before.

"Aramen Alexi," she said. "The son of President Alexi."

"Right." He told her about General Grigori's treachery.

She listened intently. "So that's how the Azakis managed to rout the Tarkestanis. It hadn't made sense until now."

"The Tarkestanis are planning a counter offensive, before the international peacekeepers get here."

"With what? The Azakis destroyed the their armory, didn't they? Aren't all of their weapons gone?"

"Just about. And somehow the Azaki army appears to have had a high-tech make-over."

"Yeah, I noticed that. So what are the Tarkestanis going to do?"

Duke shook his head. "I don't know, but they seem to think they have found a way around it."

She thought for a second, then looked up at him. "That's good intelligence work, Duke."

He was about to say thanks, but he wasn't sure he took it as a compliment. He was well aware of the importance of good intelligence, but he hadn't been trying to collect any, really. He wasn't going to withhold something like that from his own team, and though he barely knew the Tarkestanis, Duke respected them as warriors. He felt bad betraying their trust.

As they drove to the next village, Ripcord gave him a sidelong look. "You okay, man? You look like something is bothering you."

"Nah, I'm okay, Rip. Maybe I just need to get back to some actual G.I. Joe work, instead of this meals-on-wheels thing."

"Yeah, I hear you," Ripcord replied, but his expression said he wasn't buying it.

A half hour out of the village, twenty miles from the next stop, they crested a small hill and caught a glimpse of another Azaki convoy. This one looked different from the one they had encountered the day before.

There was a single troop carrier, with two luxury SUVs in front of it and two in the rear. The windows were tinted dark and the paint was clean and new, shining brightly in the noonday sun. They were moving fast, sending up a rooster tail of dust that swirled in their wake.

Ripcord pointed them out, but Duke was already watching closely.

"X-Ray Team, this is X-Ray One. On your toes, we have company at ten o'clock."

They drove in parallel for a while, but the Azaki convoy quickly outpaced them, then veered away, toward the hills off to the west.

"What are you thinking?" Ripcord asked, leaning forward to get a better look at Duke's face.

Duke didn't answer at first, then he said, "Stop the vehicle."

"What?"

"Stop, I'm getting out."

"Duke, it's the middle of the Tarkestani desert. You can't just 'Get out.' "

"I'm taking the ATV, do a quick recon."

"But—"

Duke cut him off with a look. Ripcord sighed, shook his head, then slowed to a stop.

"X-Ray Team, this is X-Ray One," Duke said into the radio. "We're stopping for a brief moment, but we'll be back on our way in no time."

The ATV was loaded on the back of the Jolt. Duke was beside the vehicle before it had stopped, and within half a minute he was backing the ATV down the ramp.

Most of the other Joes were out of their vehicles, watching him, but he ignored them. Scarlett strode right up to him.

"What do you think you're doing?"

"Quick recon," he replied, not looking up from the task at hand.

"That's not our mission, Duke. We have food to deliver and a schedule to keep. I know I said that was good intelligence work earlier, and it was, but that's not what we're here for. And we can't be sitting around waiting around for you to come back."

"You won't have to wait. I'll be on the ATV. Probably get to the next village before you do."

"I know you're invested in this, Duke, but it's not our job. Not this time around."

Duke listened, but by the time she was finished, he was sitting on the ATV, starting up the engine. "I hear you, Scarlett, but recon is always part of the job. Knowing is half the battle, right? And in my opinion, it's important that we know what's happening on the ground."

She opened her mouth to reply, but he gunned the engine and sped off.

DUKE HAD STUDIED the maps enough to know that the Azaki convoy was headed toward a pass that led to a small, abandoned mining town in an isolated valley. As far as he could tell, the pass was the only way in or out. If he followed them in, he risked being seen and possibly being cut off.

Instead, he headed straight for the hills, figuring he would take his chances with the ATV's climbing ability. It was hard going, but he knew he had to push it hard if he didn't want to fall hopelessly behind. The hills rose in front of him in waves, and after a few minutes, he fell into a rhythm, shooting up one hill, cresting it airborne, then catching the downside of the hill in time to cushion the landing and scoop up some momentum to scale the next hill.

Before long, he came to the top of a hill, and the one beyond it was smaller, not larger. Looking over the next rise, he could see the valley beyond it, and he throttled down and climbed the rest of the way on foot.

Crouching behind the top of the next hill, he got out his binoculars.

The Azaki vehicles were parked in a small semi-circle, with men in suits and dress uniforms clustered around them. One of the men in uniform was massive, with a bald head and huge shaggy mustache. General Grigori.

Maybe fifty yards away, four soldiers in fatigues stood in a line. They were holding some kind of assault weapons. A hundred yards away from them was a row of white, man-sized targets.

As the men standing by the vehicles watched, the four soldiers aimed and fired. Almost immediately, the four targets disintegrated.

The four soldiers replaced their clips and stood at the ready, like they were waiting for a signal. Another set of targets rose up on springs, and as they started shooting again, Duke saw a flash on a distant hilltop. Four fountains of sparks shot up into the air, fanning out so they were evenly spaced.

Both the soldiers and the civilians in the valley looked skyward as the projectiles, which in the distance looked like steel javelins, reached the top of their trajectories and started falling back down. But unlike simple ballistic weapons, when they started to fall, almost simultaneously they flamed and started flying, actively adjusting their courses as they plunged down toward the valley.

The soldiers stopped shooting, and one of them took off running. The others stood in place, watching him for a moment, then they seemed to tense, as if they knew they should get out of there, too, but couldn't figure out where to go.

Their indecision may have bought them a few microseconds; as they stood there, one of the small missiles shot straight down toward the floor of the valley, then pulled up at the last second and went after the runner, following the contours of the ground, maybe a meter above the surface. The soldier angled away from it, but the thing kept coming after him. He even tried a stutter step, but the agile rocket shimmied right along with him, then it caught up with him and detonated.

Duke couldn't tell if it exploded before or after it hit him. It seemed simultaneous. One moment he was there, the next he was gone, replaced by a flash and a bang and few bloody shreds tumbling across the dusty valley floor.

Their comrade's sudden destruction galvanized the others, and they took off, still gripping their weapons. Two went one way, the third ran in the opposite direction. The rockets had already pulled out of their dive, streaking across the desert floor, one splitting off from the others to follow the lone runner.

The soldier who had gone off on his own was first. He quickly disappeared in a flash of flame and scarlet spray, inspiring the other two to find an extra burst of speed, but there was no escape.

One of the soldiers pulled ahead of the other, and a missile seemed to spear him in the back before it erupted into flame. The last soldier stumbled, and as he put out his hands to break his fall, his rifle went tumbling through the air. The last missile punched through the cloud of carnage left behind him and connected. He never hit the ground, except as a fine red mist.

There was a moment of quiet as the echo of the explosions faded and the four little smoke clouds drifted away, then General Grigori started to clap and the rest of the men gathered by the vehicles joined in. Duke watched in horror and disgust as the men congratulated each other, slapping each other's backs and shaking hands.

After five or ten minutes, the Azakis got back into their vehicles and drove off, back through the pass where they had entered.

Duke felt nauseous and angry. He wanted to go after them, or round up the Joes, maybe even call in a drone strike—international incident be damned. But he knew that wasn't going to happen. What he didn't know was what the hell was going on. Part of his brain was overwhelmed with fury and revulsion, but another part was already playing with the pieces, trying to assemble them into something that made sense.

He knew he had to get back to the aid convoy, and he knew

if he left right then, he had time to do it. But instead, he went forward, weaving his way over the hills and through the gullies until he had made his way to where the weapons test had taken place. The tire tracks of the SUVs were plainly visible, and beyond them, the four darkened, spattered craters where the four soldiers had been hunted down.

He drove around on the ATV, circling first, to make sure there were no surprises. Even with the benefit of the ATV, he doubted he could outrun those missiles, and the thought of it made him nervous, out in the open like he was.

Duke kept a respectful distance from the four impact sites. He wasn't going to bury them or say a few words or anything, but he didn't want to disrespect the dead soldiers, either.

As he was turning to go, he noticed something half buried in the sand, and he touched it with the toe of his boot.

It was the rifle that the last soldier had dropped, right before he was hit. It looked like an M249, a common-enough light machine gun with decades of service. This one was meant for street fighting, judging by the forward pistol grip. The plastic stock looked new, perhaps from a recent refurb.

He stood there staring down at it for a moment, replaying in his head what he had just seen, wondering again what the hell had just happened. If it was a weapons test he witnessed, the weapon being tested was probably the antipersonnel missiles, not the rifles. But then why have them firing the M249s in the first place? Two tests in one?

It felt a bit like he was looting the dead, but he picked up the gun and put it in the ATV's utility compartment, if for no other reason than there was nothing else left to pick up. He supposed this might also come under the heading of intelligence work.

DUKE CAUGHT UP with the rest of the Joes as they were packing up to leave the next village. The villagers had their food, everybody looked fine, it didn't seem like he had been missed until Ripcord came up to him while he was securing the ATV on the back of the truck. "Scarlett is pissed," he whispered.

"What?" Duke asked. But he already kind of knew it.

"Scarlett," Ripcord repeated. "She's mad as hell. At you."

Duke started to say he didn't care, or she didn't scare him, but then he saw her approaching, and he knew he did care. And he was scared.

He was fumbling at the utility compartment of the ATV when she stepped right up to him, her nostrils flaring and her brow hard.

Duke pulled out the gun and held it up. Her face stayed hard, but one of her eyebrows went up, intrigued despite itself. "What's that?"

"Looks like an M249. Some kind of variant."

"And what's *that?*" she said, pointing to some speckles of dried blood along the barrel.

"That's what's left of the last man to fire it."

He told them both about the demonstration he had observed.

"What do you make of it?" she asked.

He shrugged. The question had been percolating in his brain since he had watched the four soldiers vaporized while their commanders looked on. "I don't know. When those rockets showed up, the VIPs in the bleachers weren't upset, they were celebrating. I think it was a test or a demonstration. And from all the high fives afterwards, I'd say it was a success."

GENERAL HAWK was not amused, but he was intrigued. Scarlett had come with Duke, partly for moral support, but mostly because she was intrigued as well.

Duke had already endured Hawk's lecture about following orders. He had even made the mistake of pointing out that technically, he hadn't violated any orders, a point that, while valid, only seemed to aggravate Hawk even more.

Duke felt bad for the general. He knew their temperaments

were similar in many ways. It was probably bugging the hell out of Hawk to be sitting on the sidelines with his hands tied.

When the lecture portion of the conversation was over, Hawk leaned forward and picked up the gun, turning it over in his hands. "The Marines have had the M249 since before the first Gulf War. The pistol grip isn't regulation but it's not uncommon either. Even with that and the new stock, it looks pretty normal to me." He turned to Scarlett. "Any thoughts?"

"Sure, lots," she said. "But I need more information."

He looked at Duke and raised an eyebrow. "How about you?"

"I don't know. The more I analyze it, the more I wonder if the rifles weren't part of the test, you know? I think there's something to them."

Hawk nodded. "We can send it back to the Pit for analysis, see if anything turns up."

Duke furrowed his brow. Sending it back to G.I. Joe headquarters would take time. "I was thinking maybe Brainstorm should take a look, get us something faster. He was pretty sharp during that op at the Cobra goldmining farm in Russia."

Hawk gave him an appraising look. "He was at that, but what's the big rush?"

"Something is going down. And I think it's happening before the Internationals can get here."

Hawk nodded. "A day or so, huh? Okay, have Brainstorm see what he can find out." He leaned forward, looking at Duke with a laser stare. "You can even keep an eye on the Azakis, but Duke, you violate our ROE and I will put you in the stockade for a long, long time. Do you understand?"

"Yes sir."

"You can look, but do not touch. That's not why we are here. And you may not fight against either side unless you are directly and physically attacked."

"Yes sir."

"Now get out of here before I think of any rules that you have 'technically' broken."

"I'M HAPPY to help," Brainstorm said, turning the gun over in his hands. Brainstorm had listened gravely while Duke told him what he had seen. "But it looks like your basic M249 with a dash of urban flavor. I don't know exactly what you want from me."

"I don't know exactly, either," Duke told him. "But I think something is up with that weapon, and I have a feeling you'll know it when you see it."

Brainstorm couldn't say how long it would take, because he didn't even know what he was looking for. But he pledged to get on it immediately. He knew it was important.

Duke stepped outside Brainstorm's tent and yawned, thinking about getting some shut eye. But when Ripcord ran up to him, he knew that wasn't going to happen just yet.

"We've got activity," Ripcord said, out of breath.

"What kind?"

"Don't know. Flint and Heavy Duty were on patrol. Spotted a convoy of vehicles headed east three klicks southwest of here. Could be the guys with the funny firearms you saw."

FIVE MINUTES later, Duke and Ripcord were tearing across the darkened desert on their ATVs. Hawk had told Duke he could keep an eye on the Azakis. As it turned out, he didn't have long to wait. The night vision goggles lit up the desert, and with the infrared, they easily found the convoy's trail. From there, it was follow the yellow brick road.

Even with the night vision, they couldn't push the ATVs as fast as they could during the day. Still, they knew they were gaining on the convoy as the heat signature got brighter and more distinct.

After fifteen minutes of hard riding, they saw exhaust plumes in the cold, dark desert sky. The ATVs were electric, running cold and quiet. Still they approached with caution and followed from a safe distance.

Two miles later, they rounded a jagged rock formation and saw other vehicles approaching from the opposite direction. It looked like a trio of large trucks, running hot and dirty and bright as beacons in the night vision.

The rock formation formed a concave wall jutting up from the desert floor, and the two convoys angled in towards it, so they would meet in a spot shielded from view on three sides.

Duke and Ripcord took an even sharper angle, to where the edge of the rock formation sloped down into the desert sand. They found a large boulder to hide the ATVs. The rocks were only about thirty feet high at that point, and it was an easy climb to find a spot that looked out over the vehicles below.

Night had fallen, but the darkness was pierced by a small cluster of dim flashlights. Through the night vision binoculars, Duke watched as the two parties lined up across from each other. He touched a pair of buttons on the side of the binoculars, activating record mode.

One member of each group stepped forward into the middle and shook hands. Two others came up behind them with flashlights, illuminating a large briefcase as it was opened. One of the men pulled a dark cloth bag out of the briefcase, opened it, and shook some of the contents into his hand. Duke zoomed in quickly, watching as the dim light glinted brilliantly off small shiny stones. The man held one of them up to the flashlight and examined it, then put it in some sort of miniature scope, like a high-tech jeweler's loupe. Everyone had their eyes on him.

After further study, the man raised his head and nodded. The briefcase was snapped shut and the figures moved toward the rear of one of the trucks, gathering around it. Again the flashlights came on, and again Duke zoomed in. The back of the truck was packed with wooden crates, and as he watched, the men opened a crate and started hauling out assault rifles, passing them around. Each one had a forward pistol grip.

After a few minutes of examination, the weapons were passed back and the men all shook hands. They got back into their vehicles, the engines started up, and the trucks drove off, all in the same direction from which they had come, except for the one with the guns in the back, which drove off with the other group.

"Was that what I think it was?" Ripcord asked.

"Won't know for sure until we can get the video analyzed," Duke replied. "But it sure looked like a covert arms deal to me. Now let's find out who all the players are."

IT WAS LATE when Duke and Ripcord returned to camp, but the dim light in Brainstorm's tent meant he was still awake, probably.

"Still working on it," he said when Duke came to the tent flap. Brainstorm had the subject weapon pretty much disassembled.

"Might not know for sure until morning, but everything looks normal so far. Someone's idea of an upgrade retrofit, I think," he told Duke.

Duke smiled sweetly.

Brainstorm suddenly looked even more tired, but he didn't complain. "What do you need now?"

Duke held up the night vision binoculars. "Home movies, starring more of those weapons. How are your video enhancement and facial recognition skills?"

Brainstorm grinned. "Top shelf. I'll get it started so it can be running while I'm doing this," he said, nodding back towards the disassembled machine gun.

"You're the best."

"Yeah, that's how I got this job."

AFTER A NIGHT of tossing and turning, Duke was just settling into a deep sleep when Brainstorm showed up at his tent, first thing in the morning. He felt a little less sorry for himself when he saw the man's up-all-night face.

"Got some results from the video," Brainstorm said, then turned and walked back to his tent.

Duke pulled on his pants and a T-shirt and went after him.

"That might have been the worst piece of video I have ever worked on," Brainstorm remarked as soon as Duke walked in. "No light, high mag. Sometimes, seriously, you guys seem to think we can just make stuff appear from the void."

"So, were you able to make anything appear?"

"Well, yeah, of course, but that's not the point, is it?"

Duke didn't answer, letting the man have his moment.

"Anyway," Brainstorm continued, "I managed to tease out a few things. First, the easy part." He tapped a few keys on his computer and the screen showed a ghostly green image of a familiar-looking assault rifle. "You understand that without making a physical comparison I can't say for certain that the weapons your subjects were inspecting in the back of the truck are the same as the one over there."

He hooked a thumb at the worktable, where the M249 variant Duke had recovered lay in an even greater state of disassembly.

"So stipulated," agreed Duke, wondering how long this would take. "So are they?"

"Absolutely," said Brainstorm as he tapped a few more keys. Now the screen showed a hand holding a small helping of bright stones. "It's also impossible to tell what else is in that briefcase, but the contents of that bag definitely appear to be diamonds."

Duke shook his head. "A black marketer's best friend."

"So that's it for the sticks and stones, now for the names that'll never hurt you." The screen split, showing a shadowy green face on the left and on the right a surveillance photo of a vigorous-looking man with a handsome face, a deep tan, and cold gray eyes. "First, Rudolph Pines, notorious arms dealer. Young, innovative, and totally unburdened by any sense of morality. Known associate to just about anyone we've ever been on the other side of a fight with, from rogue nations to terrorist splinter groups."

"Right. He's the one who showed up with the truck full of guns," said Duke darkly. He knew Pines claimed to be an honest businessman, but was responsible for untold carnage on a daily basis.

Brainstorm began tapping keys again. "Okay, so who is the other party in this transaction, you ask?"

As with the previous screen, the green image on the left was barely recognizable as a face. The image on the right was somewhat more familiar. "That's right," Brainstorm said with a flourish. "Aramen Alexi. Son of the slain president of Tarkestan."

DUKE WALKED out of Brainstorm's tent in a daze, wondering what this meant. Aramen had said his people were hungry because they had no money, yet there he was, skulking around in the dark, giving a suitcase full of diamonds to a known supplier of warlords and extremist groups. Before Duke could decide on his next move, he heard someone call his name. He looked over to see Footloose waving him over to the guardhouse.

"Hey, Footloose. What's up?"

Footloose hooked a thumb outside the perimeter of the camp. "Someone here to see you."

In the middle of the Tarkestani desert, that didn't make sense. Then he saw Irina standing just beyond the fence.

She waved her hand in the air. "Duke! I must talk to you!"

After learning about Aramen's association with Rudolph Pines, Duke didn't know what to think about Irina.

"What is it?" he asked as he walked up to her.

"I must talk to you. But not here. Come," she said, pulling his arm.

He knew she had a dagger in her tunic, and probably something else up her sleeve, but Duke figured he could take care of himself. He walked along with her, but stopped after twenty yards.

"Okay, please explain yourself," he told her.

Irina looked at the guard over his shoulder, then glanced around to see if anyone else could be listening.

"I only came to tell you this because I don't wish any of your people to be hurt."

"Tell me what?"

"The counter offensive is tomorrow," she whispered. "And it will take place very near here. I do not want the Joes to get involved. To get hurt."

"It's going to be here? Why?"

"We have intelligence. The Azakis are redeploying their forces before the peacekeepers arrive. That is our last chance —our only chance—to hit them while they are on the move."

"What about arms?" he asked bitterly. "I thought you had no weapons."

She shrugged. "We have enough."

"Because you bought enough."

Her dark eyes flashed. "What do you mean?"

"Irina, you say your country has no money for food, and I believe it, yet Aramen hands a briefcase stuffed with diamonds to Rudolph Pines. Hell, half the genocidal psychopaths on the planet have him on their speed dial."

The expression on her face made him glance down to make sure she wasn't reaching for that dagger. "That was our food money! And I would do it again in a heartbeat. We all would, if it meant saving our country."

"But Rudolph Pines? He's—"

"Yes, yes; we know who he is, who his clients are. We haven't the luxury of choosing who to do business with." Irina was not about to apologize for anything. "And I am not about to debate battlefield morality with a man whose own—"

A vehicle was fast approaching, a black SUV, seeming to appear from the desert like a wraith. Duke and Irina watched it come to a sharp stop close by. Its windows were dark, and one of them slid down to reveal a large figure wrapped in a kheffiyeh, an Arab-style headdress.

"Hello, Duke," said the figure in the kheffiyeh. "Your ride's here."

What he could see of the figure in the car was in no way familiar, but Duke knew that voice well. It was the voice of trouble.

He moved to speak to Irina, but she was already walking away. *Well, that could've gone better*, he thought before turning to the SUV's driver.

"And why would I want to ride with you? I ought to—"

"Yeah, but you won't.," said the driver. "Now hurry up, I only got two minutes before I turn into a pumpkin."

Duke hesitated a moment, then climbed into the SUV.

"Nice outfit, Chuckles," Duke said, appraising the driver's apparent disguise. "No Hawaiian shirt today?"

"Save the comedy for YouTube, we need to talk," said the man known as Chuckles. Putting the vehicle in gear, he began driving in a wide arc, away from the G.I. Joe camp. Duke had the distinct feeling they were not headed anywhere in particular; they were just driving.

"So when do these two minutes start?" Duke asked evenly, his eyes studying his former colleague. Officially, Chuckles was *persona non grata*; with any sighting to be reported to Hawk immediately. It looked to Duke that, like it or not, he was back in the intelligence-gathering business.

"I'm assuming you know that Rudolph Pines is in the region," started Chuckles.

Duke nodded. "Supplying both sides of the local border war they got going here. Isn't that what all arms dealers do?"

"Usually, yeah. But Pines isn't just any arms dealer. Not anymore. Did you know he's not taking his usual fee from the Azakis? Our boy Rudy's doing it *pro bono*. Funny, isn't it?"

"Pines is working for nothing?"

"For strategic considerations."

"So he's taking sides. Why?"

"To answer that you got to ask yourself, why did the Azakis attack in the first place."

Duke shrugged. "Azakistan is an arid country without the money or infrastructure to effectively control what little water they have. Grabbing Tarkestan's makes sense; probably go after some other resources too."

"Sure, why not, they're already in the neighborhood, right?" agreed Chuckles. "But you should remember that Azikistan is landlocked. Tarkestan isn't."

"You really think access to the sea is that important to the Azakis?"

"To them, no, but to whoever is working with them, that's something entirely different," said Chuckles. "If you're looking to establish a foothold somewhere, terrorist or otherwise, access to the sea can be pretty useful."

Duke went quiet, thinking. "And why should I trust you, exactly? Why are you even here?"

"It's *because* I am here that you *will* trust me," replied Chuckles. "Now listen and learn, my friend, the meter's about to expire. The Azakis are planning a major battle for tomorrow. I'm sure your ROE protocols prohibit the Joes from any active combat."

"A battle?" said Duke. "Don't you mean redeployment?"

Chuckles stopped the SUV. The arc they were driving had become a circle and the camp was coming up on their left. He pulled back the kheffiyeh and faced Duke, his expression serious for a change.

"I don't know or care what you think you know," said Chuckles, "just hear and understand what I am telling you. The Azakis have something very big and very bad planned for tomorrow, and Rudolph Pines is involved in ways that no ordinary arms dealer would be. You'll just have to figure out the rest on your own. Now get the hell out, I'm already late."

Duke opened his door. "Tell me, how did you know I'd be out here?"

"Not you, just *someone*. Funny, isn't it?"

And with that, Chuckles was gone, speeding back across the desert, leaving a trail of dust and questions.

Damn, thought Duke, wondering what he was going to tell Hawk about what just happened.

BRAINSTORM CAME RUNNING out of his tent just as Duke entered the camp.

"Duke!" he shouted, skidding to a stop when he saw him. "You're going to love this!"

Hawk and Scarlett were already in the tent. They looked as pensive as Brainstorm was giddy.

"This is so cool," Brainstorm said, sitting back down at his worktable. "You were right about something going on with this gun, and I finally figured it out."

Brainstorm gave them a quick run down on all the tests he had conducted.

"Everything came up negative. Nothing. Then I did an ultrasound. Saw something weird in the plastic stock, so I cut it open, pried the two pieces apart, and found a few extra bits in there."

By this point, Hawk, Scarlett and Duke were all leaning in close.

Hawk screwed up his face. "Extra bits? What the hell does that mean?"

"Couple things. This," he pointed at a small metal wafer, half an inch in diameter, maybe an eighth of an inch thick, embedded in the plastic of the gun stock. "It's a receiver. See those wires there? They run through the stock to this," he indicated a small metal disk. "It's a short-range transmitter, has a tiny built-in battery."

"A transmitter? Like for some kind of security device?" asked Scarlett.

"Well, it's damaged so I can't say for sure, but I bet that when the receiver, here, detects a specific signal, it activates the transmitter, which then sends out a tracking wave."

"So, at that test," Duke said, "with the missiles?"

Brainstorm nodded. "The transmitters probably served as homing beacons for the missiles."

"Oh man," Duke said. "That's why Rudolph Pines is selling to the Tarkestanis even though he's deeply involved with the Azakis—they're all rigged."

Scarlett looked stricken. "The Azakis are setting them up. The Tarkestanis will be slaughtered."

Brainstorm scratched his head. "You see one of those missiles coming right after you, wouldn't you simply drop your gun and run?"

Hawk smiled grimly. "In the heat of battle, you going to throw away your main weapon?"

"Well, no," Brainstorm said. "But some of them might."

"So you wipe out the entire force except for the three percent that don't have enough sense to hold onto their weapons. Close enough," said Hawk.

"Okay, so it looks bad," Brainstorm admitted.

Duke was quiet. He had hoped Chuckles had it wrong when he said the Azakis were planning something big, something bad, but they were, all right. They were laying a trap that would wipe out the Tarkestanis for good.

Duke got to his feet. "I've got to warn them."

Hawk stood as well, and he stepped toward the entrance to the tent. "Duke," he said, pausing, like it was the preamble to a lecture, "… just be careful."

Duke watched him leave, then followed him out of the tent. "General Hawk," he called out.

Hawk turned and waited for him.

"Some of that intel, about Pines being involved with the Azakis, I got that from Chuckles."

"Chuckles?" His eyes narrowed. "Where? When?"

"He was here. A few minutes ago. But now he's gone." Duke studied Hawk's face for a reaction, but there was none.

"Let's just keep that between you and me."

BEFORE HE LEFT, Duke packed a bag of tools and other supplies, the beginnings of an idea forming in his head. Now he was shooting across the desert toward the craggy mountains of the Tarkestani hideout, the tires of the ATV kicking up a massive column of dust.

As he approached the foot of the mountain, Duke spotted the stream bed he had followed the first time, hoping he would remember his way. If he made enough noise, he figured the Tarkestani soldiers would find him, even if he couldn't find them.

Duke hit the streambed without slowing down. He had been driving randomly the first time, but somehow he remembered every zigzag and turn. This time he was doing it even faster.

When he reached the first plateau, he paused for a moment to get his bearings, then started off again, attacking the crisscrossing gullies as he ascended, then throttling back, as he slowly climbed up to the next plateau. As he crested the rise, Duke saw the same stream bed, widening out to the plateau where the Tarkestani camp had been, only it wasn't there now.

For a moment, he thought maybe he was at the wrong place, but the ground had been churned by wheels and feet and hoof marks and dragging. The Tarkestanis had definitely been there. But they were gone.

He was about to leave when he heard Aramen's voice behind him. "It is nice to see you again, Duke. But I thought I said you should not come back here."

Duke turned to face him and saw he was not alone. Aramen and some of his guards had appeared from the shadows, their new weapons held or slung over their shoulders.

"Sorry for breaking my word, Aramen, but your troops are in great danger."

"It is war, is it not?" Aramen laughed. "That can be dangerous sometimes."

"I know you purchased assault rifles from Rudolph Pines."

"And I know you don't approve. Sorry about that. If nice people had what we needed, perhaps I would have purchased from nice people."

"The man is not to be trusted. He supplies your enemy, as well."

"What are we supposed to do, go into battle with the slings that our ancestors used? That our children play with? As a boy I was a champion with a sling, but I do not think that is enough this time." He shrugged. "We needed weapons, we got weapons."

"The ones you bought are sabotaged. Deathtraps."

Aramen smiled and fired a short burst of bullets into the sand next to them. The sound was deafening. "Seems to me they are working fine."

As the other men started laughing, Duke went airborne, head-butting the soldier to his left and using him as leverage to plant his foot in the stomach of the soldier to his right. When he landed, he swept the legs out from under three of the other soldiers and took cover behind the pile of tangled limbs.

Before the last soldier had hit the ground, Duke had two guns aimed at Aramen, his Kimber Warrior .45 and one of the M249s.

Aramen's face darkened as he looked at the soldiers sprawled on the ground. The soldiers still standing pointed their guns at Duke, but they didn't know what to do. Aramen's hand tightened on his own gun.

"Don't be stupid, Aramen," Duke said evenly. "You don't have a shot, and your people need you alive if they are to have any hope of survival. You can be a hero later, but right now, you need to listen to what I'm saying."

Aramen took a deep breath, then moved his hand away from his weapon. "I am listening."

Duke stepped backwards, away from the others, so that his back was against a jumble of boulders. He hoped he was right about this.

Keeping his .45 on Aramen, he flicked the rifle up into the air, catching it by the barrel, then smashed the stock hard against the rock.

Aramen stepped forward. "You idiot—"

Duke held up the .45 and he stopped. "Sorry," he said, gathering up the pieces. "You wouldn't listen. I'm hoping you will at least look."

Aramen didn't say anything as Duke walked up to him with the shattered weapon. He held up the plastic stock, split down the middle to reveal the receiver and the transmitter.

Aramen leaned forward to look, dismissively at first, but then intrigued, and then concerned.

"There's a receiver, for an activation signal, and a transmitter for targeting antipersonnel smart bombs." Duke looked at him. "I saw how these work. I saw Grigori have four of his men test these guns out in the desert. They fired them and destroyed their targets like good soldiers, then four small missiles appeared from over a nearby hill, chased them down, and took them out. There was nothing left to bury."

Aramen was paying attention now, still staring at the mysterious components embedded in the plastic stock, but hanging on Duke's words. The other soldiers had gone pale listening to him.

"One of the rifles survived the attack partially intact. We were able to discover its secret just in time to warn you."

Aramen shook his head. "My father was the victim of treachery, but he would not have fallen for this." He looked up at Duke with something close to fear in his eyes. "Can we take them out and destroy them?"

Duke reached into his warbag and pulled out a roll of duct tape. "I might have a solution."

*   *   *

THE FIRST SIGN of the Azakis was a cloud of dust in the distance, rising out of the gray predawn desert, glowing red where it hit the light from the dawn. As the cloud got bigger and closer, the red faded and the sunlight reached lower and lower until the entire Azaki force was illuminated by early morning sun.

The Tarkestanis looked on from their hiding places, some up in the mountains, overlooking the arid plain, just as they would have in a real ambush, which in a sense, this was. The rest of the force was hidden in trenches dug into the desert floor far below them.

They had been working hard all night and they were exhausted, but Duke could tell that the expectation of impending battle was keeping them sharp.

As the Azakis approached, the column seemed to widen out. As they got closer, they actually looked less formidable: little in the way of armor or big guns. There were a lot of them, though. The column seemed to slow as it reached the Tarkestani position, like they were intentionally waiting for the Tarkestanis to make a move. Daring them.

Aramen looked at Duke, maybe for reassurance. Duke gave him a brisk nod and Aramen returned it, then with a deep breath, he shouted out the signal. The Tarkestanis attacked as if it were a regular ambush—peppering the convoy with mortars and grenades, then following up with fire from their M249 assault rifles.

The Azakis fought back with machine gun fire, .50 cal, and more grenades.

For ten or fifteen minutes, the battle was fought, and plenty of firepower was loosed in both directions. To an untrained observer or a terrified civilian, it would have appeared horrific, but to Duke, watching from on high, there was a strange lack of intensity, like both sides knew this was just a preamble.

Duke was careful not to participate. Not yet, anyway.

On either side of him, Aramen's soldiers fired their mangled weapons down at the desert floor, and they did some damage to the Azaki forces. In addition to their M249s, each of the Tarkestani soldiers had at their feet a traditional Tarkestani sling, crafted from rope and animal hide, the way they had been made for over two thousand years.

The sound of the automatic weapons was great and terrible, louder than thunder, traveling through the rock and into the bones. But through it, they heard a distant whoosh—and they all stopped firing.

Hundreds of missiles, maybe thousands, arced up into the air from a valley somewhere behind the Azaki convoy, raking the sky with fire. Each missile trailed fire and smoke, and as they rose together, they formed a wall of fire and death that bisected the sky, obscuring half of it. For a moment, the Tarkestanis stood transfixed by the sight. They had known it was coming, but the immensity of it took them by surprise.

In the sudden quiet, the Azaki weapons sounded tinny and feeble. The Tarkestanis had been preparing all night for this moment, sawing and chipping, prying and splitting, and taping. Since just before dawn, they had been twisting and tying rope and animal hide, constructing their slings like when they were children, like their ancestors had done for centuries.

Now, they would use them.

Aramen was the first to snap out of it, climbing up onto the rocky lip of his hiding place, in full view of his men, and in full view of the Azaki men down below.

He held up his sling and carefully placed a rock in it. Whipping the sling over his head several times, he let go, sending the rock flying through the air, and with it the tiny transmitter that was securely duct taped to it.

Aramen had said he was a champion as a youth, and Duke was impressed. The projectile followed a parabola that would take it to the command vehicles in the rear. It disappeared in the distance long before it reached its target, but as it flew, one of the missiles broke away from the pack, curving and correcting its path as its target flew through the air.

The other Tarkestani soldiers began frantically whipping their slings over their heads, and for a moment the air was filled with the sound of hundreds of slings wheeling through the air, releasing hundreds of projectiles, and hundreds of tiny transmitters.

The precise lines of missiles screaming across the sky briefly deteriorated into chaos, with each missile frantically correcting course to keep track of its now-moving target. A few of the missiles collided and exploded in the air, but miraculously, after a moment, the tangled knot of fire reassembled into a similarly precise formation, with all the remaining missiles now streaming across the sky in the opposite direction.

Almost all of them.

One missile continued to speed along its course, and Duke stood his ground, watching it. Waiting for it. The missile was bearing down on him, and he stared at it. He told himself he was waiting because he wanted to be sure, because it mattered. But deep down he wanted to take the thing on. Deep down, he thought he could beat it.

The Tarkestani soldiers were nervously edging away from him when he finally lifted up his arm, sling in hand, and whipped it as hard as he could.

The missile quivered as the transmitter shot past it, then it pulled up sharply and doubled over on itself. A gust of hot exhaust washed over Duke. He had let the thing get too close. But now he knew, without a doubt, the missile had been coming for him.

He had been fired on. *Now*, he could fight back.

ARAMEN'S AIM was as good as he claimed. Down below, a missile bore down on one of the command vehicles, tiny figures moving away from it in slow motion. An instant later, the missile struck. The explosion galvanized the rest of the Azakis, sending them scurrying in every direction.

As Duke and the Tarkestanis raced down the mountainside

with their sidearms, the rest of the missiles landed, a rain of fire that reduced the center of the Azaki column to a flaming ruin and peppered the edges. The vehicles on the periphery scattered, and men ran in every direction from the onslaught.

Before the Azakis could regroup, the Tarkestanis in the trenches opened fire with their old rifles.

As he reached the desert floor, Duke was targeted by an Azaki soldier. A bullet slammed into the rock next to him, spraying his face with razor sharp fragments. Duke went into a roll and spotted the soldier who had fired at him, lining up another shot. If the weapon had been on automatic, Duke would have been dead, and he wondered if the Azaki knew how to use it.

Regardless, Duke put two in his chest.

After that, he was in it. Within the swirl of chaos and destruction, having only a sidearm was not much of a disadvantage. Duke liked his Kimber .45. It was quick and nimble, and there wasn't enough room for distance shooting anyway.

He had brought plenty of ammunition, but he was distributing it generously. Line one up, squeeze off two rounds, then move on to the next one.

Even after the missile strikes, the Azakis still had superior firepower, but they were in disarray and before long, they were in full retreat.

The Tarkestanis let them go. They did not cheer—too many bad things had happened for that, but there were some tired smiles, a few hugs, and men thinking about going home, and starting to rebuild their country.

Aramen found Duke and shook his hand. They stood for a moment, watching the Azakis go, then they turned and started back up the mountain.

From up on the mountain, they could see the Azakis retreating in the distance, toward the valley that would take them back to Azakistan.

Duke got on his ATV and started it up.

Aramen put out his hand. "Thank you, Duke. My people are forever grateful."

Duke shook his hand, then gestured out at the Azakis. The retreating column seemed to be falling apart. "What about them? You going to be able to handle them?"

Aramen followed his gaze and smiled. "I think it will be some time before the Azakis cause trouble again."

As he said it, Irina galloped up on horseback, trailing a second horse.

"What is it?" Duke asked.

"They're not all leaving," she said, out of breath.

Aramen looked confused. "What's that?"

"The Azakis. They are not all leaving." As he fished out a pair of binoculars and swung himself onto the other horse, she continued. "Grigori has made a detour. They're not headed for Azakistan."

"They're headed for Dubrinsk," Aramen said, lowering the binoculars from his eyes. "The village of my father."

Moments later they were plunging headlong down the mountain. Duke was on his ATV, with one of the old Mosin Nagants rifles across his back and his .45 in its holster. Aramen followed on horseback.

Irina had gone to alert the Tarkestani forces, but there was no time to wait for help or for better weapons. As it was, with the ATV, Duke would get there before the Azakis, but only just.

Gunning the ATV as fast as it would go, Duke quickly pulled away from Aramen. Maybe the horse had more sense than he did, but before long Aramen was far behind him. He pushed the ATV down the steep incline as fast as it would go without tumbling over.

The village of Dubrinsk was of no military significance; it was just a place where women and children sought refuge. And it was the place where President Alexi had been raised.

The Azaki troops had visited the village once already, and had done terrible things. They had visited a second time when the Joes interceded. If they were headed there again, it would be to take captives and to scorch the earth they were leaving behind, to brutalize the Tarkestani civilians one last time before retreating back to Azakistan. And to make good on Grigori's vow to erase any trace of the dead president.

Approaching from the rear, the village seemed more scarred by war, the plain mud huts all pockmarked from bullets. The women and children stopped what they were doing and stared at Duke as he approached.

They seemed to recognize him from before, but still they watched him warily. He skidded to a stop in front of them. Irina and Aramen were nowhere in sight.

"Does anybody here speak English?" he asked loudly. He could hear engines in the distance. The Azakis were coming.

A young woman stepped forward. She was small and her face was bruised and swollen. "Little bit," she said. It was the woman Irina had been trying to save the day before.

Duke pointed to the west. "The Azakis are coming."

Her eyes went wide and he thought she was about to lose it. "It's okay," he told her, smiling. Then, pointing at the children. "Must hide children."

Maybe her English was better than she let on, because somehow she seemed to get what he was saying. With a nervous smile that was utterly unconvincing, she ushered the kids inside the smallest of the huts.

Duke did a quick reconnoiter. There were twelve huts. None had more than one entrance, but six had windows facing away from the doors. Close enough.

The sound of the Azaki vehicles was getting louder. Still no sign of Irina or Aramen. He hoped they were okay. It was tricky footing coming down that mountain. Easy for a horse to fall.

He would have time to worry about them later. Now, he chose his best spot, a larger hut in the middle of the village. He hunkered down, checked his weapons, and waited.

He didn't have to wait long. Sneaking a peek through the hut's window, he spotted eight of them. At the center of the group was Grigori himself.

The rifle was bolt action, and he knew he would only be able to get off two, maybe three shots, tops, before they disappeared. Still, he figured he'd rather be fighting five or six unsurprised foes than eight surprised ones.

He ducked down, waiting for his targets to get within range. When he heard feet crunching on gravel, he figured they were close enough.

Popping his head up in the window, he caught an instant mental snapshot of the group. He fired before they had a chance to see him, and one of the men went down with an exploded chest. As he slid the bolt to chamber the next round, the image he had seen sank into his brain. He fired again without thinking about it, his muscles calculating the shot and executing it before his brain could even process the information.

By the time he had chambered the third bullet, his brain had caught up a little bit. Grigori was in the middle. The soldier standing next to him was carrying a large gasoline can. And the element of surprise was gone, the Azakis were already tensing for a mad dash to find cover.

Somewhere in Duke's circuitry, the decision was made, instead of taking out the next target in his progression, he would try for Grigori.

He would have liked to think the shot was good, but as he pulled the trigger, one of the younger Azakis darted in front of the general, and the bullet took off the back of his head.

By the time Duke had chambered the fourth round, the Azakis had gone to ground. Duke did the same. Slipping out the window, he ran to a different hut, away from the center of the village. As he waited at the window for the Azakis to close in on where he used to be, he heard a concussive whoosh, and saw a ball of black smoke rolling up into the sky.

Mercifully, there were no screams accompanying it, and a few seconds later, two Azakis crept into his field of view, showing him their backs as they hugged the mud wall, circling around the hut next to the one he had just vacated. Duke used the .45, taking his time to line up the first shot, then a quick flick of the wrist to catch the second one. The two men went down simultaneously, leaving two circles of wet crimson on the mud wall. Neither of them were carrying the gasoline can.

Duke paused for an instant, listening for clues to the other Azakis' whereabouts. He heard another whoosh, and another black smudge rose into the sky. Wherever the Azakis were, he needed to get between them and the children. His clip was low, so he switched it out for a full one.

Slipping out of the hut, he almost bumped into another Azaki soldier. The soldier stepped back, but immediately started firing. Duke ducked back as well, trading fire from inside the hut. He didn't have enough ammunition to be wasting it like that, and the longer he stayed in the hut, the more likely the Azakis would get him surrounded. Against all of them, he would surely lose a shootout, if they didn't burn him out first.

And it was only a matter of time before the Azakis found where the children were hiding.

He peeked out the doorway and immediately drew fire. There were two Azakis now, and surely the rest would be there soon. He brushed them both back with two bullets each, then charged, splitting the middle and diving low. One of the Azakis fired sideways into the air over Duke's head. Duke shot him in the armpit and came up into a firing stance as the other Azaki was turning to follow him.

He pulled the trigger, but the bullet ricocheted off the Azaki's assault rifle. He pulled the trigger again, but his clip was empty. The Azaki pulled his trigger as well, but Duke's bullet must have damaged the firing mechanism. They both dove for the dead Azaki, and as the one Azaki reached for his fallen comrade's rifle, Duke grabbed the knife from the man's belt and plunged it into his throat.

While the Azaki was still gurgling and thrashing, Duke grabbed the dead Azaki's rifle, but it was empty. Just as well he had gone for the knife instead.

Duke switched out his empty clip, but the one he replaced it with only had three bullets. He was sure now that something bad had happened to Aramen, but he couldn't think about that now. As he tried to get his bearings, tried to remember which hut held the children, he noticed a slight movement out of the corner of his eye. It was a boy of ten or eleven, peering at him through the window. As he saw the scar on the boy's forehead and recognized him from before, the child held up his hand, pointing to his left, telling him that's where the bad guy was.

Duke gave the kid a nod and held his hand out flat and pushed down, telling the child to get out of sight. The head disappeared.

Creeping around the next hut, Duke paused when he saw Grigori's shadow on the dirt.

Three bullets left. Should be two more than enough.

He sprinted out into the open. As Grigori came into view, Duke saw the gasoline can at his feet and the rifle in his hands, already coming up in Duke's direction, almost immediately emitting a loud growl as it spewed bullets at an unimaginable rate. Duke squeezed off a shot, but he couldn't line it up, couldn't even stop running, or else he would have been cut in half. The ground seemed to turn into liquid, churning as the bullets plowed into it.

Duke went into a roll, taking another shot as he came out of it, rushing it and almost missing. Grigori's uniform puffed out at the shoulder and a thick glob of blood hit the dust at his feet, rolling into a little ball of red mud.

Grigori smiled and brought the rifle up again. Duke jumped behind the next hut, feeling the wall shudder behind his back as the bullets hammered into it.

One bullet left. He had to make it count. As he ran around the opposite direction, trying to sneak up on Grigori's blind side, he caught a sudden whiff of gasoline, and heard a chorus of children shrieking in mortal terror. He urged his legs to pump harder and faster, and as he came around the other side, he saw Grigori's back. The gas can was lying on its side in the dirt, open, but nothing was pouring out of it.

Grigori had the rifle in one hand and a small metal object in the other, an old-fashioned Zippo lighter. As Duke looked on, he flicked it open and closed, open and closed. He was savoring the moment.

The children were still shrieking, screaming in terror, and Grigori lit the lighter, but he seemed to sense Duke's presence, and when he whirled around, the lighter went out.

Duke slid to the ground, two-handing the gun and aiming it at Grigori's heart. As Grigori brought his rifle around, Duke pulled the trigger.

There was a raspy click and nothing else. When he pulled the trigger again, he didn't even get that. It was jammed.

Grigori smiled and lowered the gun. He wasn't going to kill Duke because he wanted him to witness what was about to happen. He flicked the lighter again, looking down at the flame, breathing in the air filled with fumes and terror. He lowered his arm, ready to underhand the lighter into the hut, but when his arm came forward his hand was gone. So was the lighter.

In its place was a jagged red stump. He looked down at it for an instant, confused. Duke was confused, too, until he they heard the echoing crack of a distant rifle shot.

Grigori looked around, the intensity of his evil desire temporarily displaced by curiosity about what was going on, what had happened to his hand.

Duke had already spotted Aramen, leaning against a rock, maybe a quarter of a mile away. Grigori's eyes went dark when he saw him, too. As he brought his weapon up to fire, he muttered, "Aramen," then his head snapped back as a bullet caught him in the cheek. A second report echoed around them as he fell forward, his shattered face splattering in the dirt.

Irina darted past him and into the hut, ushering the traumatized children and their terrorized guardian out into the fresh air. The little boy who had signaled Duke waved as he walked past.

Duke gave the boy a thumbs-up as he hurried over to Aramen.

The Tarkestani general was covered with cuts and bruises. His leg was slightly twisted and bent out at a wrong angle.

Duke winced at the sight of it. "Are you okay?"

Aramen shrugged and waved him off. "I'm fine," he said. "You should see the horse, though."

"That was some fancy shooting."

"Was nothing. I told you I was good. What about you, though? When Irina told me, I didn't believe her, but I saw some of what you did, through the binoculars. What are you, some kind of super-hero?"

"A super-hero?" Duke shook his head and laughed. "No, not me. I'm just a regular Joe."

Just a Game

MATT FORBECK

ONE

BRAINSTORM DOVE for cover behind the boulders hunkered on the hard ground before him. The machine gun's bullets buzzed past him and tore through Vasily, one of the Russian phreaks who'd gotten the Joes snarled into this whole SNAFU. The local-boy-gone-bad gave up the ghost before what was left of him hit the ground.

"Keep down!" Scarlett flicked the safety off on her hand crossbow as she grabbed Brainstorm's shoulder to make sure he complied with the order.

She always treated him like that, like he needed someone to watch over him. Most days, that rankled Brainstorm more than he cared to admit. He liked to think of himself as a modern man, one who accepted women as equals—even deadly women trying to protect him—but it wasn't always easy, especially when the woman in question could kick his ass.

At the moment, though, he didn't mind it at all. Crouching low, Scarlett ran off before he could object.

"Our intel didn't mention any heavies guarding this 'abandoned' gulag," Barrel Roll whispered over the Joes' comm system. Brainstorm pictured him lying in the grass somewhere behind them, searching for an angle from which he could take out the machine gunner. The mini-earplugs the Joes wore in the field worked via bone conduction, which still weirded him out. He didn't even have to whisper to speak into them, just subvocalize, but he hadn't quite mastered that trick yet.

"Our people do the best they can," Duke said. He plucked a grenade from his belt and hefted it in his hand. "Siberia's a long way from anywhere."

"It RFE now, Russian Far East," Krivoshapkin said in his broken English. The short, round-cheeked man grimaced as he checked the body of his fallen friend for any signs of life. "Siberia back west. Warmer."

"Siberia? RFE?" Barrel Roll whispered. "WTF? I am *not* coming back here on my vacation."

Another burst of machine gun fire ripped across the rising foothills of the taiga, zipping over the Joes' heads. Duke had been about to deliver the grenade in his hand, but he held back, waiting for the right moment.

"We need to take that tango out now," Duke said, "before he brings all of the Russian Far East down on our heads."

"Working on it," Barrel Roll said, an edge in his voice.

"We brought you along to provide cover," Brainstorm said.

"Who flew you out here? I brought *you* along."

Brainstorm grimaced. He hated getting shot at. The operation wasn't supposed to go like this. General Hawk had said it would be simple.

"Get in, blow the place up, and get out, Brainstorm," he'd said during their meeting in the Think Tank. "Nothing to it."

"It's not that easy, General," Brainstorm said. "If we blow it up, we won't do a thing to them."

General Hawk arched an eyebrow at that. "I find that explosives often leave a mark."

"If that's all you're interested in, General, that's fine." Brainstorm fidgeted before continuing. "But I'd rather hurt Cobra if we could."

"You have proof Cobra's behind this?"

Brainstorm winced. "Circumstantial only. Not enough for a court of law."

"But enough to ask me to authorize an operation that could cause an international incident with the Kremlin if you're caught carrying it out?"

Brainstorm opened his mouth to speak but found his words wouldn't leave it. He closed his lips again and nodded.

He then explained the situation to the General three times. After that, he outlined his operational plan for an assault on this remote outpost just inland from the Sea of Okhotsk. With luck, they'd not only destroy the installation but maybe cripple Cobra's operation at the same time.

"Aren't you tired of just reacting to Cobra, General?" Brainstorm said. "Here's a chance to take the battle to them, to hit them on a flank that they don't suspect is vulnerable."

General Hawk nodded. "Make it happen. And good luck."

Back then, Brainstorm had grinned like a kid being let out of school for a field trip. At the moment, though, with the bullets zinging over his head, the General's hard-won confidence in his plan seemed misplaced. "Just do your job," he said to Barrel Roll over the comm. "Take the shot."

"No shot to take yet," Barrel Roll said. "The guy's good. Pops up in a different spot every time, then pops right back down."

"Crosshair told me once he doesn't take shots. He makes them."

"Hey, I may not be as good a sniper as Crosshair, but I—"

"Talk too much," Scarlett said. "Tango is down."

"What?" Barrel Roll wasn't happy. "You poached me? I *had* him. I just needed a little—"

"We're about to be out of time." Duke returned the pin to his grenade and stashed it back where it belonged. "Those shots just started the clock ticking. Once someone comes out here to investigate, our chances of slipping into the installation quietly fall to nil."

"You're welcome," Scarlett said.

Brainstorm knelt down next to Krivoshapkin as the man closed Vasily's dead eyes. "Sorry for your loss, Krivo."

The man shook his head in regret. "We all said Vasily would meet bad end." He looked up at the ridge from which the machine gunner had mowed down his friend. "Never imagined this."

"We'll have to come back for him," Duke said. He stood over Brainstorm and Krivo, motioning toward the path Scarlett had taken.

Brainstorm stood up and helped Krivo to his feet. "*Do svidanya*," Krivo said to Vasily's corpse.

"I thought you were Eveni, one of the native peoples," Brainstorm said. "That was Russian."

A wry smile cracked Krivo's brown face. "How many your Native Americans still speak their tongue?"

"Let's roll, Joes," Duke said. He set out after Scarlett, and Brainstorm and Krivo scrambled to keep up.

"You coming, Barrel Roll?" Scarlett said. Brainstorm scanned for her through the pine trees and low bushes that covered the rocky slope ahead, but she remained invisible.

"Just as soon as you top that hill," Barrel Roll said. "That's all according to the master plan, right Brainstorm?"

"I–I'm not—"

Duke clapped Brainstorm on the back as they rallied at a turn in the trail up the ridge. "Just say, 'Yes.' He's only trying to rattle you."

Brainstorm rubbed his temples. "But he's right. The plan I had, it's— Well, it didn't include anyone getting killed."

"No plan survives contact with the enemy," Scarlett said. "Happens all the time in the field. That's what we always try to tell you FOBbits."

"I like the Forward Operating Base," Brainstorm said. "Nobody shoots at you there. Well, not *too* often."

"Suck it up," Barrel Roll said. "Life gives you lemons, what do you make?"

"Lemon batteries?"

"What?"

"No, it really works. You can even connect them in series to get enough power for a pocket calculator. It's the citric acid and the way it exchanges electrons with the zinc electrodes."

"Shocking."

"Not really," said Brainstorm. "There's not much of a charge."

"With who do you speak?" Krivo said.

Winded from the climb, Brainstorm looked down at Krivo's curious face. The little man wasn't breathing hard at all.

"Quiet," Scarlett said. "I think I found the front door."

Brainstorm raised a finger to his lips and motioned for Krivo to follow him. They chased Duke up the switchback trail, keeping crouched over as they went. At one curve, Brainstorm stumbled over the body of a man crumpled across a Cold War–vintage machine gun. A black crossbow bolt of surgical steel jutted from the side of his neck, and the barrel of the simple but deadly weapon was still warm. Brainstorm scrambled off the body and dusted himself off. Krivo stepped forward and spat at the fallen man's face. He cursed in a language that Brainstorm didn't understand, but his tone made his intent clear.

No one else stood between them and the top of the hill. Brainstorm followed Duke up it, and Krivo trotted behind.

"Explain to me again why we don't just blow the place up and blame it on a natural gas explosion," Barrel Roll said. "What do we care about the publicity? There's no one out here to know."

Duke chuckled. "You destroy an enemy installation in Siberia—"

"RFE." Scarlett corrected Duke like a nun with a ruler.

"RFE—and no one notices. Does it matter?"

"Don't get all philosophical on me, soldier." From the tone of exertion in Barrel Roll's voice, he was on the move again. As high up the hill as they were now, he wouldn't be able to offer any cover from his last location. "I say we call in a bunker-buster strike, stick a U.S. flag in the center of the crater, and skate home."

Brainstorm stifled a snort. This was the bit of field action that always intrigued and mystified him. The other members of the team had been trained for this sort of deep-insertion mission for years. They'd executed countless such operations, some more successfully than others, but he refused to dwell on that. Duke, Scarlett, and Barrel Roll were such cool-headed professionals that Brainstorm never saw them worry, even under fire. Alert, sure, sometimes tense, but it astonished him that they could banter with each other the entire time and even make jokes.

Brainstorm often helped out with missions via the comm system, from the safety of the G.I. Joe headquarters in the Pit. Even while just listening to the other Joes in battle, he felt like his heart might burst from his chest. When people fired real bullets at him, he feared just the panic that inspired might kill him.

He never showed that fear in the Pit. He rarely saw a hint of it in anyone else there, and he refused to be the weak link in that chain. But it was a lot easier to keep his cool in the safety of the Pit, than when under fire in some armpit of the world he'd never once hoped to see.

He wished he could contact someone back in the Pit for support. Cobra had been jamming strong radio signals in and out of the region, though. The best range they could get with their mini-earplug comm system was limited to less than five hundred yards.

"We can't just blow the place up," Brainstorm said. "Well, we *could,* but that's not the point. This place is the nerve center of one of the largest money laundering operations on the planet. It's like the Wall Street of the underworld. Literally billions of dollars pass through here every year."

"And blowing it to hell wouldn't put a dent in that?" asked Barrel Roll.

"It might slow them down for a day or two, maybe a week if they're running without the proper sort of backup regiment, which I doubt. They're too savvy for that. We take out their operation here, and they just set up a new one in a different part of the globe—a secret place we don't know about yet."

"Until we find that one and blow it up too."

"Aren't you tired of playing Whack-A-Mole. Makes for a lot of feel-good smashing around but in the end you just can't keep up."

"I like watching things blow up."

"Beyond that. Wouldn't you rather make a difference? Pull the plug on the entire game?"

Duke put up a hand to signal a halt. Brainstorm skidded to a stop and had to grab Krivo's jacket to keep him from barreling ahead.

"Welcome to the *Otverstie*, boys," Scarlett said over the comm. "The Hole."

Brainstorm gaped up at the pair of massive steel doors set into the rocky face of a rise above the plateau that topped the hill they'd just climbed. They stood over thirty feet tall and wide enough to drive a pair of tanks through side by side. They looked strong enough to laugh off a bunker-buster, which set Brainstorm to wondering if they could withstand the firepower of the experimental field assets he'd arranged to bring with them.

A gunnery slot appeared in each of the doors at about shoulder level, but they sat open but empty, like wide toothless mouths. A fence-faced guard tower stood planted on each side of the doors, but no one peeked out from behind their half-height walls. Access to them must have been from somewhere inside the complex that lay beyond the doors, as they offered no way to reach the ground from their high platforms.

The entire area seemed abandoned, but that didn't explain the presence of the guard on the way up the hill. Had he been a hunter on the prowl? Or a member of the local militia? Maybe he'd thought they were thieves or invaders and had fired on them to protect his home. While Brainstorm could hardly blame him, the thought that they might have killed an innocent man twisted his guts into a knot.

"Anyone about?" Duke said over the comm, keeping his voice low.

"No visible hostiles," Scarlett said.

"Don't storm the place without me," Barrel Roll said, breathing hard from running. "Be there in under five."

Brainstorm scanned the region. From his intel, he'd expected to find the installation teeming with people streaming in and out of the place, but instead it was dead silent. Looking around, though, he noticed signs of habitation.

The grass around the gravel driveway that led up to the double doors had been trimmed recently. No rust showed on the guard towers or even on the doors, which looked as if they wore a recent coat of paint. No birds sang in the nearby firs clustered atop the hill or splayed out across the rest of the plateau. Perhaps the noise from the machine gunner had scared them away, but Brainstorm guessed that he had been too far away to frighten off any creatures that might be roaming around up here.

"It's too quiet," Brainstorm said into his comm. "It's a trap."

"That it is, *tovarich.*" As Krivo's voice snaked into Brainstorm's ear, he felt the cold barrel of a pistol press against the back of his skull.

Brainstorm felt a bead of sweat trickle down his back. For an instant, he feared that Krivo might just shoot him, no matter how valuable he might prove as a hostage. Then a pair of machine gun barrels appeared in the gun slots in each of the doors facing him, and he had more important things to worry about.

TWO

"I HAVE him!" Krivo shouted. "Come out, and help grab others!"

Duke turned around to face the local man, and Krivo jammed the gun into Brainstorm's skull, hard.

"Stand down," Duke said. He pointedly did not aim his

weapon at Krivo, for which Brainstorm felt grateful. The last thing he wanted was for Krivo to panic.

"You don't have to do this," Brainstorm said to Krivo. "We can help you. We can get you out of here."

Krivo snorted. "Could you save my family? My friends? My village? You saw what happened to Vasily."

"You can't hold us responsible for that."

"Could have been me. Killed him to send me message, to make sure I do not betray them." Krivo thumb-cocked his pistol. Brainstorm reflected on how primitive the revolver was compared to the gear the Joes carried, but he also realized how little difference that would make to his brains if that bullet blasted them out of his skull.

"You in position yet, Barrel Roll?" Scarlett's voice came soft and steady through the comm.

"Setting up right now," Barrel Roll said. "Give me fifteen more seconds."

"You have ten."

"Krivo," Brainstorm said. "Put down the gun."

"I can ace that goon in five seconds," said Barrel Roll.

"I regret this very much," said Krivo. "You are good man, but I have no choice."

"I have him," said Scarlett. "Go for the machine guns."

"Two right," Duke said under his breath. He brought his assault rifle up to bear, but he did not point it at Krivo.

"Deal," said Barrel Roll.

"Krivo," Brainstorm said. "You don't understand. I knew you'd betray us. We knew."

The gun pressed harder into Brainstorm's skull, so hard he wondered if he might start to bleed. Then he realized that Krivo was steeling himself to pull the trigger.

"Then *go*," said Scarlett.

As the words reached Brainstorm's ears, a steel crossbow bolt stabbed into Krivo's hand. At the same moment, a shot from a sniper rifle cracked out, and Duke sprinted to the left and let loose a burst from his rifle at the machine gunners behind the door on that side.

Brainstorm spun about and grabbed Krivo by the shoulders. The man stared at the bolt speared through his bloody, ruined hand and screamed. Brainstorm ignored that and dove into the dirt, pulling Krivo over with him.

The ferocity and suddenness of the Joes' attack must have stunned the machine gunners inside the complex. For a vital moment, none of them fired at all.

Another shot from Barrel Roll's sniper rifle thundered out, and the second of the two machine guns that had been poking out of the right-hand door fell back and away.

Duke's surprise burst had taken out one of the machine guns on the left, but the other still jutted from the gun slot there. It opened up at the Joes, spraying the open field in front of the doors with lead.

The bullets tore up the grass toward Brainstorm and Krivo, who was still screaming at his hand. Brainstorm hunkered down behind the small man and wondered if his body would be thick enough to stop the bullets. Would they at least slow them down?

Another burst from Duke's assault rifle drew the machine gunner's attention toward him and away from Brainstorm and the wailing Krivo. The trail of bullets veered off to the left where Duke stood his ground, blasting away at the doors.

"Could use a hand here," Duke said. Brainstorm could hear his voice through the comm, cutting through the clatter of the gunfire.

"I don't have the angle," Scarlett said. "Barrel Roll?"

As the bullets ranged closer to Duke, Brainstorm marveled at the man's bravery. Rather than leaving Krivo and Brainstorm to die, Duke had purposely drawn fire away from them, and now—although it might cost him his life—he stood there and kept firing rather than doing what Brainstorm would have done on instinct: turned and run.

A third thunderous shot from a sniper rifle cracked out, and the machine gun fell silent.

"I'm on it," Barrel Roll said. "Oh, wait. I already got him. Thanks for asking."

Brainstorm scooped up Krivo's gun and then let Duke help him to his feet. The Eveni man ignored them as he lay there in the short grass and wept over the ruin of his hand.

"Thanks," Brainstorm said to Duke.

"We're not done here yet," Duke said. "Not by a long shot."

Brainstorm nodded. He glanced over at the still-locked doors and then down at Krivo. "Couldn't you have held out just a little bit longer?

Krivo had screamed himself hoarse. "Show mercy," he said. He held out his good hand while he cradled his injured one to him, taking care not to stab himself with the bolt. "Shoot me."

Duke sprinted over to the doors and their still-gaping gun slots. "Brainstorm, check out our friend there. Scarlett and Barrel Roll, rally on me," he said. "I'm on the entry."

Brainstorm stuffed Krivo's pistol into the back of his belt, then knelt down next to the man and examined his injured hand. "How would shooting you be merciful?" he said.

"I fail," Krivo said. "Price badder than death."

The bolt had gone between the bones not in Krivo's hand but his wrist. If not for the bolt's tail fins, it might have passed straight through.

"Just unscrew the tip," Scarlett said over the comm. "Grab it by the barbs. Comes right off."

"Tell him he's lucky Scarlett had him in her sights," Barrel Roll's voice said. "I shot him, there'd be nothing left to clean up."

Brainstorm pushed that thought aside and set to removing the tip from the bolt. Once he managed that, he grabbed Krivo by the hand. "Brace yourself," he said.

Before Krivo could ask why, Brainstorm yanked the dismantled bolt free. Krivo bellowed in pain, then clasped his injured arm to his chest.

"Entrance is clear," Duke said. "No guarantee it'll remain that way, though."

"Time to call in the cavalry, Brainstorm," Scarlett said. "Or are you ahead of me on that?"

"Is anyone ever ahead of you?" Barrel Roll asked.

Brainstorm reached into a pouch on the front of his uniform and pulled out a glass-fronted control pad the size of paperback book but only half as thick. He activated it and flicked his fingers across the screen as it sprang to life. "I'm on it," he said to Scarlett.

Krivo struggled to his feet and peered over Brainstorm's elbow. The bleeding from his arm had slowed, and he all but ignored it, transfixed by the control pad instead.

"What that?" Krivo said, his voice filled with curiosity and wonder.

Recognizing the man's returning enthusiasm, Brainstorm smiled down at him. "Wait and see."

Duke set up next to one of the doors, a grenade in his hand, ready to toss it through the gun slot at the first sign of trouble. Barrel Roll emerged from the brush at the edge of the plateau, his rifle slung over his back. While he may not have been as good a shot as Crosshair, he still worked a rifle far better than Brainstorm ever managed. Even second best in the Joes was pretty damn good.

Scarlett tumbled down from the stand of trees above the door, landing on her feet and letting her momentum carry her toward Brainstorm and Krivo. The Eveni man cringed away from her as she approached, and she gave him a sardonic smirk. "If you don't like getting shot, don't point guns at my friends."

"So much for getting these guys to open the door for us," Brainstorm said. He glanced at Krivo between taps on the control pad. "You couldn't have waited for one more minute before taking me hostage?"

Krivo held up his bleeding arm. "You tell me nothing! How could I know?"

"If we had told you, you would have blown it," Scarlett said. "You're a rotten actor."

Krivo had the gall to look insulted. "How do you say that?"

"How do you think we knew you were going to betray us?" Brainstorm said.

Krivo frowned. Brainstorm thought he might begin to cry. "I suck," Krivo said.

"Yes," said Scarlett, "but your English is getting better."

Brainstorm swiped his hand across the control pad, blanking the screen. "Help is on the way."

Barrel Roll joined them. "Calling in an airstrike to open the doors?"

Scarlett stared at him. "Doesn't that seem a little extreme?"

"This is a converted Soviet bunker from World War II. Those doors are probably at least an inch thick of reinforced steel."

"Not a bunker," Krivo said.

Brainstorm fished a coagulant spray out of his medical pack and used it to coat the man's wounded arm. It covered the injury and the skin around it in a gummy white substance that began to harden immediately.

"Give it up with the lying, Boris," Barrel Roll said. "I know a bunker when I see one. I suppose you're going to tell me that's some kind of summer home for Putin."

"No *dacha*," Krivo said. "It is *gulag*."

Brainstorm let the man's arm go. "Don't touch that until it's dry," he said.

Krivo flexed his injured arm and winced in pain. He nodded his thanks, then pointed at the doors. "Once was *sharashka*, special gulag filled with scientists who work for glory of Soviet Union. Abandoned many years. Vasily and I discover when phone exchange in town switch to E5-carrier."

Scarlett glanced at Brainstorm. "Like a T1 Internet connection in the U.S.," he said, "only about three hundred and seventy-five times faster."

"How fast is that?" asked Barrel Roll.

"Moves about half a gigabyte per second."

"That's fast, right?"

Brainstorm ignored Barrel Roll and motioned for Krivo to ignore Barrel Roll and go on.

"We look, find Kremlin-strength firewall." Krivo allowed himself a wan smile. "Not stop us. Took months, but we broke through. Discover gold-farming operation."

"There's a mine in there?" asked Barrel Roll.

Scarlett sighed. "Do you ever read the briefings?"

"I was flying the plane out here, remember?"

"Gold-farming is a phenomena that rises out of MMORPGs."

"Wait, I got that one. Multiple Magnetically Operated Rocket Propelled Grenades, right?"

Scarlett rolled her eyes.

"Massively Multiplayer Online Roleplaying Games," Brainstorm said. "Like *Guild Wars* or *World of Warcraft* or *Star Wars: The Old Republic*."

"You're talking about games?" said Barrel Roll.

"Games."

"Like video games?"

"Like the most massive video games you've ever seen. Tens of millions of people worldwide play them, and they spend literally billions of dollars to do it. And that's just what's on the books."

"They have things that are off the books? They're not even real books to start with."

"They're real enough to have value. People can trade things inside the game, which means they automatically generate their own economy. Some games have a higher GDP than many developing nations. Even though it's usually against the rules, some people trade their time in the game for money. They gather gold pieces in the game, for instance, and sell them for real cash."

"And that's gold farming."

Scarlett nodded and smirked. "A virtual economy manifesting itself in the real world."

"With real consequences," said Duke.

"Precisely," agreed Brainstorm. "You can make a couple bucks a day just playing the game and finding gold to sell to people who'd rather not spend the time on it. To Americans, that may not be much, but to someone who'd otherwise be slaving away in a sweatshop or farming a rice paddy, it's a lot of money. In China and Mexico, they have warehouses full of people who do this in round-the-clock shifts."

Barrel Roll glanced over at Duke, who shook his head. There hadn't been any signs of activity inside the complex since the shooting had ended.

While Brainstorm was grateful that no one else had shot at them yet, the very same fact worried him. Shouldn't there have been a faster response? They'd shot at least five guards dead.

He looked up at the sky and spotted a trio of dots coming toward them from the direction of the sun. If he hadn't known they were there, he'd never have been able to see them. "Here they come," he said. "Right on time."

"So we came all the way out here to stop people from playing games?" Barrel Roll shook his head. "That's just not right."

"It's illegal," Duke's voice said.

"It's harmless," said Barrel Roll. "It's not even hacking! Who are they hurting?"

"Technically, Duke's right," Brainstorm said. "In most games, real-money trading is a violation of the End User Licensing Agreement."

Barrel Roll tucked his chin into his neck and started snoring. Scarlett smacked his arm with the back of her hand.

"It's not the fact that Cobra's cheating at a game," Brainstorm said. "It's *why* they're doing it."

The mention of Cobra grabbed Barrel Roll's attention. His eyes snapped open again.

"Money," said Krivo.

Brainstorm nodded. "These underground economies allow people to electronically move around massive amounts of cash to the point at which they become untraceable."

Barrel Roll's jaw dropped. "No way."

Scarlett nodded. "They're using the games to launder their cash."

"That's just sick," Barrel Roll said. "Only Cobra would come up with a way to use a videogame to cheat the world."

"How many times did you have to explain this to General Hawk?" Duke asked.

Brainstorm fidgeted. "He did read the briefing."

"Just answer the question," Barrel Roll said.

"Two or three. Well, two and a half." The others stared at him. "He gave up halfway through the third time."

Scarlett shook her head. "I can't believe he sat through it twice to begin with."

Brainstorm blushed. "He liked the whole idea of hitting Cobra where it would hurt most—in their bank accounts."

Barrel Roll jerked his head at Krivo. "If Boris here hadn't gotten so excited about capturing Moose and Squirrel that he jumped the gun, we might have gotten those guards to open the door for us. As it is, I don't know how you think we're going to bust our way into that place. Bunker or no, it's locked up tight."

Brainstorm glanced back up into the sky and smiled. "I think I have the solution."

THREE

THE THREE wooden crates about the size and shape of a footlocker parachuted onto the wide field in front of the complex's steel doors on large sheets of white silk. They landed hard, the impact tossing each one of them open on a single side, just as they'd been designed to do. Once each crate settled on the ground, the machine inside the box began to unfold itself, and moments later a flat-bottomed, steel and carbon-fiber lozenge rolled out of each crate on its Kevlar-curtained wheels.

Brainstorm flicked his fingers across the control pad, and its screen leaped to life again.

"What those?" Krivo asked, his eyes wide around as cue balls.

"Just something we've been working on in the Think Tank." Brainstorm grinned with pride. "We've had reports that Cobra is developing a Battle Android Trooper, a BAT. This is our response to that."

Barrel Roll and Krivo stared at the mobile shells as they trundled across the field toward the massive doors. Duke stood there, keeping his eyes concentrated on what lay beyond the gun slots. Scarlett ignored the entire spectacle, instead scanning the horizon for any signs of incoming danger.

Brainstorm followed her gaze, wondering if he could possibly spy something vital before she did. He was more used to picking out flaws in a line of code than spotting a glint off of a sniper's rifle.

The entrance to the Cobra base sat on the edge of a small clearing on top of a high ridge that ran south of Molochnaya and down through the pine-covered low mountains toward the Sea of Okhotsk. This far north—just shy of the Arctic Circle—the colors of the few hardwood trees had already started to change. Although summer had not officially ended yet, temperatures had dropped down near freezing last night, and they wouldn't be much warmer that afternoon. A few clouds hung high in the sky, but the sun seemed too distant and cold to ever bring much warmth to this frigid land.

Molochnaya was a tiny town, little more than a crossroads where the local farmers, miners, or ranchers could meet for a drink or come to gather supplies. That made it perfect for Cobra's purposes. Brainstorm guessed that Cobra must have bussed in the workers from the surrounding cities that lay nestled off in unseen valleys. With the real gold mines in the region beginning to play out, many would be hungry for work.

Perhaps some workers came from Sokol, just a short distance

to the north. A thin curl of smoke wafted into the air from that direction, probably from some sort of small factory or refinery. Still, Cobra would be sure to find better pickings in Madagan, an isolated port city of little over a hundred thousand souls to the south. People tired of braving the sea to make a living at fishing might leap at the chance to work in a climate-controlled computer array situated on solid land.

Barrel Roll nudged Brainstorm and nodded toward the robots, which had come to a stop. "They don't look like any androids I've ever seen."

"That's because the only ones you've seen were in science-fiction films," Brainstorm said. "That imagery sucked Cobra into building their BATs that way too. Robots don't need to look human to get the job done. Making them look like bad copies of people is like putting lipstick on a pig. You're not fooling anyone."

"But what good are they going to do against those doors?" Barrel Roll asked. "They can't even hold a gun."

"In the sense that they don't have hands, you're absolutely correct. But they don't need to hold something that's an integral part of them."

The sleek, low machines sat there on their ruggedized wheels. Brainstorm had hoped to outfit them with walking legs for a bit more mobility over a wider range of difficult terrain, but this early in the development process he'd gone with simpler mechanisms instead. He could raise the machines up and down a couple feet on their independent suspensions, which would get them into most places or over most obstacles —at least inside the complex. Their rotatable chassis would even let them go up and down stairs.

The machines' matte-black surfaces seemed to absorb sunlight. In the dark, they'd be almost invisible. Each of them had lights mounted around their front perimeter—as well as infrared, ultrasound, and low-light sensors—and these could be activated selectively at will to let the machines pinpoint enemy locations. Their Kevlar and carbon-fiber plastic exteriors made them bulletproof. Little short of a rocket could harm them. They were the soldiers of the future, ready for deployment on their first mission today.

Brainstorm pressed a virtual button the control pad, and slim doors atop each of the three robots slipped back and exposed their unfolding weapons in perfectly synchronized movements. The one closest to the door revealed a minigun. The next one uncovered a flamethrower. The third deployed a recoilless cannon.

"Which one should I try first?" Brainstorm could not suppress a smile as his finger hovered over the control pad, ready to send these lethal gadgets at those solid doors.

"How about you let me get out of the way before you do?" said Duke.

"Of course," Brainstorm said. He folded back his finger until Duke was clear, then extended it again. He held his breath, then stabbed the finger down at the button he'd selected.

The air shook as the recoilless cannon fired an explosive shell straight at the doors, catching them smack in the seam at which they met. Once the fire and billowing smoke cleared, Brainstorm smiled at the twisted remains of the doors, which had both crumpled like tin foil as they'd been blown back off their hinges.

Frozen in place, his injured arm forgotten, Krivo gaped at the destruction. Scarlett and Duke were already moving into position to execute their practiced maneuver for entry into a hostile space. Duke went left, while Scarlett moved to the right, each of them with their weapons at the ready.

Barrel Roll unlimbered his rifle, suspending it from his shoulder by a strap that put the trigger near his hip. "Nice," he said as he clapped Brainstorm on the shoulder. "You trying to put us all out of work?"

"Would you rather the bad guys shot at you or a Joe-Bot? These cost six million apiece, but the price will go down once they go into production—and unlike regular Joes, they can be repaired and replaced."

"Joe-Bots?" Barrel Roll made a face. "That's what you're going with?"

Brainstorm sent the minigun-equipped Joe-Bot into the breach the cannon had just opened. "You got a better idea?"

"GI-D2? C-3GI?"

"Those came up. Too derivative."

"Everybody's a critic."

Brainstorm turned to Krivo, who still stood frozen with his mouth open. He nodded to Barrel Roll, who grabbed Krivo by the elbow and hustled him toward the destroyed doorway. As they walked, Brainstorm moved the Joe-Bots into formation in front of them. The minigun stayed on point, with the flamethrower and cannon spread out behind it in a triangular formation.

"How many people are inside?" Brainstorm asked Krivo. Barrel Roll kept a steely eye on the man, ready to knock him flat at the first false move.

The Eveni scooped up his jaw and shook his head. "I–I don't know," he said. "Never inside. Only met guards in Molochnaya—my village. They kicked down door. Said they knew I e-mail you. They read everything. They know everything."

"That might explain why there's no one hanging around here," Duke said. "Smells like a trap."

"Could be the entire place is wired to blow the minute we move in," said Scarlett.

"Let's find out," said Brainstorm. Using the control pad, he linked the three Joe-Bots together to move in formation. Then he sent them forward into the waiting darkness.

The control pad showed the view through the front Joe-Bot's camera as it pressed its way through the wrecked doors and into the wide room beyond. Blast scorches splashed along the walls, with one spot showing the reverse shadow of a man who'd been standing between the wall and the detonating shell. A streak of blood ran from the center of that negative space and terminated in a battered corpse.

Brainstorm coaxed the Joe-Bots forward. Through the video feed, he located the broken remains of the other three men who'd pointed machine guns at him and the rest of the Joes. If any of them had still been breathing when the shell had struck the door, the explosion had cured them of that.

Regret welled up inside Brainstorm. He was a soldier, but he'd never enjoyed killing. His life back in the Pit kept him away from that most days, and that was the way he liked it. These men would have killed him, he knew, but that barely made it easier to stomach.

The walls of the place were made of poured concrete, probably run through with rebar. Someone had painted their smooth surfaces an industrial greenish gray and covered the ceilings with the same color. The floor was made of the same material, but roughened up for traction and colored a solid matte black.

In the back of the entrance area, Brainstorm spotted an open hallway wide enough to drive a truck down. It laced down into the darkness. Beyond the immediate destruction in the entrance, the hallway seemed clean and well maintained. This installation may have been abandoned once, but someone had come in and polished it up since, and they'd done a good job. Strings of LED lights ran along the edges of the floors, outlining where they met the walls, which stood bare of decoration. Soviet-era steel-caged light fixtures popped down from regular spots in the ceiling, but they had been painted over and no longer worked.

Rooms—none of which had doors—appeared on either side of the hallway, burrowed out of the top of the hill. Brainstorm methodically sent the Joe-Bots into each of them to search for hostiles. All they found were stacks of rotting crates, signs of water damage from occasional leaks in the ceiling, and random bits of detritus scattered about the place. Some of it clearly dated from the Cold War: eight-track tape decks, stacks of computer punch-cards, and so on. In one room, a vintage radio communications station sat moldering.

"Seems clear all the way down to the lab," Brainstorm said.

"Now tell me why we don't just go in there ourselves," said Barrel Roll. "Seems to me it would be a lot faster."

"And more dangerous," said Scarlet. "I know you're not afraid of anything, but most Joes would prefer to not get shot."

"General Hawk has been itching for a chance to field test these Joe-Bot prototypes," Brainstorm said, "but since they require a trained operator, it's been hard to find the right time and place. When he agreed to send me along on this mission, he took the opportunity to send the Joe-Bots around the block as well."

"Two nerds with one stone," said Barrel Roll.

Brainstorm sighed. "Something like that."

"If these units prove useful, it could change the face of battle," said Scarlett. "Imagine being able to send in forces to battle Cobra or other threats with no threat of casualties on our side."

The others nodded at this, even Krivo. They'd all lost friends in battle, some more recently than others. They'd all been shot at. Anything that could keep that from happening again—or at least as often—had to seem like a good idea.

Ever the soldier, Duke brought their attention back to the matter at hand. "No resistance at all?" he said, pointing at the control pad.

Brainstorm shook his head and furrowed his brow. Counting the man on the hill, there had only been five hostiles here. He wanted to enjoy how easy this field trip had been so far, but it wasn't like Cobra to leave a place like this so undefended. He didn't like the way this was going, even if the Joe-Bots seemed like an unmitigated success.

"Maybe we're already too late," Brainstorm said. "It's possible that Cobra has already removed everyone. After all," he glared at Krivo, who cringed, "they knew we were coming."

"So why did we come out here in the first place?" Barrel Roll said.

"We don't get many opportunities to confront Cobra on their own turf," said Duke. "If that requires us to walk into a trap, then in we go."

"We just need to disable that trap along the way," said Scarlett.

"How many people worked here?" Brainstorm asked Krivo. The man started to object to the question, but Brainstorm cut him off. "I know you were never inside here, but what about anyone else in the village? They must have hired some of the locals to help them out."

Krivo grimaced and shrugged. "No one I know. Molochnaya small village. Hard to keep secrets."

"So they imported all their labor?" Duke said.

"That's not too hard to believe," said Scarlett. "It's not the easy way to do things, but Cobra prizes secrecy and loyalty over low-cost solutions—at least for installations like this. I ran into one of their covert construction teams down in Costa Rica once. They're like secret Seabees."

"But that doesn't make sense for a gold-farming operation," said Brainstorm, frowning. "You need lots of cheap labor to run the machines and play the games. You can't just set up a script-bot to handle it. The mods—the in-house game moderators—they come around and check on users who play suspiciously."

Barrel Roll snorted. "How do you play a computer game suspiciously? Wear a mask?"

Brainstorm ignored the sarcasm. "Most players are in the game to level up and acquire assets, rewards for their achievements. They go on adventures, join tribes, craft or find things to sell to other players, and so on. Script-bots behave too predictably. They usually just sit in one area and do the same thing over and over."

"And that's against the rules, so they nab them."

Brainstorm shook his head. "There's nothing wrong with that, but if a mod spots it, he'll chat with the character he's suspicious about. Most script-bots don't make stunning conversationalists, so once the mod identifies one he bans the player and deletes the account."

"And that's the only way to catch them?" asked Duke.

"No, but it's the easiest. The other way is to find the money being sold online and track it back to its source. It's a much bigger challenge, but a lot more effective. You can shut down an entire operation—at least temporarily—rather than just kicking out its workers one at a time."

"Which is why they hire people to actually play the game," Scarlett said, understanding. "It's easier to put real people behind the accounts rather than engage in an arms race between creating artificially intelligent script-bots of sufficient sophistication and detecting them."

Brainstorm couldn't help but grin. "Exactly."

"But there's nobody here?" said Duke.

The minigun Joe-Bot reached a set of double doors. Bluish lights from the room beyond glowed through a crack between the doors and the threshold. Brainstorm cranked up the volume on the control pad, but all he could hear was the faint hum of the Joe-Bots' electric motors.

Brainstorm held up the control pad so the others could see the Joe-Bots' video feed. "Let's go find out."

At Brainstorm's bidding, the Joe-Bots moved forward. The door refused to give with simple pressure, so the lead robot extended a metallic arm that found the latch and pushed the door open. It led the way inside, and the others followed it close behind.

The view through Brainstorm's control pad scanned a large warehouse of a room. It was filled with computer servers stacked in black steel racks that stretched in a labyrinthine array from one end of the place to the other. The computers' lights flashed and blinked in myriad staccato patterns, crawling and pulsing like living things hunting for a way out. The soft hum of a modern climate-control system filled the room, just audible over the sound of the whirring of countless cooling fans.

"Where are all the gold farmers?" Duke said. "On break?"

Brainstorm shook his head, mystified. There should have been dozens of people at work, but no one greeted the Joe-Bots at all. He ordered them into the place to investigate.

One of the Joe-Bots moved off to an open space on the right while the other two wandered among the server racks, finding ample space to maneuver. The floor of the space had been fitted with steel grating on top of which the server racks stood. Each rack was about eight feet tall and held a dozen or so generic black servers shaped like double-thick pizza boxes and bolted into place. The wires running down the back of the racks disappeared into the floor, where Brainstorm guessed there was a shallow crawlspace through which the technicians could run the wires that connected everything together. The racks stood in rows that were bolted together in seemingly random lengths. It felt like a high-tech version of a garden maze.

"You going to get those things lost in there?" Barrel Roll said.

"They know where they are," Brainstorm said. "I just instruct them to return, and they'll retrace their steps."

The Joe-Bot that had gone off to the right emerged from the maze to find the room's long eastern wall filled from one end to the other with active flat-panel monitors. Brainstorm gasped. There had to be hundreds of them— maybe a thousand.

In one cluster of a couple dozen displays, a band of heroes wielding swords and wands stalked across a snowy mountaintop and took on a flock of fiery red dragons. Each of the monitors showed the battle from a slightly different angle, and despite the power of the monsters the heroes had chosen to pick a fight with, the good guys seemed to be winning.

In another group of monitors, several starships waged silent war deep in the heart of a glowing, rainbow-colored nebula. In others, heroes fought zombies, supervillains, Nazis, drug lords, orcs, and a staggering variety of other mysterious creatures not even Brainstorm could identify.

"Someone's in there, playing the games," Brainstorm said. "But where are they? Maybe they're just coordinating their efforts through this central hub while the workers sit in smaller, decentralized locations around the world?"

"Since I don't understand any of that, I'll have to take your word on it," Barrel Roll said.

"Does this mean the mission's a bust?" asked Duke.

Brainstorm shook his head. "Not at all. If the machines in there have access to the accounts Cobra's using for money laundering, all we need to do is go in there and find the central database they constructed to coordinate everything. If we can manage that, we can steal their accounts and confiscate their assets before they can stop us."

"Can't the Joe-Bots do that for us?" Scarlett asked.

"Not programmed for that," Brainstorm said. "They're built to be soldiers, not hackers."

Barrel Roll chuckled. "I know just how they feel."

"What are we waiting for?" Duke asked.

"Nothing." Brainstorm led the way in through the double doors. Scarlett and Duke followed right behind him. Barrel Roll pushed Krivo after them, and once the Eveni man was in motion he brought up the rear, keeping a wary eye on the outsider.

Brainstorm followed the Joe-Bots' path into the complex. Duke covered the left side of the main corridor, while Scarlett took the right. While they had seen the Joe-Bots clear out the rooms, they weren't about to place their full trust in the technology quite yet.

"Your friends," Krivo said, calling ahead to Brainstorm, "they do not trust your amazing machines?"

Brainstorm laughed. "The Joe-Bots may be state of the art, but it never hurts to double-check your work."

"What good machines then?" Krivo said. "They do work. You do it again?"

"Machines are just tools. No matter how amazing they are, they help you with the work," said Duke. "They don't do it for you."

"The Joe-Bots are close to being able to handle that," said Brainstorm. "But we're not quite there yet. We may never be."

Brainstorm reached the doors that led into the server farm, and he pushed them open. Krivo and the other Joes followed him in, and he moved over to where the Joe-Bots had rolled in front of the long bank of active monitors. Colorful action burst across every screen, forming a stunning montage of virtual battles that could never be. Brainstorm stared at it for a moment, and the others joined in.

"It's almost hypnotic," said Duke.

Scarlett sniffed at it. "It's a bit too much."

Barrel Roll grinned. "It's incredible. I have got to try some of these out when we get back to the Pit. Can we get a connection from down there?"

"How do you think I managed to find out about all of this?" Brainstorm asked.

"Once, before all this, Vasily and me come here to look. This wall—" He spread his arms wide to show where the screens now stood arrayed. "—this once was huge window that look down over valley to sea. Now it look out on many strange worlds instead."

Duke clapped the Eveni on the back. "I don't know if that's humbling or horrible," he said. "Maybe both."

Chuckling, Brainstorm moved over to a server rack and pulled a retractable USB cord from the side of his control pad. He plugged it into the closest server, and a duplication of the display it controlled popped up in a window on the control pad's screen.

Tapped into the servers' local network, Brainstorm set to finding the master account files that they'd come here for. As Brainstorm worked, Krivo moved in front of the others and stared up at the patchwork quilt of action-packed screens. "Where are they?" he said. "Players of these games? What have they done with them?"

The screens all went blank for an instant, dousing the room in darkness. The blinking lights on the server racks pinged along, though, keeping the blackness from becoming complete. Brainstorm's entire control pad went blank too, and an icy fear stabbed through his guts.

Before anyone's eyes could adjust to the dimness, the screens flared to life again. This time, though, they displayed a single image spanning across all of them. The same image of a chrome-faced man appeared on Brainstorm's control pad and glared out at him, mocking him.

"Welcome to my game room, G.I. Joe," Destro said in his thick Scottish burr. "Would you mind if I have a go?"

FOUR

"Yo, Joe!" Duke yelled. "Out of here, now!"

Scarlett and Barrel Roll did as they were ordered, moving more on instinct and a pure trust in Duke's judgment than anything else. They split off in different directions at first, each scattering away from the center then heading back for the doorway through which they'd entered the room, their boots clanking on the steel grates on the floor.

Krivo stood there in front of Destro, transfixed. The man fell to his knees in front of the image of the Scottish laird and wept. He spoke in a language Brainstorm couldn't understand, but it was clear that Krivo wanted only one thing: mercy.

Unfortunately, Brainstorm knew Krivo wasn't likely to get his wish. Destro might have been a devious businessman, an aloof aristocrat, and a charismatic leader, but his cruel streak ran a mile wide.

Brainstorm unplugged his control pad from the server in front of him. Destro's image remained there despite that, which told him that something had gone horribly wrong. An instant later, when the Joe-Bots started moving on their own, he knew exactly what it was.

The minigun Joe-Bot spun on its base and drew a bead on the Eveni man, who still knelt there, begging Destro to spare his life.

"Krivo!" Brainstorm shouted. "Run!"

The Eveni turned toward Brainstorm. As he did, his eyes fell on the minigun barrels pointed straight at him. The lethal contraption spun into motion as he stared at it, goggle-eyed. When it came up to speed, it began spitting bullets, and they stitched a line straight through Krivo's chest.

As the others reached the door, the Joe-Bot with the recoilless canon unleashed a shot straight into the ceiling above the doorway. The blast knocked back Duke and Scarlett and sent the lagging Barrel Roll diving for cover. Reinforced concrete tumbled down from the ceiling, blocking the door. Brainstorm guessed that the Joes could clear it away and be through the door in under a minute, if they were to get the chance.

Unfortunately, Destro seemed determined to not grant them that.

"What amazing devices you designed here," the Cobra leader said. "Far more sophisticated than I would have given you credit for. It's so rare to see any kind of innovation spring out of your government these days—unless they purchase it from someone else."

Brainstorm ignored the insult and scrambled for cover. The Joe-Bot with the minigun was sure to start hunting for another target now that Krivo had been killed. Destro might kill them all soon enough, but Brainstorm wasn't about to make it easy for him. He fell prone behind a server rack and crawled away from it on his hands and knees.

"You think you can hide from my new toys, do you, laddie?" Destro laughed. "Perhaps if you hadn't built them so damned well."

Brainstorm heard the telltale click and whoosh that signaled that a flamethrower had been armed somewhere off to his left. He fell flat on the floor, face down, and covered his head with his arms. An instant later, a gout of fire enveloped the server rack next to him, from top to bottom.

Destro's rolling laughter filled the room. Brainstorm had expected it to seem like that of a madman. Instead, Destro sounded like he'd just heard the world's greatest joke—not insane but rather all too human.

"Fall back!" Duke said. "Spread out! Look for other ways out!"

Scarlett and Barrel Roll moved to comply with the orders. Brainstorm wanted to, but the heat from the flamethrower's gout of fire was too close for him to risk exposing any more skin. The moment it faded, though, he planned to leap to his feet and dash away from the blazing server rack.

Before that could happen, water sprayed down from the ceiling, drenching the entire area, including Brainstorm. As the fluid ceased falling, he stared up at the ceiling, mystified. No one who cared a bit about their computers would ever use water as part of a fire-suppressant system. It would destroy everything it was meant to protect.

Brainstorm patted his hands against himself and realized he was already dry. Not water then. "Halotron."

With the synthetic fluid already evaporated, Brainstorm realized that there was nothing preventing the flamethrower from letting loose at him again. The Halotron system might put out the flames right away, but that wouldn't do him any good if they fried him through first. As the barrel of the flamethrower swiveled toward him, he flipped up onto his feet and scrambled away.

Brainstorm had led the development of the Joe-Bots himself.

He knew exactly what they were capable of. The flamethrower could only pump so much incendiary fluid into its firing mechanism at a time. Once expended, it required approximately fifteen seconds to refill the firing mechanism and become live again.

Brainstorm and his engineering team had spent many man-hours trying to whittle that recharge period down, and he never imagined he'd be so glad that they hadn't managed to do better at it. That down period didn't give him a lot of time, but he was determined to make the most of it.

He shoved himself to his feet and sprinted along a corridor of servers until he reached the far wall. Once there, he spun right and took off along the edge of the room. As he ran, he scanned the walls for any sign of an exit: a door, a window, even a large air vent might do. He just knew he needed to find a way out of there fast.

"Anyone find anything?" Duke said over the comm. "Report in?"

"Negative," said Barrel Roll.

"Nothing here," Brainstorm said.

"Double doors leading out in northwest corner, directly opposite the doors through which we entered," said Scarlett. "Meet you there."

"First one on point wedge open the doors, then turn and provide cover," said Duke.

"Already on it," Scarlett said. "Doors are locked."

"How locked?"

"Keyhole-rusted-over locked. These haven't been opened since before any of us were born."

"Can't you handle something simple like a rusty lock?" asked Barrel Roll. "Just WD-40 the damn thing."

"Already on it."

"What do you have planned?" asked Duke.

The thunder from a muffled explosion rumbled off to the northwest. Brainstorm hoped that the Joe-Bots hadn't been behind the noise. It sounded too soft to have been from the recoilless canon.

"A little strategically placed C4," said Scarlett. "Doors are open, and we're in business. Uh-oh."

"Uh-oh?" said Barrel Roll. "Tell me that's not a bad thing, please?"

"Sorry to disappoint," said Scarlett.

Gunfire growled from just up ahead. Brainstorm recognized the sound of the Joe-Bot mounted minigun. He'd wondered where it had gotten to after mowing down Krivo. It must have spun about to go cover the other doors. Of course, Destro would have known about other exits and tried to cut the Joes off.

"Brainstorm!" Scarlett said. "What the hell's going on? Call off your robo-dogs, would you?"

Brainstorm's stomach sank. "I'm not doing that, Scarlett," he said. "Destro took control of the Joe-Bots. He's shut me out of their systems."

"So the Joe-Bots have gone rogue?" Barrel Roll said. "Figures. Just when I thought I might finally be able to retire."

"Be replaced, you mean?" said Duke.

"Yeah, that's it." Barrel Roll laughed. "Hear that, Destro? You just saved us Joes from premature obsolescence."

"They didn't go rogue," Brainstorm said. "They're not smart enough to manage that. Destro took control of them."

"Well?" said Scarlett. "How do we take them back?"

"I don't know." Brainstorm smacked the side of the control pad as if he might be able to shake a bad circuit loose. "I need some more time. I just—"

The server rack looming over Brainstorm's head exploded as a cannon shot blew it to pieces. He yelped in surprise as he fell to his knees and wrapped his arms around his skull. Bits of melted silicon and hot shrapnel rained down over his head and shoulders, burning his skin and slicing open a shallow cut across an arm.

Brainstorm's training took over then. Although he might be

a FOBbit, he was still a soldier, still part of G.I. Joe. He dashed off, crouching low and slipping left and right through the maze of servers in a random pattern. Desperate to get away from the Joe-Bots, he refused to let his terror of their weapons overwhelm him. Instead, he used his fear and the adrenaline it sent coursing through him to sharpen his senses and help carry him away.

It wasn't until he stopped that he realized the others were yelling for him. He could barely hear them over the ringing in his head.

"I'm all right!" he said a little too loudly. "I don't know where I am, but I'm not hurt." He winced from the stinging of the cut across his arm. "Well, not too bad, at least."

Brainstorm put his hand over the cut, and it came away covered with red. He'd have to attend to it later. He couldn't stop to risk it now, not with the Joe-Bots still out there and hunting for him.

He examined the control pad. A crack had formed in the glass across its face. Destro grinned back at him through the flaw, his face split into two mismatched pieces.

"Run, little rabbit," Destro said. "Drag out this game of ours a wee bit longer. You and your friends are trapped. No matter how long you might evade your delightful toys, I've already won."

A sniper rifle cracked in the distance, the report rolling like thunder through the room.

"Damn!" Barrel Roll said a moment later. "What did you make these things out of, Brainstorm? Bulletproofium?"

Off in the same direction, a flamethrower roared, the air filling with the stench of kerosene and melted plastics.

"Barrel Roll, report!" said Duke.

"I'm all right." Barrel Roll's voice sounded like he'd smoked a truckload of cigarettes. "But now I'm getting mad."

"It's a pity you did such a good job building these drones of yours," Destro said, his voice reverberating throughout the gigantic room. "Otherwise, you might actually stand a chance. Once you're dead, I'll have to pull them apart and see what lessons we can apply to our BATs. You may have single-handedly doomed the entire G.I. Joe program. How ironic!"

Brainstorm glared down at the image of the Cobra leader. He couldn't recall if he'd ever hated anyone as much as he did at that moment. He fought the urge to spit at his own control pad, knowing that Destro would only mock the pointless gesture.

"I could use a little help here," Scarlett said. "The bot with the machine gun has me pinned down. It can't get to me here, but I'm caught in a dead end. There's no way out!"

Destro's malicious laughter filled the massive chamber.

"One of you may have gotten away from me, but I'm afraid that will be today's limit," Destro's voice said, booming throughout the massive room. "At least, if these robots of yours are as well designed as they seem. They really do have a delightful interface, although it's not as intuitive as I might have hoped. Fortunately, I don't actually have to bother with it."

Brainstorm wondered what the mad Scotsman meant by that.

"In any case, it's a temporary setback as far as the fair Scarlett is concerned. With the power available in this installation, the robots can hold out indefinitely. I don't think we could say the same thing about any of you. Eventually she'll have to come out or starve."

"She'd die of thirst first," Brainstorm said. He didn't know why the words escaped his lips. He didn't want Scarlett to die, but he needed to correct Destro—to be more right about at least one thing than him, at least this once before they died.

It didn't feel as good as he had hoped.

"Not helping," Barrel Roll said. He sounded like he had more to add, but a coughing fit cut him off.

"Won't they run out of ammunition eventually?" Scarlett said.

"That only works if they miss every time, doesn't it?"

said Brainstorm. "I don't think we should count on that."

"Don't you have some kind of failsafe for these things, Brainstorm?" asked Duke.

The question surprised Brainstorm. He'd been tumbling into despair, and the sound of Duke's voice shocked him out of it, at least for the moment.

"I–I did. Of course I did. Nothing should have been able to get through the Joe-Bots' protective programs. They shouldn't even be able to shoot at us. They recognize us by the comm system. The only link to them is the—"

Brainstorm looked down at the control pad, which he still held in the hand of his injured arm. Destro smirked at him through the cracked screen. "Catching on finally, are you?"

"What is it?" Duke asked Brainstorm. "What do you got?"

"The control pad." Brainstorm spoke so low he could barely hear his own voice.

"What?" Duke said. "That didn't come through. Repeat."

"The control pad." Brainwave's voice rose as he spoke. "It was the damned control pad. I plugged it into the gaming network so I could copy their accounts. That's when Destro broke into my system and took over."

"So what happens if you destroy it?" asked Duke.

"Destroy what? My control pad?" At first blush, the idea made Brainstorm feel ill, but he quickly realized that it might not be such a crazy idea after all. If Destro was using the control pad to operate the Joe-Bots, then taking it out of the loop might cut off his access and shut the machines down.

"Is that a problem?" Duke asked.

"Maybe. If I break the control pad, I don't have any means of controlling the Joe-Bots—should we somehow break Destro's control another way."

The sound of an explosion from the cannon put an exclamation point on that sentence.

"Do something!" Barrel Roll said. "Anything!"

"I'm on it," Brainstorm said. He tried to turn the control pad off, but the power switch didn't seem to be working. He assumed that Destro had disabled it, and the Scotsman's evil cackle only confirmed that theory.

Brainstorm knew one thing that the Cobra leader couldn't stop him from doing, though. He turned the control pad over and removed the battery from it with practiced ease. He'd spent enough time swapping power packs in and out of this pad and others like it over the years that he could have managed it blindfolded.

"No!" Destro's roar, came out through the control pad but also shook the walls with the network's built-in sound system. "You can't do that to me! The Joe-Bots are mine!"

"Lights out, Destro!" Brainstorm said as the battery pack fell out in his hand. The control pad wouldn't work at all now, although whatever was stored in its solid-state memory would remain safe and untouched.

"You can't do that to me!" Destro said. "You can't!"

A moment later, the Joe-Bot with the minigun opened up at someone, the bullets spattering across the walls and floor of reinforced concrete. Brainstorm's blood froze in his heart.

From where he knelt among the servers, Brainstorm could see the still-active wall of screens. Destro's smug smirk sprawled across several of them.

"As I was saying, Brainstorm, you can't do that to me," Destro said. "Not even a little bit."

FIVE

BRAINSTORM SMACKED the control pad. He couldn't understand what was going on. Without the control pad ordering the Joe -Bots around, they should have fallen into stand-by mode, which meant folding back into their closed lozenge shapes and staying still—not shooting at the flesh-and-blood G.I. Joes. Instead, they were moving around on their own, without any outside control at all.

"I don't get it," Brainstorm said. "It should have worked. That should have done it."

"Barrel Roll's down!" Duke said. "Maybe out." Ever the professional, Duke relayed the news in a flat and professional manner, as a leader assessing the situation. Even so, Brainstorm could hear an edge in the man's voice that he couldn't suppress.

"No, no, no," said Brainstorm. "This shouldn't be happening!"

"We need a new solution," Duke said. "Now!"

"I'm done, Duke." Brainstorm stared down at the grating that made up the floor. Wires and coolant tubes snaked through narrow crawlways below, keeping all the servers in the room running in tip-top condition. "I've pulled every trick out of my hat. I got nothing left."

"Don't worry," Duke said. "I still have a few up my sleeve."

Brainstorm stared down the long row of server racks lining the corridor in which he cringed. There had to be something he could do. He couldn't give up. He was a Joe.

Brainstorm stood up and stuffed the control pad and its battery into his pockets. Then he drew his automatic pistol with one hand and Krivo's revolver with the other. If he could get to the others, he might be able to help them. He didn't know how for sure, but he had to try.

Then he heard something tapping below him, and he nearly jumped out of his boots. He pointed both pistols straight down at the floor and saw a set of well-manicured fingers sticking out at him.

"Don't shoot!" Scarlett said in a stage whisper. "Brainstorm, it's me!"

Brainstorm put up his guns. He opened his mouth to speak, but Scarlett shushed him. "Don't use the comm," she said. "The Joe-Bots are using them to track us."

Brainstorm raised a hand to where the comm's plug sat in his ear. "Of course."

"Get rid of it," Scarlett said. "Toss it as far away as you can, and join me down here. Then we can work on a plan to take down the Joe-Bots."

"Barrel Roll?" Brainstorm said into the comm. "Barrel Roll, are you there?"

"He's fine," Scarlett said, understanding that he was speaking for the benefit of Destro if he was listening in on the comm chatter. She also knew what he was really asking. "He's down here somewhere too. The Joe-Bots shot at his comm until it went out. Duke's leading the flamethrower and cannon around right now, keeping them busy until you can get clear."

Action off to the right caught Brainstorm's eye. He saw that the army of heroes he'd spotted fighting a wing of red dragons were getting slaughtered. The heroes kept throwing themselves at the dragons without any coordinated strategy. While the monsters had been overwhelmed at first by the heroes' superior numbers, they had survived the initial onslaught and now were whittling the heroes down.

For a moment, Brainstorm felt sorry for the dying heroes, with their sparkling spells and flashing blades. They had charged into battle hoping to triumph but instead were being slaughtered. If he didn't come up with something fast, the same might happen to the Joes.

Brainstorm realized then that the heroes in the game were losing because they weren't fighting smart—or at least not smarter than their foes. Maybe, he thought, the Joes weren't the heroes in the battle raging in this refurbished Cold War installation. Maybe they were the dragons instead.

"Hey," Scarlett said. "You still with me?"

Brainstorm nodded, a wry and determined grin on his face. He pulled his comm's plug out of his ear and switched it off.

"Come on," Scarlett said. "We don't have long."

"Don't worry about me," Brainstorm said. "I have a plan."

"Now would be a good time to share."

He glanced over at the monitors again. Heroes fell over up and down and left and right. Monitor after monitor displayed the kill screen before sending the heroes back to their respawn points, far from the thick of the battle.

"We need to grief enough aggro to get the Joe-Bots to auto-nerf themselves. Then we can gank them like noobs."

She narrowed her eyes at him. "Now say it in English."

Gunfire rattled away, blasting apart servers only a few corridors down.

"Get back to where you left your comm," Brainstorm said. "Once you get it, turn it off, and use the access tunnels to get back to where we were standing when all this started. If you run into Barrel Roll, have him rally with us there too."

"All right," Scarlett said. "Are you sure you know what you're doing?"

"Yes. If it all goes according to plan."

"Will it?"

"I give it better than even odds."

"Good enough." She winked at him. "Yo, Joe."

Brainstorm allowed himself half a smile as he turned and scaled the nearest server rack. The racks stood about eight feet tall, leaving another eight feet or so between their tops and the ceiling. With all the heat the servers gave off, they would mess with the Joe-Bots' infrared sensors, and it was dark enough up here that their visual cameras might miss him. Best of all, Brainstorm knew that the Joe-Bots' vertical field of fire was limited. Even if they found him, they shouldn't be able to hit him up here. That wouldn't stop them from blasting away at the server racks underneath him, but it might give him the edge he needed should it come to that.

If what Scarlett said was right, Brainstorm might have been able to walk right in front of the Joe-Bots without anything happening at all. With his comm turned off, they might not see him as either a threat or a target, and it was possible that he could dance circles around them without them firing a shot. That wasn't an experiment he felt comfortable performing here in the field, though. If the theory proved incorrect, he would pay for the mistake with his life.

A server rack went up in flames to Brainstorm's right. He spotted a figure atop another rack between him and the fire, silhouetted against the flames—a human figure moving toward him fast.

Duke.

The field leader leaped across the gap between the racks: once, twice, and a third time. The last jump landed him next to Brainstorm, and Duke clapped the FOBbit on the shoulder.

Brainstorm raised a finger to his lips and pointed at his ear. Duke nodded at him, then removed his comm plug and turned it off.

"Glad to see you made it, Joe," Duke said. "Scarlett find you?"

Brainstorm nodded. "She says Barrel Roll's all right."

Duke nodded. "I figured."

"So, what's the plan?"

Duke grunted. "Don't you have one?"

"Just hoping yours is better."

Duke shrugged. "I was trying to trick the Joe-Bots into shooting at each other, but the timing is tricky." He held up a scorched arm. His uniform was still smoking.

Brainstorm reached into his pack and pulled out a small roll of duct tape. "I might be able to improve upon that." He ripped off a pair of strips of tape and attached one to his comm plug and one to Duke's.

"And how is this supposed to help?" Duke asked as Brainstorm handed him his taped-up comm plug.

"Whatever's controlling the Joe-Bots has programmed them to use these to track us. But if we can attach them to the Joe-Bots and then turn them on, they should shoot at each other."

Duke looked down at his comm plug. "It's a fine plan. Now we just need to bell those bots."

"I'll turn mine on to draw them here," Brainstorm said. "That should give you a chance to get behind one of them and attach the plug to it."

"They don't have three-sixty vision?"

Brainstorm shook his head. "It's about one-eighty. They're just prototypes. That's on the slate for the beta versions. They can turn pretty fast, though, so be careful."

"Can't you just tape your earbud to a wall and run?"

"There are three of them, and we only have the two earbuds between us."

"There's Scarlett's, if we can get it."

"That's just enough then. We can't waste any."

"All right," Duke said, moving off already. "See you on the other side."

Duke turned to leave, but Brainstorm grabbed him by the arm. "You need to stick the tape to the Joe-Bot's deployed weapon," he said. "Don't just smack it on the body of the robot."

"Why not?"

"Trust me. You'll get the shock of your life."

An extra bit of respect crept into Duke's eyes, and he gave Brainstorm a nod of thanks before he left. As Duke slipped down the side of the server rack and disappeared, Brainstorm listened. He could hear the whine of a Joe-Bot's servos not too far off.

"Hey, you Cobra-Bots!" Brainstorm shouted. "I'm over here!" He turned on his comm and held his breath. The servos he could hear stopped, then wound up to a high-pitch and headed his way.

"What are you up to, little Joe?" Destro said. His voice boomed throughout the room. "Feeling suicidal?"

Brainstorm felt like a Pac-Man. Racing through the maze, he had to get close enough to the Joe-Bots to draw them after him, but not so close that they could catch up to him quite yet. He wondered if Destro had a top-down map of the labyrinth on which he could track all the players, and if so, did it look like the Joes were winning or losing?

Brainstorm ignored Destro and concentrated on the sounds from the approach-ing Joe-Bots. He thought one of them was still busy pinning down Scarlett's comm signal. That left two to watch out for.

The machine with the flamethrower appeared around the

end of one of the two corridors below Brainstorm, and it swiveled toward him. Flames leaped from the barrel of its weapon right away. Apparently it had decided that it didn't want to wait until he was within range. It was willing to burn down everything between itself and its prey to ensure that Brainstorm wouldn't get away. As a machine, it didn't worry about things like property damage.

Brainstorm edged away from the flamethrower, trying to draw it farther down the corridor so that Duke would have a better chance of getting behind it. It came along after him like a dog hungry for a treat.

From his vantage point atop the server racks, Brainstorm could see over the flamethrower and the fiery venom it kept spitting at him, growing closer and closer with every passing second. "Come on," he said, coaxing the thing along, even though he knew it couldn't understand his words. "Come on."

Barrel Roll appeared at the end of the corridor then, behind the Joe-Bot, and let loose at the flamethrower with his sniper rifle. "Think you're taking my job and then turning traitor?" he shouted at the Joe-Bot. "Not on my watch!"

The high-powered slugs from the rifle smacked into the robot's armored carapace and moved the machine forward a few feet with every shot, but once Barrel Roll had gone through every bullet in the gun, the Joe-Bot tried to spin around to attack him. There wasn't enough space in the corridor for it to be able to manage it, though.

Frustrated, Barrel Roll hefted his rifle high over his shoulder, the butt facing forward, and charged the Joe-Bot, shouting at the top of his lungs. When he reached it, he slammed the butt of his rifle against the machine, then fell on top of it and kept smashing away.

The blows did no good at all that Brainstorm could see. When Barrel Roll landed on the machine, though, it let loose with a high-voltage shock that locked up every muscle in Barrel Roll's body and sent him slipping to the floor.

Still unable to turn around, the Joe-Bot raced forward, away from Barrel Roll's fallen form. Brainstorm knew that if he didn't do something to stop or distract the Joe-Bot, it would soon reach the end of the corridor, spin about, and then race back to kill the still-helpless Barrel Roll. He turned off his comm plug.

As the flamethrower Joe-Bot passed underneath Barrel Roll's position, he dropped down behind it. The machine was moving fast, and he had to sprint to catch up with it. He wasn't sure that he had a real chance at matching its speed, but it seemed that Barrel Roll's bullets might have done enough damage to the Joe-Bot to at least slow it down a little bit.

Even so, Brainstorm only managed to catch up with the machine just before it reached the end of the corridor. He reached out with his hand and slapped the taped comm plug flat on the back of the flamethrower itself.

As the Joe-Bot made it to the end of the corridor, Brainstorm realized two things. First, he had nowhere to go. If he turned around and started running now, the Joe-Bot would probably fire on him and engulf him in flames before he got ten feet away from it.

Second, he'd forgotten to turn the comm plug back on.

With no time at all to debate the wisdom of his decision, Brainstorm charged at the Joe-Bot again. If he could turn on the comm plug, he might at least be able to save Barrel Roll's life—even if the Joe-Bot was sure to flambé him before Barrel Roll could thank him.

Brainstorm grabbed at the taped-up comm plug just before the Joe-Bot started to turn around. He squeezed the small d evice, which he knew should activate it. Then he stumbled backward before he slipped against the Joe-Bot and had it shock him senseless too.

Instead of freezing when the Joe-Bot turned toward him, Brainstorm scrambled backward on his hands and feet. He was probably going to die here, but that didn't mean he had to give the machine an easy shot at him.

The appearance of the comm plug on the rear of its weapon must have confused the Joe-Bot for a moment. Brainstorm actually made it a full ten yards away before he heard the telltale hiss of the Joe-Bot priming its flamethrower.

"Do your worst, you malfunctioning piece of junk," he said. "Please?"

SIX

AS THE FLAMES from the Joe-Bot leaped forward to engulf Brainstorm, the machine exploded in a billowing ball of fire. Brainstorm instinctively recoiled from the ovenlike heat and covered his head with his hands. The force from the blast actually shoved him back along the gratings that lined the corridor's floor.

As soon as he could, Brainstorm scrambled to his feet and dashed away from the Joe-Bot's still-burning wreck. He wobbled a bit as he walked, which made him wonder if the noise of the explosion had been enough to damage his inner ear. Or maybe the ground was moving underneath him. It was hard to tell.

By the time he made it to where he'd left Barrel Roll, the man was already on his feet. "I don't know what you did to that thing," Barrel Roll said, "but I like it."

"I didn't do it," Brainstorm said. "Well, maybe in a way. I helped the Joe-Bot with the cannon find it, I think."

"Can you do that again?"

"Not with that earpiece," Brainstorm said. "Right now, we need to keep moving. If the machine that did all that damage manages to catch us here, we're dead."

"Then let's roll."

Barrel Roll set out in the lead, scooping up his sniper rifle as he went. As they walked, he thumbed another five bullets into the weapon and readied it again with practiced ease.

When the two Joes reached the end of the corridor, they spotted Duke coming at them. "Did you see that one go up?" he asked. "Looked like the Fourth of July."

"Did you manage to tag the other one with your comm plug?" Brainstorm asked.

Duke held up the duct-taped plug in his off hand. "Never had the chance. I guess you beat me to it."

"Now we just need to figure out how to get the last two machines to blow themselves up too."

"What do you think the chances are of that?" asked Barrel Roll. "From what I could see while I was lying dazed on the floor, we just got lucky with that last one."

"We could tape a comm to the front door," Duke said. "Trick the machines into blasting a way out for us."

"The last time a Joe-Bot did that, it brought down the roof," said Brainstorm. "It might just bury us deeper."

"Did either of you see where the Joe-Bot with the cannon went?" asked Duke. "I figured it would come right after anyone or anything in the area around the destruction, but it looks like it zagged instead."

Brainstorm and Barrel Roll shook their heads.

The purr of a minigun sounded off in the direction in which Scarlett had supposedly been trapped. Brainstorm figured she was safe, but if that was the case, then what had the minigun been firing at?

"We should go check that out," Duke said. The others nodded, not saying a word.

They were about halfway to the dead-end entrance when another massive cannon shot went off. The boom came from the same direction as the minigun.

"Scarlett?" Duke said to the others. Brainstorm and Barrel Roll shrugged.

"I told her to meet me back where Krivo got shot," Brainstorm said. "I haven't had a chance to get back there yet."

Duke glanced back in the direction from which the noise had come. "I didn't hear her voice in all that. Let's head to the rally point first."

Duke led the way, double time, and Brainstorm and Barrel Roll followed right after. When they reached Krivo's body, they saw Destro glaring out at them through the wall of monitors. Scarlett was already standing there, ignoring him.

"Aye, you're a clever lot," Destro said. "I didn't suspect you'd survive this long."

"Two down, one to go," said Scarlett. She raised her crossbow by way of example. "I attached my comm plug to a bolt and fired it into the Joe-Bot with the minigun."

Barrel Roll grinned. "And then the cannon-bot took it out. Slick."

Scarlett favored him with a sly smile.

"That's great," said Brainstorm, "but another problem just struck me. We're still trapped by all the rubble blocking the door. Even if we manage to destroy the third Joe-Bot, we're stuck in here until we either starve to death or Cobra sends in troops to finish us off."

"This bunker is pretty old, I'm sure we can find a weak spot somewhere," said Scarlet.

"It'll take some searching," said Brainstorm. "Russia is all about hard things for a hard people in a hard land. They never could keep up with us technologically, but when they built something, they built it to last."

"You sound jealous."

Brainstorm shook his head. "Impressed. The Soviets took a different route than we did: simple things for the simple farmers who became their soldiers. They never would have created a G.I. Joe program of their own. They didn't trust technology enough."

"You think maybe they were right?" said Barrel Roll.

Brainstorm shrugged. "That depends on whether or not we get out of here alive."

Duke stared up at Destro. "Why don't you just push the self-destruct button now, and blow us all to hell?"

The silvered Scotsman smirked. "This isn't a spy movie," he said. "I don't leave high explosives sitting underneath millions of dollars of equipment in a secret base. They have an unfortunate tendency to go off when you'd least care for such things."

"Aren't you afraid we're going to take your game accounts and cut off access to all your money?" asked Barrel Roll.

Destro smirked. "First, the money we run through this operation is but a small sliver of our total revenues. Taking all of it would be little more than an annoyance, hardly a mortal blow. Second, I've already cut off access to those accounts from that installation. The servers wiped themselves clean the moment your clumsy technician there tripped our electronic security measures."

Duke grimaced. Brainstorm pointedly found a scorched section of floor to examine at that moment.

"You've already failed, Joes," Destro said. "Now you're just fighting to save your miserable lives. I haven't been watching you out of worry, but sport."

"You're a real bastard," Scarlett said.

"You Yankee lasses always say the most flattering things."

Brainstorm opened his mouth to mention to the other Joes the fact that the third Joe-Bot was out there somewhere still. If Destro was taking the time to chat with them, the only reason had to be that he wanted to slow them down until the murderous machine could find them.

Duke cut him off, though, with a curt wave of his hand. "That's enough out of you, Brainy."

Brainstorm knew right away that Duke had figured out what Destro was up to as well. He might have called him Storm, but never Brainy, no matter how angry he might be. Duke must have wanted Destro to think he had them under his silvered thumb. At the very least that meant the Cobra leader wouldn't be coming up with more ways to cause them grief.

The Joes still had a chance to get out of this alive, Brainstorm knew. And if they managed that, their mission wouldn't be nearly as much of a failure as Destro might think.

The last remaining Joe-Bot—the one with the devastating recoilless cannon—appeared at the end of a long corridor of server racks. It spun toward them, coming straight at the screens from which Destro leered down at the Joes. Brainstorm could hear it speeding in their direction, and he tapped Duke on the shoulder to let him know.

"Hey, Destro," Duke said. "We have something for you we'd like you to see. Next time around, we'll drop by to deliver it personally."

The Cobra leader squinted at the Joes, trying to puzzle out exactly what Duke might mean. Then Duke held open his palm to show the comm plug sitting in the center of it. Without even asking, Brainstorm knew it was on.

Duke tossed the comm plug straight at the screens, and it stuck between the ones that showed Destro's eyes. He and the rest of the Joes scattered fast after that. He didn't have to say a word.

Destro shook his head. "I don't know why we ever worry that G.I. Joe might present any sort of problem to us. If that's the best you can come up with—"

Destro cut himself off as he saw the final Joe-Bot charging toward him, a loaded shell locked and ready. The smirk melted from his face as the machine fired a high-explosive shell straight at the man's massive image.

The screens and the wall behind them disappeared in an earth-shaking detonation. A massive cloud of dust and ashes billowed out from the point of impact and made it impossible to see. When the air started to clear, Brainstorm saw that the shell had blown a hole clear through the wall. Sunlight streamed in from the outside, falling in streaky beams through the airborne mess.

"Yo, Joes!" Duke said. "Head through that breach!"

Brainstorm grabbed Duke's shoulder as Barrel Roll and Scarlett bolted out through the brand-new gaping hole, as ordered. "We can't leave the Joe-Bot behind," he said. "Not intact, at least. We can't let that tech fall into the wrong hands."

Duke hauled Brainstorm away from the corridor down which the last Joe-Bot still moved. "Isn't it too late for that?"

"The others have been effectively destroyed. I don't think Cobra's systems managed to upload anything from their CPUs.

Destro didn't seem to have any direct control over them at all."

"Got anything handy that can stop it?"

"We're all out of comm plugs," Brainstorm said, "but I think I may have the next best thing."

He pulled the control pad out of his pack and slapped the battery back into it. The screen blipped on, but the feed from Destro had been cut off. Brainstorm wasn't sure if the cannon fire had managed it or if the Cobra leader had shut the feed off on purpose, but it hardly mattered. With luck, the control pad would still serve his purpose.

"Got any of those grenades handy?" Brainstorm asked.

Duke plucked one from his belt and hefted it in his hand. "I don't know how I'm going to get close enough to use it."

"Just climb up on top of that rack and get ready," Brainstorm said. "There's an opening in the Joe-Bot's carapace right where the weapon mount's base sticks out of it. If you see a chance, stuff that pineapple in there and run."

"And what are you going to be doing during all this?"

"Trying to give you that chance."

Duke spun about and started climbing the nearest server rack. A moment later, he walked hunched over along their top, moving toward the Joe-Bot coming at him until they passed each other. Then he came back after it.

Brainstorm looked down at the control pad in his hand. If his theory was correct, he would be just fine. If he was wrong, well, at least he wouldn't have much time for regrets.

Brainstorm steeled himself and then stuck the control pad out into the corridor in front of the Joe-Bot. He waited for a moment with the control pad waving out there at the end of his arm and wondered the entire time if a shot from the cannon would kill him instantly or just blow off his arm and leave him to bleed to death.

Nothing happened.

Brainstorm leaned his head out after his arm and saw that

the Joe-Bot had ground to a halt about thirty feet away. It seemed to be staring straight ahead at the control pad, and Brainstorm had the distinct feeling that if the thing had a head it could have cocked at him it would have done just that.

Duke slipped down behind the Joe-Bot then, silent compared to the sound of the machine. As Brainstorm watched, the G.I. Joe field leader pulled the pin from the grenade in his hand and then jammed it inside the gap where the weapon mount met the Joe-Bot's carapace.

Duke turned and bolted away down the corridor. Brainstorm took this as his cue to run in top speed in the other direction. He made it about ten yards before the Joe-Bot detonated.

The grenade must have set off the Joe-Bot's remaining explosive shells. The explosion knocked Brainstorm off his feet, and he had several racks of servers between him and it at the time. It roared like thunder that rolled forever, and Brainstorm's head was still reeling when Duke scooped him up and set him back on his feet.

The entire complex seemed to be on fire now. Duke and Brainstorm kept their heads down against the smoke and raced for the newly made exit. Flames licked at its sides, but Duke grabbed Brainstorm by the arm and dragged him straight through it. They came through scorched but intact and fell into the waiting arms of Barrel Roll and Scarlett.

SEVEN

ONCE THE JOES were safely aboard the sleek black transport jetting them out of Russia, Duke asked Brainstorm the obvious question. "What the hell just happened back there?"

Brainstorm coughed his throat clear. "I ignored it at the time, but when we made our way into the facility something struck me as strange. Think about it: for Cobra's money laundering operation to work, that game lab should have been filled with live players, not unstaffed servers."

"Maybe they heard we were coming and simply cleared out," Barrel Roll called back from the cockpit. "Krivo must have told them."

"Sure, but you remember the monitors before Destro took them over?"

"They showed characters playing the games," said Scarlett.

"Right," said Duke, "but if there wasn't anyone there controlling them, then how did that work?"

"It seems that Cobra has developed a stunningly sophisticated software bot system—almost to the level of an artificial intelligence—to play the games for them," said Brainstorm. "They're years ahead of any other faction."

"They have programs pretending to be their characters?" asked Barrel Roll.

"And doing a frighteningly fine job of it," said Brainstorm. "When I hooked up my control pad to their network of servers to copy their accounts, the AI invaded *my* system instead. After that, it took over control of the Joe-Bots, copying itself into their limited memory. It could only rely on the Joe-Bots' sensors, but it was clever enough to realize it needed to shoot at the things the Joe-Bots' original programming was supposed to be protecting."

"And vice versa?" said Duke.

"Right. That's why it didn't shoot at me when I held up the control pad. It recognized the pad as one of its own kind."

"Did you know that was going to work?" said Barrel Roll.

"Yes." Brainstorm blew out a sigh. "Kind of."

"So tell me something," Scarlett said. "If the Joe-Bots and this entire operation were such a disaster, why are you smiling?"

Brainstorm hadn't realized he'd had a grin on his face until then. "Because we came out of there with something far more valuable than several million gold pieces in a fantasy-adventure MMO. As Destro said, that wouldn't have hurt Cobra much." He waved the control pad in front of the others.

"Don't tell me you have a copy of Cobra's AI on your control pad," said Barrel Roll.

Brainstorm nodded, his grin spreading across his face to infect the others.

Only Duke didn't crack a smile.

"What's wrong with you?" Barrel Roll asked. "We just turned a blown mission into a huge win. Doesn't that do anything for you?"

"Yes," Duke said. "We have a lot to feel good about. We did G.I. Joe proud."

"So then what's the trouble?" asked Scarlett.

"It's this Cobra AI that we discovered," Duke answered. "If it's really so sophisticated, does it seem likely that Cobra would only use it for hoaxing online games? Even Destro didn't seem to think it was all that big a deal."

"What would you expect him to say?" asked Scarlett.

"A billion here, a billion there. Before long it can add up to real money," noted Barrel Roll.

"Okay, okay," said Duke. "But still, I'm not so sure. We saw how this program easily took over Brainstorm's control pad and three of our cutting-edge automated weapons systems, and we simply stumbled upon it. If Cobra has something this powerful in its cyber arsenal, I find it hard to believe that they're only using it as a kind of online scam, even if it is on a global scale. There's got to be more to it than just a game."

Brainstorm frowned. His sense of triumph drained from him and left him feeling cold. "I see your point," he said. "They might be using the MMOs to train the AI. There are few better tactical challenges in the world than to pit a bot against countless players in endless battles with human minds from around the globe. They have to be using those experiences to hone the bot, to improve its programming every step of the way."

"And would they do that just so they could better move more money around?" asked Scarlett.

Brainstorm shook his head as that cold feeling coalesced into a lump of ice in his gut. "No way," he said. "It has to be for something far more important."

"My point exactly," said Duke. "Any idea what that might be?"

Brainstorm shook his head and stared down at the cracked screen of the precious control pad in his hands. "Haven't the first clue," he admitted. "Maybe they want to improve their BAT programming, or release the AI into the wild and take over the entire Internet. Could even be that it's training itself to run Cobra's strategic and tactical planning operations on a level that no flesh-and- blood leader—not even General Hawk—could ever touch."

"So it's impossible to tell?" said Duke.

Brainstorm shook his head. "Nothing's impossible. If Cobra can come up with it, we can stop it. We proved that today, although just barely. And as soon as we get back to the Pit, I'm going to pry into this thing's programming and puzzle out its ultimate purpose so we can do just that."

Message In A Bottle

JOHN SKIPP & CODY GOODFELLOW

DUDE, YOU'VE GOT to see this video. I can't stop watching it.

The whole assembly sequence runs less than five minutes, and syncs up wickedly with Metallica's "Damage Inc.", but this time, I'm watching it in super slo-mo, with Wagner's *Tannhauser* overture blasting on my earbuds. Even though I've seen it a hundred times, every time I watch it, I fall in love all over again.

Just in the last minute, I'm positive this guy Snake Eyes gets wasted at least twice.

But rewind it.

Freeze it, *there.*

The perimeter cameras at the Gursan 3 water treatment plant have night vision that turn the rain-streaked dark inside out. The half-flooded slums of Dhaka crush up against the twenty-foot hurricane fence, like Venice with twenty times the people and none of the money.

In a place this poor and overcrowded (11 to 13 million, but who's counting?), with the rising sea shrinking the available land and raw sewage flooding the few unpolluted freshwater sources, kids die every day of cholera and diarrhea.

Bangladesh has serious water problems and constantly simmering unrest, so naturally, the place that recycles their sewage and cleans their drinking water needs heavy protection. The shiny new filtration plant looks like an alien invader.

A generous donation from a hedge fund run by guys who actually earn their astronomical bonuses. My bosses.

The camera picks him up as he soars over the fence. Don't blink. That blurry black hole in the night, right there, moving between this frame and the next…that's him.

Note the checkpoint guard, sound asleep in his booth with a Bollywood magazine on his lap. Tape shows he was wide awake sixty seconds ago. The drug in his system will have metabolized long before he wakes up. The tiny delivery dart in his neck is made of sucrose, and will have melted before the police even arrive.

No other camera spots him outside the building, and there're twenty-four channels of video, including thermals, and four local guards walking the perimeter. He's just a thickening of the shadows running up the sheet metal of the plant's exterior and vanishing into the pipe spaghetti. A shadow of a shadow.

His suit drinks in the light and sheds no heat, no reflection. The whole Sharper Image catalog of gear on his web harness slows him not a bit as he slithers down the wall and freezes, waiting.

A Spider—autonomous security drone with a taser-turret for an abdomen—creeps right past him without trying to zap him. Its swiveling lenses show him close enough to touch without registering a twitch of motion.

It's almost like the cameras are afraid to see him. Almost as if he's supposed to be here.

When he finally pops up, it's at an outlying terminal overlooking the chemical extraction process. He's quick and thorough, ripping the LAN's dirty secrets onto a thumb-drive, then taking three samples of water from the clean tanks.

Only then does he climb a duct and crawl under it the length of the plant to the elevated control room, but he doesn't go in. He can see through the windows, plain as day, why he doesn't need to go in there.

The four civil engineers and the two chemists on duty are all dead. Sitting at their ergonomic swivel chairs, with their heads in their laps. Lopped off cleanly by a professional with a sword just like his.

I wish I could see the look on his face when he realizes he's been royally pwned. But he's wearing that damnable bug-eyed mask. And besides, that's when the guards come running.

The guys outside are local cutouts. The guys inside are better equipped, came from further away; they cost a lot more, and were told to expect him.

Like any of that matters.

This three-man fire team, they're bunched too close between the massive reclamation tanks, and they're not looking straight up. He's clinging to the underside of a pipe like a nasty black spider. He drops on them with a wicked samurai katana and a shorter *wakizashi*, the defense sword.

The long folded-steel blade licks out as he falls and chops the barrel off the point man's belt-fed automatic shotgun. The man jerks up, looking in amazement at his truncated gun. His flankers jump back and shoot, just as the intruder drops into a crouch and streaks between them. If they had half a chance, they'd shoot their own point man in the back in a blind panic, but the shadow throws out both swords. Now it's going to get wet.

The swords flash and both men fall, but not a drop of blood is spilled. The butt of each sword cracks a man in the temple and slams him into the wall of a tank.

What the hell kind of ninja is this guy?

Which leaves the point man. His teammates are down, and he's a soldier with most of a gun in his hands. What the hell is he supposed to do?

He shoots at the shadow, but the shadow is gone. His shotgun explodes. The reclamation tanks burst. At least the tons of raw sewage put out the fire.

The other three teams run to the action, but the trail's already cold. See him here, there, everywhere and nowhere. The only sure solution is to blow the whole place.

It doesn't take a whole lot of C4 to blow up a sewage treatment plant, if you know where the methane is.

The first explosions peel the roof back, then multiply as the flames roar through the pipes venting the highly flammable gas. The shadow goes out a skylight and springs from tank to standpipe to girder column just before each is awash in flaming, flying debris.

A team of mercs spots him and opens fire, sweeping the air, herding him into the fire. The clowns high-five each other, now it's Miller time.

They don't see him come out. He pops out of the overflow canal with barely a ripple. A patrol boat roars up the canal and lays down a curtain of fifty-caliber life preservers. When he pops up behind the boat, they're too bulky to turn and pursue, and he's riding something like a self-powered water ski.

A helicopter picks up his wake, if little else, and follows him into the channel. Two more patrol boats try to pinch him, but their converging rooster-tails of red-green tracer fire only strike sparks off each other's bowsprits.

The skier's back pops open and a weather balloon yanks him backwards and up out of the water. The balloon lifts the skyhook up about three hundred feet, when something too small to have a human pilot drops down out of the rain clouds and scoops the hook, ripping the black shadow-warrior out of view like a puppet just before the curtain closes.

Two thumbs way up.

But like any summer blockbuster, once the magic wears off, the questions start to pile up. What kind of ninja goes around with two swords and doesn't kill anybody? Who does this clown think he is? What kind of war does he think he's fighting? If both sides were playing this kind of kid's game, they might as well run around zapping each other with red and blue flashlights. But this is war, and any way you slice it, the other side is losing.

I've got epic spycam footage my man Error zipped me, of Snake Eyes wasting a whole nest of henchmen in the Swiss Alps a couple months ago, and the few he didn't shish-kabob, he consigned to die in a fire. Maybe he gave the Bangladesh operators the benefit of the doubt before he knew he was dealing with Cobra. Maybe he's just getting soft.

I'm probably the last guy who's going to see this awesome action epic in its uncut form. It doesn't matter that he didn't kill anyone. When we get done with it, the noble ninja is the dastardly heel who killed the civilians in the control room, and burned the whole place down.

The world leaders and intelligence moguls who watch the leaked final cut will see an elite American operator break into an ordinary water treatment plant that is saving tens of thousands of lives, and blowing it up. CNN and Fox will never get to show it, but the right people will, and they will conclude that America is out to destroy anyone it cannot control.

Sometimes you have to fudge the details to reveal a larger truth. You have to hit a deep sleeper pretty hard to wake them up.

I almost feel sorry for this guy, Snake Eyes. Because he shows me that I'm a warrior, too. I've never killed anyone with my own two hands, but if not for me and the people I work for, none of this would have happened at all.

The water plant in Bangladesh was a great way to help a poor, starving people live healthier lives. It was an even better way to test experimental psychological control medications on a whole population. The impacted slums of Dhaka are one missed meal away from major unrest and rioting. Certain elements of the government of Bangladesh had a vital interest in keeping them docile. My employers were all over that contract, or so we let them believe. A rogue WHO report from a fictional doctor who "disappeared," and some carefully laid conspiracy theory breadcrumbs all over the Net.

They sent a man to investigate, and stepped right into our trap.

MY GENERATION catches a lot of well-deserved flak for its apathy, but I have always been a freedom fighter. Injustice hurts, and indifference is like an infection. My curse is that I see it, where others just see business as usual. I thought the grades my school gave out were unfair, so I changed them. The bank tried to take away my parents' house. I moved their loan to a fictitious holding company the bank had set up to hide from taxes.

Nobody noticed.

They made me sick. They were so secure in their domination over the "land of the free" that they didn't even notice when you stole it back.

I am not a traitor to my country. I was born in the United States to parents who named me Gram Fensler, but I renounced my citizenship when I was still a minor. I did not declare war on my birth country. They made me a refugee, when they took my country away. I became a sovereign citizen of the Internet.

You probably don't remember my name. It wasn't in the headlines: "Teen Hacker Cracks Pentagon Network." I didn't change anything. I was just strolling along on the Internet, when I came across their locked door, and I went around it to peek at DARPA's research archives. Hell, I thought I was on their side. If they wouldn't have been such crybabies about it, I might've gone to work for them. If they had recognized for one moment the talent it took to do what I did, instead of punishing me for having the stones to do it, I might be working for G.I. Joe today.

I didn't break the laws of my adopted country, which begin and end with the assumption that information wants to be free. If they didn't want someone to pry into their secrets, why did they leave them laying around where any kid with a knack for cryptography could crack them?

My federal jail sentence was suspended, but I was banned from Internet access. It would violate my parole to touch anything more advanced than an adding machine.

Almost old enough to drive and I was a marked man. Don't know what I would've done, if not for Cobra.

I was moving out of my parents' garage and combing the want ads when I got a call about a job interview. Somebody wanted me to go down to the Cayman Islands and help set up a data haven. I was seventeen. What would you do?

Long story short, three years later, I was living and working on an island. On a good day, I didn't see a single living human being. But every day, I handled secrets that the NSA would kill for.

IT'S ONE of the smallest of the Maldives, near the end of the Chagos Archipelago. About forty tribal natives lived on it until the local friendly dictator cleared them out after the tsunami in '04, and turned it over to us. The island isn't big enough to play football on, but they built three levels of bunkers into the coral and lava rock. Technicians and consultants would fly in and out, but most of the time, it was just me and four "hardware specialists."

On paper, the island was an unmanned weather satellite tracking station. In reality, it was the hub of the Undernet.

My new country.

From our distributed network of servers in China and Transnistria (it's a real country, look it up!), we sent encrypted streams to friendly and weak satellites, but most of the traffic went through blue laser arrays. My little underwater laser light show was the main artery of a black market information network that had its own stock market, its own Craigslist, its own eBay. One-stop solutions for the embattled dictator or the guerilla on the go. We made invisible backdoors for billions to change hands, for state secrets and terrorist threats to be traded like pork-belly futures. We ran scams that made the Nigerian 419 money-bomb look like the March of Dimes.

And we worked on our tans.

Anyway, the other guys did. There wasn't much for them to do, because nobody ever came within fifty miles of us without inviting themselves first. Fences and electronic barriers kept anything bigger than an angelfish out of the lagoon, and the sharks kept anything smaller than themselves from getting to shore. Two automated missile batteries tracked the empty skies, and if anything got past all that, my roommates were more than ready to make their island vacation a memorable one.

The guards rotated off the island every six weeks for R&R in Thailand. Maybe watching me crunch code was a plum assignment. It certainly wasn't punishment. Cobra doesn't punish slackers with island duty. It feeds them to trees.

Yeti was the team leader. He was a true professional; hated my guts, but hid it well. He spoke English with a sliver of an accent, but I never found out where the hairy bastard came from, or how he came to work for Cobra.

Rijs was an Afrikaaner, and he did a lousy job of hiding his problem with me. He spent most of the days topside, playing the role of a communications engineer and feeding hand grenades to sharks.

Blinky might've been Russian or Ukrainian, but asking him would only piss him off. His right eye was glass, and a size too large or small, or something, because he always squinted like it had sand on it. He never spoke and he had no fingerprints, but his tats screamed *Solntsevskaya Bratva*, the Muscovite Mafiya. It took a while to transcribe the jumble of Cyrillic slogans and the phonebook of names on his arms and back, but it was a list of dead comrades and slain enemies.

They weren't all badass barbarians. The other IT guy was supposed to be this hot-dog code wizard, but aside from embedding the head office's video conferences into the errors on BitTorrent traffic, I never saw him do any actual work. Rakko was an Ainu, the redheaded stepchildren of Japan. The other guys didn't like him, either.

Most of the time, I handled the whole operation myself. The other guys' primary job was to stay out of my way. Every day, federal and corporate snoops tripped over one of our many busy tentacles in cyberspace. It was my job to send them away thinking they'd found junk, and scratching away at spybots and malware like digital crablice.

After the first year, I flatly turned down R&R. I hated coming back to find someone else in my seat, and all my preferences fragged. Even more, I hated the possibility that I might miss something.

LIKE THIS:

There's an almost *Oz*/Pink Floyd synchronicity to the Costa Rican operation, when you watch it with this mashup I made of "Mars, Bringer Of War" and "Yackety Sax" on the headphones.

Costa Rica doesn't have its own military, which kind of puts them in an awkward position when a covert microchip factory and terrorist HQ turns up inside their borders.

The Joes have come a long way to get here. I almost pity them. When the Brazilian stock market collapsed three months ago under a malware swarm, two billion in investments vaporized, and Rio's financial moguls claimed it was an American attack. After combing the network data, the Americans blamed the Chinese, just as we wanted them to. The attack had all the earmarks of their state-sponsored hackers, but there was no trail. When it happened again in Singapore, the bright boys finally caught on. The attacks weren't coming from outside their firewalls, but from within their hardware.

The microchips in both stock exchanges' networks came from Stellanova, a new but already huge power player in microchip manufacture that was close to competing with Intel on the global market. You can imagine how damaging an accusation would be if it got into the press, and how hard it was to cover up, when thirty thousand chips spontaneously succumbed to a "bit rot" defect at the exact moment that the common thread in the crashes came to light.

All things considered, a chip factory would be a perfect Cobra front. They handle chemicals that the Nazis banned for use in warfare—stuff that turns water to hydrofluoric acid, for instance. No end of dangerous toys they could deploy, if cornered. G.I. Joe came armed for bear.

Before the Costa Rican government even knew what was coming, G.I. Joe had a task force in San Jose. They swept the factory floors and clean rooms, vetted all the geeks and suits before lunch, and came up with nothing. Stellanova was cooperative, and proved that the chips must have been counterfeit...but they were arsed if they could explain how someone replaced their products en masse with diabolically buggy fakes.

Pathetic. Without our help, they'd never even find their way into our trap.

A customs official in San Jose who didn't show for work turned up instead hanging in the spacious walk-in closet of his big house, with a neatly printed note detailing his shameful role in helping replace Stellanova's microchips with identical fakes for a criminal syndicate he knew only as *los culebras*. Though he didn't know who they were, he left bank account information and a cell number, and a GPS heading for the location of the chip factory, in the mountainous jungle near the Nicaraguan border.

Cue tape.

The Costa Rican Security Minister meets Scarlett and Breaker at the airport, then joins them on their helicopter. His own tactical guys are riding with the other Joes—Roadblock, Tunnel Rat, and Recondo.

Costa Rica may not have an army, but no country lasts long enough to make a flag, unless it has soldiers. Ricardo Uribe is a ramrod-stiff top cop, with a legendary record for corruption busting. They sweep him for bugs. The little wand doesn't beep when it passes over the tie-tack camera we put on him.

A redheaded vision quirks an apology of a smile at him as she pronounces him clean. The fish-eye lens effect isn't too flattering, but damn...I'm in love.

"You couldn't possibly have known," Scarlett says, the velvet edge slicing through her diplomacy, "what you're dealing with."

"We will not agree to a full-scale operation," the Minister interrupts. "This group you warn us has infiltrated our country...we are not familiar with it at all. But if they are a criminal enterprise, we have law enforcement capabilities of our own, and if they are a terrorist organization...well, wouldn't we have heard of them?"

They look at each other for a long moment, trying to decide how much to say, whether to reveal how little they really know. "Cobra has used crime and terror and chaos for profit, but not even we know for sure what their end game is. The only thing we can tell you for certain is that your country is not prepared for them."

You got that right, beautiful.

Below the chopper, the misty mountains of rain forest rise up, then plunge into valleys of perpetual fog. Somewhere down below is the spot where the customs agent received his orders. Satellite scanning shows a small tilapia farm in a clearing, with half a dozen shallow rectangular pools around a rusty sheet-metal shack. Thermal imaging shows the shack is ten degrees cooler than the outside air. It doesn't take a genius like me to figure the shack is sitting on a ventilation shaft for a major underground installation.

Breaker's running the pair of recon drones circling the insertion site. They're not supposed to be armed with any weapons. But in the right hands, they *are* weapons.

And those hands are *mine*.

Breaker. I've never met the man, but I've outbid him time and again on Lone Ranger merchandise on eBay, and I've clobbered his gimpy ass on Xbox Live more times than

I count. Kind of guy who stops at red lights when he's playing *GTA IV*.

One of the recon drones pops up out of the fog and swoops across the helicopter's nose. "Breaker, stop showing off."

"I'm not running them, Scar." He texts the Basement, where a couple geeks like me are bashing their joysticks against their tables in helpless rage.

Uribe pops up. "What's the meaning of this? Aren't those your planes?"

Not anymore!

They still have a lot of options. The chopper is bristling with missiles, and armed with a directional EMP pulse that can knock them out of the air. But none of this stuff comes into play before the scout drone pops a heat-seeking cap into their tail rotor.

The chopper spins out of control, the human cargo flung into the walls like wet laundry in a washing machine. Uribe fouls the tie-tack camera's view with his blood.

Cut to the drone's nose camera. White-out as the drone climbs out of the fluffy cumulus clouds hanging over the active Arenal volcano, then the clouds part and the cotton-candy canopy of the jungle appears and swallows the falling chopper.

The other chopper banks and cleaves close to the treetops, spraying countermeasure chaff like candy from a piñata. Any second now, they'll come around and light my drone up with Hellfire missiles. The drone is just stubby wings, twin VTOL thrusters and a fuselage stuffed with CPUs and fuel, and a missile rack and a Gatling gun pod that were a huge pain in the ass to arm. Its skin is a black polymer that's harder to track with conventional radar than the continued appeal of *Firefly*. But if he shoots as good as he maneuvers, the pilot will be able to knock me out of the sky by dead reckoning.

I sit back in my seat and sip a Black Mountain Dew and pick my nose. Then I pick up the joystick and hit the button to kill them.

The missiles lock on and swoop down and converge on the chopper. (Would it be too much to ask, to put cameras in the missile nosecones? Just sayin'…) Then they pass through the drifting cloud of sparkling chaff, and go haywire. One dips and disappears into the trees without detonating, while the other spins off like an epileptic hummingbird.

The chopper comes around and kicks off two Hellfires.

The drone climbs right into the sun, overloading the nosecone camera. The missiles smash into my belly.

I spill my soda.

DISSOLVE TO Uribe's tie-tack camera. Smoke, sparks, cursing. The pilot and co-pilot are toast. Scarlett's right arm is broken, and her face is dappled with blood from a nasty gash in her forehead. Breaker and Uribe carry her out of the wreck.

The wind stirs the trees. Howler monkeys criticize their landing. "Doesn't this place seem a little mellow for a Cobra operation?" Breaker asks.

"It's cold," Scarlett shoots back. "It's a trap, and we walked into it."

"No need for your enemies to stay around," Uribe cuts in, "if they can use your own weapons against you."

Roadblock's voice booms out of their headsets. "Had it up to here with those toys of yours, Breaker."

"I tried to tell you guys," Breaker whines, "we got hacked." Punching a touchscreen on something that only looks like an iPhone, he adds, "I'm locked out of them, and the Basement, too. Our whole IT capability has been thoroughly owned by a professional."

I know there's no action, but pardon me while I watch it again.

"Our whole IT capability has been thoroughly owned by a professional."

Uribe sets Scarlett down against a leaning tree. "We were shot down by your own reconnaissance drones?"

"The group we're fighting has capabilities—"

"That outmatch your own. I think my country could do no worse than you, in handling this group…"

"We'll take them down together," Scarlett says, groggy but resolute. Tying off a sling for her broken arm with her teeth. Damn, this lady's tough. "Roadblock, we're down two men, and need a medic. What's your ETA?"

"I'm still playing tag with the other drone…I think…I keep getting missile lock-on messages, but the onboard CPU is buggy. There can't be that many of them out there…"

The tilapia farm is only a hundred yards away, across an open field. The spawning ponds are all drained, dead fish rotting on cracked mud, but nobody has eyes to see that, now.

Uribe helps Scarlett to her feet, all smoldering Latin gallantry. You've made a powerful enemy today, hombre…

Breaker staggers back towards the wreck. "Wait, I can't leave this on the chopper."

"It'll keep, Breaker, let's move…"

Breaker climbs in the open door to reach for a big, cumbersome case. It should be too heavy for a geek like him to lug, but it comes away in his hand so easily, it cracks him under the chin. The case falls open. It's empty.

"Well, this is going to be hard to explain…"

Breaker doesn't have time to tell Scarlett what was supposed to be in the case, but I know.

An eight-foot articulated titanium snake, the Inch Worm was designed for cave reconnaissance in Afghanistan, but this new model has some sweet mods. Thermal cameras, chemical sampling sensors, a sixty-thousand-volt burst taser, a blowtorch, and a pair of linked bullpup twelve-gauge shotguns for fangs.

Friggin' sweet hardware.

It's just like eBay, buddy. Nothing you can bid on, that I can't take away.

Cut to the snake's eye view. I toggle over to manual control.

The Inch Worm's AI is so good it'll autonomously take out these clowns and anything else that moves, but I haven't played a good first-person shooter in ages.

The Inch Worm rears up out of the crushed cockpit and zaps Breaker dead-bang in the solar plexus. The arc of blue lightning blows him off his feet to crash head-first into a tree. Game over, noob.

Its blunt hammerhead swivels and pumps a salvo of depleted uranium buckshot into the spot Uribe stood on a split-second ago. He dives for Scarlett, but my girl's already rolling into the high grass, sidearm drawn and snapping off shots at my titanium dome.

They plink off my undulating serpentine body like spitballs. I can afford to be merciful. In the time it'll take Roadblock to shake the game Rakko's running on him, I can bag her and Breaker both and score huge brownie points with the company. Our recon boys are in the jungle, watching.

Which reminds me—where's Uribe?

I whip around faster than I meant to, before I realize what's going on. The Costa Rican cop has me by the tail, and cracks me like a bullwhip. My shotguns discharge into a rock. I coil around his arm once hard enough to crush his wrist bones. The taser is trashed. The blowtorch spits a blue-white tongue of oxyacetylene flame over his shoulder. I've almost got his bulging eyes and bushy monobrow in my sights.

Then my POV does cartwheels over the grass and comes to rest against a rock, looking back at my favorite frenemy, holding a machete.

What the hell is Breaker doing still standing?

Wobbly, but looking good for a guy who rode the lightning just a minute ago. I should have figured any geek who carries three laptops into combat would wear an insulated flak suit.

He cut off my head. With one stroke, the pencil-neck chopped the head off a robotic killing machine. I really need to learn to hate this guy more.

"Impressive," says Scarlett, my little mindreader.

"No big deal," Breaker wheezes. "I read the manual."

"My phone isn't picking up anything," Uribe says. "It seems we're being jammed…"

The conversation dies as they hear a faint growl grow to a roar almost overhead. Scarlett and Uribe run out into the clearing to flag down Roadblock's chopper, but they really should've listened closer. It's not helicopter rotors they hear. It's the afterburners on Rakko's drone.

It's like a beautiful reboot of *North By Northwest*, as Uribe and Scarlett race across the grass field and the empty fishponds with the drone buzzing them and hacking up the earth with its Gatling guns.

They dive and hug the ground as it passes. When the dust settles, I almost wrest control of the drone from Rakko. I've lost enough credits playing dogfight simulators with the jerk to know he could have stitched them up if he really wanted to. Either he's still trying to bring them back alive, or he's been watching the Snake Eyes video too many times, too.

Killing by remote control is easy, if you're not too fussy about who gets in the way.

Uribe gets up and grabs Scarlett by the arm, runs for the shack. As if that sheet metal roof is going to save them. Scarlett shakes him off and outruns him while scanning the treetops for the drone with that adorable crossbow.

The drone comes back around and frames a nice zooming wide shot of our quarry.

I fire off an IM to Rakko. *Finish the job.*

The ground comes unzipped under the drone's pounding Gatling gun. A cute little baby missile drops off the fuselage and then shoots ahead on a lance of white fire.

Uribe throws an arm around Scarlett and crashes through the flimsy tin door. The sound of his scream, so high for a big tough top cop, is priceless.

Two steps into the shack, he steps on empty darkness.

Holding Scarlett, he twists as they both fall into the open shaft that yawns to fill the entire floorspace. The pit swallows them up just in time.

Cut to the drone's eye view. The missile is made for knocking armored convoys off desert roads, not bunker-busting, but it blows the shack apart with an impressive fireball.

The blackness filling the Uribe screen goes Halloween orange for a moment. Lying at the bottom of a twenty-foot vertical shaft, Scarlett throws Uribe off her and covers him with her lithe yet armored body. The fireball pancakes at the bottom of the collapsed ventilation shaft, lighting up the cave. The brunt of it passes over their heads.

When she gets up, her body armor is scorched and smoking and her hair singed a few inches shorter on one side, but she's healthy enough to smile at the cop. "Still want to take them on alone?"

Uribe looks even dumber without any eyebrows. "Commander Scarlett…if there are such monsters as these at play in Costa Rica, we can none of us ever afford to be alone again."

Ugh. Gross. Cut, already.

EVEN THOUGH I didn't manage to kill them, the head office called the operation a success. The Costa Rican government wasn't as impressed with G.I Joe as Uribe was, and refused further cooperation. Venezuela, Cuba, and the other usual suspects accused the U.S. of fabricating the threat. But confidence in the world stock markets took a sustained hit for about six weeks after the Stellanova chip rot situation was resolved. I didn't score any G.I Joe heads for our wall, but my bosses still made a killing.

When I got back to my room that night, I found a nice surprise waiting for me. The supply plane had dropped off my favorite Internet swimsuit model, and she was very happy to see me. She's a redhead too. And even if she wouldn't remember who I am in the morning, tonight, she really made me feel like a hero.

AFTER THAT, I got deeper access. I didn't know there was deeper access.

I got to see so many things. They knew I was watching, reading their mail. They knew what I am, because it led me to them. They had to know I was watching everything.

I got this assignment that seemed routine at first, almost a waste of my talents, but if they tapped me for it, then it must be important. I had three fake Indian passports, and a batch of doctored articles and citations to plant in the Internet to create a trail, a fake persona convincing enough to pass the cursory (doesn't it bother you how nobody knows what that word really means?) search by TSA and Customs officials.

In the old days, you could get a passport with a birth certificate, so most fakes were issued in the names of dead infants. Now, digital technology allows any mouth-breathing TSA luggage-monkey to fumble in the dark like a real private investigator. But because they're still just amateurs, they stop looking as soon as they find something. A nervous immigration agent could Google these guys and find out everything I wanted them to find in ten seconds.

I had done this before, but these trails had to be more sophisticated, because these guys weren't just smugglers and thugs posing as foreign exchange students. They were to enter the U.S. as medical doctors from Mumbai, with records and degrees and even articles and blogs in Hindi about curbing STDs. They were going to the United States on six-month visas to attend seminars on epidemiology and public health at the CDC in Atlanta.

I got their trails planted in half a shift, and if they didn't want me to start getting snoopy, they should've sent me more busy-work.

I nursed my burning curiosity for all of a half hour. Rakko was in his hammock, watching cartoons. I didn't know the real names of the three geeks I was smuggling into the States, so I took their pictures and sequenced the pixel data, then searched the day's boundless gigs of encrypted communications for a match.

I found three. I only opened the latest one.

It had a long, vague progress report on something called Operation Stagger that put me to sleep halfway through, but the pictures of my three new friends all appeared.

They were doctors, all right, but none of them ever made anyone healthier. All of them were recruited or abducted from a radical splinter faction of the Hindi nationalist party Shiv Sena, which pledged to reduce their Muslim neighbors to the "outer aspect of dogs."

Though dismissed as an urban legend, they were blamed for a slew of viral outbreaks that wreaked havoc in Pakistan but stopped with uncanny efficiency in Kashmir, at the Indian border. These geeks were supposed to be unmatched at splicing viruses that targeted specific ethnic groups. Their real records were wiped off the Net by somebody with a bigger magic wand than me.

And there was a big fat juicy video file, just begging to be unzipped and played.

It's from a traffic camera, overlooking a busy intersection in Indonesia or Thailand. Tuk-tuks and bicycles swarm around water trucks and hundred-headed snakes of rushing pedestrians charge into crosswalks under the shrill whistle and waving baton of a traffic dictator.

Slow it down. The man in the crowd crossing the street is just a hat among dozens of others, and the puff of mist that wafts up around him could be the smoke from a cigarette, or the exhaust from a car.

The dense discipline of the pedestrians dissolves into a deranged mob. The cop blasts his whistle and tries to part the crowd like Moses, but his military bearing goes all freshman spring break on him. His spastically waving arms tell everybody to go at once.

Men and women stumble into the grills of trucks and thrust their vomiting faces into the open windows of cars. A tuk-tuk charges across the intersection, knocks down a woman with a baby, and tips over. The infected pedestrians struggle to get into the thick of traffic, their movements as frantic as they are impaired, crazy to spread their disease.

With drunken maniacs climbing up the sides of his tanker truck, one driver finally loses it and charges into the intersection, crushes the overturned tuk-tuk, and mows down dozens of walkers on his way out of the frame. As a truckload of policemen arrive to clobber sense into the growing chaos, a tour bus stops in the middle of the intersection...

I can't take any more.

AND THEN I got this e-mail from my Mom.

Just a link to a news item. She doesn't say much because she's still kind of sore about my problems with the Pentagon, and she has no idea where I am or what I'm doing, and she still doesn't know the Internet too well.

It was a link to a news article about this recent university study, the kind of perennial junk science that makes for good water cooler talk. She sent me every one of these linking too much computer use to schizophrenia or cell phones and brain tumors, but this one, I read.

It showed how these doctors were able to suppress the moral judgments of test subjects by stimulating the temporo-parietal region of the brain. For those non-brain-surgeons in the house, this is the bunch of gooey gray stuff above and behind the right ear. In the tests, patients with electrodes on their heads got mild electrical jolts, too mild to feel on the scalp, that disrupted the neuron firing in their brains. As a result, they were way more likely to approve of violence committed against others.

I took off my headphones. Big Bose TriPort noise-cancellation ear-goggles. Magnets in them the size of car stereo speakers, and a bead microphone transmitting and recording my every breath.

I thought about the water treatment plants in Bangladesh. It seemed like a good idea at the time. I mean, how else to pacify an angry, overcrowded city as it slowly drowns?

I thought about the chip rot scam in Costa Rica, and the counterfeit anti-virus updates we made that crashed every hospital in the Western hemisphere, last New Year's Eve. All the ways we—I—had worked to make my bosses richer, and give them power over the disasters the rest of the world called acts of God.

I thought about the choices I'd made, and let them make for me.

And damn me, if I didn't start to feel bad.

Thanks, Mom!

I MADE these choices myself. I hadn't gone in blind. I thought that the people who were getting hurt were stupid, so they deserved it. I thought that if someone was worth saving, they'd never even show up on our radar.

I could live with the decisions I'd made. But suddenly, I started to suspect that my choices had not always been my own. I was the worst kind of blind man: the kind who thinks he can see.

I wasn't sitting at my workstation bawling my eyes out. I went back to work, but didn't seem to get anything done for another hour. And I didn't put on my headphones.

I put them on the minute I got out of bed every day, on the rare occasions when I didn't fall asleep in my ergonomic office chair. I sometimes had bad dreams, but I took meds for them, thoughtfully provided by our company's generous health plan. What was in them? I only knew they worked.

What the hell was wrong with me? The company had never given me reason to doubt, never hid anything from me before, but did that mean there was nothing to hide? Or just that they had hidden it from me as successfully as I helped hide them?

If paranoia is really perfect awareness, then my Mom had just made me a Buddha.

And why should I care? Because they were bringing these guys to America, the country that had cut me out of its heart for doing what I thought I was born to do? It served them right, all the trouble I could cause for them, and if my work didn't wake up the American people to how screwed their leaders were, then they didn't deserve to be saved.

Right then, I found myself hoping that someone had been brainwashing me.

Rakko came into the control room with a big mug of green tea. His sleepy eyes were hooded, but more shifty than usual. "I been pinging you, home slice. What's up with your ears?"

I looked up at him, trying to remember what innocence looks like. He was pointing at my headphones. I shrugged. "Ear infection, man. Been kind of tender all day."

"You want some tea?"

"No, I took some antibiotics. I'll be fine." Why was he suddenly so concerned about my health?

Rakko sat at his terminal and checked his e-mail. He wore an earbud headset. I'd never seen him without it. He was always whispering to someone in Japanese. Despite all those years of anime, I never picked up more than a few phrases.

On a remote desert island, cell phones shouldn't work at all, but Rakko had set up a secure microcell off our computer network that used a tunneling proxy to access Google voice texting.

I'd checked out his records, and found he was shooting the bull with other *otaku* on a party line, swapping bootleg torrents and funky fan mods that render the characters in *Final Fantasy IXX* naked, or something. Rakko was an old-school phone phreak, and apparently the head office didn't consider this unsanctioned activity a security risk, so why should I be worried?

"You look beat, my main man," Rakko offered. He was an hour early for his shift. "Why don't you catch a nap? I'll take over."

I usually had to drag his ass out of his hammock to get him to cover me. "Why, am I going to miss something good?" The French President's wife might be sunbathing in Cannes, again. Or they were already suspicious and wanted Operation Stagger out of my hands.

He took something out of his medicine bag and pressed it into my palm. "Take these," he said. His drooping eyes were fixed on me, trying to impress on me something he couldn't say. "It'll fix you right up, dude."

"I told you, man, I'm fine!" I'd said it too loudly, so I tried to make it a joke. "Get off my case, toilet-face!"

Rakko cracked up. He loved American potty humor.

"Just come back in a while, man," I told him. "I'm working on a special project." Finger to lips, I added, "I could tell you, but I'd have to kill us both."

That, at last, seemed to put him off. "Okay, dude...buzz me when it's go time, okay?"

Rakko shuffled out of the control room. I waited until I heard him get in the elevator—headed up, to the surface—then I opened another file.

The modified encephalitis virus is easily transmitted via aerosolized mist, and aggressively penetrates the sinus membranes and the blood-brain barrier to begin incubation in brain cells in Stage I.

Stage I lasts an average of forty-five seconds.

In Stage II, the rapidly proliferating virus causes traumatic swelling of the brain, inhibiting motor reflexes, pain receptors, and short-term memory, while flooding the body with acetylcholine, creating a fight-or-flight panic response that maximizes transmission of the virus throughout Stage II, which concludes when the virus has consumed too much of the victim's brain to allow continued activity.

Stage II lasts an average of two to six hours. Mortality projections from 72 hours on are above 90%.

Dr. Chandrasekhar admits that the modified virus is too volatile to follow the prescribed Pathan vectors he wrote into its code, but it should be more than sufficient for deployment in Operation Stagger...

I paused for a moment with my headphones in my hands. These Hindi lunatics had tried to make a disease that would only eat the brains of Pathan, or Afghani, victims. And when it turned out too deadly, or their own people turned on them, they had come to Cobra. And Cobra was sending them and their little gift to America. It wasn't a prank. It wasn't a scam, or a trap to make America look foolish. It was biological warfare.

Did I really have a problem with that?

I sat down and wrote Mom a note.

Hi Mom,

Long time no see… Nice to know you still worry. I'm fine, but it'd be good to hear your voice.

I sent the message. It was encrypted and forwarded through a chain of dummy addresses before it ended up in my mom's AOL mailbox. I had never replied to one of her messages before, because I knew it couldn't be her.

Even before my troubles, Mom was about as computer literate as a New Guinea headhunter. When she said she wanted help starting a blog, and I opened a blank Word document and told her that was her website, it took her two years to figure it out.

After I made them infamous, Mom hated computers like her mother hated the cigarettes and whiskey that killed Granddad. I doubt she went out and bought herself one after I ran away. I figured those messages, sent to my old CTS.net address every year around my birthday, had to be someone fishing for me.

I sat back and cleared the screen, opened up my next assigned task, but I was looking right through it when my e-mail avatar appeared and mooned me.

Call the old number. We're still there. You can still come home.

HOME.

I've seen my home by piggybacking on a KH-7 satellite, and I know that it was foreclosed two years ago, like almost every other house on my old block. The windows are boarded up and someone burned an anarchy symbol into the brown lawn, and some killjoy filled the drained swimming pool with sand so kids would stop skateboarding in it.

What I was about to do was too important to stop and think about. I needed to be convinced. I still remembered my old home phone number. It was a stupid thing to do, but I thought I was covering my tracks pretty well by using Rakko's microcell line.

She picked up on the second ring.

"Hi, Mom."

"You know better than that, don't you?"

I took a good couple of breaths before I could speak. I hadn't expected to hear my mother's voice, but I hardly expected to hear *her*.

The beautiful redhead I tried to kill last month.

"Is this a secure line?" I asked.

"Are you trying to be funny? It's not my end of the line you need to worry about."

"I can guarantee it for about two more minutes, so talk to me, Scarlett."

"We know who you're working for, and we know them better than you do. You think this is all a game."

"I'm not in a position to turn on the people who took me in when America screwed me."

"You're on Island 179 in the Chagos Archipelago. You like to go skinny-dipping at night. Your *World of Warcraft* character has way too much manna invested in chaos magic. And you could have killed me and my team in Costa Rica, if you really wanted to."

Lady, you had me at skinny-dipping...

"Listen, honey. I'm not saying I know what the hell you're talking about, but I don't owe my country anything, and I owe you guys even less. You're just another gang of goons defending the right of your country's bastards to walk all over the rest of the world. If you've been around the same places

I've seen, you know people are starting to realize that global survival is a zero-sum game. They're not going to keep dying for the American way of life. If you clowns have to work a little harder to protect the status quo, maybe things will have to change."

"That's a nice speech. Did they write it for you?"

"You don't even really know who they are, do you?"

"And you do?"

"You've got less than thirty seconds. What are you prepared to offer me?"

"Safe passage home. Amnesty, if you cooperate."

"If I rat on my employers. Enter witness protection and hide for the rest of my life from people you can't even find without a guide. Thanks, but—"

"How would you like a new job?"

"Your time is up."

She didn't try to say anything else before I cut her off.

My avatar mooned me again. I opened another e-mail from Mom, called Mom's Recipes.

I dug in and found a decrypted batch of our old internal files—all, I must add, from before I took the job.

It was the kind of stuff I'd been ordered never to touch, but hacked on my first day. Most of it was mind-numbing junk: coded invoices from Destro to various anonymous clients; oblique personal communiqués from Xamot to Tomax, whom I've always believed were dual identities to one highly toxic lunatic; dossiers on the perversions of various third-tier world leaders and CEOs.

This batch was different. Bills of lading for weapons to both sides of every civil war and tribal massacre in Africa. Gloating reports on terrorist actions in Moscow, blamed on Chechen rebels. Foiled plots to steal nuclear waste from Yucca Mountain to make a dirty bomb...which would've been extra embarrassing for Uncle Sam since, officially, there was no nuclear waste at Yucca Mountain.

My stomach chewed on broken glass. My eyes burned, but I couldn't blink. These people I worked for...they didn't hate anyone, they fought for no one's liberation, and they wanted only one thing from the world: its total surrender.

Someone grabbed me by the neck and shook. "Dude, the Keyhole's over Miami Beach! Spring Break-U!"

I closed the screen with a wave of my hand, opening a zombie movie forum to hide my shame.

He shoved me gently out of the chair. "My line was busy, dude. Who was that on the phone?"

"My mom."

Rakko looked at me like I'd just said, *I quit.* "You called your home?"

"It was scrambled and I didn't tell her anything. You talk to freaks in Japan all damn day and night. And anyway, do you think I want my mom to know where I am, or what I'm doing?"

"My mother thinks I'm dead." He sounded kind of proud. Rakko plugged his headset into the console and cleared the screens without looking at them, brought his current game up. A version of *Katamari Damacy* using the NSA's global satellite models, it let him roll a giant sticky ball down the streets of Dubai, rolling up endless fleets of Mercedes and Ferraris as Bedouins mournfully ululated from the roof of the Burj.

I felt a need to explain some more, to cover my trail, but he'd already forgotten me.

I double-timed it back to my room. The elevator from the surface came down just as I closed my door. I watched Rijs come down the corridor and go into the control room.

I stood in the corridor, just out of sight, just in earshot.

"How long you been on duty, man?" Rijs demanded.

Rakko just put his feet up and made a farting noise with his mouth.

About three seconds later, I heard two shots.

For another three seconds, I hid behind my door, trying to

get into character. What would a totally clueless, innocent person do, in this situation? He wouldn't be here at all.

I charged out into the corridor and almost knocked heads with Rijs. His gun poked a new belly button in my churning gut. "What the hell, man? No guns in the house—"

Before I could react, Rijs grabbed me by the collar of my sweatshirt and dragged me back to the control room. "Your yellow boyfriend just screwed us, man."

Rakko sat in the captain's chair with his head back. Whatever else he'd done, I couldn't fault Rijs for making a mess. He must've put the barrel of the gun right to the crown of Rakko's skull before he pulled the trigger. The screens before him were only lightly dappled with blood.

When I saw—and smelled—Rakko, I didn't have to pretend. "Why—what did you—what did he do, that you had to kill him?"

Rijs went to the console and punched in a code I didn't recognize. The telecom queue popped up. "This little bastard just made a call to the United States."

"So what? You think it's your job, now, to second-guess what we do?"

"That's *exactly* my job, man. You think anyone here trusts you little weasels, you got another think coming." Highlighting the phone number for my old house, Rijs double-clicked, and a global map showed up. The number I'd called showed up somewhere in Nevada, but then it bounced around the world. "Whoever he called wasn't really in America, it seems. They're in the air over the Indian Ocean, about two hundred miles north, but closing fast."

"Who—who was it? What did he say?"

"I don't know, but you'd better believe we're going to get to the bottom of this." He punched up the internal security cameras and hunted until he found Yeti and Blinky in the gym. They were sparring, and they kept dancing around punching each other in the head as Rijs tried to hail them. "Bloody damn intercom. Didn't you fix it?"

"You've made a big mistake, Rijs. The company's going to cut off your ears."

Spinning Rakko's chair around so the corpse stared accusingly at me, Rijs lit a hand-rolled cigarette. "When they hear I clipped a spy, they're going to give me a bonus. Unless…" He took out his knife and a whetstone and made the blade sing like a tuning fork, pointed at me. "Unless maybe I got the wrong spy."

"So, so what…what're we going to do now?"

"Our missiles are going to shoot them out of the sky, man. But this operation is totally compromised."

I went to the backup console, opposite Rakko. "I'd better let the head office know what's going on…"

Rijs's fingers around my neck lifted me off the floor. "D'you think I'm new, computer-boy? If the company finds out we're on lockdown because somebody talked, they'll kill all of us, just to be sure. We're going to the gym to see Yeti, and then we'll decide who gets to know what."

I had to get ahead of this thing. Rijs knew about the call, but he obviously hadn't heard me. If he was less of a bigoted moron, he wouldn't have killed the first brown person he saw, and he would've seen right through me.

I needed to think fast, but all I could do was ask myself, over and over, *What Would Snake Eyes Do?*

If I was going to stay alive, I needed to start speaking ill of the dead.

"That scumbag!" I jumped out of Rijs's grip and kicked Rakko's corpse out of the chair. "If he's turned traitor, we need to know who he's working for." I started going through Rakko's pockets.

Rijs tried to stop me, but I talked him out of punching my teeth in the same way I always did…by talking faster than the other guy could think.

"Wait, dude! You said it yourself, if we tell them we've been breached, they'll just liquidate the whole operation. We need to hand them an asset. If I have his phone, I can get a line on his contact. He's texting and phone phreaking all day and night. We have to give them something, or we're useless."

His face screwed up with doubt, but he was confused enough to let me finish searching my dead friend. "Got it," I said, pocketing it and sprinting ahead of him for the elevator, like I couldn't wait to get to Yeti.

The elevator is never a comfortable place to spend time with someone like Rijs, but tonight, there was something special in the air. "Don't see why we need you little bastards out here, anyhow," he snarled in my face. "You have no skin in this game, boy. You think you can just put in another quarter."

I think I figured out, right then, that we weren't really going to see Yeti.

I hadn't been in a real fight since eighth grade. This lumbering steakhead mouth-breather, Jeff Sestak, heard me calling him Jeff Sleestak, and ordered me to meet him by the bike racks after school. I don't know what the hell got into me. Sestak had terrorized his peer group since kindergarten and, if left alone, probably would have bullied himself to death. I had been pushed, kicked, spat on, and chased home, and learned to keep my head down. But a straight fight? Never before, and I was no hero that day, either. I hopped the back fence and took the canyons home. Jeff Sestak and his posse were waiting in my driveway.

He made me throw the first blow. I knew he'd trap my pathetic roundhouse and stomp me into a puddle. I had no fighter's instincts whatsoever, but I had a lifetime of bottled rage.

I screamed like a fruit bat and charged right through him. I slapped. I scratched. I got a mouthful of his hair in my teeth and ripped it out by the roots. His friends had to pull him off me. They got a few licks in, but I was past feeling it. I was lost in a red fog of nerd rage, and would've killed them with my hands if I could.

Nobody messed with me after that, but I kept my stupid

nicknames to myself. I learned a hundred other ways to solve my problems, but I never learned to control myself in a violent situation. In paintball, I emptied my gun into the first tree I saw, and always got capped first, often by my own hand.

The elevator doors opened and we crossed the surface bunker—an unassuming repair bay with a bunch of spare parts, boat motors, and scuba gear. But instead of pushing me out onto the sand to head for the guards' living quarters, he shoved me down the ramp to the lagoon.

The moonlight on the water was nice, but it didn't get all magical for me, in some samurai poetry *satori* moment. It was just the last moonlight I was ever going to see.

"You know, Rijs, we're going the wrong way—"

"Shut up!" Rijs kicked me in the kidneys, sending me tumbling down onto the dock. "You think I'm stupid? Rakko didn't have the stones to sell us out. I killed him because he looked at me cockeyed. I'm going to do you special, because you're a dirty traitor."

My legs were lunchmeat. I felt something deep inside me twist and rupture when I pulled myself to my feet, but I knew worse was coming if I didn't reach into my pocket.

It almost slipped out of my hand and fell into the water, but I held onto it and pointed it at Rijs, who didn't seem to recognize that it wasn't a phone. "Who you calling, boy?"

I shot him in the neck with Rakko's taser. I didn't expect him to just drop and flop, but honestly, I expected a little bit more of something. He had a spear gun pointed at me, and when I juiced the electrodes, he shot me through the leg.

The spear wasn't really a spear, of course—more like a crossbow bolt, with a simple point that pierced the meat of my thigh, grated off the bone and poked out a good two inches through the other side.

I went down squealing and jerking the trigger on the taser.

Rijs dropped the spear gun and popped his knuckles. "Stop it, boy. You're giving me the giggles."

"You shot me! Damn you, that hurts! You shot me!" I know, belaboring the obvious.

"They can smell blood in the water for hundreds of miles, boy." He didn't even pluck the electrodes out of his neck. He seemed to *really* enjoy being tased. "I was about to go fishing, so I let them in."

I was terrified. Sure. But right then, I couldn't help laughing. It hurt to laugh, but I was learning a new appreciation for the little things.

"What's so funny, boy? You think I'm joking?"

I knew he wasn't. None of this was even the least bit funny, right then. Forgive me if I chose to go to my happy place instead.

Rijs had a thing for sharks, and he'd ragged the company to let the natives come back, so he'd have something "tasty" to play with. I was no Mike Phelps even when I *hadn't* been perforated, and I knew he'd stay to watch.

"Nothing…just something funny Rakko and me talked about doing…"

Rijs picked me up by my sweatshirt and held me out over the water. I could hear the wavelets break against the dock, and could picture what was making them.

The waters around our island are pristine and as blue as an airplane toilet bowl, but when you live anywhere downstream from a corpse-clogged pollution pump like the Ganges, you're going to have a shark problem. The lagoon had a fence and sonic barriers, but Rijs shut them off and threw chum into the lagoons to start a feeding frenzy, then tossed grenades in the water and got out the skimmer. He grilled them superbly, if you had a magnet handy to find the shrapnel.

"What's so funny, boy?"

In my hand, I held Rakko's real phone. "We made joke ringtones for you guys… This was our ringtone for you."

I pressed the button and called Rijs's communicator. The guards got these super-durable walkie-talkies, sheathed in rubber, that would ring underwater and keep ticking after a direct EMP hit.

Rijs's ringtone was the bleating cry of a baby seal. It sounded kind of cute. Rijs certainly thought so.

He threw back his head and laughed. Then he slammed his forehead into my nose.

My head whipped back so hard muscles tore in my neck. I saw stars. Planets. Nice ones, where nobody was getting beat to death. I shopped around for a while before I came back to this one.

He laughed and headbutted me again.

I wasn't thinking anything besides, *oh crap, not again.* And like I said, I have no instinct for violence. What happened next can only be explained as pure-D *deus ex machina.*

As his face came rushing at mine, I threw my head down with my teeth bared, and I bit his nose.

Rijs was an old-school bully from way back. When his prey fought back, he was even more at sea than I was. He pulled back, instead of sensibly trying to bite me back. I twisted my head around and tore his nose off.

At the same time, I thrust my impaled right thigh into his groin. The protruding inches of steel spear jabbed right through something soft between his legs.

Rijs body-slammed me on the dock, then staggered and tripped on the mooring line for the Waverunners and fell into the water. His anguished moans were, if anything, a full octave lower than before. Another cherished cartoon myth dispelled.

I was seeing spots and fireworks from the pain. I took a deep, whooping breath and almost swallowed Rijs's nose. I spat it out and fumbled around for Rakko's taser. The battery was practically flat, but I jolted Rijs again, who enjoyed it a lot less this time.

Then I downloaded the baby seal ringtone to Rijs's communicator. And called him.

Thrashing around in the water, Rijs cursed me in Afrikaans

and tried to make his spastic arms lift him out of the water. "Gonna eat you myself, boy," he said, which made it even harder to feel sorry for him when something even bigger and meaner than him bit his leg and dragged him under.

I don't know if it was the barking seal ringtone or the blood from his nose and groin, but I like to think they knew who blew up all their cousins.

Seeing him get eaten alive only made me laugh even harder. Call me callous, but if you can laugh with a spear through your leg and a broken nose, then something must be really, *really* funny.

It took me a while to get up the dock and back to the control room, and none of it the least bit humorous. I locked down the elevator with my master key and fetched a Mountain Dew from the fridge.

Now I was in my element. But I was still bleeding to death.

I got the first aid kit. I got blood all over the medications, and couldn't read them. I took a couple Percocets, but I didn't have time to wait for them to work. On the monitor, Yeti and Blinky were still sparring. Stupid. I locked down the living quarters and flooded them with gas.

I was not trying to be a hero, then or ever. The Snake Eyes Show taught me nothing I could use. I know now that he didn't leave his enemies alive out of weakness, but because even the death of a dirtbag like Rijs is not worth carrying around for the rest of your life. And all things considered, it's a much harder job, just trying to keep people alive. It's all too easy to lose your cool and just start killing people, and Cobra makes it easier than shopping at home.

I didn't have the guts for what I had to do next. Pulling the spear out was the hardest, most painful thing I've ever done, and I hardly remember it, but before I blacked out, I sealed the holes with a suture gun and packed the wound with gauze.

I was still crying in a ball on the floor when the console phone rang.

It was my "Mom."

"You bastards used me...you, you're coming here, anyway, and you just—people are dead—"

"I'm sorry, Gram. But we had a narrow window to hit this operation, and we thought that you would...that when the truth was made clear to you...that you would help..."

"I can't believe you people. They know you're coming. They killed my...my friend, and they tried to kill me. Our automated defenses will shoot you down..."

"What do you want, Gram?"

"I WANT TO GO HOME!"

"Then listen to me. You got yourself into this situation, and you're the one who can get yourself out of it." Her voice was cool, but not cold. She was just a voice on the phone right then, but she was also the red-haired beauty who never lost her nerve when I tried to kill her with every toy in Breaker's toybox. Was she just humoring me about my holding back, or did she know me better than I knew myself? Maybe Rijs hadn't hit me enough times, but I wanted to believe her.

"I can crash the missile batteries," I offered hopefully, "but if our perimeter's breached, the home office will fry the whole system by remote. This is not a metaphor. The walls are packed with thermite and RDX."

Three incoming bogeys popped up on our radar, but I'd ordered the defense grid to ignore all targets. Whether it told the home office about them was a question way above my pay grade.

"What kind of system are we talking about, here?"

"It's a cold laser array...part of our covert data network. And the database...we don't have the servers here, but we have periodic backups cached...the stuff we have is worth way more than the sixteen million in hardware."

"Can you back it up?"

I looked at our network. Eight nodes, all booby-trapped like Blackbeard's treasure, loaded with untold hellabytes of criminal activities. "I can try…but you need to know something. They're sending a team of scientists to America to mass-produce a new disease…"

"It won't be the first time."

"They're not sneaking them in. We—I—helped build false identities for them, and they're going to the CDC and WHO, and you need to know who they are—"

"Send the relevant files to the Basement. If it's as important as you say…"

"I've seen it…it's important." I didn't feel like it was so very important right now. Percocet kicking in like gangbusters. But I wanted to make Scarlett trust me. I wanted to be one of the good guys, if only so they'd save my conniving, cowardly ass.

"Do it now, then. And be ready to evac in thirty."

I was already typing. Attaching the test videos, the fake and the deleted biographies, and their fake passports.

Hi!

STOP THESE GUYS, PLEASE!!!

(see attached files).

Have A Nice Day,

L1Q1D8TR

"It's away. Happy now?"

"Thank you, Gram. What other kinds of resistance can we expect?"

"Not much…there's automated defenses, but I can sit on them."

"What about the other staff?"

"Oh, you don't need to worry about them…" I felt a swell of bravado, and had to hold myself back from going into gratuitous detail. At just that moment, I looked at the closed circuit monitors again, and almost swallowed my tongue.

The halls and guards' rooms were smoked out. But in the gym, Yeti and Blinky kept boxing. They hadn't even broken a sweat.

Stupid like a couple of steroidal foxes.

The camera in the gym was feeding me a loop. Their tracking tags still showed them there, so they must've ditched them, too. They could be anywhere, and they probably weren't sleeping in their quarters.

"Um, Scarlett? I've got problems…I need to…"

But she was already gone.

PICTURE THIS:

Our hero limps down the corridor, weapon brandished to vanquish any foe. Note the fiery determination in his spastically blinking, tear-choked eyes, and the bloody stain on his cargo shorts.

There's a gun in my room. I've kept it under my bed ever since I first got here, when a guard who used to work here told me he'd gut me if I didn't spring his kid brother out of a Turkish prison. Long story. Anyway…

I have a gun in my room. With a gun, I won't need to worry. Yeti and Blinky only have about twenty guns between them, and they clearly knew something was going down before Rijs did. Probably before *I* did.

My room. The door stands open. I forget if I left it open. Rakko always borrows DVDs, steals toilet paper. I don't sweat it, I just walk in. My bed is five feet away, but I never get there.

The door slams into my shoulder and throws me sideways into the wall.

Funny joke. In Soviet Union, door knocks on *you*! Blinky could've dropped that on me. This would be Michael Bay material, right here.

But he just comes out and grabs me by the legs like he's going to use me for a wheelbarrow. Or swing me around in circles.

Plan B, then. My airplane ride ends after two twirls. I smash into my 52-inch plasma screen and roll on the floor. The rest of my entertainment center comes down on my back.

Another problem with movies: the villain never just snaps the good guy's neck. He keeps throwing him around the room until the hero lands on a conveniently lethal object and dutifully jabs it through the stupid villain's face.

Blinky follows the playbook like a seasoned pro henchman, but I can't live up to it. My frantic hands find and fling Xbox controllers and clamshells, an iPod and some Ultraman figurines, but nothing more lethal than a Peckinpah box set comes available.

Blinky shrugs all of it aside and picks me up by my neck.

It's never too late to try being nice. "Hi, uh…Anatoly. You know, there's been one hell of a misunderstanding…"

"Is all good, then, yes?" Yeti slouches in the open doorway, holding an MP5. "You can fix."

"I don't have a magic wand, dude. The task force is in the air—"

"But you *do* have magic wand. You can knock task force out of air. Arm the security system. Let it do its job."

"And, uh…then what?"

"Then we leave with your computer boxes. Is good plan, yes?"

I nod emphatically. "And uh, so…where are we going?"

Yeti laughs. Blinky tries to join in, but almost instantly gives it up as a mistake. His roid-ripped muscles strangle each other, and his glass eye almost pops out.

Finally, Yeti lets me in on the joke. "My English is not so good, but yours… Ha! *We* are going. *You* are staying."

"Then, uh, yeah, in that case, I'd have to say…no?"

Yeti looks at Blinky. "I did not understand his English. You ask him."

Blinky slaps my ear with a cupped hand. The sting of it is almost bad enough to make me pass out, but when he rips his hand away, it feels like he's holding my brain in his palm.

I can't even hear myself screaming, "Yes, OK, OK, OK, OK! Just stop—"

Blinky has to carry me out of my room and dump me into the captain's chair. Three choppers are well inside our perimeter, ETA sixteen minutes.

"Fix it," Yeti says.

I punch up the security menu and enter my code. They didn't need me to do this. The code is right there in the bar code on their tracking wristbands, except they took them off in the gym, and they probably can't read mine.

As soon as I rescind my *Ignore* order, the radar screen goes Technicolor. The recessed red alert lights flare up and the fire alarm hoots all through the bunker.

Blinky twists my arm like an angry kid with his sister's Barbie. "Let go, man! That's normal! We're under attack, right?"

The missiles lock on. I pray somebody smarter than Breaker is on one of those choppers.

The closet nobody but me knew was there opens behind Yeti, and a faceless soldier steps out and shoots Yeti in the back.

"That's normal, too," I say. Like a boss.

At the same time, the hidden door in the hall opposite the elevator also opens, and two more BATs goose-step into the corridor to block the exit.

Cobra's security people work in layers that would make the Pharaohs look like trusting chumps. In the event of mutiny or infiltration or somebody like me monkeying with the security protocols, the bunker has a built-in failsafe system. On full lockdown, BATs come out of the woodwork to wipe out anything that moves without a tracking tag. We never deployed them in our drills, because they have a tendency to blow up at the slightest provocation. Like the strain of trying to figure out what to do about Blinky, an untagged threat, holding me up in front of him as a human shield.

I've never given Blinky a whole lot of credit. He always seemed like the big dummy of our little crew. I never figured he or Yeti had the brains to plan ahead, but they rolled my ingenious ass, so who was I to judge?

The BAT takes aim at us, then jerkily lowers its weapon and sweeps the room, to point at us again. The poor thing looks like it's having a seizure.

I try to reason with him. "Dude, you're gonna get us killed."

"Not both of us," he says. In one blinding motion, Blinky does something very smart, and something very stupid.

His gnarled fingers pry the tracking band off my wrist. Before I even feel the sting of the band tearing off, he throws me at the stupid robot and bolts for the elevator.

I sail through the air with my arms out to break my fall. What the BAT makes of it, I can't imagine, but its 16-bit fight reflex kicks in, as it realizes the unarmed screaming civilian flying at it headfirst is now OK to shoot.

I tackle the robot across its chest. It's like trying to take down a telephone pole. Its programming clearly doesn't have a subroutine for plucking craven cowards off itself. I cling to it like a baby koala. It rocks back on its heels and locks in on Blinky, "thinking" it's me.

Blinky's getting away. He picks up my backup drive from where Yeti dropped it, and then turns to look at me. At least, I think he's looking at me. "You should have stuck to your video fighters."

And you should've kept your own wristband.

Blinky turns and walks down the corridor towards the other two BATs.

I whisper into my phone. "Computer, update employment status, Gram Fensler."

"Lockdown alert is activated. All access denied."

"Security override Omega. Rhubarb pie." Hey, it's easier to remember than a PIN number.

He's waiting for the elevator. The robots are just standing there, letting him walk out with all my data.

"Computer, I quit. You guys can take this job and shove it."

The effect of my resignation takes a little more than three seconds to kick in. The elevator doors open. The BATs point at Blinky and shoot. He dives for the elevator, raking them with his machine pistol. My BAT shoots up the corridor. I spring off it and roll behind the server rack. The other two swivel and shoot at it, and they're just standing there in a perfect little triangle, shooting each other until they all explode.

I hug the floor and try to play dead until it feels like my hair's turned white. Then something weird happens.

The red flashing lights all shut off. The screens all go blank.

I get up and pat myself down. I wasn't shot or burned or blown up. Maybe videogames taught me something useful, after all.

I don't go packing a bag. I just crawl for the elevator. I hit the button and the door shuts, and Blinky slams me into the wall.

He was practically cut in half by the BATs, but is still strong enough to break my neck in his bare hands.

I don't have any more slick tricks or wiseass remarks. At this point, it's just gratuitous violence.

He squeezes my throat until my trachea closes. My vision shrinks down to a vanishing point. My hands bat at his face like moths, until a lucky shot with the heel of my hand dislodges his glass eye.

The red hole in his head winks at me, as if to say, *It's okay, what were you going to do with the rest of your life, anyway? Probably something stupid. This is better...for everyone...if it ends here.*

I stick my thumb in it, up to the hilt. It feels like—no, forget it...you don't want to know, and I don't want to think about it.

It's not like in the movies. He doesn't bust out any raw last words or anything that makes it easier, makes me look like a good guy. Something in Blinky just fizzles out. His hand spasms and squeezes even harder, then goes limp. His last breath in my face smells like garlic.

I push him off, massaging my throat to try to get a breath in.

I came, I saw, I conquered. So why am I dying now? Getting a breath in is like trying to suck a tennis ball up through a crushed bendy-straw.

I am still lying on the floor in a clench with the dead gangster when the elevator doors open and I hear helicopters.

That's bizarre. Our missiles should've shot them down. But I've tried to kill these people myself enough times to know how hard it is.

I stagger out of the bunker and fall to my knees, clutching my broken throat, where I can still feel Blinky strangling me.

A Chinook and two Apache choppers sit on the sand. A tall, slender form in a tight flight suit and a green helmet jumps out and runs to me. She lifts the briefcase-sized backup drive and takes my arm.

"Is this everything?"

"That's…everything," I try to tell her, but I can't talk.

I can't see her. A brilliant wormhole of strobing purple supernovas fills my eyes, promising me exactly what I deserve, at the end of the tunnel. The last thing I think I'm ever going to see in this world is a serrated Ka-Bar knife, stabbing me in the neck.

She cuts a hole in my trachea and plugs a broken ballpoint pen into it. My first breath tastes like liquid fire. She and another soldier pick me up and carry me to the Chinook.

We dust off and I'm floating. I got out. I'm free. I ripped their brains out and I got out of that snake pit…

"You're a very lucky young man," she says. A playful purr in her voice. Scarlett was all business, but this lady is enjoying herself a little too much…and what's with her accent?

I sit up, but she pushes me back into my seat and winches down my restraints until I can barely breathe through my plastic tube. Then she takes off her helmet

Her hair tumbles out and spills down her back. It's not red.

It's black. She smiles and puts on her glasses. "Lucky—but not very smart, I'm afraid."

The Baroness. I've seen her picture enough times, I should have recognized her when she picked me up off the beach. If I hadn't almost died a half dozen times in the last hour, if I hadn't been living in a fantasy for the last three years, I might've recognized her right away. I might've known this whole thing was too good to be true.

My voice is a hollow, reedy rasp. "You set this whole thing up...to rip off yourselves?"

"Oh no, Gram. Cobra is a fiercely competitive entity, and we deal in absolute solutions. We cannot afford to have our strategic assets stagnate or soften in their commitment. This is how we test our employees, to see who is ready to move up, and who is deadweight."

"And you're probably not, uh...grading on a curve, are you?"

She reclines on the seat opposite me and crosses her long, lethal legs. Her glasses flash with tiny symbols as she reviews the contents of my drive. "You surprised us, Gram. We knew your loyalties were tissue-thin, but we did not anticipate your capacity for violence. A pity you turned on us at the first blush of a woman's attention, but you hurt us only as much as we wanted you to, and you have helped us a great deal."

She touches a screen in the bulkhead and it lights up to show a CNN Special Report: *Suspected Terrorists Arrested At LAX.*

"So...I never was in touch with G.I Joe at all...?" Duh.

"You sent them the message that made the real operation possible. The false identities you gave them were a secondary cover. Their terrorist ties were planted on the net by another team, for you to find."

"So there's no plague?"

She laughs. "There will be plagues and wars and famine, where and when we need them. But when America reacts to the credible threat of a plague by jailing innocent foreigners, it becomes unable to tell truth from fantasy, it alienates its allies, and it loses its way without ever facing the real enemy."

"You guys—"

"No, Gram," the Baroness takes out a syringe and taps the bubbles out of it. "The real enemy is people like *you*. Who think the American way is to take all you can, and damn everyone else. As long as America is well stocked with selfish, apathetic fools like yourself, it will always lose."

So now she's going to kill me. I can't even twist away from the needle. My heart beats so hard I think I'm going to die before she even sticks it in me. I deserve to die.

But she knows what I'm thinking. And like a true pro, she knows how to make me feel even worse, just before she sticks it in.

"Why would we throw you away, Gram? You're untrustworthy, but we've always known that. You're also young and resourceful, and so you will be extremely useful for a very long time."

AND I HAVE.

My new digs aren't quite as nice as the Maldives, but I don't have to worry about skin cancer or bullies. I live in a coffin-sized container. My computer is set into the wall. I have a keyboard and a mouse, and a slot that cheap Korean food comes through twice a day, and the foot of my bed flips up to reveal a snazzy space age toilet. My computer does not have a clock, and only gets heavily screened, glitchy Internet service. I see everything I need to see.

I think I have been here for eighteen months. When they take me out of my coffin to exercise, they put a hood on me. There are at least a hundred coffins on the floor in my building. There must be twenty floors, or more.

I wake up and eat, then I write code until I fall asleep. I do what I always did, without any of the perks. I create fake IDs, fake news for psyops campaigns against Third World countries Cobra wants to shake down. And viruses, lots of viruses: e-mail reading spybots for various sex ads, invisible worms lurking in virility come-ons, and grand Trojan horse attacks like the one that contains this message.

I'm not begging to be rescued. I earned this box. I'm trying to save you.

I'm trying to get you to see the box you are in, and who put you there. You don't know what you're dealing with, and you're fighting it wrong, and if you keep it up like you have been, you're going to lose.

I'm trying to save you from *me*—

Contributors

CHUCK DIXON is a long-time comic book writer with thousands of comic scripts to his credit, including properties as diverse as *The Punisher*, *The Simpsons*, and a run on Batman-related titles that lasted over a decade. He currently writes both the regular *G.I. Joe* monthly as well as *Snake Eyes* for IDW. He can be found on the web at dixonverse.net, and comicspace.com/chuckdixon.

"Writing prose is tough for me. I'm a dedicated comic book guy. But no one had written a Snake Eyes story and Andy Schmidt (my editor) shamed me into it."

— *Chuck Dixon*

JONATHAN MCGORAN, writing as D. H. Dublin, is the author of the forensic crime thrillers *Body Trace*, *Blood Poison*, and *Freezer Burn*. He writes short fiction, nonfiction, and satire under his own name, and is editor of *The Shuttle*, a monthly newspaper in Northwest Philadelphia. A proud member of the Liars Club, the Mystery Writers Association, and the International Thriller Writers, McGoran is currently working on the stand-alone thriller *Drift*. Visit him online at www.jmcgoran.com.

"As a kid, I got a huge kick out of G. I. Joe, but I was the youngest child, so they were pretty battle-scarred by the time they got to me. I enjoyed writing 'Unfriendly Fire' because I got to pit state-of-the-art weapons against ancient ones, but also because I finally got to spend some time with Joes that were still intact."

— *Jonathan McGoran*

MICHAEL MONTENAT graduated from MICA with a BFA and then dabbled in magazine illustration, as well as displaying and selling his work in galleries and offices along the East Coast;. He only recently returned to the beloved realm that helped get him into art in the first place —comics! Montenat plans on living and thriving in this rediscovered world of epic stories and personalities.

"Having grown up watching G.I. Joe cartoons, this was a really cool opportunity to put my own visions of some of these awesome characters to life. This has been a great project for me, and I look forward to working more with the Joes and Cobra in the future!"

— *Michael Montenat*

JOHN SKIPP & CODY GOODFELLOW have written three novels together: *Jake's Wake*, *The Day Before*, and *Spore*. Their short stories have appeared in *Hellboy: Oddest Jobs*, *Up Jumped The Devil*, and IDW's *Classics Mutilated*. John Skipp is a *New York Times* best-selling author and editor, whose 19 books have sold millions of copies in a dozen languages worldwide. His latest anthology is *Werewolves and Shapeshifters: Encounters With the Beast Within*. Cody Goodfellow has sold three novels and a collection, *Silent Weapons For Quiet Wars*, which won the Wonderland Book Award in 2010. He also writes comics and is the co-founder and editor of Perilous Press, a small publisher of modern Cthulhu Mythos horror fiction.

"When we heard about this project, we immediately thought this would be a treat, to peer at what Cobra's really like behind the scenes. Ever since Shipwreck found that brochure detailing Cobra's superior health care coverage, it's been something we yearned to know more about.

"As with most truly evil enterprises, many, if not most, of those who make it work don't really know what they're supporting, or at worst, they have no idea how vast, and how nihilistic, it really is. And the growing emphasis on surveillance and remotely operated drones for warfighting cried out to be fused with our need to insulate ourselves from real violence, while getting as intimate as possible with the unreal thing. Can a lifetime of video games really prepare you to become an instant ninja, if forced to fight for your life? We sure hope so."

— *John Skipp & Cody Goodfellow*

DUANE SWIERCZYNSKI is a well-known crime and thriller writer whose next three novels, *Fun & Games*, *Hell & Gone*, and *Point & Shoot* will be published back-to-back during Summer 2011. Visit Duane at twitter.com/swierczy.

"I aimed to write the fastest-moving story possible, especially since the protagonist would be one of G.I. Joe's fastest-moving characters. The name Skidmark gave me pause at first (because...well, you *know*), but his family background and his skill set really appealed to me. One bit of trivia: I wrote a great deal of 'Speed Trap' while driving cross-country with my family last summer. Skid and I traveled the same roads. Fortunately, nobody tried to run us off the road or hit us with a pain ray."

— *Duane Swierczynski*

MATT FORBECK is an award-winning author and game designer with some fifteen novels to his credit. His latest—the critically acclaimed *Amortals* with Vegas Knights—are currently available. Visit him at www.Forbeck.com.

"I've worked on several computer games, and I've been fascinated by the gray-market virtual goods surrounding MMOs for a long time. The chance to make all that part of a Cobra plot seemed too perfect to pass up—both for me and Destro too."

— *Matt Forbeck*

JONATHAN MABERRY is a *New York Times* best-selling author, multiple Bram Stoker Award-winner, and Marvel Comics writer. His novels include *Ghost Road Blues, Rot & Ruin, Patient Zero, The Dragon Factory,* and *The King of Plagues.* His nonfiction works include *Zombies CSU* and *Wanted: Undead or Alive.* His comics include *Doomwar, Captain America: Hail Hydra,* and *Marvel Universe vs. Punisher.* He's a contributing editor for *The Big Thrill,* and a member of SFWA, MWA, and HWA. Visit his website at www.JonathanMaberry.com, or find him on Facebook, Twitter, and LinkedIn.

"I'm a science junkie, always have been. Lately I've been indulging that part of me by writing the Joe Ledger series of science thrillers. I grew up reading science fiction and pulp reprints in which heroes squared off against illains who had advanced weapons that were just beyond the current reach of science but which were definitely going to be real one day. The Doc Savage novels, Dick Tracy, H.G. Wells, Tom Swift. Most of the stuff in those stories is commonplace now. For 'Fling and Steel' I did a lot research into what was on the cutting edge of drone warfare and military application of artificial intelligence. Most of what's in the story is either in development or already in the field. We live in a science fiction age. How cool is that?"

— *Jonathan Maberry*

MAX BROOKS is the author of the zombie-themed books *The Zombie Survival Guide* (2003), *World War Z: An Oral History of the Zombie War* (2006), and *The Zombie Survival Guide: Recorded Attacks* (2009), a graphic novel. An Emmy Award-winning writer for his work on *Saturday Night Live* (2001–2003), Brooks recently wrote the IDW mini-series *G.I. Joe: Hearts & Minds.*

Exorcist

MAX BROOKS

To: HWK1010010110
From: SCRLT0010110101
Subject: EXORCIST

General,

Per your orders, I have conducted an exhaustive inquiry into possible candidates for Project Exorcist. Per your instructions, rank-and-file team members have not been informed of its genesis. Senior command staff responded, as you predicted, with initial resistance, acquiescing eventually into tepid tolerance. It should be noted that team member Doc supports this project wholeheartedly and was instrumental in recommending one candidate that, in my professional opinion, surpasses the others by a considerable margin. I believe his skill level and expertise, as well as his character, exemplify "the imperative assets for 21st Century Warfighting" (your words). I have included the full transcript of my "interview" with said candidate in the following document. I believe you will find our "exchange" enlightening.

BEGIN TRANSCRIPT:

Why do I bother!?! I mean, what the hell's the point!?! Am I making a difference, I don't know, am I just goofin' off, I

317

don't know! Maybe I should just walk away. I could, you know. I could go into the private sector, set my own hours, make a buttload of money, wear my hair the way I want! Why don't I just do it? Cause I can't make a decision? Real inspiring, huh? I can tell *eeeeveryone* else what to do except for me.

You ever heard that Jimmy Durante song "Did you ever have the feeling that you wanted to go, still have the feeling that you wanted to stay, start to go, change your mind"…sorry, I have to sing it in a Punjabi accent. I can only hear it in my head with my mom's voice. She LOVED that song. Don't ask me where she heard it, maybe late at night, when she was just coming off work, when all those old black-and-white movies used to be on. She used to sing it to my dad all the time when we first moved to this country, when he used to complain about life here. You know, "I used to be a barrister, now I work in a hardware store!" Typical immigrant story…well…now. Remember the early 90s, when the Soviet Union imploded and we got flooded with all those whiney Russians, "Oh, I used to be physicist, now I drive taxi cab" yada yada yada… Well, we were about ten years ahead of the curve. I used to call my dad a trend- setter. He didn't get it. I think he just wanted to forget those days. I sure as hell wish I could. An Indian kid, half Muslim, half Hindu, growing up in Atlanta in the 1980s, yay!

"Dude, where's your magic carpet?" "What do you hear from Arafat?" "Musta sucked for you when we bombed Libya!" Ah, those were the days. You know, I didn't mind getting my ass kicked, I guess I kind of expected it. How f'd up is that? The part that still sticks in my ass is that I would be the one to always get in trouble. Mr. Cormode, the vice principal… ohmygod "Minaaaahhhj"…he never tried to learn my name. "Minaaahhhj, the other kids just don't know how to relate to you. People are scared by what they don't understand." Okay, fair enough but…drum roll: "Ya just gotta learn to fit in more, be more like them, not as threatening." And get this, I was so stupid, I actually believed him! I thought it was my fault! I did everything I could to try and "fit in"; playing baseball, eating apple pie, playing baseball WHILE eating apple pie...okay, so I stole that part from Maz Jobrani, that Persian-American comedian. Funny bastard, but at least he didn't change his name. I did, legally! How I conned my parents into agreeing, or the spending the time to do it...not like they had a whole lot of free time. But suddenly, I went from Minoj to Michael, or Mike! And, big shock, didn't make a damn bit of difference...well...at least it was easier for the kids to say "Let's kick Mike's ass" instead of "Hey, let's kick...whatever his name is! The dune coon!" Good times.

So I'm at the store one day, getting groceries for my folks. It was my mom's birthday and I thought I'd do her chores. And I'm trotting up to the counter, and this was right after the Lockerbie Bombing, remember that? So, of course, what does the Bubba behind the counter say, "We don't serve no damn camel jockeys here." And, of course, I don't say anything, even when he throws the money back in my face. Dimes and quarters really hurt, by the way. So I'm bending down to pick up the cash and suddenly, BAM, there's, like, this explosive banging noise, and automatically, I figured he'd hit the counter with a bat or something, and was gonna use it on me next, and as I'm turning to run, I see his face, smashed into the counter, facing me, with this hand...this...looked like King Kong's, big and hairy and pressing this sweaty hillbilly's flesh into the particle board. And I look up and there's this 'creature'...that's the only way I could describe him. He was nine feet tall, no seriously, you know how people can exaggerate the height of authority figures; their doctor, their parents, a cop, whatever. He was nine feet tall, with this monster black leather vest and ponytail and goatee. Did you ever see *Erin Brockovich*...I had a girlfriend who made me watch it, okay! Well, this guy looked like the Aaron Eckhart character.

"You take his damn money and then you say THANK YOU!" That's what he said to the guy at the counter...and he did. "Uncle Jesse" takes my money, still with his head smashed down on the counter, not even trying to struggle, and when he's done, he says, "Thank you, come again." And the giant says, "Nice touch!" and pulls him back so fast he hits the wall behind him. I don't even know what I looked like, probably the closest I ever came to actually being white. I didn't say anything when the giant gave me my bag of groceries and put his hand on my shoulder and walked me outside.

He said, "I'll give you a ride home." I think he must have worried about what would happen when he left and I was stuck walking home. I didn't argue, not because he scared me, not because I hadn't seen that Ricky Schroeder PSA, because I had, remember that one? He's on his bike and he shows you some vignettes of what happens to kids who…whatever, point was, in theory I really, REALLY shouldn't have agreed, but I did, and you should have seen my mom's face when her little boy comes thundering up to her porch on the back of this big ol' hog.

And the last shock of the day, as if I needed more, was when he said, "Hey Mrs. Khan, Mike and I were just running some errands." And he dropped me off, patted me on the back, so hard I almost fell over, and rode right across the street to his house. He knew who I was! He knew who my family was! He'd actually bought some stuff from the hardware store my dad worked at. He'd even said hi to my mom a couple times! And, get this, when the adrenaline started to wear off and my brain started working again, I remembered that I knew him too. His name was Steve Morgan, and I'd seen him plenty of times in our neighborhood. He'd always been out in the front driveway, working on his bike. He'd even waved to me a couple of times and, of course, I was always too shy to wave back.

So, the next morning I went over there, oh this is so pathetic…I'd baked him an apple pie. I know, so heartbreaking, this little boy, walking across the street to this big Hells Angels-lookin' dude with this pathetic, uneven-looking mess of a pie in my hands. Thank God, he pretended to like it.

Flash forward, we become friends, you know, like an afterschool special, "The Immigrant and the Biker: Starring Aaron Ekhart and some Puerto Rican actor with a passable Indian Accent." But no, seriously, he was my friend…he was my friend.

I'd help him with his bike on the weekends. He helped build my bike, bicycle. We'd scavenge parts from wherever and mesh them into something I could ride.

He taught me how to fight. Not martial arts, not the way I knew them. He used to tell me that all the stuff I would see in kung fu movies was all show. "In the words of Master Bruce," he'd say, "if you can't take a man down in sixty seconds, you can't fight." Something like that. He taught me some dirty tricks, who knew there were so many ways to damage the human testicles. I still got my ass whipped, okay, this wasn't *Karate Kid,* but every time I took at least one bastard down with me. "Make sure to hurt one of them bad, real bad, so bad that he's a living example to the other kids, so bad that next time they'll wonder if it's worth it ending up like their friend. It's called 'deterrence,' and it works."

More importantly, Steve taught me how to fight the system. He told me to bypass the vice principal, go right to top, which I did, with a letter. I said… this little kid, trying to sound brave, I said, "Mister Sommers, I've written this letter to 'Ask Nell,' "—she was our local paper's version of "Dear Abby"—"and I'd like you to proofread it for any mistakes." And he took one look at it and…the letter was about what was happening to me, how I was being picked on every day because I was "different" and how the vice principal kept telling me that it was my fault because I didn't fit in. To this day I have never seen a bureaucracy work so fast! And after that, I didn't even mind the fights 'cause I knew I wouldn't be the only one in detention.

Steve even helped me with my homework, nothing major, just quizzing me on my flashcards and maybe reading a book report or something. My parents really wanted to help too, but, they were just too damn busy. Immigrants. Not a lot of free time. I thought Steve was just being nice, but I think, now looking back, that there was a part of him that was craving that kind of life; having a kid, being a father. He was in his 40s and he wasn't married. He'd been married, twice, but it didn't work. I thought…well…I thought because he told me, "Some stallions just can't be broke." I actually believed him, what the hell did I know? God, I was dumb. It took me so long to put all the pieces together, even after I started hearing the screams.

I was up studying one night at the kitchen table…we had this little two-bedroom house. My mom was in my bedroom with my baby sister, she had an ear infection, and my dad was in their bedroom, studying too, for the Georgia Bar. I used to like to read out loud, so I could work on my American accent, so instead of bothering my dad, I was at the kitchen table. It was late, I'm not sure what time, but late enough for me to be asleep.

And I hear this scream, high pitched, like a girl. I thought I didn't hear it at first, you know, like when you're not sure, so you stop to listen, then I heard it again, then lower, grunting like an animal. I opened the window, I listened hard. I heard it coming from across the street. It was coming from Steve's house. You know what's funny, I didn't even think of going to tell my parents. It wasn't just that I didn't want to bother them, but at that time, there was such a divide between us. They were such FOBs…Fresh Off the Boat? They were so lost in this new country, even more than me. It's a hard thing, to lose confidence in the people you trust to protect you. You see your parents as gods, all knowing, all seeing, just…invincible, and then you come to a strange country and suddenly they're as helpless as you. That's how I saw it back then, that's why I didn't tell them about the screams.

So I didn't do anything that night. Just opened the window and listened. It went on for at least an hour. What really freaked me out was that no one else in the neighborhood did anything. I was expecting to see what I'd seen in all those movies about America; lights going on, doors opening, people coming out in their bathrobes and nightgowns. Nothing. I think I heard someone shouting for him to shut the hell up, but I might be retrofitting the memory.

I asked Steve about it the next day. I didn't say "screaming," more like, "Uh, mister Morgan, did you hear anything last night?" Maybe he knew what I was talking about. I do remember his face changing a little bit, I'm not retrofitting that. He asked me something like "like what" and I just shrugged, and he let it go. Whatever it was, he didn't want to talk about it any more than I did, and even if I wanted to, he didn't have time. I met him coming out of his house with a black metal box in his hand that he put in the saddlebag of his bike. After the first question, I asked him what was in the box. He said, "Just goin' huntin'."

I didn't ask where he was going or what he was hunting. I didn't really understand the whole process. I thought about asking him if I could go, but I knew my mom would have a cow. She was Hindu. I didn't ask any more questions, and I didn't ask why he didn't catch anything the next day when he came home. I let it all go.

But then it happened again, maybe a month or two later? The weather was warmer so I had the window open and this time I know what I heard. It was definitely a man screaming, and it was coming from Steve's house. I didn't ask him about it the second time, the next day, when he went hunting again, or the next day, when he came back empty-handed. I didn't know enough to put the pieces together, but I was curious, and like a stupid kid, the next time it happened, I crept across the street, right under his bedroom window to listen. It was really fragmented, or gibberish…English was almost my first language by then, so I knew what gibberish sounded like. I also knew what hard-core American profanity sounded like and there were a few of those words sprinkled in as well. There were a few words I didn't understand; "Incoming!" "Snake and Nape!" "Puff is inbound!"…"Puff," that was a word he said more than a few times. "PUFF!" sometimes in quick succession "PUFFPUFFPUFF." And again, I didn't say anything, and again, the next day, he went hunting and came back empty.

And this went on, for a year, maybe longer? I'd hear the screams, I'd sneak out to listen. Each time I'd pick up something new, people's names, phrases out of context, but PUFF was always there. One time I heard "Puff" then something, then "Dragon." And then I started asking around. Obviously, to paraphrase Sam Kinnison, "Mom and Dad are no freakin' road map," so I asked some of the friends…well, not really friends, basically the white kids who spoke to me. That's when I first heard the phrase "Puff the Magic Dragon." Most of them said it was a children's song. One kid, Matt Blank, real last name, kept insisting it was code for smoking weed.

They were both right and I probably would have thought that that's what Steve was talking about except for a few months later when I was eating dinner in front of the TV and this movie came on called *The Green Berets*. You ever see it? As Vietnam movies go, it is the LAMEST one ever made! Ohmygod, even I—and I knew next to nothing about that conflict—I couldn't believe the utter lameness. Inaccurate, racist, inaccurate…the end of the movie's got John Wayne and some little Vietnamese kid watching the sun set IN THE EAST! BUT…but…that was the first time I heard "Puff the Magic Dragon" in reference to an AC-47 gunship.

And you can guess where this is going. I finally got up the courage to ask Steve about Puff. I saw this look on his face, something that didn't look like him. More like, someone inside him looking out at me through a window. I know, hard to describe, but suddenly for a second, Steve wasn't Steve anymore. "Where'd you hear that?" That was the first time I lied to him. I told him that some of the kids were arguing in school about what it meant. He laughed, and suddenly the look was gone. He told me that, yes, one of the references was to an aircraft that flew combat missions in Vietnam. I tried to play dumb and asked what Vietnam was. He answered me back in this uber-serious gravelly voice, "What is Vietnam. Honoring isn't enough. Remembering isn't enough…" He saw I didn't get the reference…you don't either, it was a Time-Life book series and he was doing a Martin Sheen voice from the commercial. He kept smiling and told me I should know about Vietnam from school. I told him that was next year, in Western Civ II. We were still talking about the French Revolution. He just shook his head and made some very homofrancophobic remark. Is that a word? It is now.

And that's when I started learning about Vietnam. He brought out this big, battered green Army footlocker…his house didn't have much furniture, did I mention that? For a biker type, he kept things really clean, really Spartan. He kept the footlocker hidden under his bed. I remember thinking it was like a treasure chest when we opened it; medals, photos, I remember this pair of homemade flip flops that looked like they'd been cut out of truck tires. He called them "Ho Chi Minh Sandals." He showed me this knife, more like a spike with a brass knuckle handle on it. There was some French writing and the date was from 1917. He said, "Imagine how many owners this little pig sticker's had." There was the box, the one he always put in his saddle bag when he went hunting. He didn't let me touch that, but he let me touch everything else.

We sat on his front porch for…hours, just looking at the photos. "That's at Ahn Khe, that's Saigon, that's this little beach where the water was like warm glass…" We spent a lot of time on that front porch. He'd tell me about weapons he'd used and battles he'd been in. I honestly didn't know much about any war at that time. I knew my dad lost a brother in one of the wars with Pakistan, but he never talked about it. So for me, it was kinda cool. I mean, here I am getting firsthand stories about firefights and helicopter assaults from a guy who'd actually been in it. There were a lot of Vietnam movies coming out, mostly about going back to Vietnam to rescue POWs, you know, like *Missing in Action* or *Rambo II*. I asked Steve if he'd take me to see them, and he just laughed. "You want a fantasy movie, we'll go see *The Goonies*." He did get serious, though, when he saw how disappointed I looked. "Look, kid, those movies, they're not about the war, because they're made by people who never went anywhere near it. I promise, when someone who was actually there makes a movie about what actually happened, I promise, I'll take you." He probably figured that was a safe promise. He probably figured that, Hollywood being Hollywood, nobody was going to let a real Vietnam vet make a real movie about Vietnam.

You're too young to have seen *Platoon* when it came out. It was really, REALLY real. I probably shouldn't have seen it, but Steve'd made his promise, and my parents said it was okay. I remember sitting there, all jacked up on Pepsi and the Milk Duds, and it was during that first firefight in the beginning, when I looked over and I saw Steve sweating…a lot. He kept rubbing his cheeks and forehead and I noticed he actually started to smell different. Not regular sweat smell, not the kind when he'd be out in the sun working on his bike, different, sharper, acidic. I kept trying not to notice, or look at him. I tried to focus on the movie, but that scene halfway through, when Tom Berenger is going through the tunnel, nothing's happening, before he even shoots the guy, but Steve suddenly turned to me and said, "I gotta take a piss," and left. And I didn't think anything about it until I realized later that the movie was almost over and he hadn't come back.

He never came back. He was waiting for me, outside, on his bike, and didn't even try to explain why he left. And I didn't ask. I started asking later, not about the movie, but the next time he was telling me a war story. I think I started interjecting comments like, "That must have been scary" or "That's terrible," and he'd either ignore it or shrug out some answer like, "Yeah, but you deal." I kept trying, I kept probing. "But weren't you scared?" "Didn't that freak you out?" That was the first time I'd used the term "freak out," I was really proud of that. And he'd always come back with, "You do what you gotta do" or "Nothing I can't handle" or "A real man doesn't freak out." He used that term "real man" in a lot of different answers. The last time he used it, the time I saw "that look," was the last time I asked about being scared. By the way, the night after seeing *Platoon*, I heard screaming most of the night. The next morning he went hunting for two days.

I could have let it go. Stupid kid. I just HAD to dig deeper, HAD to know more, curious little fartbag. I started asking my teachers, some of the other kids. Basically, in Atlanta, in the '80s, Vietnam fell into two categories. There was the hardcore, right-wing shouting about "We coulda finished the job if dot dot dot." Those were the people who LOVED *Rambo II*. And then there were the very quiet whispers, the ones about people who came back "really messed up." That was the term I kept hearing, "really messed up." And to my further questions I got a lot of "you know"s and a lot of changed subjects. I did hear the term "Shell Shock" from my Western Civ teacher, but that was as far as he'd go.

Long story short, I hit the books, spent a lot of time in the school library, such as it was, and even the local library, such as it was, and I got enough info to figure out that, duh, war can drive people crazy. I got the names and addresses of some VA hospitals and wrote them a bunch of letters about how I was doing a report on "combat trauma." I thought that phrase sounded SOOOO adult. Only one guy wrote back to me. Dr. "Black," no, that's his real name, from L.A. He gave me the names of some books, all WAY above my reading level. I was in ninth grade, and he was really helpful in explaining them to me. We had this penpal relationship for months and he was awesome in breaking everything down for me.

He taught me about the 1800s when army doctors starting seeing cases of what they called "Exhaustion" and how they didn't do much about it… probably because they were too busy sawing off legs that had a splinter in the toe. Then World War I rolls around and suddenly hospitals are just flooded with "Exhaustion" cases, like 60,000, and that's just the ones they caught. Finally it's a legitimate medical condition and they called it "Shell Shock." Then comes World War II and they change it to "Battle Fatigue." Sounds more medical, more "official," don't you think? But a LOT of people still aren't on board with it, like it's just a scam or some medical excuse for cowardice. You know that story about General Patton slapping that G.I. Some poor bastard whose nerves have smashed to Jello and Patton thinks he's just wussing out. Douche bag. Yeah, I said it, General George S. Patton was a flaming DOUCHE BAG! But he wasn't the only one, hell, he was in majority, even twenty years later when we hit the worst mind-(EXPLETIVE DELETED) of all wars. That's when I learned about the K.O. teams. Dr. Black told me about them. He actually had a couple friends who were part of them and how, during a bad jungle dustup, when a grunt's mind began to implode, the brass'd helicopter out some Army shrink who'd…I still can't believe this…who'd give him a shot to make him sleep for 18 hours. When he woke up, he might have to go right back into combat. "K.O." "Knock Out." And by the end of the war, when they'd changed "Battle Fatigue" to "PTSD" eighty-five percent of patients were eventually returned to combat! Did you know that? EIGHTY-FIVE PERCENT! Way to "do no harm," guys!

Dr. Black treated a lot of those cases at his hospital on the coast. The more he talked to me about the symptoms, the more they started to sound like Steve. I didn't mention him, or my real motives, for a long time. I was really conflicted for a long time. But then Dr. Black told me about one patient, who, instead of self-medicating with booze or drugs, would treat his nightmares by going out into the wilderness with his gun and